Anne Herries lives in Cambridg[...]  watching wildlife, and spoils the [...] frequent visitors to her garden. Anne [...] of nature, and sometimes puts a li[...] they are mostly about love and rom[...] own enjoyment, and to give pleasure to her readers. Anne is a winner of the Romantic Novelists' Association Romance Prize. She invites readers to contact her on her website: www.lindasole.co.uk

Regency Surrender

Christine Merill — Regency Surrender — *Wicked Deception*
August 2018

Laurie Benson — Regency Surrender — *Powerful Dukes*
September 2018

Janice Preston — Regency Surrender — *Scandalous Return*
October 2018

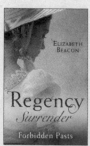
Elizabeth Beacon — Regency Surrender — *Forbidden Pasts*
November 2018

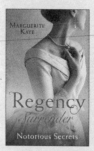
Marguerite Kaye — Regency Surrender — *Notorious Secrets*
December 2018

Sarah Mallory — Regency Surrender — *Infamous Reputations*
January 2019

Annie Burrows — Regency Surrender — *Rebellious Debutantes*
February 2019

Annie Herries — Regency Surrender — *Defiant Lords*
March 2019

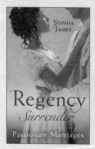
Sophia James — Regency Surrender — *Passionate Marriages*
April 2019

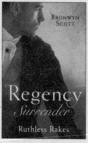
Bronwyn Scott — Regency Surrender — *Ruthless Rakes*
May 2019

Georgie Lee — Regency Surrender — *Debts Reclaimed*
June 2019

Louise Allen — Regency Surrender — *Sinful Conquests*
July 2019

Regency Surrender: Defiant Lords

ANNE HERRIES

MILLS & BOON

First Published in Great Britain 2019
By Mills & Boon, an imprint of HarperCollinsPublishers
1 London Bridge Street, London, SE1 9GF

REGENCY SURRENDER: DEFIANT LORDS © 2019 Harlequin Books S.A.

His Unusual Governess © 2013 Anne Herries
Claiming the Chaperon's Heart © 2016 Anne Herries

ISBN: 978-0-263-26794-5

52-0319

MIX
Paper from
responsible sources
FSC™ C007454
www.fsc.org

This book is produced from independently certified FSC™ paper to ensure responsible forest management.

For more information visit: www.harpercollins.co.uk/green

Printed and bound in Great Britain
by CPI Group (UK) Ltd. Croydon, CR0 4YY

HIS UNUSUAL
GOVERNESS

I would like to dedicate this book to the memory of my great friend Paula Marshall, whom I loved dearly, as did so many of you.

Prologue

'What was so important that you summoned me here?' Lord Rupert Myers arched a languid eyebrow at the Marquess of Merrivale. ''Tis an unseasonable hour and I was up late last night.' He smothered a yawn and levelled an elegant gold-rimmed eyeglass at the older man. Seeing that the marquess looked strained, he dropped the air of boredom and said in a very different tone, 'What may I do for you, sir?'

'Good grief, sir,' his uncle said, looking at a coat that had so many capes it made Rupert's broad shoulders look positively menacing. 'Where did you get that monstrosity?'

'Uncle!' Devilish eyes mocked him. 'My feelings are deeply lacerated. Don't you know I'm a very tulip of fashion? I dare say at least six young idiots have copied this cape only this week, for I saw Harrad's boy wearing one with nine capes and this has only seven.'

'More fool him,' the marquess grunted. 'Sit down, m'boy. You make me feel awkward, towering over me like an avenging dervish. What happened to the eager young fellow I saw off to war six years ago?'

'I dare say he grew up, sir,' Rupert replied carelessly, but there were shadows in his eyes as he sat in the chair opposite and his mouth lost its smile. He did not care to be reminded of that time for the memories were too painful. 'Is something bothering you?'

'I fear it is,' the marquess said. 'I'm in somewhat of a pickle, m'boy—and I'm hoping you'll sort me out.'

'Anything to oblige. I do not forget that you stood as a father to me when my own...' Blue fire flashed in bitter regret, for the late Lord Myers had been a rogue and a cheat and had brought his family almost to the edge of ruin. That Rupert had been able to save himself and his sister from disgrace was in large part due to this man. 'No, I will not go down that road. Tell me what you wish, sir, and if it is in within my power I shall do it.'

'It's Lily's children,' the marquess said with a heavy sigh. 'You know my daughter's story, Rupert. She would marry that wastrel. I warned her that he would run through her fortune and break her heart. She wouldn't listen and he did all that and more—he killed her.'

'You can't be sure of that, sir.'

'He drove her out into the rain that night. Her maid told me of the quarrel between them. Scunthorpe broke her heart and she stayed out all night in the rain. You know what happened next...'

Rupert nodded for he did know only too well. Lily Scunthorpe had died of a fever, leaving a daughter of six years and a son of three, but that had been more than ten years previously and he could not see what the urgency was now.

'You took the children when Scunthorpe deserted them, installed them in Cavendish Park with a governess, tutor and the requisite servants—what has happened to throw you into a fit of the blue devils?'

'The governess and tutor both gave notice last month. I've tried to find replacements, but with very little success. I fear my niece and nephew have acquired a reputation for being difficult. I have managed to find a woman who is prepared to take them both on—I suspect because she has no choice—but I'm not sure she'll stay above a few days.'

Merrivale cleared his throat. 'They need a firm hand, Rupert. I fear I've spoiled them. If I read them a lecture, they would apologise sweetly and then go straight back to their old ways. Would it be too much to ask you to stand as mentor to them for a while? The boy may go to college at the end of the year and the girl...well, she ought to have a Season next spring, but I fear I shall find it hard to secure the services of a woman influential enough to give them a good start.'

'Play bear-leader to a girl on the edge of her come-out and a rebellious youth? Good grief, Uncle! Have your wits gone begging? I'm hardly a role model for either of them. Besides being a tulip of fashion, I'm a notorious rake—or hadn't you heard?'

Merrivale ran nervous fingers through his white hair. 'I know you have your mistress, but I'm not suggesting you should take her with you to Cavendish.'

'Thank you for small mercies,' Rupert said, the light of mockery in his eyes once more. 'She would take it as an invitation to marry me. Annais is too greedy for her own good. I have been looking for an excuse to finish the affair and I suppose one is as good as another...she has no love of the country.'

'Do you mean you will do it?' A look of such relief

entered the marquess's eyes that Rupert laughed out loud. 'I should be so grateful, m'boy.'

'I'll do what I can for them,' Rupert said. 'But I must have a free hand. Discipline is never popular and I dare say one or the other will write and complain of my high-handed behaviour or some such thing.'

'Lily was very precious to me and her children are all I have left—apart from you, m'boy. Francesca is very like her mother, but I think the boy may be more like his father. I hope John won't turn out to be a rogue like Captain Scunthorpe—but that is why he needs a firm hand now, to knock him into shape a little before he goes to college. I suppose I should have sent him earlier, but I preferred to educate them at home—some of those schools are very harsh to boys, you know.'

'We've all suffered at the hands of bullies at school,' Rupert said. 'John needs to learn to stand up for himself. I could teach him to box, gentleman's rules—and perhaps fencing lessons. I'm not sure about the girl, but perhaps the governess will be what she needs.'

'I pray she will be suitable. Her references from Lady Mary Winters were good, but Lady Mary's daughter was leaving for finishing school in France so she may just have wanted to get the woman off her hands.'

'How old is this governess and what is her name?'

'She's in her late twenties, I think, and a sensible woman. Her name is Miss Hester Goodrum and she teaches the pianoforte as well as French, literature and needlework.'

'Miss Goodrum?' Rupert nodded. She sounded sensible enough, though her skills were limited. 'I'm not sure what help she would be to John. He needs rather more than that—but for the next six months he shall have the benefit of my knowledge, such as it is.'

'I'm not sure what you mean.' The marquess looked puzzled. 'I thought you would just run an eye over them, give them both a lecture and then pop in once in a while?'

'I hardly think that would do much good, sir.' Rupert arched his right eyebrow. 'I've been feeling jaded for a while and this sounds like a challenge. I shall reside at Cavendish Park until the boy goes to college and by then you will have found someone to take Francesca on, I imagine. I can be John's mentor and tutor and keep an eye on this governess until Christmas. After that I dare say I'll be thoroughly sick of it all, but I've never refused a challenge.'

'Then take my hand on it. If I can be of service to you, you have only to ask, m'boy.'

'You have done more for me than I could ever repay,' Rupert assured him, clasped his hand firmly and smiled. 'It will be a change for me. My estate is in good heart and almost runs itself these days. Besides, I shall be no more than a day's ride from my home if I'm needed.'

'I fear you may find they do not take kindly to authority, Rupert.'

'I dare say John may kick a bit at the start, but he'll gentle to the bit in time.'

Rupert waved his uncle's gratitude aside carelessly. After all, what trouble could one young boy and a girl on the brink of womanhood be to a man of the world? He hoped the governess would be presentable and not one of those sour-face spinsters, but whatever she was like they would bob along together easily enough....

Chapter One

'It was so good of you to take me up with you, Miss Hardcastle,' Hester Goodrum said as she climbed into the comfortable chaise. 'Lady Mary promised to send me to Cavendish Park in comfort, but she was called away to her sister's bedside and forgot all about me. I have to be there by the end of the week, because the marquess sent word the young people would be alone by then, except for their servants, of course.'

Sarah Hardcastle looked at the woman sitting opposite her and nodded. Hester was in her late twenties, attractive, though not pretty, and kind- hearted. She had heard of her predicament and been moved to offer assistance.

'Well, I'm returning to my home in the north of England and we must pass within twenty miles of Cavendish Park. It is no trouble to take a detour, Hester.'

'My fiancé told me I was a fool to agree to this position,' Hester went on as she settled in her seat. 'He wanted me to give up work and go home to Chester and marry him.'

'Why didn't you?' Sarah asked and caught at the rope

as the chaise moved off with a lurch. 'I fear Coachman is in one of his moods again. If he continues this way, I shall have to call a halt and give him a scolding.'

'Please do not do so on my account,' Hester said. 'I should like to get married, miss. I've been saving for years, but Jim needs more money to set up for himself in an inn. He's got some savings, but we both know we need to wait for another year at least.'

'That's a shame...' Sarah looked at her thoughtfully. She'd been told the governess's story and it was part of the reason she'd offered her the ride in her chaise. 'How much more do you need to save?'

'I suppose a hundred pounds might be enough...' Hester sighed. 'If we both save hard this year, we may just manage it, though I contribute very little and it may take much longer.'

She was not a young woman. Sarah felt sympathy for her, because time was passing her by and her youth was fading. It was so ironic that Hester should be longing for marriage, but did not have enough money while she, Sarah Hardcastle, was doing her best to avoid being married because she'd had rather too much of it.

Was her plan too outrageous to have a chance of success? She'd thought about it all the previous night and her stomach was tying itself in knots. No doubt Hester would think she'd run mad.

'Supposing I offered you two hundred pounds and gave you two of my best dresses in return for your reference from Lady Mary and the gowns you have in your trunk? Would you change places with me? I mean, let me take your place as the governess at Cavendish Park—and you go home to marry your fiancé?'

There, she'd said it out loud. Did it sound as mad as she imagined?

Hester was staring at her in bewilderment. 'What did you say, miss? I don't think I heard right.'

'I offered you two hundred pounds to let me have some of your clothes and the reference Lady Mary gave you. You can do what you wish with the money.'

'You want to be a governess? Why?' Hester was stunned. 'You're a rich young woman, Miss Hardcastle. Why would you wish to be a governess?'

'I need to disappear for a while and it seems an ideal situation to me. Your employer has never seen you. The girl is almost seventeen so will be easy to manage and the boy is going to college in six months—so how could I go wrong? My tutors considered me a bright pupil. I imagine I can teach the boy mathematics and geography and the girl music, literature, French, Latin, drawing and dancing. What more does she need to know?'

'Nothing, I shouldn't think,' Hester said, but looked anxious. 'I don't know what to say, miss—it doesn't seem right. We should be deceiving my employer…'

'But if he didn't even bother to interview you he can't be that bothered about his grandchildren. All he wants is to keep them out of his hair—and I can do that as easily as you.'

'Perhaps better, miss. You've a way with you. People pay attention when Miss Hardcastle speaks.'

'That is because my father left me a fortune invested in mills and mines and I've run them myself since he died when I was just nineteen.'

'How old are you, miss—if you don't mind my asking?'

'I'm five and twenty,' Sarah said and sighed. 'My

aunt and uncle have been trying to marry me off for months. They say I need a man to help me and they're afraid I shall die an old maid.'

'Do they bully you, miss?'

'No, I shall not lie. Aunt Jenny is kind and my uncle is well meaning, but I have no intention of marrying simply to please them. I came away because my uncle would not let the subject drop.'

'What will happen to your mills if you're not there, miss?'

'I have managers and a man of business I trust. I shall keep in touch with him by letter—and it will just be for a short time, until I've made up my mind about something. After that I'll give notice and your pupils will have a new governess. Surely my influence cannot harm them in that time?' Sarah leaned forward. 'Will you think about it today? This evening when we stop at the inn you can tell me. If your answer is yes, we'll change clothes. In the morning I'll send you on in my chaise to Chester—and I'll go by post-chaise to Cavendish Park.'

'I don't know what to say...' Hester looked worried, clearly torn between taking this wonderful chance and fulfilling her duty. 'It's such an opportunity for me. It would mean the world to my Jim to have his inn this year instead of waiting.'

'Well, the choice is yours. I shan't twist your arm. If you say no, I'll simply find another way to disappear for a while.'

Hester nodded, settling back against the squabs with a sigh. She was obviously tempted and Sarah crossed her fingers under the folds of her elegant travelling gown. Being a governess would be a safe environment for a wealthy heiress to hide in until she could shake off the feeling of being persecuted for her money.

Why had her father had to die in that accident at the mill? Tobias Hardcastle had always been a hands-on employer, not above taking off his frock coat and rolling up his sleeves. He'd started out with fifty pounds left to him by his grandfather and built up his huge business using his brains and his ability to work twenty hours out of every twenty-four for years.

Before she died, Sarah's mother had complained bitterly that she wasn't sure when he'd had time to give her a child. It wasn't true, of course, for he came home for meals and occasionally had Sunday off, but he'd certainly put in long hours to ensure that his business empire was solid. Sarah couldn't claim to do the same, but she had a knack of choosing her employees well and of inspiring loyalty. She'd taken up the challenge at the start because it was there and she did not wish to hand over her father's empire to someone who might abuse it. However, she had begun to grow a little tired of the constant rounds of meetings and bookkeeping that were an ever-present part of her life. It was time to sit back a little, for her life was slipping away and some might already consider her as being past the age of making a good marriage. Her managers would make sure the mills continued to prosper during her absence and also the two copper mines she owned in Cornwall. It was on her return from her biannual visit to the mines that she'd stopped off to visit her own governess and there met Miss Hester Goodrum.

Something about the young woman had appealed to Sarah immediately. Had Hester been a woman who wanted a lifetime career she would have offered her a position as her companion, but Hester had confided her hopes for marriage and that had set Sarah's quick mind working.

It was a little deceitful to pretend to be someone she wasn't, of course, but she wasn't harming anyone. She wouldn't steal the silver or teach the children to swear and drink gin. A smile touched her lips, for the idea of being the children's mentor was pleasant. Sarah had worked hard since her father's death, giving little thought to pleasure of any kind. She'd been asked to dinners and evening affairs at the homes of her father's friends, but since she knew that the ones with wives wanted to buy her mills and the widowers wanted to marry her to get them cheaply, she normally found such evenings tedious.

Even at school she'd been aware that she wasn't really one of the gentry. She was the daughter of a rich man who'd bought the right to live in a big house and own land, but she wasn't one of the blue bloods. The other girls were friendly to a degree, but she'd felt the barrier between them and knew that they laughed at her northern accent, which had all but disappeared now. Sometimes, if she was upset, it returned, but her teachers had earned their money. Mr Hardcastle had wanted his daughter to be a lady and to all intents and purposes she was—except that she wasn't fully accepted into their society. They welcomed her on the boards of their charities and they were even friendlier towards her money, which they grabbed as soon as it was offered, but she was seldom invited to an intimate affair at their homes. Occasionally she would be invited to a large dance because of her influence, but she wasn't the kind of woman that gentlemen thought of marrying.

Well, that wasn't quite true, either, Sarah mused, glancing out of the window. She did have one rather persistent suitor. Sir Roger Grey had asked her to marry him three times now and he didn't like being refused. Sarah was aware that he was in financial difficulty, though he'd managed to hide that fact from her uncle and most of his acquaintance. Sarah had asked one of her agents to make enquiries and his report was disturbing. Sir Roger gave the appearance of being wealthy and respectable, but in reality was a rake and a gambler, and the last man she would ever wed. However, he was difficult to shake off, for he seemed to have taken it into his head that she would come round to the idea if he continued to press her. Unfortunately, her uncle was completely taken in and believed him to be a man of his word.

It was Sir Roger's tactics at the charity ball in Newcastle that had made her decide to leave for Cornwall a month earlier than usual. He'd tried to kiss her and he'd fumbled at her breasts. She'd had to fight him off and had scratched his cheek in her efforts.

'You little hellcat.' He'd put a hand to his cheek in shock. 'You will be sorry for that, Sarah. I'll teach you to respect your betters.'

'I do not consider you my superior, sir,' she'd retorted. 'I have no intention of being seduced. If you thought to compromise me and force me into marriage, you are far off the mark. I would rather have fingers pointed at me in the street than marry you.'

That was perfectly true, for she would rather die than marry a man like him, but it was also true that she didn't wish to lose her good name. Nor would she care to be whispered about or pointed out as an object of shame.

'If you would marry Sam Goodjohn, or Harry Barton, you'd be safe from rogues like that,' her uncle had told her when she'd told him what had happened. 'They're good men and run mills of their own so you could stay home and be a wife and mother as you ought. It's time you married and thought about a family, Sarah—unless you want to die an old maid.'

'I know you want to protect me, Uncle William,' Sarah replied. 'But I should hate to be married simply for the sake of my fortune. When I find a man I love who loves me, I'll get married.'

'Love,' her uncle scoffed at the idea. 'When did love ever get you anywhere? You need a man to protect you and look after your business, young woman. Don't leave it too late or you may find that even money won't get you the kind of man you need.'

Her uncle's scolding had jerked her from her complacency. It was true that time was slipping by and she was no longer a young girl. If she wanted a family she must marry—and Sarah had begun to realise what she might miss if she did not.

Was she so ill-favoured that she needed money to buy her a husband? Sarah knew she wasn't beautiful by any means. Her hair was dark brown, and her nose was straight. Her mouth was bigger than she liked and she wished she had thin lips like Hester. Miss Goodrum was prettier than she was, but Sarah didn't feel ugly. When she dressed in her best she was attractive enough and people said she had a nice smile.

Was it impossible that she would find love?

She felt she might have more chance of it if she were not her father's heir. When men looked at her they saw the rich Miss Hardcastle and they wanted what she could give them. The hard-headed ones wanted to build up her business and get richer; the spendthrifts wanted a ticket to the easy life.

Sarah wanted… A little sigh escaped her. She wanted a man who would make her laugh. A man who appreciated music, poetry and beautiful gardens…someone who would love her for who she was, not for her money.

Was she asking too much? Perhaps her uncle was right. It might be sensible to accept one of her suitors and have the lawyers draw up a contract that gave her the right to retain control of her business and protect her fortune.

It was the simple way out of her predicament. A business arrangement that would protect her from fortune hunters and unscrupulous businessmen who wanted the vast wealth her father had bequeathed her. Until recently, Sarah would have thought it a perfectly sensible idea, but for some reason she had begun to feel a slight dissatisfaction with her life as it presently was. She had not thought of marriage whilst her father lived and in the first years after his death she'd been too wrapped up in her work to consider it. Of late she'd begun to notice children playing in the parks and sweethearts walking together in the sunshine. If she did not marry, she would miss so much.

Was she lonely? Certainly not! She had friends and loyal employees and was too busy to be lonely.

Yet surely there was another way to live? She must have time to consider, to decide what she wanted of life. What Sarah needed was a place to escape, to hide and to be someone else for a while.…

'Yes, I'll do it, miss. Like you said, it can't hurt anyone—and Jim will be so happy to have me home.…'

Sarah blinked, dragging her thoughts back to the present. For a moment she couldn't believe that Hester had agreed, then, as she saw the other woman was in earnest, she smiled.

'Thank you so much, Hester,' she said and leaned forwards to touch her hand. 'You won't regret it. I shan't do anything that could harm your good name, I promise you.'

'Lord, miss, as if you would.' Hester laughed, looking younger as her eyes lit with excitement. 'I can't thank you enough for giving me this chance—and I hope you'll get on with your charges. Lady Mary arranged it for me. She said they're a little bit difficult, but I'm sure you'll be fine.'

'Yes, I'm certain I shall,' Sarah agreed and laughed. 'How hard can it be to look after a young lady and a boy of thirteen?'

Chapter Two

'Why do we have to have a mentor as well as a governess? I thought you said it would be all right when we got rid of the last two? You said Grandfather would give up sending us tutors and take us to live with him in London.'

'I said he would take me. It's time I had my come out,' Francesca Scunthorpe said and made a face at her brother. She was a pretty girl with soft hair and bright eyes, and a mouth that was wide and sensuous. Her yellow-silk gown was attractive, but not as fashionable as she would like, and made for her by a local seamstress. 'You will be going to Cambridge after Christmas. It looks as if I'll be stuck here on my own with some stupid governess.'

'I don't mind going to college,' John said and threw a paper dart at her across the schoolroom. He was a sturdy boy, attractive with dark hair and eyes and a stubborn chin. His tutor had given him a list of Latin verbs to learn to keep him busy until the new mentor arrived, but John was bored with lists. His tutor had given him new lists every day for the past eighteen months, but he hadn't explained anything. His lessons consisted of setting a new exercise and then tests to see what he'd learned. 'It would be better than staying here on our own.'

'It was all right at first,' Francesca said. 'When we were younger we had Miss Graham and Mr Browne. I liked her and she taught me lots of interesting things, but she left and the last governess was useless. She couldn't play the pianoforte or the harp and she chose all the wrong books.'

'And she didn't like frogs in her bed,' John said, a gleam of mischief in his eyes. 'I've never heard anyone scream as much as she did when she saw that grass snake.'

'She thought it was poisonous.' Francesca looked scornful. 'She didn't know it was a grass snake and harmless.'

'Anyone knows the difference between a viper and a grass snake,' John said and looked up at his sister. 'What are we going to do, Fran? I'm so bored—aren't you?'

'Yes, some of the time,' Fran agreed. 'I like to read poetry, but I know you'd rather play games or go fishing.'

'Can we go fishing today? He will probably stop us having fun when he gets here—and your governess will say it isn't a fit occupation for a lady.'

'We'll outwit them somehow,' Fran promised. She picked up a volume of poetry she'd been reading earlier, then threw it down with a sigh of discontent. 'They are both supposed to arrive later today, though not together. We'll go fishing this morning and come back when we feel like it.'

'Grandfather's letter said we had to be on our best be-haviour—to be waiting in the parlour when they arrive.'

'Well, he should have come down himself and stayed for a few days.'

'He said it was getting a bit much for him. Do you think he's ill?'

'I don't know.' Fran's brow creased because she worried about her grandfather. The marquess was all they had—the only one who bothered about them anyway. Her father had gone off abroad somewhere when his money ran out. His house and estate had been put up for sale and the marquess had brought them here. At first he'd spent time with them, but of late he hadn't bothered to come down other than at Christmas, though he always sent birthday gifts. 'I hope he isn't, because I don't know what would happen to us if he died. We haven't any money of our own, John. Everything comes from Grandfather. If I get my Season, I'll marry a rich lord and then we'll have money. I'll look after you then. You won't have to work for a living.'

'Do you think Grandfather will leave us anything?'

'I don't know. I don't want to think about that...' Fran's throat caught at the idea that they might be forced to leave this house. She'd loved it from the moment they came here and didn't want to live in a horrible little cottage like some of the children on the estate. 'Come on, I refuse to be miserable on a lovely morning like this. Let's get some stuff from the kitchen and go down to the stream.'

'Yes.' John grinned at her. 'At least we've got each other. I'll put frogs in her bed and you can think of something to do to this lord whatever- his-name-is...'

'Lord Rupert Myers,' Fran said. 'Don't worry, we'll

think of some way to get rid of them if we hate them. Let's go fishing. It will serve them right if there's no one to greet them when they get here.'

Sarah got down from the chaise and looked at the house. Cavendish Park was a pleasant country house, much the biggest one she'd ever visited, larger and more impressive than her father's on the outskirts of Newcastle. She'd visited a few country houses as the guest of her school friends, but never one quite like this. It was so beautiful that for a moment all she wanted to do was to stand and stare at the mellow golden walls and long windows that sparkled like diamonds in the sunshine.

'If you'd like to come into the house, Miss Goodrum.'

Sarah came to herself with a start. The housekeeper must have been speaking to her for a few minutes, but she'd been lost in thought—and it was difficult remembering that she was no longer the wealthy heiress, Miss Hardcastle. She'd packed that particular persona into her trunks and sent them back to her home with a letter for her uncle explaining that she was taking a little holiday and they were not to worry. All she had with her was a small trunk containing the clothes she'd purchased from Hester.

She was wearing Hester's best gown, because she'd been assured it would be expected for her first arrival. It was pearl-grey with a slender skirt and tight bodice, and it had a white lace collar. Sarah had fastened a small silver brooch at the neck to cheer it up a little. Hester's other gowns were not as good and certainly not what Sarah was accustomed to, but she would get used to them—and it was only for a few weeks or so.

'Yes, thank you, Mrs Brancaster. I was just thinking what a lovely house it is. You must enjoy living here?'

'It's a nice enough house, Miss Goodrum, but...' The housekeeper hesitated and then pursed her thin mouth. 'Things are not quite what they ought to be. His lordship doesn't come down often enough and the children are left to do much as they please. The house needs a master or a mistress, if you ask me—preferably both.'

'Yes, I expect it does. A big place like this takes some running and it shouldn't be left to the servants.'

Unaware of the odd glance her remark had brought from Mrs Brancaster, Sarah walked into the house by way of the kitchen entrance. Since she made a habit of visiting her kitchens regularly at home this did not make her uncomfortable. She might be wealthy and she'd been educated as a lady, but Sarah knew she was a long way from being one. You could take the girl out of Newcastle, but you couldn't take Newcastle out of the girl; it had been one of her father's favourite sayings and made her smile. She'd been so close to her father, his right-hand man, and she missed him so very much.

She supposed she was looking for someone she could admire and respect as she had Tobias Hardcastle. If such a man were to present himself, she would not hesitate to hand over her person and the day-to-day running of her business to him—but as yet she'd never met anyone who came close to filling his shoes.

'I'll take you straight up to your room,' the housekeeper was saying. 'You can settle in and then come down to the kitchen for a nice cup of tea. Miss Francesca and Master John were supposed to be here to meet you, but they slipped off early this morning. I suspect they went fishing in defiance of the marquess's instructions that they should sit in the parlour and wait for you and their mentor.'

'Their mentor? I thought the Marquess of Merrivale was their grandfather and guardian?'

'So he is, Miss Goodrum. Mr John is to have a tutor and he is to be their mentor. As I understand it, he's to be in charge here and we shall all report to him.'

It was the first Sarah had heard of this arrangement and she wondered if Hester had known. This new man might enquire more closely into her background than she'd imagined and she was glad she'd asked for the reference as well as Hester's clothes.

'I see. Do you know this…mentor's name?'

'I wasn't listening properly when Mr Burrows told me,' the housekeeper admitted. 'I'd just discovered that the pair of scamps had disappeared again and my mind wasn't on it, but I'll find out when he arrives and let you know.'

'Thank you, Mrs Brancaster.' Sarah was thoughtful. 'Do you think I could leave the tea for an hour or so? I should like to take a walk about the grounds before I unpack—get my bearings.'

'Well…' Mrs Brancaster looked a bit put out. 'I'm sure it's up to you, miss. I thought you might want to see the schoolroom?'

'When I return you can give me directions or I'll ask one of the footmen. I don't want to take up too much of your time, because I know you have so much to do in a house like this—and with two new visitors it must have turned your routine upside down.'

'It has…' Mrs Brancaster nodded. 'Well, off you go then. Your trunk will be taken up and you can find your own way here when you're ready, I dare say.'

'Oh, I'm sure I shall. I'm really quite capable, you know.'

Sarah left the housekeeper staring after her. She knew that she had perhaps risked offending her new colleague, but she'd felt as if she must escape before she did something stupid. All at once the enormity of what she'd done—and what she was attempting to do—had hit her square in the face. In her comfortable chaise with all her familiar things about her it had seemed a clever idea. She'd imagined the children were left much to themselves with just their grandfather's servants—but who was this new mentor and what would he be like?

If he was just another superior servant, she might manage to get away with her masquerade by keeping her own counsel. If, however, he'd been placed in charge of the children's future by the marquess, he might want to know too much about her. Sarah couldn't afford for him to dig too deeply into her background. Should he discover she was lying, he might imagine her to be a person of low integrity and dubious virtue.

Her stomach was fluttering with nerves as she strolled through the kitchen garden, noticing how well everything was kept. If she'd expected to find an air of neglect here, she was far off the mark. What if this mentor had met Hester Goodrum in the past?

Oh, this whole thing was madness! She should go back to the house, ask for directions to the nearest post house and leave. What on earth had made her think she was capable of carrying out a masquerade like this? She hadn't been thinking clearly, of course. Sarah wanted time out of her life, time to come to terms with what she needed from the future: should she marry for the sake of companionship or should she wait until she fell in love?

A smile touched her mouth. There was no guarantee that the man she chose would reciprocate her feelings. Sarah knew that she wasn't the prettiest girl in the world and if she found someone she wanted, he would probably not be interested in her.

She must not rush her decision. Looking about her as she walked, Sarah fell in love with the beautiful rose gardens, the herbaceous borders and the sweeping lawns. Some of these trees must have been here for centuries. Hearing the sound of laughter coming from what appeared to be a small wilderness, she turned instinctively towards it and then stopped as she saw a young woman of perhaps sixteen years and a boy some years younger. They were sprawled out on the grass, watching as a fish cooked slowly over a smoking fire.

The camaraderie between them and the sound of their laughter caught at Sarah's throat, making her aware of how much she missed in not having a family. They were so beautiful, so wrapped up in themselves and their amusement that she hesitated, not wanting to intrude. If she introduced herself now they might resent her intrusion into their private time and she would start off on the wrong foot. No, it would be better to wait and meet them later when they had washed the dirt from their hands and faces. Yet how she longed to be a part of that scene.

Turning away, Sarah felt the ache inside her. She had been thinking it best if she made some excuse and went away, leaving the new mentor to arrange a new governess for his charges, but now she'd changed her mind again. Something inside her called out to the young people she'd discovered having fun and she wanted to stay. She had no wish to harm them and she would keep her distance from their mentor, be friendly but reserved, as a proper governess should be.

Lifting her head, she took her courage in her hands. Her father's lawyers had advised her to sell her father's mills to the highest bidder and not to think of trying to run them herself. She hadn't listened to their prophecies of doom and gloom, and, though she'd come up against prejudice and men who resented a woman in their midst, she'd overcome their opposition and her business was thriving. She wouldn't turn and run at the first obstacle now.

It was time to have that cup of tea with Mrs Brancaster. Sarah wouldn't lie more than she had to, to sustain her masquerade as a governess, but she wasn't going to walk away from those delightful children, either.

Rupert was getting down from his curricle when he saw the woman walking back from the gardens. The sun was shining on her head, picking out the red tints in her dark hair and giving her a kind of halo. From her dress he guessed her to be the new governess and surmised that she'd been for a little walk to acquaint herself with her surroundings. He knew very little about her, except that she had been recommended by Lady Mary Winters.

Well acquainted with Cavendish Park from visits to his uncle as a young man, Rupert had no desire to follow her example. He'd known his uncle's grandchildren when they were all younger, but it was years since he'd seen them. He wondered whether they were waiting dutifully in the parlour, as they'd been bidden, or, as he would have done in their place, escaped for a last day of freedom.

'Your lordship,' Burrows said, his face wreathed in smiles as he came out to greet him. 'It is a pleasure to see you, sir. I've been informed that you intend to stay with us for a few months.'

'Yes, until John goes to Cambridge,' Rupert replied. 'It's Burrows, isn't it?'

'Fancy you remembering that, sir.' The butler looked gratified. 'Most of the staff are still here, though some of the maids and footmen are new.'

'Is Mrs Brancaster still with you?'

'Yes, sir. She'll be up in a minute…ah, here she is now. I dare say she was busy…'

'Are Francesca and John in the house?'

'They went off early this morning, sir. Shall I send someone to look for them? One of the gardeners thought they'd gone fishing.'

'Perfect day for it. Wouldn't have minded a spot of fishing myself this morning. No, don't make them feel guilty. We'll soon have a routine established once I've had time to sort things out. I think I should like some cold ale if you have any and a bite to eat—didn't stop for nuncheon.'

'Lord Myers—' Mrs Brancaster looked stunned as she came up to him '—how are you, sir? I didn't realise it was you coming down today. I've prepared the wrong room. I thought…' Her cheeks turned pink. 'Forgive me, I'll have your own room ready in half an hour.'

'Plenty of time,' Rupert assured her, amused by her obvious embarrassment. 'I should like to meet Miss Goodrum. I believe I saw her return to the house a moment ago?'

'Yes, sir. She went for a little walk to get used to her surroundings. We were just about to have a cup of tea when I was told you'd arrived and it set me all of a fluster.'

'No need to stand on ceremony. I'm the same as I was when I came here as a lad, Mrs Brancaster.'

'No, that you're not, sir. We all heard how you were decorated for bravery for what you did over there in France—and you were wounded in the leg.'

'Which is so much better I hardly know it happened. It's only when the weather turns cold that I feel it.' Rupert's smile dimmed. He did not like to hear himself praised for something he felt best placed in the past where it belonged.

'I'll tell Miss Goodrum to wait on you in the front parlour immediately, sir.'

'Please request her to visit me there when she has had time to take her refreshments. I should wish to be on good terms with the young woman. Tell me, Mrs Brancaster, what are your first impressions?'

'Of the new governess?' Mrs Brancaster frowned. 'I've only just met her, sir, but…she seems very calm and sure of herself.'

'Do I detect a note of disapproval?'

'Oh, no, sir, nothing like that I assure you.' The housekeeper was thoughtful. 'It's just…she isn't quite like any of the others we've had. They usually have a look about them…sort of resigned and disappointed… but she's not like that at all.'

Rupert quirked an eyebrow, amused. 'I see. An unusual governess. How interesting. I hope she is intelligent enough to know that you cannot keep a girl of

Francesca's age always in the schoolroom. However, we shall see.'

'You mustn't take against her for anything I've said, sir. I've only just met her and I'm sure she's perfectly respectable.'

'Oh, I'm certain of it. Lady Mary would not otherwise have employed her. She comes with impeccable references. I am quite looking forward to meeting her.'

'I'll send her along in about ten minutes—and your refreshments will follow as soon as they're ready. I'll have your room prepared immediately.'

'Thank you. You always did spoil me, Mrs Brancaster. I can see I've been missing a treat by not coming down more often.'

Mrs Brancaster positively glowed and scurried away to set everything in motion. Rupert smiled to himself as he went into the house. Nothing much had changed here. It still smelled of roses and lavender; the furniture was mostly good oak and polished to within an inch of its life, though in the main salon he recalled seeing some mahogany Chippendale pieces.

It was what it had always been, a pleasant country house, comfortable rather than elegant, and he could feel its welcome as he made his way to the parlour. Vases of flowers stood everywhere and the smell of roses was even stronger in the parlour. Merrivale had good servants and it was a pity the marquess didn't spend more time here, but Rupert supposed the memories were too strong for him. He'd grieved for his wife for years and the loss of his daughter had nearly done him in, bringing on a heart attack that had left him with a weakness. Rupert suspected that the old man found it too upsetting to visit often for reasons of his own, but it hadn't been wise to let the children run wild. Francesca in particular would need to be schooled in the manners she needed for society and he could only hope that he would find some support in the new governess—because he was more used to dealing with ladies of a different kind.

Rupert laughed softly in his throat. His latest mistress had been most disappointed to hear that he was leaving town and did not expect to return for months.

'What am I to do without you?' she'd asked, as she ran her long nails down his naked back. 'Do you expect me to languish here alone?'

'I expect you to take a new protector within a week,' Rupert told her with a mocking smile. 'We both know this was merely a convenient arrangement for us both, my dear Annais. You will find yourself adequately compensated by my parting gift, so do not pretend to feel more than you do.'

Her nails had scored his back, her eyes glinting with temper. Rupert had known she was angry at being given her freedom to find a new lover, but the diamonds he'd gifted her should soon dry her tears and he was aware that she'd been casting glances at Lord Rowley for a while now. He would bet that the gentleman found himself in her bed within the week. His own feelings were not touched. It was a long time since he'd found more than a fleeting pleasure in the arms of a woman—since Madeline had broken his heart before he went off to fight for his king and country.

A picture of Madeline's beautiful face and long blonde curls passed through his mind and was ruthlessly dismissed. When she'd married the old Duke of Marley for money, he'd put her out of his heart and mind. At first he'd been angry, bitter, broken by her scorn and her betrayal, but then he'd found something more worthwhile—and that was the camaraderie of his friends. It was only when he'd lost them that his heart had become encased in ice.

His one-time friends believed that he had done something careless that had led to the deaths of several of their comrades. Rupert knew that he was innocent of their charges, but he refused to explain or to tell them the truth about what had happened that night. If they could see only what was in front of their noses, then they were not worth bothering over—they were certainly not his friends and not the men he'd thought them to be. Where was the trust that should have existed between them? Where was the respect he believed he was entitled to expect? Since they had chosen to believe evil of him he would not defend himself. Let them think what they chose. He'd shut out the memory of their friendship, becoming in truth the man society believed him: a hardened rake and a ruthless card player.

'You wished to see me, Lord Myers?'

The voice was soft, but there was just the trace of an accent. Rupert turned to look at the young woman who had entered the parlour as he stood gazing out at the park. Although no beauty, she was of medium height, slim, attractive with dark hair that he knew carried tints of red in the sunlight. Her eyes were a bluish-green and her mouth pleasantly full. She carried herself well and there was a hint of pride in her face—also something else?

Did she seem wary? A little uneasy, perhaps?

'You are Miss Hester Goodrum?'

He thought there was a slight hesitation before she inclined her head. 'I am the new governess, sir.'

'Miss Goodrum?'

'Yes.' This time her voice was firm and without hesitation. 'I believe you are to be the children's mentor?'

'My uncle has requested me to be John's mentor until he goes to his college. I am also here to see that Francesca is ready to enter society next Season. She will be seventeen then and I believe arrangements will be made for her to stay with a suitable lady next spring. Until then you are here to keep her from getting into mischief.'

'I dare say I can find ways to do that, sir. Once I have established the level she has reached in her studies, we can plan a new schedule.'

'I hardly think you can expect to keep a young woman like Francesca in the schoolroom all day, Miss Goodrum.'

'I would not be foolish enough to try,' she replied, her head up, eyes meeting his. All sign of the hesitation had gone now. 'Perhaps some poetry, music and dancing lessons would not go amiss. I imagine she already has some knowledge of French, Latin and drawing. We can find some way of making the lessons more interesting, I dare say. John may need more tuition, but I think that will be your province, Lord Myers. I am prepared to give him certain lessons if you wish, of course. I could take history and literature and mathematics. However, geography and the sciences were never my strong point, though I am willing to attempt them should you wish?'

'I am amazed you are able to offer such a wide curriculum. I am sure my uncle did not tell me you were so accomplished.'

Did he detect a hint of colour in her cheeks—a lessening of her confidence? Why? He'd just paid her a compliment, yet he seemed to have made her uneasy. For a fleeting moment she looked uncertain, but then her head came up and she bestowed a cool smile on him.

'I dare say you are able to take the boy's education to a higher degree than I could, my lord. However, I am willing to help should I be required.'

Rupert's instincts were alerted. She certainly was an unusual governess. Her manner was far from that one might expect of a woman in her late twenties who had little expectation of life other than to work for a succession of employers until she retired. This young woman did not look a day over four and twenty and she had a confident manner beyond her years, which was strangely at odds with her calling. Something about her did not ring true.

'I understand you have been employed by Lady Mary Winters for some years?'

'Yes, sir. I was her daughter June's governess until recently. Miss June has gone to Bath for a visit with her mother and aunt. She no longer requires a governess, which meant that I was free to take this position.' He noticed that her eyes seemed to be fixed on a spot beyond his left shoulder.

'Fortunately so was I.' Rupert smiled. 'We must try to keep these young rascals in order. They have been allowed to run free, I fear, and their last tutor and governess left at rather short notice.'

'I was told they might be a little difficult at times?'

'I do hope you are not frightened of frogs? John apparently has a habit of putting them in the governess's bed.'

'Ah, I see.' She smiled. Rupert caught his breath. There was something very engaging about this young woman, a way she had of holding her head and of sometimes looking straight at you. 'Thank you for the warning. I do not dislike the creatures, but would not wish to find one in my bed. I shall make sure to inspect it each night before getting in.'

'If you find something unpleasant, let me know. I'll deal with the culprit.'

'Oh, I dare say I can manage,' she said. 'My cousin was forever playing such tricks when we were both children. Uncle William was glad to pack him off to E…to school.' A hint of pink touched her cheeks. She drew breath, lifted her head and met his curious gaze. 'Do you wish me to prepare a curriculum for you to inspect, sir?'

'Good grief, no. I shall leave Francesa's lessons to you. However, I think we should arrange for her to have dancing lessons—perhaps someone will know of a local man who could come in once or twice a week.'

'I would be happy to play the pianoforte. If there is no master to be found, you might supply the lack. I can teach her the steps if you would practise with her.'

'Is there no end to your talents?'

'I…have an interest in music and dancing, also deportment. I think I may be able to teach Francesca how to enter a drawing room in society and how to conduct herself, to engage others in conversation…enough so that she does not feel strange when she meets her chaperon next spring.'

'Indeed? I would not have thought you would have had much experience in the drawing rooms of society hostesses?'

Rupert saw her colour deepen and knew he'd scored a hit. It was perhaps a little unfair of him to say such a thing to her, but he had not been able to resist it. This confident young woman had aroused his curiosity. He was quite certain that she was not what she was pretending to be. Governesses did not meet the eyes of their employer so boldly nor did they have much experience of society.

'I have acted as companion to a lady of quality,' she replied, her head up. 'Besides, one is accustomed to being with ladies and young women of…breeding.'

'Tell me, Miss Goodrum—where were you educated?'

'I…my father employed a governess for me and I went to Miss Hale's school in Newcastle for young ladies for a period of two years. It was a highly respectable academy, I assure you.'

'What manner of man is your father?'

Her body stiffened. 'My references are all in order, sir. I have them to hand if you wish to see them.'

'I am not your employer.' Rupert's gaze moved over her. 'It was just idle curiosity. You are not obliged to answer me.'

'My father ran a mine, sir. We were respectable and he was able to give me benefits that not all girls of my class receive. He died a few years ago and…I was obliged to earn my living.'

'The manager of a mine and from the North of England, I think?' Rupert nodded, pleased because he'd detected the slight inflection in her voice, especially when she was disturbed. 'You *are* an unusual governess, Miss Goodrum. I believe we shall rub along well enough—providing that I do not discover you have lied to your employer and to me.'

Her head came up at that and her eyes flashed with

temper. Rupert was tempted to laugh. He'd thought her merely attractive at the start, but he was beginning to see that there was much more to Miss Hester Goodrum than met the eye. He would swear that there was fire banked just beneath the surface.

'Was there anything else, sir?'

'Oh, yes,' Rupert replied with a smile. 'I believe we've only just begun, Miss Goodrum. However, we shall leave it for the moment. You will do me the honour of dining with me this evening, I hope?'

For a moment she hesitated, then she gave him a straight look that took the wind out of his sails. 'As I am sure you know, that would not be appropriate, Lord Myers. A governess may be asked to dine with the family on occasion, but only when the mistress of the house is present—and certainly not alone with a gentleman.'

'How disappointing. Now you are being a proper governess. I had hoped we might get to know each other better. Besides, Francesca and John will be dining with me. Did you really imagine I was asking you to dine intimately, Miss Goodrum? I assure you I would only do that if I had seduction in mind.'

Now the colour was high in her cheeks. She took a moment to control herself, as if afraid of speaking too quickly and betraying herself into unwise words.

'I think you like to mock, sir. I am certain you had no such thing in mind. Why should you?' She hesitated, then, 'If Francesca is to dine with you, perhaps I should also be present. You may be here as John's mentor, but you are a single gentleman and Francesca is an impressionable young girl. I think I must act as her chaperon.'

'How wise of you to change your mind,' he murmured softly, adding, as she left, in a voice she could not catch, 'And who, I wonder, will chaperon you, Miss Goodrum?'

Chapter Three

Sarah went straight up to her room. Mrs Brancaster had asked her to return to her sitting room after the interview, but she needed a little time alone to calm her nerves. When she'd suggested that she change places with Hester Goodrum she had not dreamed she would have to run the gauntlet of those steel-grey eyes and that razor-sharp mind. Lord Myers was a man of the world and very intelligent. As herself, Sarah would have felt his equal, well able to parry any darts he fired at her, but she was at a disadvantage because she was here under false pretences. Lord Myers had warned her that he would not take kindly to lies on her part and she could imagine what he would think and say if he discovered the truth.

Cold chills ran down her spine. What on earth would she do if she were exposed as an impostor? It would be so very embarrassing and could ruin her reputation. For a moment she was tempted to turn tail and run away now before she was dragged into something beyond her control, but pride would not let her.

No, she was doing nothing wrong…not terribly

wrong anyway. Having embarked on her masquerade, she could at least stay to greet the children. If the challenge became too much for her she could always hand in her notice and leave and no one would be any the wiser. Besides, it was unlikely that anyone she knew would visit Cavendish Park and, providing she gave good service, her employer would have no cause for complaint.

Having calmed her fears, Sarah changed into a fresh gown. It was clean, neat and clearly the kind of plain no-nonsense dress that a governess would be expected to wear. She pulled at the bodice because it was a little tight across her breasts. Although of similar heights, she and Hester were of a different build, Sarah being rather more curvy.

However, the dress fitted well enough and perhaps she would have time to let out the seams a little. Had she been impersonating a maid there would have been a uniform but governesses were expected to provide their own gowns.

Sarah wondered how much Hester had been promised as her wage. It was one of the many things she hadn't had time to discuss and now regretted. Money was not a problem for the moment, because she still had several guineas in her purse and would need very little while she stayed here. She might miss her clothes and favourite pieces of jewellery, but had decided to have her trunks stored until further notice. Had the housekeeper decided to investigate her closet, it would not have done to have a dozen silk dresses hanging there. Mrs Brancaster would have immediately thought the worst, because there was only one way a governess could come by such gowns.

Hester Goodrum had given her the reference from

Lady Mary, also the schedule she'd intended to set for
Francesca and John. A swift perusal had left Sarah feeling that it was sadly lacking in imagination and she
made a few notes in the margins of lessons she thought
a young woman might enjoy.

Making her way downstairs to the kitchens, she
heard voices and, since her name was mentioned, hesitated outside the door.

'What do you think of her, then?' a woman's voice
asked. 'Will she last longer than a month, do you think?'

'Well, Cook, all I can tell you is that she seems very
sure of herself—and that's what I told his lordship. She's
not like any of the others so she might just succeed
where they failed.'

'I hope as you're right, Mrs Brancaster. Those young
devils were in here earlier and they took all the cake
I'd baked yesterday and I had to start all over again.'

'Well, let's hope she can keep them in order—'
Mrs Brancaster broke off as Sarah opened the door
and walked in. 'Ah, there you are, Miss Goodrum. We
were just talking about you, wondering whether you
would settle here.'

'It is a lovely house and the grounds are magnificent,' Sarah said. 'Have Miss Francesca and Master
John returned yet?'

'I believe they went upstairs just a few moments ago.
His lordship said we're to serve tea at the normal time—
and he asked that you should join them in the drawing
room. Says he's going to introduce you to your pupils.'

'Oh…' Sarah's heart hammered in her breast. 'I
thought I was to have tea with you, but if I've been
summoned… Where is the drawing room, please?'

'You recall the parlour? Well, the drawing room is at

the far end of the corridor and looks out over the park. Shall I send one of the maids with you?'

'No, I dare say I can find my own way.'

'Well, Miss Goodrum, I'm pleased you've come,' Cook said, wiping her hands on her apron. 'In my opinion it's time those youngsters were taught some discipline.'

'I shall do my best to make them behave, but I can't guarantee it.' Sarah smiled. 'I think Lord Myers will soon have Master John under his control. I hope I may have some success with preparing Miss Francesca for her future role.'

'She's been allowed to run wild and that's the truth of it,' Cook said. 'Their grandfather has spoiled them too much in my opinion.'

'Well, perhaps they just need someone to take an interest in their needs. If you will excuse me, I shall find my way to the drawing room before they ring for tea.'

Sarah left the kitchen and walked up the back stairs, letting herself out into one of the back halls. For a moment she looked about her, trying to get her bearings. Had they turned left or right for the parlour? It was a large house and if she took a wrong turning she might lose herself.

'If you're looking for the drawing room, Miss Goodrum, you turn to the right,' a voice said. Sarah turned and found herself being addressed by a footman. He was young and attractive, with dark blond hair and blue eyes and his smile was friendly.

'Oh, thank you,' she said. 'I visited the front parlour earlier, but couldn't quite recall which way to turn.'

'It's easy enough once you get used to it,' he said.

'I'm Trevor Bent, Miss Goodrum. Your name is Hester, isn't it?'

'Yes, but I don't like it,' Sarah said, her cheeks faintly pink. She hesitated, then, 'My father called me Sarah. I prefer the name, if you don't mind.'

'I don't mind,' he replied and grinned. 'May I call you Sarah—or am I being too forward?'

'I don't mind at all,' she said. 'Thank you for your help, Trevor.'

Turning in the direction the footman had pointed out, Sarah was pleased by the respectful admiration in the young man's eyes. He seemed to like her and it was refreshing to know that he had no idea that she was rich. She was tired of being courted for her fortune—and, of late, a certain person's pursuit had been nothing short of menacing. He was determined to push her into marriage and she was equally determined to resist—but her uncle and aunt were on his side, forever telling her what a good husband Sir Roger would make.

'He's a gentleman,' Uncle Matthew had told her. 'He won't interfere in the running of the mills, but he'll be there at your side to give you more authority. A woman alone can't hope to mange everything your father left you.'

'But I told you what he did—that he is a rogue. How can you say he would make a good husband for me?'

'Reformed rakes make the best husbands,' her aunt had told her with a foolish and rather coy smile. 'I dare say he got carried away a little at the party by his love for you, Sarah. Gentlemen can be like that sometimes.'

'Love is neither here nor there,' her uncle had said. 'A woman should be married and caring for her children, not managing the mills. Sir Roger has mills of his own and would take the burden from your shoulders.'

It was no use telling her uncle that Sir Roger left his mills to the care of neglectful overseers and was in danger of losing them—or that she would never subject her people to the kind of treatment they received from Sir Roger's managers. Of course, Sir Roger never went near them himself. He was far too busy enjoying himself in London—and no doubt he imagined her money would allow him to continue with the life he desired.

Sarah had bitten back the hasty retort that rose to her lips. She had been managing her mills alone quite well, with the help of her managers. It was true that she had found it time- consuming, giving her little leisure for herself, which was why she'd decided to take this time out. Yet she would hate to relinquish them to a man like Sir Roger.

As she approached the drawing room, she heard the sound of voices raised.

'Why doesn't Grandfather come himself?' a girl's voice said on a truculent note. 'John and I are tired of being given boring lessons and told to get on with them. We want to see other people—to have some fun.'

'Well, you have me now. I think John is old enough to start fencing lessons and I'll teach you how to shoot— and we'll go fishing and play cricket, but of course you will have to do some lessons. Your governess will take you for those, but I'll take you both for drives into town. If you behave yourselves, that is.'

'What about me? Why should John have all the fun while I get stuck with a boring governess?'

'I'm afraid that is a woman's lot in life,' Lord Myers

said, but with a teasing note in his voice. 'I dare say Miss Goodrum may allow you some fun if you behave.'

'We don't need her here. Why can't we just have…?'

Sarah walked into the room. A very pretty fair-haired girl and an equally attractive youth were standing in front of the open hearth with Lord Myers. They looked cross and upset, a contrast to the carefree children she'd observed in the grounds. The girl's English-rose colour heightened as she turned and saw her.

'Ah, here is Miss Goodrum,' Lord Myers said into the hushed silence. 'As you can see, ma'am, the truants have returned. I have decided they will receive no more than a warning for this day's escapade, but I shall not be so lenient in future.'

'I dare say no harm was done,' Sarah replied. 'It was a perfect day for fishing after all. Since we did not arrive until half the day was done, it would have been a shame to waste it all indoors. I am hoping to walk with you both on pleasant days. There is no need to sit at a desk to learn. We can observe nature and practise our Latin verbs while on a walk, John—and I think you, Francesca, may find the discussion of your favourite poets as interesting in a meadow as a musty school-room.'

The girl's cheeks went white and then pink. She was clearly undecided whether to show appreciation or hold on to her reserve.

'Mr Morton made me spend the whole morning doing exercises while he sat in his chair and read a book,' John exclaimed indignantly. 'I want to play games and do things.'

'So you shall.' Sarah and Lord Myers spoke at the same time. 'There are many ways to learn,' Sarah finished while the mentor looked at her through narrowed eyes.

'What about me?' Francesca gave them a sulky look. 'What am I supposed to do?'

'Learn some manners for a start,' Lord Myers said. 'You've neither of you welcomed Miss Goodrum to Cavendish Park.'

'She didn't have to come here.' Francesca said rudely. 'I'm too old for the schoolroom.'

'That is why I intend to teach you to dance,' Sarah said, unruffled by the girl's sulky manner. 'We should discuss society and what kind of people you may encounter—and the conversations you may have with friends and acquaintances. Also, you will need to know how to spot a rake and how to avoid being compromised by ruthless gentlemen.'

Francesca's eyes opened wide. She stared in disbelief, her mouth slightly parted. 'What did you say?'

'We shall naturally discuss poetry and literature and you will need to practise your drawing, embroidery and the instrument of your choice—but learning to dance, to enter a room, to curtsy and to hold your own when a gentleman flirts with you is very important. You will need those skills before you have your Season.'

'You don't want me to write an essay on the decline of the Roman Empire or conjugate French verbs?'

'I imagine you've had a varied and extensive education. We can discover the boundaries of your knowledge together in conversation. A young woman of fashion must be able to converse intelligently, do you not agree, my lord?'

Sarah risked a look at Lord Myers, who was watching her with narrowed eyes. She was not sure whether they expressed suspicion or disbelief.

'Most young ladies of my acquaintance are too missish to say boo to a goose. They repeat phrases parrot-fashion and then lapse into embarrassed silence if asked a question.'

'Too harsh, my lord!' Sarah laughed, her face lighting with amusement. 'Well, I shall hope that Francesca will have more to say for herself on her debut. If she has not, I shall have failed in my duties.'

'Remarkable...' Lord Myers's eyes held a look of calculation. 'Francesca, I think you have been more fortunate than any of us imagined in your new governess. My only question is—how did Lady Mary ever bring herself to part with you?'

Sarah refused to lower her eyes. He was probing, trying to get beneath her skin, but she would not allow him that privilege.

'Lord Myers is using mockery, Francesca,' she said in a calm and composed manner. 'Were I a young woman of fashion I might do one of two things. If I wished to encourage him, I might give him an enigmatic smile and flirt with my fan—or, if I wish to discourage his advances, I should raise an eyebrow and move on without answering.'

'Here endeth the first lesson,' Lord Myers drawled. 'It is actually good advice, Francesca. May one ask which you would have chosen, Miss Goodrum?'

'I shall leave that to your imagination, my lord,' Sarah replied, but was relieved when the door opened and the housekeeper entered accompanied by two maids, each of whom carried a tray. 'Ah, here is our tea. Would you like to play the hostess, Francesca?'

Francesca shot her a nervous look, but took her seat next to a small occasional table. Mrs Brancaster set up her butler's tray, exchanged a few words with Lord Myers, looked curiously at Sarah and left, taking one of the maids with her.

'You are aware that you begin with the lady of first rank,' Sarah told Francesca as her hand hovered. 'However, since I am the governess, you should begin with Lord Myers and then me and then your brother. Were there several ladies of rank you should attempt to serve the highest rank first and then, when all the ladies are served, go on to the gentlemen and begin again in the same way.'

'Miss Goodrum may be correct,' Lord Myers said. 'But in my opinion ladies are always first—of whatever rank. You may serve Miss Goodrum tea first, Francesca.'

Sarah shot a look at him, but did not contradict him. 'I take my tea with lemon, no milk or sugar,' she said and smiled as Francesca lifted the heavy pot. The girl's hand trembled slightly but she accomplished the ceremony without accident, handing the cup to the maid who delivered it to Sarah, and serving Lord Myers next. He asked for milk and one sugar and then accepted a sandwich and fruit tartlet from the hovering maid.

After everyone had been served with tea and cake, Francesca looked at Sarah. She inclined her head and the maid was dismissed.

'Did your last governess take tea with you both?'

'No, she preferred to take hers in the kitchen,' John answered, a trifle indignant. 'Fran and me had most of our meals in the nursery together. The only time the drawing room was used was when Grandfather came down and we had guests. Mrs Brancaster served us then—or sometimes Cousin Agatha.'

'Fran and I,' Sarah gently corrected. 'Your cousin visits you from time to time?'

'Only at Christmas,' John said. 'We've been on our own for years, haven't we, Fran?'

'Yes.' Francesca sipped her tea. She had crooked her little finger in an affected way, but as she looked at Sarah and saw that she held her cup in a more relaxed manner she did the same. 'We're both bored. Why can't we have friends here to picnics and dances?'

'We might have a dance on your seventeenth birthday. It's a few weeks before Christmas,' Lord Myers said. 'If you attend to your dancing lessons and whatever else Miss Goodrum has to teach you, you may be ready then. We might start to entertain a few visitors, though—just to dinner and cards or some such thing.'

'The weather is beautiful,' Sarah said. 'I think a picnic for your neighbours would be ideal as a way of letting people know we are receiving calls and visits. The best way to become accustomed to company is to invite them into your home. Does a picnic appeal to you, John?'

'Can we have games and races? We went to the fete at the vicarage last summer—Fran and I won the three-legged race. It was fun.'

'I am sure something could be arranged, but you must ask Lord Myers. I am just the governess. I can suggest, but it is not for me to decide.'

Sarah opened her eyes at him, inviting him to respond, her manner carefully controlled. His frown deepened and his gaze narrowed, as if he were trying to read her thoughts. Lord Myers was clearly not convinced that she was a governess.

Just how far would he go to discover the truth?

'A picnic?' His gaze moved from one eager face to another and then back to Sarah's. 'I seem to have been outnumbered. A picnic it is, then—but I shall expect you to write the invitations, Miss Goodrum. And you will organise the games, if you please.'

'I'll help you write the invitations. I know where Grandfather keeps his list of people to invite for Christmas,' Francesca volunteered. 'And we'll both help with the games, won't we, John?'

John looked at his sister and nodded. He was very much under her influence, Sarah realised. If Francesca gave the new governess her approval, half the battle would be won.

They were talking excitedly about what they wanted at their picnic. Sarah smiled inwardly while helping herself to a dainty almond comfit. This was exactly how she saw family life in the country and she was enjoying herself. However, she knew the battle was not yet won. At the moment the children were getting their own way and were therefore prepared to be amenable, but at the first hint of authority they might change like the wind.

Sarah was very conscious of being scrutinised by Lord Myers. She felt that he did not know what to make of her and was taking his time in deciding. Sarah found herself wishing that she was the governess she professed to be, because she wanted to stay here and be a part of this charmed circle.

A little shiver started at the nape of her neck as she imagined what they would say and think if they knew she was the rich Miss Hardcastle escaping from the pursuit of an overeager suitor. Would they feel betrayed or angry? Of course they would, because she'd lied to get her position here. She had no qualifications for her position as a governess, other than the fact that she had herself been schooled by an excellent governess and spent two years at a finishing school for young ladies.

Sarah hoped that Lord Myers would not discover just how expensive her school had been, because he would wonder how the daughter of a mine manager could afford the fees.

'Will you teach me to waltz?'

Francesca brought her mind back to the present. 'I shall do my best and when you're ready you may practise with your tutor.'

'My tutor?' Francesca gave a little laugh. 'Lord Myers is my cousin,' she said, making the situation clearer. 'Grandfather is his uncle.'

'We are second cousins,' Lord Myers told her. 'Your mother was my cousin.'

'Oh…' Francesca nodded. 'It's the same thing. My last governess told me that all the aristocracy were part of the cousinry—everyone is related to everyone else through marriage, if not by blood.'

'I've heard it said.' Lord Myers inclined his head. 'I'm not sure it's true—though many are related in some way. You don't have a male cousin, Francesca. I'm your nearest male relative apart from your grandfather. I have a married sister. Have you met Lady Meadows at all?'

Francesca shook her head. 'Grandfather asked her to stay last Christmas, but she refused.'

'Jane was having her first child at about that time. She had been married just over a year and wanted to rest to make certain there were no accidents.'

'Will she come for my birthday dance?'

Francesca's expression was uncertain, a little plead-ing, and Sarah's heart went out to her. She was surely in need of female company and advice.

'I shall certainly ask.' He looked thoughtful. 'You must not worry, Francesca. In a few months you will be out and you'll meet lots of people—ladies and gen-tlemen.'

'It's so long to wait.'

'You must learn patience,' he said. 'A properly brought-up young lady does not expect everything to happen to suit her. It will not be like that when you are married.'

'If I ever marry,' Francesca said and sighed.

'You will when you're ready,' Sarah assured her. 'Marriage is to be expected and hoped for in your case, Francesca—but there is no hurry. You should enjoy being courted and meeting people. Once you're out there will be dances and lots of exciting things to do. One day you will fall in love and marry the man of your dreams.'

'My last governess said I should be required to marry for money and position.' Francesca tossed her head de-fiantly, as if to challenge them.

'Why should you? I think that was a foolish thing to say. A girl like you will be able to take your pick. When you are invited into society you will meet lots of gentle-men, and I'm sure you'll find one that will make you happy, if you give yourself time. Do not throw yourself away on the first to ask you.'

'Have you been asked more than once?'

'Yes, several times…' Sarah answered without think-ing. 'I refused because…I wasn't in love.'

'Love?' Lord Myers snorted his disgust. 'Marriage is for property and money, Francesca. Do not expect too much from life and you will not be disappointed.'

'Is that true, Miss Goodrum?'

All eyes turned to her and Sarah felt warm. She guessed that her cheeks were very pink.

'Money and property are useful, but I would prefer to live in a cottage with a man I loved than be a fine lady in a manor.'

She had given her pupil a false impression by implying that she cared nothing for money. Her own situation was entirely different—and yet she would not advise marrying for position alone.

'Of course having money is very useful,' she added conscientiously.

'I think I shall marry for love. I want more than just a convenient arrangement,' Francesca announced and her head went up as if defying her cousin to challenge her.

'I think you are wise. You should think carefully before committing yourself.'

'I shall not marry unless I fall in love.'

'You cannot throw yourself away on an adventurer,' Sarah said. 'But I would hold your heart in reserve until you find someone who will show you love rather than mere affection.'

Francesca was silent, but obviously thoughtful. Lord Myers was frowning, perhaps shocked by the new governess's unconventional opinions. Sarah realised that she was speaking her mind, but perhaps in a way that might not benefit her pupil.

'Of course you would wish your husband to be a gentleman and of reasonable fortune.'

'So love in a cottage might not be everything after all?'

Lord Myers threw her a mocking look that stung Sarah. She wanted to retort sharply, but decided she had been indiscreet enough for one day and merely inclined her head, as if acknowledging his hit.

After tea, Sarah asked to be taken up to the schoolroom and both Francesca and John accompanied her, leaving Lord Myers to do whatever gentlemen did until it was time to change for dinner.

Sarah glanced at some of the work her pupils had done, thought it uninspired and dull, but made no comment. They looked at the books that had been provided and she shook her head over the lack of history and literature.

'Does the marquess have a library here?'

'There are shelves of books,' Francesca said. 'The last tutor spent most of his time there and told us it was off limits, because the books were too valuable to be touched by ignorant children.'

'Good gracious!' Sarah was shocked. 'How could he have been so impolite! I feel his attitude showed a lack of both manners and sense. I shall ask Lord Myers if we may use the library for our lessons when there are no guests staying. This room is too isolated and dark. If the library is on the ground floor, we can have the windows and doors open on nice days and take our books outside.'

'You're different,' John said, looking at her oddly. 'Not like a governess at all. Do we have to call you Miss Goodrum?'

Sarah hesitated, then shook her head. 'In company it might be wise to do so—but when we are together you may call me Sarah if you wish.'

'I thought your name was Hester Goodrum?'

'My father called me Sarah and I prefer it.' Sarah felt the open-eyed scrutiny of the young girl and guilt struck her. She had not given enough thought to this escapade before changing places with the governess. It felt uncomfortable to lie to this girl, more so than the eagle-eyed man who was here to overlook their education.

She wanted to be Francesca's friend. She sensed that the girl was lonely and needed the love of a mother or an elder sister. Sarah would like to give her friendship, to have her trust and like her—but their friendship must be based on a lie, and that hurt.

She would make up for her deceit somehow. As she heard the eagerness in the young girl's voice, Sarah vowed that she would do all she could to make her happy and to prepare her for a life in society. If things went as she hoped, no one need know that she was not Hester Goodrum and when she left them no harm would have been done.

Chapter Four

Sarah lost no time in changing for the evening after her pupils had gone to their own rooms. John was clearly excited at the prospect for it was the first time he had been allowed to have dinner in the dining room, with the exception of Christmas dinner, which was always earlier so that the staff could enjoy a little free time in the evening. Francesca was pleased, but trying hard to be grown-up and take it all in her stride.

Having changed quickly into a simple grey-silk gown, which was the only one of her own that Sarah had brought with her and suitable for dinner should she be summoned to dine with the family, she went downstairs to find Lord Myers. One of the footmen directed her to the library and she found him perusing the shelves, which were set out on three sides of the room. There were several long windows to let in the light and a set of French windows, which might be opened to allow access to the garden. A perfect room for studying.

'Forgive me for disturbing you, my lord,' she said in what she hoped was the tone a governess might use. 'I see you enjoy reading, which may make you more disposed to granting my request. I find the schoolroom inadequately provided for my pupils' education and I hoped we might have permission to use the library for an hour or two each morning.'

He turned to look at her, his eyes narrowing as they studied her. Sarah wondered if her gown was too smart. It was the simplest she had and she would not have worn it had he not made it impossible for her to refuse to dine with him.

'I am not sure what my uncle would think about his privacy being invaded should he decide to come down—but while he is in London I see no reason why we should not share the facility. I like to read in the evenings when we do not have company, but I shall be busy in the estate office in the mornings. Shall we say from nine-thirty to eleven-thirty the library is yours and the children's?'

'That is most generous, my lord.' Sarah approached the shelves. 'Is there a good poetry section? I dare say there is little new here…'

'Oh, I think you may find enough to keep yourselves amused. My uncle may not visit often, but he is a collector of books. You will not find books bought by the yard here. All of them have been read and handled—and there are a few new novels here. I imagine my uncle bought them for his niece.'

'John told me their last tutor forbade them the use of this room.'

'Then he exceeded his authority.' Lord Myers looked annoyed. 'It seems to me that my uncle has been ill served as regards to his grandchildren. They were neglected, Miss Goodrum. I do not intend that it shall happen again.'

'John will benefit from your tuition, sir. I hope I may do the same for Francesca.'

'She admires you.' His gaze was stern, his sensual mouth set in a hard line. 'You will not let her down, Miss Goodrum. I shall be watching her progress.'

'I hope to prove my worth to you.' Sarah raised her head. 'Thank you for your generosity.'

'The library should be available to all.' His gaze intensified, dwelling on her in a way that sent little shivers down her spine. 'I am not sure who you are, Miss Goodrum—but I intend to discover the truth.'

'I am not sure I understand you.'

'Do you not? Then perhaps I am wrong—but I sense a mystery. If I discover that you are not what you profess to be, I shall be merciless. As I told you before, I do not take kindly to liars.'

Sarah found it difficult to suppress the shiver that ran through her. Had she given herself away already? How could he know that she was not a governess—and what did he imagine her to be?

'Francesca is an impressionable young girl,' he continued. 'She has begun to trust you. Please do not give me cause to dismiss you. I should be loath to destroy her faith in the first person to offer her friendship.'

'I have no intention of harming either John or Francesca.'

He moved towards her, staring down into her face for a moment before reaching out to tilt her chin so that she was forced to look into his eyes. Sarah felt a tingle of some strange new sensation; it started low in her abdomen and spread throughout her body, making her feel hot. Her cheeks were warm and she wanted to jerk away, but held her ground.

'Are you an adventuress?' he asked, quirking a dark eyebrow. She could not help noticing that his mouth looked perfect for kissing and she trembled inside. A man like this was dangerous. Despite his sensual appeal, he had a look of iron about him and she feared what he might do if he guessed she had deceived them all. 'What do you hope to gain by coming here? Did you think you might capture yourself a wealthy husband? Had you heard Merrivale was a lonely old man who might fall for your charms?'

Sarah caught her breath and then the absurdity of his question made her laugh. It was so far from the truth that she felt her tension melting away.

'You have a vivid imagination, Lord Myers,' she said. 'I do not count my charms so high that I would ever seek to advance myself in the way you suggest. I am sorry I have given you such a poor opinion of my character. I assure you it is undeserved.'

'Indeed?' He bent his head and kissed her, his mouth soft and yet demanding, evoking a swift response. For a moment she felt light-headed, her heart racing as he deepened his kiss, and she wanted to swoon into his arms. Something inside her longed to respond to his demand and she felt a rising need, a sweet heat between her thighs that she had never experienced before.

Suddenly realising that her response must be confirming his opinion of her, she placed her hands against his shoulders and pushed him back. As anger replaced the feeling of bliss, she raised her hand and would have slapped him as hard as she could had he not caught her by the wrist.

'So there is fire beneath the cool calm exterior,' he murmured and there was devilry in his eyes. 'You intrigue me, Miss Goodrum. I am not usually wrong in my first impressions and I know you have not always been a governess. You are hiding something, but I shall find you out.'

'You are no gentleman, sir,' she replied coldly. The look she gave him had quelled the mill managers who had tried to dismiss her authority when she took over her father's business empire. They had sought to cheat and ridicule her, but she'd faced them down—and she would put this rogue in his place. Even if she had felt close to swooning at his kiss—but that just showed she was a foolish spinster starved of a man's love. What on earth was she thinking of to have allowed it to continue before pushing him away? He was far from being the kind of husband she needed, were she to decide to marry. 'I am aware that you have a privileged position in this house but that does not give you the right to question my morality or to attempt seduction in this manner. If you ever behave this way again I shall give in my notice—and I shall make it plain to the marquess why I was forced to leave.'

'She has claws,' he said, looking amused. 'Come, Miss Goodrum, you did not find the experience so very unpleasant, I think?'

'You insulted me and then tried to take advantage of me. I should like to make it plain that I will not stand for such behaviour. If you feel me unsuited to the position, you may dismiss me.'

'Dismiss you?' His gaze burned her to the core and her stomach clenched. 'Oh, no, I have no intention of sending you away until I discover the truth. I thought I might find an extended visit to the country a trifle boring, but it is no such thing. I shall enjoy crossing swords with you, Miss Goodrum.'

'I would prefer that you keep your distance. We must remain on good terms for the sake of the children, my lord—but I see no reason for our paths to cross other than in their company.'

'Do you not?' He smiled oddly. 'You rest on your dignity, but it was a different matter when I kissed you. Yet I would not harm you if you are truly what you claim to be. We shall endeavour to be polite to one another for the sake of John and Francesca—but you are the most unusual governess I have ever met.'

'Is that necessarily a bad thing?' Sarah raised her eyes to his. 'I give you my word that I am not an adventuress, nor did I come here to entrap anyone into marriage.'

'Shall I believe you?' He looked at her steadily. His strong features had relaxed and there was a teasing light in his eyes, as if he were playing with her, as a cat with a mouse. 'Yes, perhaps I shall. So what is it you are hiding? Are you in trouble? I might be able to help you if that is the case.'

'I am perfectly capable of looking after my own affairs.' Sarah raised her head proudly. 'I believe that was the dinner gong. We should go in or we shall keep the others waiting.'

He inclined his head, offering her his arm. 'As you say, Miss Goodrum. Please accept my apologies if I have wronged you.'

Sarah hesitated and then placed the tips of her fingers on his arm, her head high as they walked towards the dining room. She could only keep her distance and hope he would do the same.

The last thing she'd expected when she came here was to find herself having to fend off the advances of a man she suspected was a rake. Charming and undeniably attractive, he would make most female hearts flutter, but Sarah had come here to escape from the unwanted attentions of a similar man.

Had she been less stubborn she might have fled the next morning, but she had no intention of letting Lord Myers drive her away.

Rupert watched the governess across the table as she talked and laughed with her pupils. She seemed very at home, very much as if she were accustomed to dining in style, and showed no hesitation in choosing the correct glasses and silver. Her manner was calm and assured, and, apart from the dark looks she sent his way now and then, she seemed perfectly at ease. He knew himself at fault for that kiss, but she'd looked at him with such a challenge in her eyes that he'd been tempted. If she were truly what she claimed, he had wronged her, but his instincts told him that she was far from the downtrodden drudge that most women in her situation became after a few years.

The dress she was wearing this evening was far too stylish to belong to a governess. It was plain and simple, but in perfect taste, and must have cost as much as she would earn in a year. How could she possibly own a dress like that if she were what she claimed to be? It must have been given to her, possibly made to fit her—and who would give a governess such a gift? Yet it was not what he would have purchased for a mistress. Instead it had an understated elegance that a lady with refined taste might choose.

The gown had made him think she must be an adventuress, which had led him into that foolish kiss. He was here to mentor his uncle's grandchildren and the last thing he should contemplate was an affair with their governess. Perhaps a grateful employer had given her the gown, as a gift?

If that were the case, he had definitely wronged her, but it did not explain her manner. Summoned to eat with their employer, most governesses would show reserve or some awkwardness even if their manners were excellent, as hers were. No, she was accustomed to dining like this—and she felt it her right.

Only a woman who felt assured of her place in the world could be so at home in the situation he had forced her to accept. Had he met her in society he would not have placed her in the upper echelons, but she would certainly be accepted. Why, then, was she a governess? Had her family fallen on hard times? Yet if she were in desperate need of a job she would not be so confident—so assured. His suspicion deepened. Rupert had reason enough to distrust the female sex. His heart broken when he was no more than a lad, he'd never offered it again. Since then he'd amused himself with ladies of a certain kind, most of them married or widowed. A few of his mistresses had been courtesans, prepared to sell themselves to the highest bidder, and were usually not to be trusted.

Miss Goodrum did not follow the pattern for a downtrodden governess, which made him certain that she was not what she claimed. It followed that she was hiding something—but rather than fear he'd seen a challenge in her eyes. And she had responded to that kiss.

Her manner had aroused Rupert's hunting instincts.

He found her intriguing, and, yes, had he met her in other circumstances, he might have attempted to make her his mistress.

Who was she and why was she here? Their eyes met across the table and he smiled, seeing the uncertainty in hers. Had he made an enemy of her? Rupert suddenly found himself hoping that he could recover the lost ground. She looked so right somehow as she laughed and teased John and encouraged Francesca. He experienced a strange emotion that he could not place— as if he had found a place of content, of belonging.

For the first time in an age he wanted to be a part of that family scene. It struck him then that Miss Goodrum was more like an aunt or an elder sister to Francesca, and the smile on her lips was both generous and sweet.

Yet there was a mystery here. He'd sensed it from the start and he took hold of his emotions, reining them in. A woman's smile could deceive so easily. He'd been burned as a young man, his pride ripped to pieces and his heart damaged. Since then he'd chosen carefully and made sure that none of the ladies he took to his bed had buried their claws in his skin.

The governess had claws. There was passion and fire beneath the cool exterior. It would certainly prove amusing to discover who she really was and why she'd come here.

What was she hiding from?

John was sent to bed as soon as dinner was over. Francesca was allowed to drink a dish of tea in the drawing room with her governess, but as soon as Lord Myers joined them, he sent her off to bed. Sarah immediately rose to her feet to follow. He caught her wrist, as she would have passed him.

The candles were burning low in their sconces and the fire had ceased to burn fiercely. Shadows seemed to creep over the room, making it feel intimate and tempting her to stay—but she must not!

'There is no need for you to leave, Miss Goodrum.'

'I think there is every need, sir. Please allow me to pass.' Sarah's heart raced at his nearness, the mystique of his scent powerful and attractive. She ran the tip of her tongue over her lips, knowing that this was a dangerous situation. She must go before he tried to seduce her.

He let go reluctantly, his expression odd and almost regretful. 'I am sorry for what I said earlier. I was testing you. You must admit that dress is not the usual attire for a governess.'

'No, I suppose not. It belongs to the time when my father was alive. He bought it for me as a gift. My father was careful with his money, sir, and he spent it on me.'

Sarah avoided his searching gaze, though her words were not far from the truth. She'd purchased the gown when her first period of mourning was over with the money her beloved father had left her and because it was a favourite she'd kept it. Had she worn some of her other newer gowns she could not have hoped to keep her secret.

'Then I apologise for casting aspersions on your character. Come, Miss Goodrum, will you not forgive me?'

'Consider yourself forgiven, my lord. I only wish to be on good terms with you.'

She deliberately made her voice flat, calm and

emotionless, hoping that her reserve would make him step back.

'Then I shall not tease you again. We must not allow our charges to sense animosity between us.'

'No, that would be unfortunate,' she agreed, bringing her eyes up to his. His expression set her heart thumping. She had seen that look in a man's eyes before and it disturbed her. Normally she had no hesitation in dealing with unwanted seducers, but this man was different, more powerful and compelling than any other she'd met. 'We shall try to be easy in one another's company for their sakes.'

'May I not be counted as a friend?'

'I think you ask a little too much, sir. I hardly know you—but perhaps in time we may progress to friendship.'

'Very well. I was wrong to assume you were an adventuress—but my offer remains. If you are in trouble, I should be glad to be of service.'

'Thank you. I shall bear that in mind. Now, if you will excuse me, sir.'

'Very well. I shall not detain you against your will. I shall take John riding first thing in the morning, but he will be back in time for his lessons.'

'You must do as you think fit, sir. I believe he has a great deal of energy that needs an outlet. Riding, fencing and other sports may help him to settle to his studies.'

'I believe so. Goodnight, Miss Goodrum. Pleasant dreams.'

'Thank you.'

Sarah inclined her head and walked on past him. Her heart had raced at his touch, but she had clamped down on her foolish emotions. Gentlemen in his position too often took advantage of female employees who could not easily escape their attentions. He had promised not to bother her again, but the look in his eyes had said something different.

She could not deny that she had felt the pull of his attraction, but he was not for her. As Miss Hardcastle she might attract proposals from gentlemen who needed a fortune to finance their extravagant lifestyles, but if she was not prepared to buy herself a husband, she certainly had no intention of becoming any man's mistress. Sarah might choose marriage if the right opportunity presented itself—but not to a man like Lord Myers.

She did not know his fortune, but she recognised the sensuality of the man, the attraction that must make him popular with ladies of his own class—and others. Sarah had no doubt that he was a physical man who took mistresses whenever he chose—and that was not the kind of man she needed in her life. Such a man could not be trusted. As charming as he was, she would never be certain that he would not stray into another's bed. Sarah knew that only a very beautiful and clever woman would capture the heart of a man like that, and she could not hope that he would want more from her than a brief affair to enliven a dull stay in the country.

Nor did she wish it, of course. When Sarah married, if she ever did, it would be to a quiet man who enjoyed books; a man who would be there if she needed him but also be content to stay in the background and allow her to continue to run her mills, should she wish to do so. Sarah had fought for the right to run her mills, but was not sure whether she wished to continue. Were she happily married with a family she thought she might be content to let her husband take over her affairs. However, she did not intend to be dictated to and told she must relinquish them entirely. She could not imagine that Lord Myers would ever be content to let his wife do something he would consider beneath her dignity.

He was a very attractive man, but his character left much to be desired from what she'd seen thus far. He would not make a suitable husband for Miss Sarah Hardcastle and might run through her fortune in an instant, given the opportunity.

She had not run away from one fortune hunter to fall into the arms of another, even if she did find him attractive. No such thing! She was not truly attracted to him.

It was merely that she had been lonely since her father died, of course. Her father had been such a loving companion and what she really wanted was someone to take his place, to care for her and watch over her, but demand little other than warm affection.

Lord Myers would not have received more than a moment's fleeting attention from her had they met in company. It was only that she was forced to live in what was undoubtedly an intimate situation with him.

What had brought him here? He did not seem the kind of man to relish the obligations that his uncle had asked of him. She would have thought him more at home in the drawing rooms of London society, rather than playing mentor to a young boy. Why should he give up his time and his way of life to come down here?

He accused her of hiding, but perhaps he too had something to hide? What had made him the man he was? Sarah wondered if some secret lay in his past. He was of an age to have been married for some years. Surely he must want a wife and children of his own—

though of course she was assuming he had not for she knew so little about him. However, Francesca would surely have mentioned it if he had a wife?

So why had he stayed single? What had brought that hard glitter to his eyes and the brittle layer that hid the real man from the casual eye? He had a sense of humour, she knew—so what had made him so suspicious of her? Was it just that he did not trust women in general?

Oh, this was ridiculous! She must dismiss him from her mind for it was dangerous to allow a man like that into her thoughts.

Despite her determination to be sensible, Sarah found her thoughts dwelling too often on the handsome Lord Rupert as she undressed. She pulled down the covers on her bed, looking for any unpleasant objects that a teenage boy might have placed there as a prank, but found nothing untoward. Obviously, she'd passed her first test with the children at least.

She would forget their mentor and concentrate her thoughts on them. She was here to be of service to the children.

Francesca wasn't a child, though. She was on the verge of womanhood. In past centuries she might have been married by now; she might even have had a child of her own. To treat her as a child would be foolish. Sarah had taken to the girl and, as she slipped into bed and leaned forwards to blow out the candle beside it, she was determined to do what she could to make her life better. She would enjoy getting to know her charge and she would find it pleasant to share her own love of reading, poetry, history and even the occasional novel.

There was a wealth of books on the library shelves,

including some with pictures of mythical beasts that she thought might appeal to John. Perhaps she wasn't a conventional governess, but she was quite capable of giving them both an education. Sarah loved to play the pianoforte and she thought Francesca might enjoy playing a duet with her.

Life here could be extremely comfortable and pleasant. She would be able to walk first thing in the morning if her lessons were not to start until nine-thirty. She would have liked to ride, but wasn't sure that privilege would be granted to a governess.

For a moment she felt a pang of regret. Her own horses would miss her and so would her dogs—and some of her servants. She had written to reassure everyone that she was quite safe. She would have to make sure that she kept in touch with her agents or they might become anxious about her and set up a search to find her.

Closing her eyes, Sarah drifted off to sleep, though her dreams were unaccountably disturbed by the look on a man's face.

'Who are you?' he asked. 'I shall find you out…you cannot hide from me…'

Rupert frowned as he brooded over his glass of wine after the governess had gone up. The shadows seemed to fold about him and he was aware that the room seemed empty. He was a fool to allow the woman under his skin, because very likely she would turn out to be the adventuress he'd imagined her at first. Yet something about her had captured his interest and he'd wanted her to stay after the children had gone up.

It was years since Rupert had enjoyed feminine company—other than in bed. Most society women bored him and he was wary of foolish young misses who were out to capture a husband. To have sat talking into the night with an intelligent woman would be pleasant, he thought.

In London he was seldom aware that he was lonely because he spent his evenings either at his club in the company of male friends, drinking, gambling or talking of politics and the price of stocks, or with his mistress. Had his uncle been here he might not have realised his lack, but in this situation it had come to him forcibly that his life was far from satisfactory.

As a young man Rupert had imagined that he would fall in love, marry and rear a large family, but a woman who preferred money and a superior title had shattered those dreams. He'd taken his bruised heart and damaged pride off to war and had for a time found content with his fellow officers—but when they turned against him…

Rupert's mind shied away from the memories. Mixed with the pain of seeing his men broken and dying, their blood spilling out on the hot dry earth, what happened later was too painful to contemplate. He'd shut away his pain and hurt, just as he'd shut out the humiliation he'd received at a woman's hands, determined to rise above the petty spite of others. And he'd succeeded so well that he'd come to be what he wanted others to think him—careless, stern and reserved. Rupert needed no one's approval. He was his own man, ruled by principles of iron and he answered to no one. Only a few ever saw the other side of him—a side he had almost forgotten.

Once he'd known how to enjoy the small pleasures

in life. He'd known how to love, to show caring and to give and take joy from being intimate with another.

That was years ago, before he'd learned that no woman was to be trusted. They were all the same—greedy, grabbing, jealous little kittens that liked to be stroked and given a saucer of cream, but would scratch you if you annoyed them.

Undoubtedly, the governess was exactly the same, though for the moment he confessed to being more than a little intrigued, if only by the mystery he sensed in her past.

Yet she had reached out to him in a way few other women ever had, arousing feelings of need and desire with just one flash of her gorgeous eyes.

Sarah awoke when a maid drew back the curtains. She yawned and stretched, her mind still lost in dreams as she said, 'Good morning, Tilly. Have you brought my chocolate?'

'It's Agnes, Miss Goodrum—and you told Mrs Brancaster you would take breakfast downstairs.'

'Yes, of course,' Sarah said, the realisation of where she was returning with a rush. She had given herself away and could only hope the maid would not repeat her words to others. 'If I go down immediately I shall be finished by the time the family is up. I do not see why you should wait on me.'

'I've brought your hot water, miss—as Mrs Brancaster told me.'

'Thank you, that was kind.' Sarah threw back the covers. On waking she'd thought she was at home and her own maid was bringing her the hot chocolate she took every morning before she rose.

It would be a while before she accustomed herself to the life she had chosen—a very different life, but one that had its own compensations.

After Agnes had gone, Sarah washed, dressed in one of Hester's sensible gowns and, on looking from the window to see the sun was shining, decided against a shawl. Since she was walking on private grounds she saw no reason to wear a bonnet and left her room without one.

She found her way down the back stairs to a side entrance that led into a walled garden. The bricks were faded, trailed with roses and clematis, and would look a picture in a few weeks from now. However, she was accustomed to long country walks near her home and left the pleasant garden to explore more of the estate. She had insufficient time to walk as far as the village she'd seen, but would certainly do so on her day off. Hester had been promised one a month, which could be saved and taken together for visits home. Sarah would require only a few hours of freedom, perhaps in the early mornings or at night. If necessary, she might have to visit her home to reassure her anxious friends—if she continued here for more than a few weeks, of course.

Should Lord Myers discover her true identity she might find herself summarily dismissed. Sarah would be truly sorry if that happened. She had a lovely house herself and friends, but at home there was always the sense that she was being watched…that people were waiting for her to make mistakes.

She would forget her worries and enjoy her walk. The air was fresh and there was a hint of real warmth for later. Sarah walked as far as a small lake, where she watched ducks and swans gliding on its still waters.

There was an intriguing wood to the right of the lake and a summer house that looked interesting. Perhaps she had found the site for their picnic, she mused as she returned to the house.

Her walk had made her hungry and she entered the breakfast room, thinking she would have it to herself, but a little to her dismay she discovered Lord Myers sitting at the table. He got to his feet as she entered, came round the table and pulled out a chair.

'I was hoping you might join me, Miss Goodrum.'

'I thought I might have finished before the family came down.'

'You will not disturb me. I enjoy company at meals and I am an early riser, unlike most of my friends, who rarely show their faces before noon.'

Sarah's cheeks were warm. She kept her back towards him as she looked beneath the silver covers and chose from scrambled eggs, kedgeree, devilled kidneys and bacon, making her choice before returning to the table.

'I did not wish to make more work for the maids by having my breakfast brought up. Mrs Brancaster thought it would be suitable for me to take my meals here since you invited me to dine last evening.'

'Why make more work for the servants? I've told John and Francesca that they may join us for all meals. We are a small family, Miss Goodrum, so why not make the most of each other's company?'

'It seems ridiculous to have meals taken to the nursery when we do not intend to spend much time there.'

'Exactly. Others may find the practice unconventional, but I can see no reason why the children of the

family should not join their parents—unless they are
ill-behaved and would annoy the guests.'

'We have no guests....'

'How perceptive of you, Miss Goodrum,' he said and
there was a gleam of mockery in his eyes.

'Do you enjoy mocking everything and everyone?'

'If one could not laugh at the world it would be a dull
place, do you not agree?'

'Yes, perhaps.' Sarah's mouth was unaccountably
smiling despite her determination to keep her distance.
'Do you intend on inviting guests to stay?'

If he did so she would need to change her arrangements, for guests would not expect to see the governess at every meal.

'We may have that picnic John was so keen on and
we shall encourage people to visit for tea—but I think
no house guests at the moment. Unless my uncle decides
to visit; he might come down at any time, of course.'

'You were not thinking of holding a dinner?'

'Not for the moment. Unless, as I said, my uncle
decides to visit his grandchildren. He told me he has
no intention of it until Christmas, but he might change
his mind.'

'Yes, I can see that would change things.' Sarah swallowed a little scrambled egg and a piece of kidney. She
touched the napkin to her mouth and glanced at him.
'Would it be rude of me to ask why a gentleman like
you would agree to be John's mentor for six months? I
should have thought you might prefer to be in town—
or have business at your own estate.'

'Should you?' His brows rose. 'I see no reason why
I should answer your question, but I shall tell you that

my estate is within a day's ride should I need to visit it—and I do have agents and managers to run it for me.'

'Yes, of course, but there is always some little detail needing attention, do you not find? Things that only you can decide...' Sarah dipped her head as his eyes narrowed in suspicion. 'My father always said he could not leave his business for long...'

'I thought you said he was a mine manager?'

'Yes, he was,' Sarah agreed. 'He was always very busy and had little time for his family. Especially after my mother died.'

'Was that long ago?'

'I was twelve at the time. I grew closer to my father and sometimes accompanied him on...' She had been going to say journeys, for her father had travelled between the mine and the mills. 'On his way to work,' she finished lamely.

'That was before you went to school?'

'Yes, I had a governess. She did not approve of me spending so much time at the m...mine.' Again she had been going to say mills and bit back her words. This was a dangerous subject and if she were not careful she would betray herself.

At that moment the door opened and both John and Francesca entered. After exchanging greetings with Sarah and Lord Myers, they went to the sideboard and began to choose from the various dishes. John was clearly impressed by the choice and spent some time filling his plate.

'Can you eat all that?' Sarah asked. 'You must remember that we shall eat nuncheon later—unless we just have some fruit and biscuits? I thought we might ramble later this afternoon. We can collect wild flowers and stones, things that we can draw or make into a collection. If Lord Myers has no other plans?'

'I couldn't resist,' John said honestly. 'We never get all this in the nursery. I should like to go rambling if Rupert has nothing else planned.'

'As a matter of fact, I had planned that we should start your fencing lessons after nuncheon. We shall spend an hour teaching you the first moves and then I had thought you might wish to play a ball game on the lawn. However, you may go walking after the fencing lesson if you prefer.'

'No, I'd rather stay with you,' John said and attacked his food as if he had been starved for the past year.

'Better slow down a bit,' Lord Myers advised and John immediately sat back, chewing more thoroughly.

'I'd like to play ball games,' Francesca said. 'I'd like to watch the fencing, too—but it may be best if I wait until John has learned a few moves. We could ramble for a while and then come back and join the others, couldn't we, Sarah?'

'Yes, of course,' Sarah said and saw Lord Myers's brows shoot up. 'I told Francesca she might use my preferred name when we are alone, my lord.'

'Indeed, Miss Goodrum?' He looked at her through narrowed eyes. 'I thought your name was Hester?'

Sarah felt her cheeks growing warm. 'I never liked the name and my father had a pet name for me. It was my mother's name also....'

'I see. Are we all allowed to call you by this...pet name? Or is it only for Francesca?'

'In company I think it would be best if I remained Miss Goodrum. I leave the rest to your good sense, Lord Myers.'

'Ah, I see.' A gleam appeared in his eyes. 'I shall give the matter my full attention, Miss Goodrum.'

Sarah felt her cheeks flame. Had they been alone she might have made a sharp retort, but decided to change the subject.

For the remainder of their meal, she addressed her remarks to John and Francesca and was relieved when Lord Myers got up and excused himself.

'I have some estate business to attend to while I am here,' he said. 'I shall see you after nuncheon, John—and we shall play some kind of ball game on the lawns at about three this afternoon.'

Soon after he departed Sarah left the others to finish and went to the library. She had chosen the books they were to discuss by the time Francesca and John arrived. Having found a bestiary for John to peruse and some poetry books that she thought Francesca would like, she spent the next half an hour reading poetry. As she chose a poem that told of daring deeds and men's lives laid down on the field of battle, she was not surprised that John paid full attention to her reading.

'It was a brave thing Horatio did in laying down his life for the men he fought with, wasn't it, miss?' he said when she put down the book. 'I think I should like to be a soldier and fight for honour and glory.'

'Perhaps you will when you are older.' Sarah smiled at him. 'Now I am going to read a romantic poem for Francesca's sake. You may wish to peruse your bestiary, John—but I should like you to write me a short piece about the battle scenes we just discussed in your own time. Can you do that for me?'

'Yes, miss. May I write it as a story?'

'If you wish. Yes, I think that would be an excellent idea.' She opened her book and smiled at Francesca. 'This is Colonel Lovelace's letter to Lucasta on the eve of Battle. Although it has the same theme, it is romantic and I think you may enjoy it.'

She began to read, noticing that although John had opened his book, clearly disgusted at the idea of a sloppy romance, he soon began to listen to the poem and the others Sarah read to them.

'For your essay I would like you to write about what romance is—and what you think Lucasta meant to Colonel Lovelace to make him write such a poem, Francesca.'

'Oh, yes…it was so romantic,' Francesca said and sighed. 'Love is a wonderful thing, is it not? Have you ever been in love, Sarah?'

'No, I haven't. I loved my father, but I think being in love is very different.'

'How does one know whether love is real?'

'I am not sure—but I think when it happens one feels it in here.' Sarah placed a hand over her heart. 'If you think it is happening to you one day, you must give yourself time to be sure, Francesca—but I think you will know in your heart if it's real.'

'Men can let you down, though, can't they? I heard about one of the servant girls…' Francesca glanced at John, who appeared to have his nose firmly in his book. 'Something happened to her and she was sent away in disgrace. I asked Mrs Brancaster why and she said a man had let poor Alice down. I wasn't sure what she meant.'

'Ah…' Sarah swallowed hard. She hadn't realised

the girl was so innocent. 'That is something we ought to discuss another day—perhaps in private.'

'It meant she was having a baby and she wasn't wed,' John said, proving that his ears were still listening even if his nose was in the book. 'Timothy the groom told me Alice wouldn't say who the father was, but he thought—'

'Yes, well, perhaps it is best if we do not speculate on such matters,' Sarah said. She herself had learned from her old nurse where babies came from when she was sixteen and one of her father's maids had also been dismissed for having committed the terrible sin of lying with one of the grooms.

'I sort of knew that,' Francesca admitted. 'But not why she was in trouble… I mean, what made her?'

Sarah's cheeks were warm. 'There are a few books on anatomy, which might explain how it works. However, making babies happens when a man and a woman make love—and that starts with kissing. There is more, which it would not be appropriate for us to discuss at the moment—but it is the reason your mama would have told you not to let men kiss you, if she were still here.'

'Mrs Brancaster said something of the sort, but I didn't understand her. If people are in love, why is it wrong to kiss and make babies?'

'I dare say it is not wrong. In fact, it is perfectly right and natural—but society and the church say that it must only happen when the man and woman are married. That is why Mrs Brancaster said poor Alice had been let down by a man. He may not have wished to marry her after…afterwards.'

'Then he was unkind and cruel,' Francesca said. She

frowned. 'I think I should like to read those books on anatomy, please.'

'I will find them for you.' Sarah got up and went to the shelves. She ran her finger along them and took out two, which after looking at the pictures, she judged to be matter-of-fact tomes, which dealt with such matters. She handed them to Francesca. 'This explains how it happens and the workings of a woman's—and a man's—body but not why. If the attraction is there, feelings are aroused…but you should never give in to them before marriage. If you did so, you would lose your reputation and you would never find the kind of husband your family would wish you to have. Also, you would be shamed and many hostesses would not admit you to their drawing rooms.'

'Yes, I see.' Francesca put away the books along with with her poetry volumes just as the bell sounded for nuncheon. 'I should go to my room first. Thank you, Sarah. I've learned more this morning than I did in all the time my last governess was here.'

'But I saw some of the work you did with her. You can write quite well in French, Francesca, as well as being advanced in your Latin verbs.'

'What good will such things do me in life?' Francesca asked. 'Someone told me gentlemen do not like clever girls. I need to know about love and having children.'

Sarah made no reply. The morning had proved more eventful than she'd intended and she was busy with her thoughts as she ran up to her room to wash her hands. Both of her pupils had lively enquiring minds and it seemed they were thirsty for knowledge. She had answered their questions honestly, but she wasn't sure that her teaching was exactly what their uncle might wish them to learn.

Nuncheon was a pleasant interlude. No one was particularly hungry and Sarah noticed that Francesca followed her lead and ate mostly fruit, drinking a pleasant cordial and eating some gooseberries that were deliciously ripe and stewed with a rich pastry crust and custard.

After the meal John departed with his mentor to begin his fencing lessons and Francesca took Sarah on a long ramble about the estate, showing her parts of it that she had not yet ventured to alone. As they walked, Sarah explained more of how babies were made and what she knew of love, which was, she admitted, very little.

'I have felt tempted,' she said when Francesca pressed for more. 'But I knew it was wrong. I have been asked to marry, but as I had no feelings for the gentleman I refused. I should not want him to kiss me—or do any of the other things of that I have been told, but have no experience.'

'I just wanted to know what Alice had done to be sent off like that,' Francesca said. 'It doesn't seem fair that she lost her job, but he—well, she wouldn't tell anyone who it was.'

'She was being loyal to him, but I think it a mistake. If he promised her marriage, he should have been made to wed her.'

'But he might have lost his job, too. Mrs Brancaster said that the maids were not allowed followers.'

'You can understand why. If they get into trouble,

they have to leave and then the housekeeper has to train a new girl.'

'Yes, I see that—but why not let her stay until she has the baby? Afterwards, she could work part of the time, couldn't she?'

'I dare say Mrs Brancaster is doing what she thinks right. You see, Alice had been immoral by her standards—and that is how most people see it.'

'Do you not think it unfair?'

'Well, yes, I do. However, one has to live by the rules, Francesca. If it had happened to a girl in my employ, I should have tried to help her—but she would still have had to leave, because of the example it sets to others.'

'I still think it's unfair,' Francesca said. 'I liked Alice and I cried when she left.'

'Yes, I can see that it would upset you. I dare say Mrs Brancaster did not like to do it, but she might have lost her own job if she had neglected her duty. Your grandfather would not have wished for a girl like that to continue in his service. It's the way of the world and we shall not change it.'

'Women can't change anything, can they? Men rule our lives. If we have a fortune, our father or guardian controls it until we marry and then our husband takes over and it belongs to him.'

'Not always…' Sarah frowned, because her uncle had tried to control her and failed. 'If a woman has a fortune and is strong enough and clever enough, she may control it herself.'

Francesca was silent, as if absorbing this knowledge.

Sarah hesitated, then, 'My father was not a poor man, Francesca, and what he had he secured to me in his will. It remains mine even if I marry.'

'Why do you work as a governess if you have some money of your own?'

'Because it suits me. I have done other things—but I wanted a change of scenery and...I came here on a whim, but when I met you and John I knew I wanted to stay.'

Sarah took a deep breath as she waited for the girl's reaction. She had told her as much as she dare and felt better for it. Francesca did not know the whole truth, but Sarah no longer felt so guilty over deceiving her.

Francesca looked at her curiously. 'You're not like any governess I've had before.' She tipped her head to one side. 'Do you have a secret, Sarah?'

'Yes, there is something—but I would rather you did not tell your uncle, because he might send me away if he knew.'

'Are you in trouble?'

'I am hiding from a man who is trying to trap me into marriage. I do not like him, but my family thinks it a good marriage. I came here to avoid him while I consider what I should do.'

Francesca's gaze narrowed. 'You're not truly Hester Goodrum, are you?'

'My name is Sarah Hardcastle,' Sarah said. 'Hester wanted to get married. I gave her a little money and exchanged places with her. Do you think me very dreadful to have deceived you?'

'No, I think you are amazing.' Francesca looked thoughtful. 'Lord Myers would send you packing if he knew—and Grandfather would not be pleased, but I want you to stay. You tell us the truth instead of making up lies to protect us from what we want to know.'

'I suppose I do have different ideas.' Sarah looked

at her awkwardly. 'Do you feel compelled to tell your uncle? I know you ought, but if you do I must leave.'

'It will be our secret,' Francesca promised. 'I shall not tell John, because he would be sure to let it out. My uncle may be angry when he discovers the truth.'

'I have told myself that if I give you a proper education I am doing no harm.'

Francesca laughed. 'I do not care who you are, Sarah. I do not think you mean us any harm—and I want you to stay. You are my friend.'

'Yes, I should like to be that,' Sarah said. She glanced at the little silver watch pinned to her gown. The time was getting on. 'We'd better return or we shall be late for the games.'

'Yes.' Francesca's eyes sparkled with mischief. 'I shall enjoy keeping your secret, Sarah—it's fun.'

Sarah smiled. When Francesca had guessed so much she'd felt compelled to tell her the truth and was glad she need not lie to at least one member of the household— but was she setting a bad example by encouraging her pupil to keep secrets from her uncle?

Perhaps she ought to confess the whole to Lord Myers and leave the decision to him—yet the house was so beautiful and she'd already become fond of her pupils.

Surely she could not harm people she wanted only to help?

They returned to the house, speaking only occasionally. Francesca was deep in thought and Sarah had her own thoughts to keep her busy. Being a governess had seemed such a simple matter, but it was no such thing. Sarah had no training to guide her and she had used her own instincts, her own experience, to answer Francesca's natural questions—but had she exceeded her authority? Had she perhaps put ideas into the girl's head that her grandfather and other ladies might think wrong for a young lady of quality?

Sarah was independent because of her father's will, which had given her complete control of her fortune and his business empire. Had he willed it so that her uncle had become her guardian she did not think she could have borne her life, for she would have been hedged about by convention and would not have dared to voice her opinions as freely as she did. Was she harming Francesca's chances by teaching her to be as free in her thoughts?

The sound of laughter shattered her more serious thoughts. When they came upon Lord Myers, John and two of the footmen playing with an oval-shaped ball on the green, Sarah was intrigued, for she had not seen such a rough game before.

She watched as John caught the ball and then ran off with it, only to be pursued by his uncle, who tackled him and brought him down. John managed to pass the ball to one of the footmen, who took it and ran while the second footman tried to stop him. He was unable to and John gave a shout of joy as he threw himself down at a certain spot and touched the ground with the ball.

'A try. We scored a try,' he said. 'Well done, Jenkins. Well done.'

'Yes, good show.' Lord Myers applauded. He turned and saw the ladies, frowning for a moment before turning to John. 'I think we should play cricket now so that Miss Goodrum and Francesca can join us.'

John agreed and one of the footmen started preparing the wicket. Francesca joined Lord Myers's side and Sarah joined Jenkins and John. Apparently, Jenkins was as good at the game as at the earlier one and he was elected to bowl at Lord Myers.

Sarah had no idea what game they had been playing when she arrived with Francesca, but knew the game of cricket and was happy to field. She was forced to run after balls that went into the shrubbery several times until she suddenly saw it coming straight at her, put out a hand and caught it.

'Out. You're out, Uncle Rupert,' John crowed. 'Now it's Francesca's turn and then Mason's. We'll soon have you out, won't we, Sarah?'

'Yes, certainly,' Sarah agreed with a smile for his enthusiasm.

However, Francesca played well and scored five runs before Jenkins caught her. Mason took his turn and proved to be a clever batsman; it was some minutes before he became too adventurous and was run out for twenty-five.

A tray was brought out by one of the maids then and they all sat on blankets on the grass until John's team went in to bat. Sarah had enjoyed her glass of barley water and was on her feet again when Lord Myers came over to her.

'I should like to speak to you in the library before you go up, Miss Goodrum.' His expression was grim and Sarah's heart caught. He was angry, she was sure of it and could not for the life of her think what she had done.

Surely he had not discovered her true identity?

Chapter Five

Sarah followed behind the others as they all trooped into the house. The tea ceremony had been dispensed with for the day since they'd all enjoyed cool drinks on the lawn and no one was hungry. Sarah would have liked to escape to her room to tidy herself, but a look from Lord Myers sent her straight to the library. He followed her in and closed the door behind him. One look at his face made her catch her breath.

'What is this I hear about your lesson this morning, Miss Goodrum? Can it be right that you condoned the behaviour of a maid who was dismissed for immorality—and did you really give Francesca books that described the procreation of children?'

'We were talking about poetry and Francesca happened to say that a man could let a woman down. I hadn't realised how innocent she was and I thought it better she should know the truth.'

'And John—is he old enough to hear it like that?'

'I did not explain anything in detail and he seemed to know more than Francesca. I gave her books on anatomy, but tried to explain about feelings and the consequences of being carried away by them.'

His gaze narrowed. 'What kind of books did you deem suitable for a young woman of sixteen?'

'They have pictures, which show the workings of both the male and female body, and explain about childbirth and…the rest of it.'

'And you think that suitable reading for a young lady of quality?'

'It is better she should know than go to her wedding night in ignorance, wouldn't you say? We talked further on our walk and I was careful to impress on her the consequences of having…intimate relations before one is married.'

'Good grief!' Lord Myers seemed stunned for a moment. He ran his fingers through his thick dark hair, his grey eyes wintry. 'I was told you were an unusual governess and you certainly are, Miss Goodrum.'

'Would you prefer I'd lied? Would you have Francesca ignorant of the facts of life? She will know now precisely why she ought not to give in to the persuasion of rakish men—and what may happen if she does. She will also be more prepared for her wedding night.'

'You take my breath away.'

Sarah swallowed hard, her hands turned inwards, the palms sweating. 'Forgive me. I did what I thought was right. I know some ladies might think I was too direct…'

'A great many men would feel the same. Such revelations would undoubtedly have led to instant dismissal in most households.'

'I did not intend it to be part of the lesson, it just happened. I realise that convention decrees that these things remain hidden from a young woman—but I think it unfair that girls should marry without the faintest idea of what to expect. In some cases the shock may damage their marriage. Besides, most girls hear it from a servant rather than their mother. John had some garbled version from a stable lad and I thought it best to be open.'

'Yes, I see that…' Lord Myers was staring at her. The heat in his eyes seemed to burn her skin. 'Well, it is over now and perhaps no harm has been done. I would ask you not to indoctrinate your charges with your radical ideas too often, Miss Goodrum.'

'No, of course not—though I feel Francesca's mother would have told her the facts of life by now had she lived.'

'In a rather different way and not in front of her brother, I imagine.'

'Yes, perhaps that is true. John did not seem surprised or particularly interested. I imagine he's heard more in the stables than he heard from me.'

'And that is to be regretted,' Lord Myers said. 'The language of the grooms is something most boys learn, but it must be tempered with proper explanation so that he understands what it means to be a gentleman. He must learn where the dividing line comes between taking one's pleasure and guarding one's honour and that of a lady.'

'Yes, of course. It is a good thing that you came here, sir. He very much enjoyed himself this afternoon.'

'I have decided that in future I shall take over John's lessons. I do not disagree that Francesca should be prepared for life—and she will be aware of the consequences, as you say—but John needs a firm hand.'

'I am sorry you feel I have let him down, my lord.'

Sarah's cheeks were stinging for she felt herself at fault, though in her opinion she'd done nothing to merit such censure.

'No harm has been done that a few lessons with me cannot put right. We shall continue to have games or other pastimes that we share, Miss Goodrum, but I no longer want John to join you in the mornings.'

'As you wish, sir.' Sarah stood stiffly, her hands in front of her. She felt his censure unfair and yet understood his point of view. John did need male guidance and would do better not to gain his knowledge of the world via the stables. 'May I go now? I should like to write some letters before I change for the evening.'

'Yes, you may go,' he said, then, as she walked to the door, 'Wait a moment, Sarah—I did not wish to censure you. I felt it my duty after what John told me.'

Sarah turned to look back at him. There was no hint of tears in her eyes, though she could feel them inside. 'You were doing your duty, sir. If I failed in mine, I am sorry.'

She went out and closed the door before he could answer, hearing him curse as she did so. She was feeling subdued as she walked up to her room. Her first day had seemed to go well, but clearly she had made mistakes and aroused Lord Myers's disapproval—and that hurt. It hurt more than she would have imagined.

What he would think if he knew of her deception she dared not think. No doubt he would believe his opinion of her as some kind of adventuress thoroughly vindicated.

At dinner that evening Sarah wore her same gown. She had no other evening gown suitable and would not have dared to venture downstairs in it if she had. She had already aroused doubts and suspicions in Lord Myers's mind. Next he would be thinking her a courtesan or some such thing. She did her best to seem natural and held her head high, answering any questions that came her way, but keeping her opinions to herself. Even when Lord Myers mentioned the Regent and Francesca asked if it was true that he had been married to Maria Fitzherbert, she refrained from joining the conversation until directly addressed.

'Well, I think it was very unfair of him if he did,' Francesca said when Lord Myers merely shrugged and said he didn't know. 'What do you think, Sarah?'

'In any other case I would say it was wrong and that she had a right to be upheld as his wife—but because of the law about royal marriages it may not have been a true one. I do not know the truth of the matter.'

'If he did not truly marry her, he tricked her into being his mistress.'

'Francesca.' Lord Myers glared at Sarah. 'This is not the right subject for the dinner table. Please refrain from discussing this in mixed company. You may speak to Miss Goodrum in private on the matter if you wish.'

Francesca blushed and Sarah threw Lord Myers an angry glance. He was taking a moral stance that was hardly necessary. Such things were often discussed openly in society, though rarely in mixed company and not before children or innocent girls. He was perhaps thinking of John, for he had decided to mentor him on matters of morality. Now Sarah saw her own fault in being too easy with Francesca and looked down at her plate.

As Francesca would have protested, she reached out

to touch her hand. 'Later, my dear. Lord Myers is right on this occasion.'

He threw a speaking glance at her across the table. Francesca saw it and subsided into silence. She did not speak again until John was sent to bed and they were alone in the drawing room, waiting for Lord Myers to join them.

'Are you in trouble with Uncle Rupert because of what you told me about love this morning?'

'Perhaps I should have been more wary—waited to explain until we were alone. John is young and impressionable after all.'

'Nonsense! He knows far more than I do. We talked about everything when we were alone, but there were things he wouldn't say. He said it wasn't fit for a girl's ears.'

'Lord Myers is afraid he may have heard things in the stable that may give him the wrong idea about such things. We are to have our lessons alone in future.'

'That's so unfair of him. It wasn't your fault. You are the only person who has ever treated me as a woman— the only one to tell either of us the truth.'

'A conventional governess would not have done so. She might have given you some information in private—and perhaps it is what I should have done. Well, it is not my decision to bar John from our lessons, but I am sorry if it upsets you. I believe in speaking my mind—but it is not always wise to do so in company, especially at the dinner table.'

'No, I see that—but it was just us, family...' Francesca stared at her. 'Are you crying?'

'No, of course not.' Sarah blinked away the wetness

that had unaccountably come to her eyes. 'Do you truly think of me as your family?'

'You're the sister I never had.' Francesca smiled at her. 'She would have told me the things I needed to know—especially when she was married. It's silly the way they hide things from unmarried girls, isn't it? How can we make a sensible choice for a husband if we don't understand what it means to be married?'

'Oh, my dear,' Sarah said and was suddenly amused. 'You are supposed to enjoy your Season and have fun— and you would normally ask your mama what she felt about the gentleman you liked. She would give you her advice.'

'Will you be my chaperon when we go to London? Please, Sarah. I would rather it was you than someone I didn't know.'

'You hardly know me—though I feel as if I've known you always. I doubt if I would be thought suitable. You need someone of more consequence. Besides, I shall have to leave you before then.'

'You won't let Uncle Rupert drive you away?'

'You mustn't take against him because he corrected you at table, Francesca.'

'I shall hate him if he sends you away. I'm going to tell Grandfather that I want you as my chaperon when he comes down at Christmas.'

'We'll think about that later,' Sarah said, her throat tight with emotion. Francesca was becoming so special to her and the idea of being her chaperon appealed, but of course it was not possible. Sarah could not enter society as Miss Goodrum and, as Miss Hardcastle, she would not be acceptable to the girl's guardians. 'We have lots of time before then. I must teach you so many things—and the first is to think before you speak. Whatever we may discuss in private, and whatever your opinion of a situation or fact, it is sometimes better not to repeat it to others, especially in company.'

'Oh, you do not need to tell me. I was so mortified I could have died.' Francesca turned to her and hugged her. 'You mustn't be hurt, Sarah. If Rupert is mean to you, I'll tell John to put something horrid in his bed.'

Sarah laughed. 'Now that you must never do, dearest. Besides, it might result in the cane for John and you would not want that. Lord Myers takes his duty seriously and I think you must both respect his wishes.'

'I was looking at those books you gave me. Is that what really happens? It looks awful. I can't see why anyone would want to do anything like that…'

'I think that feelings come into it,' Sarah said with a smile, but then the door opened and she shook her head. 'You might wish to go up now, dearest, and I shall follow.'

Francesca nodded. She approached Lord Myers and bobbed a curtsy. 'Goodnight, sir. I am sorry if I offended you earlier.'

'Good grief, child. I was not offended, but your reputation might suffer in company. I wanted you to be aware.'

'Yes, Uncle Rupert. Sarah has explained that I may ask her anything in private, but not speak so openly in front of others.'

'Good. Run along now. I wish to speak to Miss Goodrum.'

Francesca threw a speaking look at Sarah and went out.

'Miss Goodrum—' Lord Myers stood looking at her

uncertainly. 'Will you honour me with a game of chess this evening? You do play chess, I hope?'

'Yes, my lord. My father taught me. I played often with him.'

'I thought that might be the case. Will you oblige me?'

'If you wish.'

'I do wish. I also want to apologise for my display of bad manners earlier. I did not intend to squash the child—and I thank you for putting things right.'

'It was a misunderstanding all round, my lord. I do not think it will happen again.'

'I suppose I cannot prevail on you to call me Rupert in private?'

Sarah hesitated, then, 'I hardly think it wise, sir. If I could add uncle I would do so, as the others do, but I cannot—and so I feel that it would not be right.'

'Make it sir, then. I cannot stand to be my lorded all the time. I would even prefer Captain Myers, as I was known in my army days.'

'Yes, sir. You were in the army?' Sarah asked politely, as she set out the beautiful ivory-and-ebony chessboard with delicate carved figures. 'I thought perhaps you might have been. My father always said it was easy to tell a military man by his bearing.'

'Indeed? I think I should have liked to know your father, Sarah.'

'Yes, you might. I think he might have liked you—he was very direct and to the point and honest.'

'Like you, I imagine?'

'I resemble my father in some ways. I cannot say all.'

Sarah was acutely aware of her lies. She was beginning to hate them and wished that she dare tell him the truth—explain why it had seemed such a good idea and why she wanted to stay here as Francesca's governess. Yet he would not understand. He would revile her for lying and worst of all he would dismiss her and install a new governess in her place.

Even though she had made mistakes on her first day, Sarah felt that she was helping Francesca. She had gained the girl's confidence and affection, too. It would hurt her if Sarah left—and she might become sullen, taking against Lord Myers and the new governess.

Sarah was doing no harm. She would be careful in future to temper every opinion she gave with the counter-argument and explain why Francesca must conform to what society expected even though she might disagree privately, but she could not desert her.

She dismissed her qualms and brought her mind to the game. Lord Myers showed his mettle by his first few moves, but she was with him.

Sarah had learned from a chess master and she was well able to keep up her end. By the end of an hour she had beaten him twice and been beaten herself once when an early move on his part had sealed her fate almost from the beginning.

At the end of the third game, she stood up.

'I believe I should leave you now, sir. Goodnight.'

'Goodnight, Sarah,' he replied. He was on his feet, standing so close to her that she could scarcely breathe. Her heart was beating fast and she felt the heat start low in her abdomen and sweep through her. She was being drawn to him like a moth to a flame. In another moment she would be in his arms. He would kiss her and then…

She stepped back, breaking the fine thread that had bound them.

'I should go.'

'Perhaps you will let me try for revenge another evening.'

'Yes, of course, if you wish.'

With that she walked to the door and went out. He made no move to stop her or call her back, though she thought she heard a muffled groan as she closed the door behind her.

Alone in her room, Sarah closed the door, locked it and then stood with her back against it. She felt weak and knew that she had escaped by a hairsbreadth from a fate that was described as worse than death—another few seconds and he would have seduced her. She would have allowed it. She had wanted it, longed for his kiss—and what came after.

It was those feelings she'd warned Francesca of—feelings that would lead to her downfall. Even as Miss Sarah Hardcastle she would not have expected a marriage proposal from Lord Myers, unless he needed a fortune, of course. Somehow she did not see him as lacking wealth or the determination to make it if he had none. He was not the kind of man to need a Cit's daughter as a wife.

Sarah was well aware that as the daughter of a mill owner she would not be thought suitable to marry into the best families—unless of course they happened to be desperate.

Sarah was trembling as she undressed and dived beneath the sheets. The awful thing was that she suspected she would enjoy being seduced by Lord Myers—and that would be stupid.

'Foolish, foolish, foolish!'

Yet the temptation to remain, to let him kiss her and do what he would on the rug before the fire had been strong. Why did he have this effect on her, something that no other man had before now?

She pounded her pillow. Before this, Sarah had resisted every advance, deflected every unwanted offer with ease—but something told her that if she stayed here she was in danger of succumbing to her wretched feelings. Even worse than being seduced was the fear that she might learn to care for him—and that must lead to terrible unhappiness.

'No, I shall not. I refuse to care about him,' she whispered and closed her eyes on the tears as they insisted on falling. 'I am not so silly as to care for a man who merely wants to seduce me.'

In future she would have to be constantly on her guard. Friendly but cool, even aloof.

She would be the perfect governess. In private, she would be open and friendly with Francesca, but whenever Lord Myers was around she would keep her distance.

God damn it! Rupert groaned as the door shut behind her, leaving him with the scent of her perfume in his nostrils and the want of her surging through his blood. What was it about Miss Hester Goodrum that had sent his senses haywire? He could hardly remember feeling such urgent lust before in his life. For a moment it had taken every last ounce of his strength to keep from dragging her into his arms, kissing her to within an inch of her life and carrying her to his bed.

His thoughts were outrageous and he knew it. If she was the governess she claimed to be, he would be doing her an extreme disservice and she did not deserve such treatment from him. Yet what if she were indeed an adventuress? There were things that did not sit well with her claim to be merely a governess—and why had she told Francesca to call her Sarah? Surely if her name was Hester a pet name would be Hetty or some such diminutive?

If she had been another man's mistress, then she was fair game and he would be justified in hunting her down until she agreed to be his. It was odd, but he did not wish that to be the case. Indeed, he feared that her appeal would be tarnished if he discovered that she was a schemer and a liar.

Why would she come here if she were not what she professed to be? The question bothered him, chasing round in his mind like a puppy after its tail. He could see no advantage to it—unless she hoped to seduce her employer, but she could have hardly hoped for that since the marquess was nearly three times her age and seldom visited his country house.

Was she hiding from someone or something? Had she been accused of theft or worse? Lurid thoughts chased through his mind—had she murdered her protector, stolen her employer's heirlooms or been snubbed by society?

A smile touched his mouth for he did not see Sarah as a fugitive from the law. Yet he would swear her name was not Hester Goodrum, nor had she been a governess until recently. So where was the real Hester and why had they changed places?

Yes, of course, it was what must have happened! Rupert felt certain of it, though he could see no reason for the masquerade. Sarah did not strike him as a society miss who would do something like this for a jest or a wager. No, she had a perfectly good reason for what she was doing.

If that turned out to be the case, she was a consummate liar and Rupert hated liars. His mouth thinned. In his experience women lied without thought for the harm they caused or the pain they inflicted.

He determined that he would discover the truth and unmask her and then—then he would show her no mercy. He would offer her an ultimatum: become his mistress or risk exposure and the scorn it would bring.

For a moment in his anger he dwelled on the prospect with pleasure, but then the picture faded and his expression hardened. He had never forced a woman into his bed and it would bring only a hollow victory. No, he would put the woman out of his head and, if he discovered she had indeed been lying to them, he would dismiss her.

Sarah Goodrum, or whatever her name was, would discover that she had made a mistake when she decided to try to fool him. By the time he'd finished with her she would wish she'd never been born.

It had rained during the night, which meant the grass would be wet if she chose to walk first thing. Sarah decided to forgo her exercise. Perhaps the afternoon would be warm and dry. In the meantime she would take an early breakfast and then spend some time in the library, preparing lessons for that day. She would try to be more conventional, and perhaps in the afternoon, if it were still damp, they could play the pianoforte. Francesca had told her she played, but needed help to achieve a higher standard. Since it was one of Sarah's chief pleasures and something she did well, she had hopes of achieving at least this much for her pupil.

She was the first in the breakfast room and had eaten when the door opened to admit Lord Myers. He looked at her coldly, his manner markedly reserved as he perused the chafing-dishes and then brought his plate to sit opposite her.

'Good morning, Miss Goodrum. I trust you slept well?'

'Yes, sir. I took my breakfast early since it was still wet out.' She pushed back her chair and stood, hesitating a moment. Why had he changed so much since the previous evening? He seemed a man of many moods.

'There is no need to leave on my account.' He frowned at her.

'I had finished, sir. If you will excuse me?'

'Yes, of course. You should prepare your lessons for the morning—a little more carefully today, if you please.'

'Yes, my lord.'

Tears stung behind her eyes, but she gave no sign as she lifted her head and swept from the room like a queen.

How dare he speak to her that way? For a moment anger rolled over the hurt, but then she remembered that he was here in place of her employer and had every right to address her as he chose. He could send her away if he wished.

Sarah bit her lower lip. She had no idea why he was angry with her. The previous evening she had sensed that he was on the verge of making love to her—so why had he changed so suddenly?

Obviously, he was a law unto himself. He was an aristocrat and had no interest in the feelings of a lowly governess—any more than he would in the daughter of a Cit, even a wealthy mill owner's daughter.

Sarah would be a fool to allow herself to care for a man like that—even if one of his sensual looks could make her feel weak at the knees and keep her sleepless in her bed.

She had made up her mind to keep her distance during a restless night and his manner this morning had made that easier. If they both kept their distance, except when in the children's presence, everything would be fine. She would conquer this temporary weakness and her heart would remain untouched.

Sarah would spend a few months in retreat from her own life and do what she could for Francesca—John, too, if he needed her, though he seemed to have taken to his mentor and hung on Lord Myers's every word. She would stay for as long as she could, but if life became unbearable she would leave.

Chapter Six

The rain had lasted for almost a week, making it impossible to hold the picnic John had wanted so badly. However, he spent most of his time either fencing, studying or riding with Lord Myers and seemed well pleased with the change. Francesca had told Sarah that he was learning to shoot.

'I hardly see him now,' she complained as they closed the pianoforte after an hour spent most enjoyably. 'I am so glad you are my friend, Sarah. I do not know what I should do if you were not here.'

'I dare say John will seek your company when he is ready. You must understand that this is the first time he has received the attention of a man like Lord Myers. He must feel pleased, excited and even flattered by it. After being neglected by his tutors he is suddenly of importance.'

'How understanding you are,' Francesca said and got up, wandering over to the window. 'Did you know that Uncle Rupert has decided to employ a dancing master for me? He is French and should be here any day now.'

'Oh…' Sarah bit her lower lip. Lord Myers had neglected to tell her, but then, she'd hardly seen him all week. At dinner he spoke to Francesca and John, but, other than asking if she were well and had what she needed, he had not directed a whole sentence at her for seven days. 'I had thought he might teach you himself.'

'He said he had considered it, but felt himself unable to convey the finer points. I think he finds that John takes up most of his time—and he has friends. You know he has dined out twice this week and he spent most of yesterday afternoon with them.'

'Yes, I dare say he wishes for some company of his own age, men he can converse with,' Sarah agreed. 'John was out with the groom all afternoon. I hear he is doing very well with his new pony.'

'Yes. He finds Blackie much more of a challenge than dear old Dobbie was, which was why Uncle Rupert purchased the pony for him.'

'Yes, that was thoughtful.'

Sarah could not fault Lord Myers for the way in which he was directing the youth's studies, giving him enough sports and activities to make the written work acceptable. She had paused outside the marquess's study on one occasion and heard Lord Myers reading aloud in Latin. Every now and then he'd stopped to ask John what he understood and to explain the story. His blend of authority and charm had carried John along and the boy seemed completely under his spell.

Francesca was respectful of the man she addressed as Uncle Rupert, even though he wasn't actually her uncle, but some sort of cousin.

'Rupert thought it better if I called him uncle. He says it is a matter of keeping up a respectable household that will give no one a chance to gossip about us. I told him that as long as I had you as a chaperon no one could possibly imagine there was anything improper in our domestic arrangements.'

Sarah resisted the temptation to ask what he'd replied. Since that night when they had played chess alone he had been reserved, even cold towards her, and she had followed his lead. It was better this way than allowing herself to imagine there might be something warm and exciting between them. If she had thought so a week ago, she did not think it now. She knew that it was the only way she could remain as Francesca's governess, but there was an ache in her heart that she could not quite banish.

Sarah stood up and joined her pupil by the window. The afternoon was pleasantly warm with just a slight breeze.

'I have some letters I should like to go first thing in the morning. I think I shall walk down to the Royal Oak and leave them. There might be something for me.'

'One of the footmen will take the letters in the morning and they bring back anything that has come for us.'

'Yes, I know, but I want these to go off—besides, I should have to rely on Lord Myers to frank them for me and I would prefer to pay some sixpences to send them myself. I was wondering if you would like to walk with me?'

'I think I would rather stay here and practise my music, if you do not mind?' Francesca looked at her. 'You will be back in time for tea. Perhaps Uncle Rupert and John will join us today.'

'Yes, perhaps. I must go up and put on my bonnet. I shall not linger, but walk straight there and back.'

Sarah left her pupil sitting at the pianoforte and the

sound of music followed her up the stairs. Francesca was still playing when she returned and left the house by a side door. She had the piece almost right, but there was one passage that she rushed every time. Sarah would show her how it should be played another day.

It was the first time she'd gone for a walk alone since it had rained. The air was fresh with the scents of early summer and the hedgerows were bright with flowers, wild roses twining amongst them and bringing the countryside alive with colour.

She had reached the village without incident and entered the inn, having noticed a horse with a white mark on its rump. She thought it might have belonged to Lord Myers, but wasn't sure. If he were here, she hoped they would not meet. It would be embarrassing if he thought she'd sought him out. As far as she'd known, he'd ridden over to a neighbour's house on some business.

She was met by the host's wife, who took her letters and asked her for four sixpences, to cover the cost of sending them post.

'It would be less if they waited for the mail coach, miss, but if you want them sent urgently it must be two shillings.'

'That is perfectly all right,' Sarah said and handed over her two shillings. 'Do you have any letters for Miss Hardcastle care of Miss Hester Goodrum?'

'Yes, as a matter of fact one arrived by post this afternoon.' The innkeeper's wife looked at her curiously. 'You're Miss Goodrum, governess to the children up at Cavendish Park, aren't you?'

'Yes, I am.' Sarah saw the curiosity in her eyes. 'Miss Hardcastle is…well, I am accepting letters for her.'

'Oh, well, I suppose it's all right, as it says "care of",' the woman said a little doubtfully. 'I normally like to be sure a letter is given to the right person.'

'I assure you I am the right person to receive this letter—and any others that are similarly addressed.'

'Is something wrong, Miss Goodrum?'

Sarah jumped and glanced round as Lord Myers spoke. 'No. I am just collecting some letters. Everything is as it should be.' She took the letter from the woman's reluctant hand as she seemed paralysed by Lord Myers's arrival and was staring at him, seemingly mesmerised.

Sarah slipped the letter, which was quite a thick packet, into her reticule, but she feared that Lord Myers might have caught sight of the wording of the address before she could do so.

'Is Francesca not with you?' he asked, walking to the inn door and opening it for her. He walked out into the yard, standing for a moment in the sunshine as she hesitated.

'Francesca wished to practise the music she is learning. I had some letters I wished to post.'

'Do you write many letters, Miss Goodrum?'

'Yes, several.'

'To your family? Or are you seeking another post?'

'I am not seeking another post at the moment. I have no reason to leave—have I?'

'Only you can know that, Miss Goodrum.'

Sarah hesitated, then, 'I understand you have engaged a dancing master for Francesca?'

'Actually, her grandfather did so himself. I wrote and said I thought it might be a good thing and he sent word that he had seen to it. I heard this morning and told Francesca. I believe he is French—Monsieur Andre Dupree, I think he is called.'

'Ah, I see. I had thought you might teach her yourself?'

'I decided it might be wiser to employ a dancing master—for various reasons. Besides, most of my time is taken up with tutoring John—and there is estate business.'

'You have been busy, I know.'

'Yes.' His gaze narrowed. 'I should be returning to the house. My business here is done—and John should have had his riding lessons for the day.'

'Yes.' She hesitated, then, 'Francesca wondered if you would both join us for tea today. I think she misses her brother.'

'Yes, things have not quite gone to plan. We must have our picnic before the fine weather disappears again. Have you written the invitations?'

'They need only the day and date. I was waiting for your approval.'

'Then make them for this Friday. We must hope that the weather stays fine. I am told some of the strawberries will be ready for picking and that might amuse both the children and our guests.'

'It will not amuse Francesca to be called a child. She will soon be seventeen.'

'Not for a few months. I shall try to remember.' He inclined his head to her. 'I shall not keep you, Miss Goodrum—if that is your name...'

With that he walked away, leaving Sarah to stare after him in dismay. It was the first time he'd talked to her for a week, but she could not deceive herself; his manner was decidedly cool towards her. She was not sure if he was angry or whether he simply did not trust her.

Shrugging off her painful thoughts, she walked on towards the house. She would read her letter later, alone in her room. Sarah had recognised the hand and knew it came from the agent who oversaw her mills. Since he had written extensively there might be a problem.

Sarah sighed. For the past few years she'd dealt with the problems as they arose, but it had been pleasant not to have to think of them for the past week. It might be nice to be married and leave business to her husband, but it would have to be the right man for the sake of all those who relied on her for their living. Sir Roger would squander her money and care nothing for her people. Until she found someone she could trust and like enough to marry, she would have to carry on—but her agents must manage without her for a while. She would not leave Francesca in the lurch unless she was forced.

What was she up to now? Rupert was thoughtful as he put his horse to a canter. His business that afternoon had concerned the governess and he wondered why he had not mentioned it to her. Something in her manner had been guilty and it had made him hold back the news he thought might be interesting for her. She had definitely hidden that letter and so quickly that he hardly caught sight of the lettering, but he was sure it had been addressed to someone care of Miss Goodrum.

He'd sensed a mystery from the start and now he was certain that she was hiding something. Could she be collecting letters for Francesca? Had the young girl formed an attachment before he arrived, one she now wished to hide from him? Rupert frowned. Francesca was surely too young to have a lover—would her governess be complicit in such a deceit?

Or was it simply that Miss Goodrum was not what she claimed to be, as he'd suspected almost from the start? Why had she lied about her identity?

The mystery deepened and he decided he had been right to keep his distance these past few days. To allow himself to like the governess rather more than was sensible would be to invite all manner of problems.

Whatever she was hiding was bound to be unsavoury. He felt disappointed to discover that she was almost certainly the adventuress he'd thought her at the start. She might seem innocent, delightful and charming, but she was undoubtedly playing a part for his sake—to deceive him, or to ensnare him?

The thoughts had gone round and round in his head as he had ridden rode home. Dismounting, he entered the house and immediately encountered John, who was full of his afternoon's outing. The youth's enthusiasm put the mystery of the letter from Rupert's thoughts. He told John to wash his hands and meet him in the drawing room for tea, taking the stairs two at a time in his haste not to be late.

Rupert must simply continue to keep the governess in her proper place for all their sakes. If she were truly innocent, his need to seduce her could only bring her to ruin—and if she were a courtesan it would lead to distress for Francesca.

Yet he lay restless in his bed each night, thinking of her in her chaste bed and burning with need that drove him mad. He wanted her as he'd wanted no other—and he could not put her out of his head.

Oh, damn the woman! He would not allow her beneath his skin. No woman had been allowed to ruffle his feelings in this way for years and he would not give this enchanting minx the satisfaction of knowing how she had affected him the night they'd played chess together.

'Oh, good,' Francesca exclaimed as she saw her brother and Rupert waiting for her in the drawing room. 'I'm so pleased you are to join us for tea. It isn't the same when you don't.'

'Blackie jumped the fence at Three Mile Bottom.' John's enthusiasm carried him away. 'You should come out with me one afternoon.'

'Yes, I should like that—but I'd like Sarah to come as well. I'm not sure we have a suitable horse for her.'

'As a matter of fact—' Rupert broke off as Sarah entered. She was wearing a plain, dark-grey gown, very suitable for a governess, but somehow managed to make it look as if a lady of quality was wearing it. 'I bought one this afternoon. So you will all be able to ride together.'

'Did you hear that, Sarah?' Francesca turned to her with a smile of delight. 'Uncle Rupert bought a horse you could ride. You will ride with us, won't you?'

'Oh… Yes, of course.' Sarah smiled. 'Sorry, my mind was elsewhere. Did you say the horse was bought for me to ride?' She looked at Rupert in surprise. 'That was extremely thoughtful of you, sir.'

'Francesca wanted you to be able to ride with her. She said you were accustomed to riding when at your home—is that true?'

'Yes, I ride whenever I have the time.' Sarah's cheeks

were warm as she took her seat. 'Shall you ring for tea, Francesca?'

'Yes, of course.' Francesca did so and looked at her enquiringly. 'Is something wrong, Sarah? You look worried.'

'I had a letter that was a little worrying, a family matter,' Sarah said. 'Forgive me if my mind wanders. It was something of a shock to me.'

'No one is ill, I hope?' Rupert asked, his gaze narrowed.

'Not exactly. There is a family problem, however. I hope to avoid it, but I may have to leave for a while should things develop.'

'Oh, no, I don't want you to go,' Francesca said instantly. 'Please don't—unless you have to, of course.'

'I have no intention of it,' Sarah replied and smiled at her. 'I think the problem may be dealt with by a series of letters—but should it not, then I might be away for a week or two.'

'Is there anything I may do to help?' Rupert asked. 'Any service I could perform for you?'

Sarah's eyes moved to his face and for a moment she seemed to hesitate, but then, as the door opened to admit the maids with the tea trays, she shook her head. He waited until after the maids had retreated and then persisted.

'We could speak later in private, if you wish?'

'You are…kind,' Sarah said and looked hesitant. 'I believe I can deal with the matter myself for the moment.'

Rupert accepted a cup from Francesca's hand and helped himself to rich fruitcake, which was always his favourite. He could see that the governess was more disturbed than she would say and his sense of frustration increased.

Was she in trouble or was her friend—the friend for whom she had received that letter? It had looked more like a packet and he was curious as to what was in it. He would be most interested in reading the contents of Sarah's package.

'Why don't you all go riding in the morning?' he suggested. 'I think we might forget lessons for once. Miss Goodrum should get to know her horse and yours will suffer if you do not exercise the poor beast more, Francesca.'

'Yes, let's all go riding in the morning,' John said, excited at the prospect. 'You will come too, Uncle Rupert?'

'Unfortunately, I have some things to attend to,' he replied. 'I may ride out and join you later, once it is finished.'

'It would be pleasant to ride again,' Sarah said and some of the anxiety seemed to leave her eyes. 'Although I do not have a habit with me, unfortunately.'

'I think there may be something in Mama's trunks,' Francesca replied and smiled at her. 'You are not dissimilar in height and build and may make a few adjustments if they are needed.'

'If we could look for it before dinner, I could make the alterations this evening,' Sarah agreed. 'Riding is such good exercise and I have felt its lack of late.'

Rupert felt pleased that he'd been able to help her in some small way, even though there was guilt at the back of his mind. With all the children out of the way he would have the opportunity to enter the governess's room and make a brief search for that letter.

A part of his mind was horrified at the idea and yet the other was telling him that as her employer's representative he had every right to discover what she was hiding.

'It was so kind of you to purchase the horse for my use,' Sarah said when she came down the next morning. She was wearing a borrowed habit, which had belonged to Francesca's mother. Sarah had taken down the hem a little, but it was otherwise a reasonable fit. Although not fashionable or exactly Sarah's style, it looked well enough. 'It is a pity you cannot come with us. I think John was anxious to show you how much he has learned.'

Rupert looked into her clear eyes and felt his guilt deepen. It would be pleasant to ride with them and he almost gave in to temptation, but his suspicions needed to be answered.

'Yes, well, perhaps my business need not take long. Which way do you intend to ride?'

'Francesca said we might ride past the water meadows and come back through the village.'

'Very well, perhaps I shall join you later on your ride.'

'I do hope so,' she said, smiled again and went to join the others. He heard the sound of voices and laughter outside as the grooms helped them to mount and the party set out.

Walking upstairs, Rupert fought down his rising sense of guilt. He paused outside the governess's room, knocked and then entered. Looking round, he saw that it was very neat, the bed made and nothing out of place.

Obviously, she was in the habit of keeping things tidy and did not make extra work for the maids.

He could see no sign of any papers. The desk that had been provided for her use was empty of letters or personal items, displaying only the inkwell and pen trays, also a pad for leaning one's paper on. His heart thudding and a sick feeling in his stomach, Rupert walked to the desk. He had never done such a despicable thing in his life. Feeling like the worst sort of rogue, he picked up the pad and saw that the soft surface had indentations, but though he studied them for a moment he could not pick out any words. He hesitated, then opened the long top drawer. It was empty. Each of the first two drawers on the side was similarly unused, but in the third he found a small wooden box, which was obviously used to store papers and letters. It was locked.

Rupert glanced round the room. Where would the key be hidden—or did she have it with her? He considered making a search and then the enormity of what he was doing swept over him.

This was despicable! Miss Goodrum was entitled to her privacy and he was not behaving as a gentleman ought. If he wanted her confidence, he must earn it. Replacing the box, he closed the desk drawer and left the room. As he reached the end of the hall, he saw a maid approaching. She looked at him curiously, no doubt wondering what he was doing so far from his own rooms.

He would change into his riding breeches, walk down to the stables and go in search of his pupils and their governess.

Sarah had been pleasantly surprised in the mare she was given. It was a spirited creature and far superior to what she had expected might be offered to a mere governess. Lord Myers was clearly a good judge of horses and she was going to enjoy the experience.

She had spent some hours thinking before she was able to sleep the previous evening. Her agent had sent her a package containing several business matters, most of which she had managed to settle easily in a few words. The letter was lying unfinished in her writing box, because she had not been able to decide about what to do on the other matter.

Sam had told her that he had received an offer to purchase all her mills.

It comes from a solicitor, Miss Harding. He has not revealed the buyer's name, but says that his client is well able to purchase all the mills and the price he is offering is far better than anything you've been offered before. My only hesitation in urging you to sell would be to do with his keeping his identity secret. There are certain men— rivals of your father—who might decide to either shut down the mills and sell off the property to reduce competition for their own trade or reduce wages and increase working hours. Your father was widely believed too generous and some of the mill owners thought that he had made it impossible for them to make the profits they wished, because key workers demanded the same rates as your father paid. However, I feel that while you have managed thus far you may find it hard to maintain the level of efficiency needed if you marry and have a family, as your father would have wished. Your husband might not have the

same feeling for the workers as both you and your
father have shown.
I await your decision as always,
Samuel Barnes

Sarah knew that the price offered was a good one.
Perhaps not the full worth of the mills, but near enough
to make it a viable proposition. It would be the easy
way out for her, particularly since she had been wishing to make a change for a while. Had she been content
with her life, she would not have felt the need to change
places with Hester Goodrum.

However, coming here had made her see how pleasant a similar life might be. She would not wish to simply hand over everything to someone else. Even if she
married, she would wish to be informed of all that was
happening and to be consulted about any changes in the
way things were run. It had come to her of late that in
the right circumstances she could happily amuse herself with a family and friends, leaving business to her
husband for the main part. If she were involved in the
decision-making and consulted before the workers were
put on short time—or, indeed, more were taken on, if
the mill prospered—she did not need to be involved in
the day-to-day running of the place.

Her uncle had always insisted she should take a husband and leave her business to him, but Sarah had felt
compelled to keep her hands on the reins. She no longer
felt as if she wished to spend all her life coping with the
problems of running her father's business empire and
would be happy to hand much of it to another.

Yet she could not simply abandon her people and her
principles to someone who might abuse them. Sarah

was well aware that despite rumblings in Parliament, where the plight of mill workers and others in similar jobs had been debated, nothing of any consequence had been done to force the owners to treat their people decently. Women and even children worked in terrible conditions for long hours; they were given only a few minutes' break to relieve themselves or drink some water and their mealtimes were restricted to a quarter of an hour in many cases. If they complained they were sent home and would be blacked by the other employers so that they found it impossible to get another job. The men fared little better and any that dared to speak out against the conditions might have to travel miles to find work to keep their families from starving. Sarah had recently taken in a family who had been thrown out of their home and refused work. Sam had told her that once Mr Arkwright discovered what she'd done, he would be very angry.

'Matt Arkwright is a hard man, Miss Hardcastle. He fell out with your father over the wages he paid and they almost came to blows. He'll not take kindly to you giving succour to a man he's dismissed.'

'If he does not like it, he must learn to live with it.' Sarah had shrugged off her agent's warning, but the next day she'd received a visit from Mr Arkwright. He had spent an hour haranguing her and left after issuing threats.

'You're a haughty piece, Miss Hardcastle, but you'll come unstuck. You think your wealth entitles you to act like a lady and carry on with your head in the clouds, but one of these days you'll go too far.'

'I fail to see what business it is of yours whom I choose to employ, sir.'

'We mine owners stick together. If you give these troublemakers an inch, they'll take a yard. Before you know it, we'll have rioting and people will get hurt. You've been warned, Miss Hardcastle. Think on it!'

Sarah had put the unpleasant scene from her mind. She did not think the man she'd employed was a troublemaker and had no intention of letting a rival owner tell her how to run her affairs. However, she now wondered if it was Matt Arkwright who had offered for the mills. She'd almost made up her mind to reject the offer, but if it was Arkwright she would have made herself an enemy.

Yet to allow him to destroy all her father had set out to do was unthinkable.

'Isn't it lovely out?' Francesca asked, coming up beside her. 'How do you like your mare?'

'She is perfect. Very responsive,' Sarah said. 'John is ahead of us—shall we catch him up?'

'Yes.' Francesca did not immediately suit her actions to her words. 'Are you still upset? You won't have to leave us, will you?'

'No, I shan't leave you for a while,' Sarah said. 'Come on, let's try them out…'

She touched her heels lightly to the mare's flanks and set off in pursuit of John, who had ridden on with his groom at a faster pace. She would not let the problem of the mills upset her. Although this interlude could not last long, she was determined to make the most of it for as long as she could.

Rupert saw the group just ahead of him. He had set out after them, expecting that it might take some time to catch up, but obviously they had ambled along for much of the ride. They had separated out a little, John and the groom ahead and the two girls at the rear. He saw they were just about to set out in pursuit when something caught his eye. A man was watching them, and as Rupert watched he drew out a pistol and fired in their direction.

'*Look out!*' The warning made the rogue's arm jerk. He turned, stared at Rupert, then set off at a run, disappearing into the trees. 'Damn it!'

Rupert saw that the shot had caused one of the ladies to fall from her horse. He was tempted to pursue the rogue who had fired at them, but knew the ladies came first. Swearing to himself, he rode up to them, his feelings mixed as he saw it was Francesca on the ground. Relieved that Sarah was all right, he was off his horse and kneeling over Francesca in an instant.

'Are you all right? Did that rogue wing you?'

'No…' Francesca accepted his hand and stood up. 'The shot went wide of us, but my horse reared and I slid off. I feel such an idiot. I should have managed to hang on.'

'Not your fault,' Rupert said. 'Have you broken anything? Do you feel any pain?'

'No, just a little bruised. I think my pride is hurt more than anything else. I thought I was a good horsewoman.'

'So you are,' Sarah assured her. 'That poacher's shot spooked your horse, that's all. Anyone could have fallen off the way you did.'

'Sarah is right,' Rupert agreed. 'You mustn't blame yourself or your horse. Damned poacher! I would have gone after him, but I was concerned you might be hurt.'

'No, I'm all right. I thought Grandfather's keepers had scared off all the poachers.'

'Apparently not this one,' Rupert replied grimly. 'I'll have them double the watch. I know this isn't technically a part of the estate, but it's still private property. It belongs to Lord Henry James and he will have to be told. He will not want poachers on his estate.'

'Lord James is hardly ever here,' Francesca said. 'I think he spends most of his time in London. However, I heard that his nephew, Sir Roger Grey, had come down to oversee the property for him for a little while.'

'Sir Roger Grey?' Sarah asked, looking at her oddly.

'Yes, do you know him?' Rupert asked, gaze narrowing as he saw the expression in her eyes.

'Oh…yes, I may have met him once,' Sarah admitted, a flush in her cheeks. 'If Lord James is often away, I dare say he does not bother about protecting his game as he ought.'

'Well, perhaps he should. I must ride over and speak to his nephew about it. We cannot allow this kind of thing to continue. One of you might have been badly hurt,' Rupert replied and frowned. 'Are you able to ride, Francesca?'

'Yes, of course,' she said.

'Up you get, then,' Rupert said and dismounted. He gave her his hand and threw her up in the saddle, looking at her with approval. 'That's my good brave girl.'

'I've fallen before. Please do not worry about me,' Francesca said and looked at Sarah. 'Are you all right? I thought the shot was nearer you than me.'

'It passed quite close. I felt the wind on my cheek,' Sarah said and Rupert looked at her again.

'Has it shaken you?'

'No, not particularly, though it was not a pleasant experience. I am glad you arrived when you did, Lord Myers.'

'Indeed.' He looked at her hard and saw something in her eyes. She didn't think that shot had been an accident—and Rupert was damned sure it hadn't, though he was prepared to let Francesca believe it. 'The rogue saw me and ran. His arm jerked and that may have made his aim go astray.'

'Was he aiming for a bird or a rabbit?' Francesca asked. 'There's plenty of game in these meadows, but I should've thought poachers preferred to set traps.'

'Some of them,' Rupert said. 'Shall we continue our ride? It is not likely to happen again. I think whoever it was will not do it again.'

'I'm sure he won't now that you are here,' Sarah said. 'It would be a shame to let him spoil our day and so we shan't.'

'Certainly not,' Francesca said. 'I've been looking forward to this and no poacher is going to put me off.'

John rode up to them and stared at his sister. 'Are you all right, Fran? Who do you think was firing at Miss Goodrum?'

'It was a poacher,' Sarah said. 'Just a foolish mistake.'

'No. I saw him,' John insisted. 'I looked that way. He took his pistol out and fired at you, Sarah. I know he did. Why would anyone want to kill you?'

'I am sure they wouldn't,' Sarah said and forced a smile, but Rupert saw that she looked shaken.

'It looked that way, John,' he said, 'but I dare say it was just an accident. Please do not frighten the ladies. Come on, I want you to show me your pony's paces.'

John frowned, then inclined his head and obeyed his mentor. As the two of them set off, Francesca looked at Sarah.

'Is there anyone who would want to kill you?'

Sarah hesitated, then, 'I'm not sure. I would not have thought so—but if John saw him aim at me...'

'If there is anything, you should tell Uncle Rupert,' Francesca said. 'He likes you, Sarah. I am sure he would help you if you are in trouble.'

'Yes, perhaps. Forget it for now,' Sarah said. 'Let us catch up with the others. It will soon be time to return for nuncheon...'

Chapter Seven

Sarah was thoughtful as she parted from the others and went to her room to change before nuncheon. The shot had been very close to hitting her. The mare had shied, but she'd been able to control it and no one had noticed her difficulty because Francesca's horse had reared up and unseated her. It had been a most unpleasant incident and Sarah could not help thinking that the shot might have been meant for her. Yet who would want her dead?

Her uncle would inherit her estate as things stood, because she hadn't made a will. There was no one else she'd wanted to leave her fortune to and Uncle William had been kind after her father's death, even if he would have liked to tell her what to do. She did not believe for one moment that he would murder her for her money. So who else could it be—and why?

She had, of course, made some enemies since her father died. She'd refused several offers of marriage and a couple of offers to buy her property. That might cause some people to dislike her—but murder? As for Sir Roger…he hadn't taken kindly to being turned down, but she could not see how her death would benefit him.

Besides, how would any of her enemies know she was staying here—or where she would be that particular morning? The answer must be that they would not so it followed that the shot had been a mistake even if it had seemed to John that the poacher had fired with intent.

Sarah would be foolish to allow the incident to play on her mind. It was an unfortunate accident and unlikely to happen again.

She changed quickly out of her riding habit. No one had been hurt so they could go on as if nothing had happened.

Why would anyone want to kill Sarah? Rupert puzzled over it after having had a word with the groom.

'Did you see the poacher, Jed?'

'Yes, my lord. He seemed to act on impulse, if you ask me. Just fired quickly and then ran for it. I would've gone after him, but I thought I should stay with Master John.'

'Quite right. And I was concerned for Francesca. I fear the rogue got away too easily. It will not happen again. In future I want another groom to follow at a distance when the ladies go riding—and he is to be armed.'

'Do you think it was intentional, sir?'

'More like someone seeing his chance and acting impulsively. The question is, why would anyone want to harm either Francesca or Miss Goodrum?'

'We've never had anything like that here before, sir. Miss Francesca is an innocent—never been out in company much. Begging your pardon, sir, but none of us know much about Miss Goodrum. Not that I mean any offence, my lord.'

'None taken. One thing I am certain of, whoever this

rogue is he should not be allowed a second chance. I do not believe Miss Goodrum to have done anything that should make anyone want to kill her. She has excellent references.'

'Yes, sir. It was just a thought.'

It was indeed a thought, Rupert mused. He'd defended her to the groom, naturally, but it was perfectly true that they knew little enough about Miss Goodrum. She had been given an excellent reference, but—was she truly who she claimed to be? Could she have done something that had made someone want revenge— enough to pay an assassin to kill her? It would have to be something serious.

Rupert had drawn back from searching Sarah's room for the key to her writing box, but there was clearly a mystery and, after this morning's incident when Francesca had come so close to being injured, he needed to know the truth. He would ask to speak to her that afternoon and get to the bottom of this affair.

Sarah walked over to her desk. She had been mulling over the offer made her that morning, torn this way and that by indecision. Selling would be the easy way out, but she was not sure she wished to sell to someone who refused to identify himself. Perhaps if he were more honest she might consider it—and she would tell her agent that...

The drawer of her desk was not quite shut. Sarah stared at it and frowned. She was certain she'd shut it properly before she went out that morning. Had one of the maids been looking through her things? She pulled the drawer open and saw that her box was still there, but it had been taken out and replaced the wrong way round. She was quite certain it had been facing the other way when she'd left it.

Sarah checked it and found it was still locked. Whoever had been searching her things had balked at breaking the lock and would not have found the key in her room for she kept it with her at all times. The box contained money and her valuable pearls, as well as her papers, and she never let the key out of her sight, even at home.

Frowning, Sarah replaced the box as the gong sounded in the hall. It was time for nuncheon. She wondered whether she should speak to Mrs Brancaster, but, looking round her room she thought nothing else had been touched. Whoever had started the search must have drawn the line at going through her clothes. Besides, there was nothing of value for anyone to steal—other than her box and that had not been breached. Perhaps she had been mistaken. She might have placed the box differently that morning because she'd been anxious about her reply to Sam's letter.

Pushing the matter to the back of her mind, she went downstairs to the small dining parlour, where the others had already gathered.

'Forgive me if I've kept you waiting.'

'I've only just arrived,' Francesca said. 'I'm hungry. The ride out must have done me good.'

'Yes, you have colour in your cheeks. It was pleasant to ride together. We must do so again when the weather is fine.'

'You should give your attention to the picnic now,' Rupert said. 'Once the invitations go out we are bound to have people calling to leave a card and someone ought to be here to receive them. It will be good for

Francesca to greet our guests and give them refreshments. You will help her, Miss Goodrum?'

Sarah heard the question in his voice and was puzzled. 'Of course, sir. I shall be there to give Francesca any assistance she needs and to lend propriety to the occasion should a gentleman call.'

'Yes, that was what I meant, of course. I wondered if you might have business of your own elsewhere?'

How could he know that? Sarah hesitated, her spine prickling. Was it Lord Myers who had entered her room while she was out? She had known he did not quite trust her for a while now.

'If I do, I shall let you know in plenty of time, my lord. At the moment I think I am able to manage my affairs by letter.'

'Indeed?' His eyes seemed to probe into her mind, searching for answers that she had no wish to give. 'I wonder if I might speak to you before tea, Miss Goodrum. I do not wish to interfere with your plans for the afternoon, but I should like a few moments of your time in private.'

'Certainly, my lord.' Sarah gave him a frosty look and then moved to the sideboard to select her meal from the array of cold meats, cheeses, small boiled potatoes and green leaves picked fresh from the kitchen gardens.

She sat at the table and ate her meal, concentrating on her plate and trying to ignore the pounding of her heart. What could he possibly have to say to her this time?

Sarah had asked for basket chairs to be placed outside on the lawn and they took a pile of poetry books and a blanket in case the wind turned cooler. For the next hour or two they discussed the merits of the modern poets, comparing Coleridge, William Blake and Lord Byron, against the work of Shakespeare and Colonel Lovelace.

Finding themselves in almost complete agreement over the various romantic poets and their work, they laughed a great deal, their heads together as they pored over the slender volumes, some of which were worn with age and obviously loved.

Sarah was able to forget the impending interview with Lord Myers until she glanced at the time and realised they must go in and tidy their gowns for tea.

'I must speak with Lord Myers,' she said, gathering up the books. 'We shall continue this discussion another day. We must not neglect your music and of course you will begin dancing lessons as soon as the dancing master arrives.'

'I'm not sure how we shall fit it all in,' Francesca said, her pretty face alight with enthusiasm. 'The days seemed so long before you came, but now there are hardly enough hours to go round.'

Sarah laughed, but she agreed with her pupil. Her days had never been long enough for there was so much business for her to attend in the period following her father's death, but she had begun to grow tired of working on her ledgers all the time and of tiresome arguments with managers and foremen. If she listened to her head, she would sell her father's empire, but her heart would not comply. It would seem like a betrayal of his standards and the people he had employed, many of whom might lose their jobs if Mr Matthew Arkwright had his way. No, she could not destroy the trust her father's employees had placed in her—but perhaps she could find a suitable husband.

'Why does Uncle Rupert want to talk to you in private?' Francesca asked as they walked up to the house. 'You haven't done anything wrong, have you?'

'I do not think so,' Sarah replied. 'I dare say it is to do with the picnic or some such thing.'

'Yes, perhaps,' Francesca said. 'My gown is very creased, I am going up to change.'

Sarah nodded and turned towards the library, where she expected to find Lord Myers. He was standing by one of the shelves, looking through the books. As if he sensed her entry, he turned with a frown on his face.

'I doubt if these books have ever been catalogued. There is no order to them at all.'

'No...' Sarah moved towards him. 'If I had time, I should like to organise them, but I am not sure...' She faltered as his gaze narrowed, seeming to disapprove. 'Have I done something to deserve your censure, my lord?'

'Have you? I thought I asked you not to "my lord" me all the time.' There was an irritated note in his voice as he snapped shut the book he was holding and replaced it on the shelves. 'What are you up to, Sarah—and why did you come here?'

'I don't understand you, sir,' she replied, but of course she did.

'John's groom saw that rogue fire this morning. He thinks you were the target, though the rogue fired in haste, as if tempted by a chance opportunity to frighten or wound you. Who wants to harm you? Have you done something to make someone hate you?'

Sarah hesitated, then, 'Yes, perhaps. I haven't stolen anything or cheated anyone, nor have I committed a crime—but I may have some enemies, though I cannot see what any of them could gain by killing me.'

'Perhaps it was just meant to be a warning of what could happen if the assassin really intended you dead.'

Sarah shuddered. 'I have considered that because I do not know why anyone should want me dead. I suppose someone might wish to scare me into doing something he wants...'

'Did you break it off with your protector? Is he trying to force you to return to him?'

'I should be insulted, my lord, if I did not understand your concern over this matter. I assure you I have not been any man's mistress. I have turned down offers of marriage...'

'Do you not think you should tell me the truth, Sarah? If there is someone out there who means you harm, I need to know. Francesca could also be at risk through association. If she were not so fond of you, I think I should ask you to leave.'

Sarah swallowed hard. She had always known there was a chance she might be unmasked and to continue the lie now would be impossible. She had already revealed most of her story to Francesca and might as well confess the rest. Clasping her hands in front of her, she met his hard gaze.

'My name is Sarah Hardcastle. I changed places with Hester Goodrum, because she wanted to marry and I wanted a place to stay where I was unknown for a while.'

'You were never a governess, were you?'

'No. My father wasn't just the manager of a mine. He owned both mines and mills. When he died, leaving everything to me, I refused to hand over the management to my uncle and I have been overseeing my own affairs ever since. I have agents and managers, but I find much of my time is taken up with business matters. Because my father left me a fortune I have had to fight off men of all classes who think they are more entitled to run my affairs than I am. Some offer marriage in the hope of gaining my fortune that way—others try to bully me into selling my father's mills.'

'You are an heiress?' Rupert stared at her in amazement. 'Good grief. I've thought of almost everything else, but not that.'

'You thought me an adventuress or worse.' Sarah laughed softly, ridiculously relieved to have told him the truth. 'Is that why you searched my room this morning?'

She saw the awkwardness in his manner and knew she'd scored a hit. 'I began to search your room because of that letter... I saw you hide it when you noticed me.' Rupert frowned at her. 'Searching your room was not an honourable thing to do and I abandoned the idea. For that I ask you to forgive me—but do you think you have behaved in an honourable manner, Miss Hardcastle? You have lied to us and deceived us.'

'I know the deceit was wrong.' Sarah's cheeks flamed. 'At first it seemed to do no one any harm. I was well able to oversee Francesca's studies, as able as Miss Goodrum would have been, I think—but I have not been truthful with you, Lord Myers, though Francesca knows some of it.' She raised her head, looking into his face. 'Do you wish me to leave?'

'I ought to say yes. You know that, do you not?' He paused for so long that she was turning away when he stopped her. 'Who would that help?' he asked in a cold clipped voice. 'Francesca is fond of you and I believe you are helping her. I do not condone the deceit, but I see no point in distressing her and putting my uncle to the trouble of engaging a new governess. Are you able to remain here until Francesca goes to live with a chaperon?'

'Until Christmas?' Sarah hesitated, then, 'I might need to go home for a few days, but I could return—if you wished me to do so?'

'It is not a matter of my wishes. I am thinking of Francesca—and you.'

'Me?' Sarah was astonished. 'Why are you thinking of me?'

'You came here because you needed a break from your life, a chance to think and relax, did you not?'

'In part, yes.'

'Also to escape from fortune hunters and the like?'

'Yes. Sir Roger Grey did not take kindly to my refusal of his obliging offer. The fact that he is visiting his uncle's estate makes it awkward and may not be a coincidence. If he had discovered I was staying here…though I cannot see how he could.…' She hesitated, then, 'I have recently received a generous offer to buy my father's business empire, but the buyer remains anonymous. If it is the man I think it may be, I should be reluctant to sell. He would close the less profitable mills, leaving both men and women without work or a home.'

'Would you wish to sell to a reputable buyer?'

'Perhaps. I am not sure…' Sarah hesitated. 'Since coming here I have discovered a different way of life. I have thought I might perhaps marry if I could find a gentleman who would agree to keep the mills running and to treat my workers decently. I should like to be part of a family like this, you see. I was an only child and my mother died when I was quite young. Father treated me as if I were his son.'

'That would account for your confidence.' Rupert nodded. 'Are you looking to buy yourself a husband—someone who needs a fortune to repair his ancestral estate, perhaps?'

For a moment her heart raced. She thought he might be going to offer his services and the thought both frightened and thrilled her.

'I thought something of mutual benefit…perhaps a widower with a young family,' she said in a voice no more than a whisper as his eyes continued to dwell on her. They seemed to sear her flesh and penetrate her inner being. Her whole body was tight with tension. 'I know that I am a mill owner's daughter. I received the education a gentleman's daughter might expect, but I do not come from gentle stock. I cannot look too high for a husband.'

'You have the manners of a lady of breeding. You should not put yourself down, Sarah—nor sell yourself short. Sir Roger may have been after your fortune, but I dare say there are plenty of gentlemen who would take you for yourself if you presented yourself in the right circles.'

'I do not have time to be a lady of leisure. Removing myself from my home and my family was a spur-of-the-moment thing and I imagine my uncle is angry with me for sending him a letter informing him that I shall be away for some months.'

'Would you not consider handing over the reins to your uncle?'

'I have sometimes wished that I might. He is a dear,

but he has no head for business. My father always said it. Uncle William would probably sell to the highest bidder and think he was doing me a favour.' She frowned as the words left her mouth. 'Indeed, were I to die I have no doubt he would accept an offer for the mills, for he is my heir.'

'Then perhaps we have the answer to the question I posed earlier. It seems likely that, with you out of the way, your uncle would accept the offer you are considering.'

'Was considering. I shall most certainly turn it down. Anyone who would employ a rogue to frighten me into selling is certainly not fit to care for my workers.'

Rupert nodded, his eyes narrowed, expression thoughtful. 'I cannot supply your lack of a husband, Miss Hardcastle. However, I might settle with this rogue—if you tell me his name.'

'Mr Matt Arkwright of Newcastle,' Sarah said, looking at him uncertainly. 'He did not give his name, but I happen to know he was very interested in purchasing the mills. Would you wish to become involved in this business, sir?'

'I imagine I might bring pressure to bear on the man—make him back off and aware of the consequences if anything were to happen to a lady under my protection.'

Sarah felt a thrill of pleasure shoot through her at his words, then realised that he was speaking of Francesca. 'I doubt he would harm one of your charges. However, if I had been killed, my uncle would have been in a position to sell to him.'

'Perhaps you should make a will, tying your property up in a trust that may not be sold? In the meantime, I could look into these matters for you and see what can be done to protect you against similar attempts to relieve you of what is yours by right.'

'Is that possible?'

'A clever lawyer could make all sorts of legal trusts and conditions that would cause Arkwright or your uncle a devil of a time trying to sort them out. I imagine it might deter either of them from thinking of your estate again.'

'Uncle William would not be a party to my murder.'

'He may have mentioned that he thinks it wrong for you to be in sole charge, Miss Hardcastle. An obliging husband would, of course, be the best solution to your problem.'

'Yes…if I could find a man I could bear to marry who would be willing to make such a commitment.'

'I dare say we might find you one.'

'I beg your pardon? I do not understand you.'

'Francesca will enter society next year. It was planned that my sister would be her chaperon, but she has been set back by a difficult birth. I dare say she would be glad to be relieved of duties she might find onerous. If you and Francesca were to stay in my house in town for the Season, with an older lady to act as chaperon—we might find husbands for you both.'

Sarah gasped. He was being generous to consider such an idea, but she felt as if he'd poured a bucket of cold water over her.

'Why should you put yourself to so much trouble? Besides, I am not certain I could spend so much time away from my business affairs.'

'I am willing to do much to see that Francesca has

the companion she trusts and loves—and I would never stand by and see a woman abused.'

'I see…' Sarah licked her lips. 'I should like to oblige you, but I cannot spend too much time away from the mills or they may suffer.'

'If you had someone to oversee them for you, to make certain that this Arkwright—if he is the man behind the offer—was sent packing, and that you were well served by your agents, you might consider it.'

'I don't see—' Sarah broke off as she saw the gleam in his eyes. 'Are you suggesting…?'

'I will visit your agent and speak to him, make certain he has all the necessary instructions he needs from you. Until you take a husband I shall stand as your… *guardian* is not the word, but in place of a male relative. I believe that once it is known I have a hand on the reins you will not be bothered by the attentions of rogues. And I will speak to Arkwright, make him understand that the mills are not for sale.'

Sarah breathed deeply. His offer was so startling that she did not know how to answer him. 'Why should you do so much for me, sir?' she asked at last.

'Someone tried to harm you while you were in my care. As an employee here you are entitled to my protection. As a young woman alone apart from a foolish uncle, and at the mercy of unscrupulous rogues who want to take what you have for themselves, you are entitled to my help as a gentleman.'

'Oh…' For a moment she had thought that perhaps he cared for her, but if she'd hoped for it her hopes were dashed. He would offer his protection, but he was not offering her his heart or even a marriage of convenience. 'I am not sure I could ask so much of you, sir.'

'You have not asked.' Rupert smiled and her breath fled. Her knees felt as if they might buckle and she had to hang on to her senses tightly. He was so handsome and, when he chose, utterly charming—the perfect gentleman. She would not be a woman if she could remain untouched by that smile. 'I feel it my duty to help you. The only other alternative is to send you away and break Francesca's heart. I believe she is happier now than she has been for most of her life. I do not wish to see her unhappy.'

He was doing this for Francesca? Remembering his concern when Francesca had fallen from her horse, Sarah wondered if he felt something warmer than mere affection for his cousin, but then decided that he had shown no sign of it. His manner towards the young girl was that of a kindly uncle, nothing more.

'I should be reluctant to hurt Francesca,' Sarah faltered, because she could not help thinking that much of his concern was for her. If she accepted, she would be breaking down the barrier between them. Was that wise? He had seemed to be intent on seduction at one point, but that was when he suspected her of being an adventuress. How did he feel now that he knew the truth? 'Yet I feel that I am asking too much of you. After all, you know so little of me—and I did deceive you by coming here under false pretences.'

'I think we should keep your true identity to ourselves for the moment. When we go to London, I shall reveal the truth to Francesca's grandfather and I am sure he will forgive you when he learns your story and knows that you have been good for his granddaughter.'

'If you are sure he will not think me a scheming adventuress. Perhaps I ought to leave as soon as a replacement could be found...'

'You will do me a favour by remaining here under this roof,' Rupert said. 'I gave my uncle my word I would mentor John and protect Francesca, but he knows I have business from time to time. I can attend to yours and my own with only a small detour.'

Sarah swallowed hard. 'I can only thank you for your consideration, sir. I think most gentlemen in your position would have simply dismissed me.'

'I am not most men,' Rupert said and there was mocking laughter in his eyes. She felt coldness at her nape. What made him look that way? Had a woman hurt him so badly that he could never trust another? 'Do not review your opinion of me, Sarah. I am still the rake you thought me, but I do have a code of honour that I respect—and that concerns young ladies in need of protection.'

'I am not so very young, but I understand your concern for Francesca—and I have become so fond of her. She is to me the sister I never had.'

'Yes, I thought that might be the case.' His smile was intriguing. 'I shall not leave until after the picnic—and now I think we really must join the others for tea.'

'Yes, of course. I can only thank you—'

'Oh, there may be something more you can do for me—but we shall discuss that at a later date. Do not look alarmed, I promise I shall not harm you. When I thought you an adventuress or a courtesan I might have taken advantage, but that is no longer the case. Come now, we shall start again. If I may call you Sarah—and you will address me as sir or Rupert in private. No more my lording me, if you please.'

'I shall try to remember.'

Sarah could not resist smiling. Her heart was beating very fast, for she could not dislike him even when he was cold and reserved. Something must have made him that way, for underneath she had now and then glimpsed a very different man. Sarah knew that she could easily fall in love with the man she'd seen on those rare occasions—but was he the real Rupert or was he the hard-eyed rake he claimed to be?

Only time and further acquaintance would tell.

She turned and left the room, preceding him to the drawing room where the others were gathered for tea.

'Ah, there you are,' Francesca said. 'Is everything all right? I was afraid you might have to leave us or something.'

'No, no, not at all,' Sarah replied. 'I had a small problem, but Lord Myers has promised to see to it for me.'

'I have some business of my own I must attend to,' Rupert said and gave the girl a warm look of affection. 'I shall do what I can for Miss…Sarah while I'm gone. It will not be until after our picnic and I know you will be quite happy here together while I've gone.'

'I wish I could come with you,' John said. 'I shan't know what to do when you're not here.'

'You have your riding lessons—and you may join Sarah and your sister for lessons and other pursuits until I return. I shall not be long and I shall give you some reading to catch up on while I'm gone—something you will enjoy. Do not look so sulky, boy. You must learn to conquer that habit for it will not wash when you go to public school. I promise you that you will enjoy the books I choose for you to study. And when I come back we shall ride together.'

John was mollified and accepted a muffin from the plate his sister offered him, biting into it and chewing as the melted butter ran down his chin.

Sarah looked round the elegant drawing room, feeling truly at peace. She was glad to have confided in Lord Myers and relieved that she would not have to deal with the objectionable Mr Arkwright herself. Sam would need a letter from her, introducing Lord Myers as a friend who would oversee things for a while, leaving her free to enjoy the next few months.

It was an excellent arrangement, though temporary. She could not expect Lord Myers to continue it for longer than necessary. Once they were in London for Francesca's Season, she would have to look around for a suitable husband. One who would be happy to run her affairs in the way she liked, and to give her a family.

The thought sent a tingle down her spine. A husband would expect the marriage to include intimate relations and she wanted children—so she would have to respect and like this man. Perhaps it would be easy to find such a person once she was mixing in society, but she'd mixed with gentlemen and men of her father's class before and found no one she could even contemplate marrying. Except…her eyes focused on Lord Myers's features and she felt a spasm of something she knew to be physical desire in her stomach.

Sarah would not object to a marriage of convenience with Rupert Myers, but he'd made it clear where the boundaries of their relationship ended.

He was prepared to offer her his protection, but love and marriage were very different things. Therefore, she would be a fool to let herself fall in love with him… and she would do well to dampen the physical feeling she'd had towards him on several occasions. Lord Myers might be a gentleman, but she was still not certain that he would not seduce her given the right opportunity.

Chapter Eight

The morning of the picnic was fine and warm, a perfect day for it. All the invitations had gone out and everyone had replied, accepting with pleasure, it seemed. Francesca was excited and John was beside himself. Several youths of his age had been invited and he was looking forward to the games he'd been promised.

Francesca and Sarah had been wrapping small gifts in secret for days. The games of running, jumping, throwing hoops over prizes and shooting arrows at a board would all be rewarded by sweetmeats and things like a silver penknife, a silver pencil and other similar trinkets, including a riding whip with a beautifully engraved silver handle, which Rupert had donated to their little hoard.

'I think this is an excellent idea,' he'd said to Sarah when giving her the gift. 'It was time this place came to life again. I'm sure you will have callers while I'm gone—and when I return we'll give a reception of some kind. I might ask a few friends of mine down, men I can trust not to try seducing Francesca before she has her Season.' He hesitated, then, 'What do you think of the dancing master? I've scarcely seen him, but he seems pleasant enough.'

'Yes, he is charming,' Sarah replied, keeping her reservations to herself. 'He has given Francesca one lesson thus far, but I think she enjoyed it. I played for them, of course, so was unable to watch all of the dancing, but I think she has a natural grace.'

'He is French, of course, and young.' Rupert frowned. 'I am trusting you to make certain he does not try to take advantage of her. She will never have met anyone like this Monsieur Dupree and may foolishly think herself in love with him. Make sure he does not get ideas above his station, if you please.'

'Most young girls have a crush on their dancing master,' Sarah said and smiled. 'He is a very handsome young man, but I think Francesca is looking forward to her Season too much to be foolish over him.'

'Well, I rely on you to keep an eye on her while I've gone.'

Sarah had promised she would. With the excitement of the picnic and the promise of her Season to come, she thought Francesca's heart was safe enough for the moment and nothing the girl had said concerning the dancing master had given her any cause for concern. Lord Myers would naturally feel more concern because he was very protective over Francesca and did not want her breaking her heart over a man her family would never allow her to marry.

Monsieur Dupree seemed to be a very honest open young man, who had proved a hit with John from the start, showing himself willing to join a game of rounders or cricket. He had also taken on himself the task of tidying the library shelves.

'It is a task after my own heart,' he told Sarah when she found him rearranging a shelf early one morning. 'I have too little to do, you see. As charming as it is to teach the adorable *mademoiselle,* I wish to earn my salary—no?'

Sarah nodded, inspecting the way he was arranging the books in better order. 'This is a task I have wanted to do. If you could put all the poetry, plays and works of fiction together, I should be grateful—and I am sure Lord Myers would be, too.'

'If I 'ave your approval, Miss Sarah, I am the 'appiest of men.'

The look in his eyes had given Sarah some qualms. She could not be certain for it was early days yet, but she rather thought he might be flirting with her. Lord Myers had feared he might try to seduce Francesca, but Sarah suspected she might be the object of the Frenchman's amorous intentions. She hoped not, for she would have to deter him and that made for an uncomfortable atmosphere in the house.

However, for the moment he made no advances, though he was swift to open a door, pull out a chair or compliment her. Sarah thanked him while maintaining a cool but friendly manner.

On the day of the picnic she could not help but be glad of his help, for he voluntarily took on the management of the games for the children, leaving Sarah and Francesca with little to do but present the prizes.

Lord Rupert had greeted all the guests, introducing them to Sarah and to Francesca using just Christian names. She noticed that he allowed people to think of her as Francesca's companion rather than a normal governess, who would naturally have remained in the background.

'I am delighted to see Francesca looking so happy,' Lady Rowton said to Sarah when they stood watching some of the sports. 'At Christmas when Merrivale was here she seemed a little dispirited. You have been good for her, Miss...I did not quite catch your name?'

'Sarah Hardcastle,' Sarah said without thinking, then realised what she'd done. 'Please, call me Sarah. Everyone does.'

'How delightfully informal. I shall do so in the spirit of the occasion, my dear. It is a pleasure to see the girl happy—and her brother. You have worked a little miracle.'

Sarah thanked her. Since she'd given her own name there was no point in hiding it and she decided to give the housekeeper a curtailed version of her story that evening. It was best if everyone understood she was in the house as a friend rather than an employed governess.

All of their neighbours seemed friendly people, including Squire Browning and his lady, Mr Honiton and his sister Gillian, the Monks family of three lively children and Mr Monks's brother James, also his wife Susan. At least thirty of the family's acquaintances had accepted invitations and Sarah had difficulty in recalling all the names, but Mr James Monks had made himself known to her.

'I say, you're rather pretty,' he said as he joined her when she was applauding John and one of his nephews in the egg-and-spoon race. 'This is quite jolly. How long have you been staying with the Merrivales?'

'Only a few weeks,' Sarah replied, amused to find herself being quizzed through an eyeglass. The young man was quite a fop, a tulip of fashion if she were not mistaken. 'I am glad you are enjoying yourself, sir.'

'One needs a spot of entertainment in the country, what? I find it dull after the town, don't you know.'

'Oh, I think there is so much to do in the country. Do you not like walking and riding, sir?'

'Well, I dare say that is well enough…' His attention was drawn to Francesca as she presented the prize for the race her brother had lost by falling over just before the line. 'Growing up, ain't she? I imagine the old marquess intends leaving her a bit in his will, what?'

'I'm afraid I have no idea,' Sarah said. Something about the man made her take him in instant dislike. 'Francesca will have her Season, but I have no idea of her prospects, sir. I think she will marry well whether she has a fortune or not.'

'Oh, I say. Only an idle question, you know.'

He wandered away, clearly annoyed with her for taking him up on the remark. As she watched, he approached Francesca and said something, which made the girl smile. She was frowning and did not notice Rupert approach.

'Was he annoying you just now?'

Sarah started and glanced at him. 'He was speculating on whether or not the marquess intended to leave Francesca a fortune.'

'Was he indeed?' Rupert glowered in the direction of the young fop. 'Impudent pup! I dare say he has run through the fortune his grandfather left him and is hanging out for a rich wife. I'd heard he was rusticating because his creditors were dunning him. Watch him if he comes calling while I'm away.'

'I would hope Francesca would have more sense than to be taken in by someone like him.'

'I'm not so sure. She seems to be enjoying his company.'

Sarah saw that the girl had taken his arm and was going in search of a drink. The maids had just brought out trays of iced lemon barley and orange juice for the younger members of the party. For the older guests there was champagne and a cool white wine.

'I think Francesca will be courted by many gentlemen,' Sarah said. 'She is lovely of face and nature. Once she comes out I think she will be very popular with the gentlemen. I have spoken to her about these things and I think she has enough sense not to let anyone seduce her.'

'Well, that is all we can hope for.' Rupert's eyes came back to Sarah. 'Are you enjoying yourself? Lady Rowton described you as Miss Hardcastle—have you told anyone else yet?'

'I shall explain to Mrs Brancaster tonight and hope that she will forgive me.'

'I am sure she will. I dare say she will understand if you explain you were in need of a place to hide. It may be best if she believes I have been aware of the truth all the time.'

'Yes.' Sarah looked at him uncertainly. 'Have you forgiven me for lying to you?'

His brows rose and his smile was absent. 'The jury is out, Sarah. I shall reserve judgement until I see how you conduct yourself in future.'

She caught her lower lip between her teeth, feeling unaccountably near to tears. 'I am sorry to have lost your good opinion—if I ever had it?'

'I am teasing you,' he said and smiled, sending her

heart rocketing. 'Not that I condone lying, for I generally abhor it—but I believe I understand why you did what you did.'

'Thank you.' Her throat caught. When he smiled like that it was enough to break her heart—but she must never forget that he could never wish to marry a woman of her class. At one time he had considered seducing her, but that was when he believed her an adventuress. Since she'd confided the truth in him, he had treated her as he would any other lady, showing her politeness, but keeping a certain distance between them.

It was all she could expect, of course. Sarah suspected that her own heart was not untouched and she knew that her heart raced whenever he smiled down at her. However, he had given her no reason to think he might feel anything more for her than the natural concern of a gentleman for a woman in trouble.

Why did he guard his heart so well? Sarah wondered about the woman who had hurt him. She must be very lovely—and a lady, of course. Sarah was neither of those things. Why should he ever look at her?

He had thought of seduction, but he was a self-confessed rake and she could not think a light affair with a governess would have meant anything to him.

Her breath in her throat, she fought her own desire to rest her head against those broad shoulders.

'Will you be gone long, sir?'

'I'm not sure—at least a week, I imagine, possibly a little more.'

'John will miss you—and Francesca.'

'I think John has already found a good substitute in Monsieur Dupree.'

Sarah followed his gaze. 'He has certainly been a

great help today. Some dancing masters would consider games with the children beneath them, but Monsieur Dupree has proved his worth.'

'Do you like him? Do you trust him?'

'Yes, to both questions.' Sarah glanced up questioningly. 'Do you doubt him for any reason?'

'None—except experience. When my sister was young her dancing master attempted to run off with her. She was foolishly infatuated with him and would have eloped had I not discovered his little plan. I paid him to disappear and he took the money.'

'Your sister must have been in some distress?'

'For a time, I believe, but she soon recovered once she became the toast of the town. She fell in love with a decent man and is very happy—so do not think me a monster for sending her would-be lover away.'

'I think you may rest easy in your mind. Monsieur Dupree has shown no interest in seducing Francesca. In fact, he seems—' She broke off and shook her head.

'What were you about to say?' His eyes narrowed. 'Please do not lie to me, Sarah. If you know something, tell me.'

'I was about to say he has shown more inclination to flirt with me—but that sounds conceited.'

'I trust you gave him no encouragement?'

'No, of course not. Why on earth should I?'

'He would not make you a suitable husband, Sarah. You must look higher than a dancing master, even if he is handsome.'

He sounded a little put out, which made her smile, but when she looked at him she saw no sign of jealousy, just annoyance.

She put her chin up at him. 'I have no intention of

it—and please do not lecture the poor man. He has merely been charming. I should not have mentioned it.'

He nodded, but his frown did not lessen. 'You should think carefully before you make your choice. I know your preference is for a widower with a family. I have been giving the matter some thought and when I return I may be able to introduce you to certain gentlemen of merit. You would do well to choose wisely and not let yourself be charmed by a dancing master.'

'Thank you.' Sarah's smile felt fixed. She was grateful for his help, of course she was—but how could she consider any candidate he might produce as a suitable husband when she was beginning to think… But she was being so foolish! Lord Myers was not for her. Even if his smile could make her pulses go wild, it was merely the foolishness of a lonely woman. Once she met other gentlemen she would soon discover that Lord Myers meant nothing to her.

'Excuse me, I must see that the children all have enough to eat and drink. Shall we see you at dinner this evening, Lord Myers?'

'Yes, of course.' His gaze narrowed. 'What have I said now, Sarah? I do not mean to dictate to you—but you did say that you needed help with your problems?'

'Yes, I do and I'm grateful. You have said nothing to upset me, sir—nothing at all.'

It was her fault for allowing her imagination to provide her with pictures of the kind of marriage she would most enjoy—because his was unaccountably the face she saw every time she considered the idea.

Dressing that evening, Rupert frowned at himself in the mirror. Why had he made the offer to find a suitable husband for Sarah? Had his pride been hurt because she seemed to favour the dancing master? It was really none of his business whom she chose to marry for she could never mean anything to him—or could she?

Rupert pondered the thought. He had considered himself uninterested in marriage, knowing that he must marry one day for the purpose of getting an heir, but he'd deliberately shut the idea from his mind. The right woman would present herself to his notice one day in the future and then... But perhaps he need look no further. Sarah had aroused feelings of hot lust in him and something more. If he wanted a wife to be a companion in his advancing years and to give him a family, why not her as well as any other?

He frowned at himself in the mirror. No, it was impossible. Sarah deserved more than he could give her. She ought to have love and the kind of happiness that comes from such a marriage—and yet she was considering a marriage of convenience.

He'd promised to help her find a husband and he must keep his word, bring some of his friends down so that she could meet them and perhaps find a man she wished to marry. A part of him persisted in thinking that it might suit him to marry her, but there was still a barrier in his mind—still a part of him that was wary of taking the irrevocable step of asking any woman to be his wife.

A handful of their neighbours had stayed to dine that evening. Lady Rowton was one, Squire Browning, his wife and Mr Honiton and his sister, also the Reverend Hoskins. Sarah found herself placed between the vicar and the squire, who was a little hard of hearing and tended to boom at her.

Sarah had answered all the questions directed at her, but was conscious of watching Rupert for much of the evening. He had been the perfect host, keeping everyone amused and making sure that it all went smoothly. She had noticed that he paid attention to all the ladies, but particularly to Lady Rowton. The lady was more than thirty, but still youthful in her looks and attractive, her smile warm whenever she had replied to something Rupert said to her.

'Did you notice Rupert flirting with Lady Rowton?' Francesca whispered as they went into the drawing room later. 'I think they had an affair a year or two ago. It was just after her husband died—and I heard Grandfather telling someone that Lord Myers was consoling her.'

'You mustn't repeat overheard gossip, dearest,' Sarah said.

'Very well.' Francesca's eyes sparkled. 'Then I shan't tell you what Monsieur Dupree said about you.'

'Please do not, and do not tease,' Sarah said, but she was laughing. She had noticed the dancing master looking at her several times during the evening, even though he'd been seated next to Miss Honiton.

Monsieur Dupree had no notion of her being an heiress. He imagined her a friend of the family, not quite a governess, but not the heiress to a fortune. That must mean he liked her for herself alone. The idea was novel and pleasing. It made Sarah smile to think that a young and handsome man found her attractive for her own sake and, when she discovered him staring at her, she smiled.

Glancing then at Lord Myers, she saw him scowling and wondered what had caused him to look so annoyed. Surely not because she'd smiled at the dancing master? Sarah might be flattered by the young man's admiration, but her heart was completely untouched. He was not at all the kind of husband she would ever consider—though she did quite enjoy being flirted with across the table.

When the ladies were assembled and tea was served, Francesca was asked if she would play for the company.

'Only if Sarah plays a duet with me,' she said, blushing prettily.

'Yes, of course,' Sarah agreed and took a seat beside her on the stool.

'Allow me to turn your music, *mesdemoiselles,*' Monsieur Dupree said, coming up to them with alacrity. 'I will sing later if Mademoiselle Sarah will play for me.'

Sarah could not do less than agree. She and Francesca played a lively melody, then the girl got up and left the entertainment to Sarah. After some discussion, it was decided that Monsieur Dupree would sing 'Greensleeves' in English and in French.

He proved to have a delightful voice and they were asked for three encores. He sang two further songs in French and then a love song in English.

At the end of this melody Sarah rose from the pianoforte and walked away, leaving Monsieur Dupree to take over. His playing was as proficient as his singing and she was about to say goodnight to Francesca when Rupert came up to her.

'His song was for you,' he said. 'I think you have made another conquest, Sarah.'

'Another? I assure you none of my other admirers have wanted me for myself.'

'Can you be sure of that? Might you have misjudged some of them?'

Sarah wrinkled her brow. 'Perhaps. I thought it was all Father's money, but some of them…' She shook her head and sighed. 'I had no interest in any of them, even if—'

'I've told you before, you should not sell yourself short.'

'I have no intention of doing so. I like Monsieur Dupree, but I have no intention of listening to an offer from him—of any kind.'

'That's very much better. I like to see my Sarah standing proud.'

His Sarah! A tingle went down her spine and her stomach clenched. What could he mean—his Sarah? For a moment a feeling of joy spread through her. If he cared for her… But, no, his attention had wandered. He was watching Francesca, who had gone to join the dancing master at the pianoforte. The two of them were now playing together and seemed to be amusing themselves with the lively piece.

Sarah squashed the nonsensical hope. Lord Myers was a gentleman and it had merely been a figure of speech. When he looked at her again it was merely to raise a quizzical eyebrow.

He was still treating her as Francesca's equal, a young woman of some consequence. Sarah almost regretted telling him the truth. He had shown more interest in her when he'd believed her an adventuress.

* * *

Alone in her room, Sarah undressed and sat before the mirror, wearing a soft robe. She hadn't been able to part from all her clothes when she left her trunks behind and had brought her own under- and night-things, because no one was going to see her when she was alone in her room.

Sitting before the mirror, she brushed her hair so that it fell on her shoulders, shining and straight with just a little curl at the ends. She wasn't truly tired and was regretting that she hadn't thought to bring a book up with her. It would be easy enough to walk down to the library, but she could not bother to dress again and did not think it appropriate to wander at night in her night robes.

She was just about to retire when she heard the tap at the door, stopped and walked to it, her hand on the catch as she said, 'Yes, who is it?'

'Rupert. May I speak to you for a moment, please?'

Sarah's heart pounded as she opened the door. What could he mean by coming to her room? She felt her pulses race as she saw him standing there, still dressed for the evening. Suddenly, she felt an overwhelming longing for him to take her in his arms and kiss her. It would undoubtedly lead to him seducing her, but at that moment she almost felt it worthwhile.

'You are ready for bed. Forgive me for disturbing you—but I am leaving very early in the morning. You were going to give me a letter to your agent. I suppose with the picnic and then our guests for the evening you forgot?'

'I have it ready. It was my intention to give it to you in the morning.' Leaving her door ajar, Sarah walked to her desk, pulled open the bottom drawer and took out her writing box. She took the key from the pocket of her robe and opened the box, extracting the slim paper sealed with wax. As she turned, she saw that he had followed her in and closed the door and her breath caught in her throat. 'Lord Myers…should you have done that?'

'Probably not,' he said. 'You look so lovely, Sarah. You make me want to do this…' Before she knew what he was about, he reached out and drew her into his arms, lowering his head to kiss her on the mouth. It was a sweet soft kiss that made her pulses race, but she stepped back, putting her fingers to her lips.

'You must not. You really must not, sir.'

'Rupert. Please, call me Rupert.'

'You should go at once. This is impossible.'

'Is it really so impossible, Sarah?'

'You know it is. It must be…in the circumstances.'

Did he think she was prepared to have an affair with him? What was he thinking of? Did he imagine that she would become his mistress out of gratitude? The thought was painful and she pushed it to a tiny corner of her mind.

'Have you been drinking, Rupert?' She could taste the brandy on his lips.

'Yes, just a little,' he said and then laughed ruefully. 'Too much. The way you look and the wine…a powerful combination, my dear. Forgive me. I am merely human—and you are very desirable. You do not realise the effect that cool exterior with just a hint of the fire below can have on a man. Thank you for the letter and your trust. Goodnight and sleep well.'

'Goodnight, Rupert.'

Sarah closed the door behind him, pressing fingers

that trembled slightly to her mouth. His kiss had been so sweet—so tempting. She had wanted it to go on… to be so much more than a kiss. A hunger so swift and so powerful swept over her that she cried out as if in pain. She had never felt like this before in her life, never wanted anything so badly that it hurt. Her whole being longed to call him back, to take him by the hand and lead him to her bed.

No, she would not be foolish. Rupert had admitted that it was merely the wine and the sight of her in her nightclothes. He was a confirmed rake and accustomed to taking a mistress whenever he chose. She must not condemn him for a mere slip of manners. He had not tried to force himself on her and had apologised for his lapse.

Sarah's problem was not that he had insulted her by kissing her, but that she had wanted more. Earlier she had been regretting that he kept a distance between them. Her heart had leaped at his touch, but her good sense had told her she could not conduct an affair with him while they were both staying under the same roof as Francesca. It would be most improper and might lead to a scandal that could reflect badly on the young woman.

Would she have had an affair with him if it hadn't been for Francesca's reputation? Sarah thought about it as she slid into bed and pulled up the covers. Her lips still tingled, and at the thought of the caresses that might have been, the rest of her body felt suffused with heat. She was desperately attracted to him. His absence these next few days would cause her grief, but his presence might be even more distressing.

Sarah had promised to stay with Francesca until she'd had her Season in town. In return, Lord Myers was sorting out her problems. She could not renege on her bargain even if she wanted to—so she was just going to have to keep a tight rein on her emotions.

Alone in his own room, Rupert threw himself down on the bed, lying staring at the ceiling. What had possessed him to kiss her that way? She'd looked so delectable in her night attire that he'd been seized with a sudden need. Had she not drawn away from him, he might have carried her to the bed and made passionate love to her, thereby sealing both their fates.

He'd flirted with Lady Rowton that evening in an effort to put Sarah out of his mind, but she had taken root there and was beginning to haunt him day and night.

Surely he wasn't thinking of marrying her? Taking her as his mistress was not an option now that they had become friends and he knew she was a respectable young woman.

It was marriage or nothing. Was he ready to cast off his past and take that step? Was he ready to trust again?

As well that he was going away on her business and his own. He needed time to get things into perspective and decide where his future lay.

Chapter Nine

'Monsieur Dupree is so funny,' Francesca said as they picked roses for the house that morning, clipping the long stems and taking care not to prick themselves as they placed the buds carefully in their baskets. 'But he's sweet, too—and he likes you so much, Sarah.'

'I agree that he is charming. I hope you are not infatuated, dearest?'

Francesca laughed delightedly. 'Oh, he doesn't want to seduce me. Andre has far too much sense. He knows that he must make his living and any such nonsense would result in his being dismissed without a reference. He might never work again. No, you are the one he wants to seduce, Sarah. He says you are a rose without compare.'

'Well, he is French,' Sarah said and her friend went into another peal of laughter. 'Besides, I told you. I need a widower—a nice sensible English gentleman who will take care of my business.'

'I still cannot believe how rich you are,' Francesca said and inhaled the perfume of a dark red rose. 'It is such a romantic story—you coming here to escape a persistent fortune hunter. I was so lucky that you changed places with Miss Goodrum. If you hadn't, we might never have met.'

'I should have regretted that,' Sarah said and looked at her with affection, feeling glad she had decided to confide her whole story in the girl. 'I think these past weeks have been some of the happiest of my life.'

The one thing to mar her content was the way she felt about Lord Myers. A part of her wanted to give in to the need he aroused in her, but she knew that she would be a fool to give her body—and perhaps her heart—to a rake.

'Do you think we have enough roses?'

'Yes, quite enough, because it's nice to have fresh ones often. Shall we go and arrange them…?' She paused as they turned the corner to the front of the house. 'It seems we have visitors….' Two gentlemen had just dismounted and grooms were leading their horses away.

'I wonder who it can be?' Francesca said and her eyes sparkled. They had received visits from most of their neighbours in the past week and Francesca was enjoying herself, because several gentlemen had been paying her compliments. 'Oh, I do believe it is Mr Monks.'

Sarah smothered a sigh, because Francesca looked so pleased. The young man had visited three times already and seemed intent on fixing his interest with Francesca, though as yet Sarah was not sure how she felt.

'There's someone with him…I think it's Sir Roger. He must have come down for a visit.'

Sarah's throat caught as she looked at the second gentleman and knew him. It was the very man she'd come here to avoid. Could he know she was here or was it a coincidence?

The gentlemen had become aware of them and turned to wait for them to reach the steps leading up to the portico. James Monks had eyes only for Francesca, but Sir Roger was staring at Sarah, his gaze narrowed and intent. Sarah felt certain he'd known she was here all the time.

'Ah, Miss Hardcastle, Miss Francesca,' James Monks said and bowed. 'I was sure you would not mind my bringing Sir Roger with me? He was most anxious to present himself when he knew you were staying with the Merrivale family, Miss Hardcastle.'

'Mr Monks…Sir Roger.' Sarah gave both gentlemen an equally cool nod. She had not told Francesca the name of her persistent admirer and so the girl was completely unaware as she greeted their guests with a warm smile and invited them to stay to nuncheon.

'Will you not come in, Sir Roger—James? You must stay to eat with us. It will be a simple meal, but we shall be happy to share it with you, shall we not, Sarah?'

Sarah could only agree to Francesca's request, though her stomach was tying itself in knots as Sir Roger inclined his head, his gaze narrowed and wary.

'Miss Hardcastle—Sarah, how pleasant to see you again, and you, Miss Francesca.'

'I trust you are well, sir?'

'Not as well as I might have been had a certain person smiled on me more,' Sir Roger said in a low voice as the others went ahead into the house. 'Forgive me if this visit makes you uncomfortable. Should I go away at once? Or may I hope that you will allow me to renew my offer? I know the ladies like to change their minds.'

'Not this one,' Sarah said and gave him a straight look. 'Forgive me, sir, but I shall be blunt. I do not wish for another offer from you and my answer remains the same.'

'You are hard, Sarah. My feelings have been hurt by your coldness. I find it difficult to enjoy life as I was wont to do—I must languish in your shadow since you will have none of me.'

Sarah felt a rising impatience. How many times must she tell this man that she had no interest in becoming his wife? If she had been at home, she might have been rude, but she was a guest here and could not insult Francesca's guest. The girl had invited him to eat with them and Sarah would simply have to endure his company as best she could.

'If we are to remain friends, sir, I would ask you not to flatter me with insincere compliments.'

'Surely you do not accuse me of insincerity?' Sir Roger looked indignant and for a moment she saw anger in his eyes, which was quickly hidden behind a false smile. 'I assure you, my feelings have always been completely sincere.'

Sarah refused to answer. It was impossible when he seemed determined to ignore her refusal. All she could do was to remain cool and indifferent, to hope that he would eventually tire of being rebuffed.

John was in the front parlour with the dancing master. They had taken a book of plays from the library and Monsieur Dupree was declaiming aloud from one of Shakespeare's works as they entered, which made Sarah smile inwardly as the words sounded very different in a French accent.

'I must give these roses to one of the maids to put in water,' she said, excusing herself. 'I shall return in a moment.'

She wished that she might take the time to arrange the flowers herself, but she could not leave Francesca to cope with the visitors alone and returned quickly, to find them all laughing and discussing the book of plays. Apparently, the gentlemen fancied themselves as actors and it seemed they were amusing Francesca by vying for her attention.

'We should put on a play in the gardens,' Francesca said. 'We could all act out parts and entertain our neighbours.'

'What a wonderful idea,' James Monks said and sent her a look of foppish adoration. 'You would be adorable as the fairy queen, Francesca.'

'Are you reading *A Midsummer Night's Dream?*' Sarah asked. 'It is one of my favourites—so amusing. I like it when she falls in love with Bottom...'

'You must play the queen,' Francesca urged. 'I should not like to take the leading part, but will take on the role of one of her attendants.'

'I shall be Bottom,' Sir Roger said. ''Tis vastly amusing, I vow.'

'No, no, I could not. Besides, the play is far too long and we should never learn all the words.'

'We could play just the scene where Titania awakes to find herself bewitched,' Francesca said. 'I think it is so funny because she loves Bottom despite the fact that he has been turned into a donkey.'

'*Mais non,* it is a tragedy,' Monsieur Dupree objected. 'The *pauvre* lady is bewitched as a punishment by her so-cruel husband.'

His words were greeted by heated exchanges and the next few minutes passed pleasantly enough, as all the aspects of the play were discussed and analysed. Sarah was pleased to see that Francesca held her own, having read the play with her, and relieved that by the time they had all been called to nuncheon and eaten their meal in a spirit of festivity, the idea of actually performing the play had been forgotten.

By the time the gentlemen took their leave, Sarah had relaxed sufficiently to forget to be on her guard and it was something of a shock when Sir Roger held her hand too long and then raised it to his lips.

'I shall visit you again soon, Sarah.'

'Francesca is always pleased to see her guests.'

The look he gave her was supposed to be ardent, but to Sarah it merely seemed menacing. Even if Monsieur Dupree liked her for herself, she was convinced that Sir Roger wanted something from her.

She shivered and wished that Lord Myers was here rather than on what might prove a wild goose chase. If Sir Roger wanted the mills, she believed that he might be willing to hire a rogue to either frighten her into signing or…might he actually want her dead?

If Sarah were dead, her uncle would sell to the highest bidder.

She was relieved when both gentlemen turned away and she returned to the house. About to go in search of Francesca, who had gone to look for a book she wanted, Sarah was surprised when Monsieur Dupree waylaid her in the hall.

'A moment of your time, *non?*'

'Was there something I can do for you, *monsieur?*'

'It is I who may perhaps do something for you, *mademoiselle*.' The Frenchman's dark eyes dwelled on her face with something like adoration. 'I think you did not like the so-charming Sir Roger? He distresses you, *non?*'

'I would not say I was distressed, *monsieur*—merely wary. I should not like to be left alone with that gentleman.'

'No, of a certainty,' he replied and made a face of disgust. 'If the so-charming Sir Roger attempts to force his attentions on you, Mademoiselle Sarah, you may call on Andre Dupree. With the pistol I am—how you say?—a dead shot.' He made a shooting motion. 'I will kill him if he harms you.'

Sarah resisted the temptation to laugh, because, looking at his expression, she could see that he was in earnest.

'You are very kind to offer your protection, *monsieur*— but I hardly think we need come to such measures. Sir Roger is a nuisance, but I think I am able to fend off his advances.'

'If he harms you, he will answer to me.' Andre took a step towards her, quite clearly intending to make his devotion to Sarah's cause even plainer, but before he could speak the knocker sounded and in the next moment the footman had opened the door to Lord Myers.

'You are back, my lord.' Sarah turned to him, a smile of welcome on her lips. She felt relief surge within her and something more. How much she wished she could run to his arms and give him a welcome-home kiss.

'Yes, Sarah, I have returned.' Rupert's brows arched. 'Have I been missed?'

'You must always be missed—' Sarah would have

said more, but at that moment John came flying into the hall and threw himself at Rupert, giving him an exuberant hug. 'I saw you from the window. You've been gone such an age.'

'Nine days, I think.' Rupert laughed and disentangled himself. 'Steady on, old chap. Surely things are not so bad?'

'Oh, I've had loads of lessons and I like being with Fran, Sarah and Monsieur Dupree—but no one is like you. I've missed my fencing lessons.'

'Well, you shall have one tomorrow,' Rupert promised. 'I might have a gift for you in my trunk—but if you continue to ruin my coat I shall consider whether to give it to you.'

'You wouldn't.' John saw he was smiling and laughed, but stood back. 'I'll keep you to your word about the fencing.' He turned to the dancing master. 'Will you give me another French lesson, *monsieur?* It sounds so much better when you speak the language.'

'Oui, mon petit,' the Frenchman said. 'Come, we shall go to the library and find a book of French plays.'

Rupert glanced at Sarah. 'I see our dancing master has many talents. I think he has relieved me of some of my duties.'

'But not all. John is willing to accept a substitute when you are not here, but of course we all miss you. Francesca was only asking this morning when you would return.'

'Your affairs took me a little longer than I had anticipated, but I am able to set your mind at rest concerning Mr Arkwright. It was not he that made you an offer. He has bought more mills and now has all he requires.'

'So it was not he that made it? You are certain?'

'Oh, I think you may be sure of it. He was reluctant to speak to me at first, but I persuaded him to my way of thinking. I made it clear that you have placed your affairs in my hands and that—should anything untoward happen to you—your estate would be subject to many trusts and clauses that would make it difficult to buy. He told me in no uncertain terms that he could not give a brass monkey's…'

'Then I may forget him. How good of you to take so much trouble over my affairs,' Sarah said. 'I am not sure how I may thank you.'

'Do not trouble yourself over it. If I needed a reward, I would ask.' His gaze intensified. 'You still look troubled—has something happened while I was gone?'

'Sir Roger visited in the company of James Monks this morning. He seems to imagine that if he persists in his pursuit it is only a matter of time before I cave in.'

'I shall speak to the man—and, if need be, give him a thrashing.'

'No, you must not. If I am unable to make him see I shall never give into his blandishments, I might ask you to warn him—but no violence.' Sarah smiled. 'Monsieur Dupree has already offered to shoot him for me if he attempts to seduce me.'

'Indeed? And what business is it of his? You are not considering him as a husband, I hope?'

'No, of course not. He is a pleasant young man—but perhaps a little young for me. Not much more than two and twenty I would imagine.'

'And you are so long in the tooth, of course—four and twenty? Five and twenty?'

'I was five and twenty on my last birthday,' Sarah replied, a little smile on her lips. Her pulses raced and she felt a surge of joy. Oh, she had missed this banter so much. It was wonderful to have him home, even if his expression was already a little stormy. 'No, I dare say I am no great age—but some people think a woman is on the shelf if she is much past twenty.'

'Stuff and nonsense,' Rupert said. 'Young girls can be delightful, of course, but I prefer a woman of sense.'

Sarah glanced away quickly. The heat in his eyes suggested he wished to take up where they had left off the night before he went away. She was torn by a swift violent longing, a burning desire to be in his arms and to know the sweetness of his kisses. Sarah was ready to become a woman in his arms, to learn why her body sang every time he was near. How they had haunted her dreams since his departure.

She knew she must tell him of her suspicions concerning Sir Roger, but now was not the time. All she could think of for the moment was the look in his eyes and what his lips would taste of if they touched hers.

'You must excuse me,' Rupert said. 'I am stained from the journey. I must change and then speak to my uncle's agent before tea. I shall leave you to continue with whatever pleasures you have planned for this afternoon.'

'I think we may take a turn round the gardens as it is so warm. I shall take a book of plays, which Francesca has gone to fetch...and here she is now. I am sure she will be so pleased to see you.'

'Rupert... It is so good to have you home,' she said and then blushed. 'We've missed you, haven't we, Sarah?' Sarah nodded, noticing the blush and slight hesitancy. John had rushed to embrace his mentor, but

Francesca merely dipped a little curtsy and smiled. She was growing up, Sarah thought.

'You look well, Francesca,' Rupert said, going to greet her. He leaned forwards and kissed her cheek. 'I am pleased to tell you that I have invited some friends for this weekend. I believe you will find companions that will bring excitement and pleasure to your life. I have a gift for you, as well as John—I will give it to you this evening. Now, if you will both excuse me...'

Rupert glanced at Sarah before walking away. She was confused by the signal he was giving her. Before he left he had shown her plainly that he meant to keep his distance, but now...having seen her home and realised that she was not a lady despite her education and wealth...did he now feel it was permissible to seduce her?

What could he be thinking of? It was quite out of the question, even if her body did clamour for his and her nights were disturbed by the feverish longings he'd aroused in her.

She could not but think that he was a dangerous flirt, a rake who could not help exercising his powerful charm on the ladies, even if he were not serious about pursuing them.

A part of her mind told Sarah that he was no such thing—that he was decent and honest and misunderstood—but she knew that he had had several mistresses, because Mrs Brancaster had warned her of the fact.

She had visited the housekeeper in her parlour one afternoon, taking a dish of tea with her when Francesca had been practising at the pianoforte. Mrs Brancaster had given her a particular look and she wondered if the staff had noticed something about Rupert's manner towards her. They must think it odd that she continued in the house since she was not a governess and no longer in the marquess's employ.

'Such a pleasant gentleman,' the housekeeper had said as she passed a cup. 'Good-looking and in possession of a handsome fortune, so they say—but it will be a clever woman that catches that particular fish. I've heard he's broken a score of hearts in his time.'

'Well, I dare say he's like most gentlemen,' Sarah said, outwardly calm. 'He has enjoyed being single and may settle once he's married. Do they not say that reformed rakes make the best husbands?'

'I've heard it said, miss,' Mrs Brancaster said, pursing her lips. 'But as I said, it will take a clever mind to trap that one—and he would never marry out of his class. His family is very proud. I suppose if he were desperate for money—but from what I hear of it, he has done very well for himself since he left the army.'

'I expect he will fall in love one day, Mrs Brancaster. Who knows—perhaps he has done so already.'

'He's more likely to marry for property and rank than love,' the housekeeper said darkly. 'You mark my words, his sort always do.'

Sarah had not argued, for her mind told her it was the truth—though sometimes her heart whispered a completely different story.

Sarah was surprised when she went up to her room and discovered that her trunk had been taken up without her being aware of it. She'd sent most of her things home in this trunk, but when she opened it, she discovered that it had been repacked, probably by her maid.

Indeed, she found a short note from Tilly, asking if she should join her mistress at Cavendish Park.

Sarah considered and then decided against it. Francesca was aware of her true standing, but she had not told the housekeeper or the maids that she was an heiress, only that she had come here to escape from an importunate suitor, and thought it best to keep things as they were. After the trip to London, she would never return here and no one need know about her masquerade.

Looking at some of the gowns that Tilly had packed for her, Sarah was tempted by one in particular. It was a yellow silk that she'd never worn. She hadn't taken it with her on her business journey, but it was lovely and would look very well for an informal evening. However, since Rupert had invited guests to stay she would save it for a special occasion.

Sarah's own gowns were all simply cut, but the quality lay in the fit and the material. Most of them were far too elegant for a governess and would occasion comment if she were to wear them here.

When they left for London, she would send for her maid to join her and ask for some of her best evening gowns to be sent to her—though it was the chance of a lifetime to buy herself a new wardrobe. Most of her gowns had been made in Newcastle, by a wonderful French seamstress, who had somehow found herself in the northern city and established her business there. However, it would be pleasant to have a new stylish wardrobe made in London.

She dressed for the evening in her usual gown and was just putting the finishing touches to her *toilette* when someone knocked at the door. With one last glance in the mirror, she went to answer it, feeling a shock as she saw it was Rupert.

'Forgive me, I wanted to give you this in private,' he said and handed her a parcel. 'I've brought gifts for Francesca and John, which I shall give them before dinner—but I wanted you to have yours first.'

'A gift for me?' Sarah was surprised. It was most unconventional for a man to offer someone like her a gift. 'Really, you ought not—I'm not sure that I can accept….' But she wanted to and her heart skipped a beat.

'It is merely a token of my appreciation. Perhaps not what I should have liked to give you, but a simple gift like this should not bring censure on you for accepting it.'

'Perhaps…' Sarah breathed deeply. 'Thank you, I shall accept it in the spirit it was given.'

'Then I am in your debt. I shall leave you to come down in your own time. I must see John and Francesca.'

Sarah nodded and retreated into her room, closing the door behind her. When she could breathe properly again, she untied the string holding the brown paper in place. Inside the package was a small prayer book in white leather chased with silver and set with what looked like a diamond clasp. Not a small gift by any means, but not an intimate gift—not the kind of gift a man might give to his mistress.

Of course, Sarah wasn't his mistress yet. Now what had put that thought into her head? It was never going to happen!

She ran her fingers over the smooth leather, thinking how much she would like to use this when they went to church on Sundays. It was a thoughtful gift and just the kind of thing she liked—the kind of gift her father had often given her for birthdays and Christmas. Mr Hard-castle had not often given impromptu gifts and Sarah wondered why Lord Myers had chosen to do so; he'd only been away a few days, even if they had seemed like a lifetime to Sarah.

'Look what Rupert bought for me,' Francesca said, glowing with pleasure as she showed Sarah the pretty fan she'd been given as her gift. The sticks were pierced ivory with gold chasing and painted with French pastoral scenes. 'Is it not lovely?'

'Yes, very pretty,' Sarah agreed, pleased to see the girl so delighted with a simple gift.

His gift could hardly have been more appreciated, for it was something the girl had lacked. She spent most of the evening fanning her cheeks and peeking over the top at them, as if she were practising how to flirt.

Sarah found her innocent pleasure most attractive and a little amusing and, her eyes seeking Rupert's, she saw the glisten of laughter there, as if he shared her thoughts. Then his eyes met hers and his expression changed, becoming so intense that it burned her. He half raised his glass to her and then turned away to speak to John.

Sarah looked down at her plate. Just what was in his mind? She was finding it difficult to judge because the signals were mixed. Rupert seemed so gallant, so kind and considerate at one moment and the next he was the charming rake, intent on making a conquest.

And if she did not stop thinking such foolish things and pay attention to what was being said, they would all wonder what was the matter with her.

John had been given a pair of York tan riding gloves

and a sturdy whip made of good leather, but without embellishment. He had worn his gloves to table, but a nod from his mentor made him remove them in order to eat his dinner.

Looking about her, Sarah thought she had never been so content. She'd always regretted the lack of a sister or brother and this was the family she would always have wished for had she been given a choice. The only thing that could make things better was if Rupert actually cared for her…but that was dangerous territory and she pushed it from her mind as the talk turned to a discussion of their guests.

It appeared that they were to have four ladies and six gentlemen, all of whom were Rupert's particular friends, and, Sarah was certain, handpicked for their reliability.

At least with guests in the house, Rupert was unlikely to start an affair with his charge's companion.

Chapter Ten

Mrs Brancaster had had the maids polishing and cleaning like fury ever since Rupert's return. It was obvious that she was delighted at the prospect of having guests and fussed over every detail.

'It's always awkward when the house has no mistress,' she told Sarah in confidence when they were sharing a dish of tea. 'I know what the master likes so it's easy to prepare the menus for Christmas, but it is a long time since we had ladies to stay in the summer. They will want ices and a lobster mousse and an iced soup, besides all manner of sweet trifles....'

'I am sure you will get everything just right,' Sarah said and smiled.

'Would you mind taking a look at what I'd planned—just to give me an idea whether I'm doing right or not?'

'Yes, of course, if you wish, though you always give us a varied menu.'

Mrs Brancaster had seemed pleased with her interest, especially when Sarah approved all the menus, but added one or two fancy puddings for the ladies. She wasn't sure whether or not she'd imagined it, but of late the housekeeper had seemed more respectful… as if she had recognised that Sarah was more than just Francesca's companion. She was aware that Sarah had money, but of course she had no idea that she was a wealthy heiress.

'I think you've planned everything perfectly,' she said and returned the neatly written menus.

'I'm glad of your advice, miss, for I think you understand the running of a big house and we've lacked a mistress for a long time. A lady's touch makes all the difference.'

'I am used to the direction of a large house, though nothing as splendid or important as this,' Sarah told her. 'I am respectable, Mrs Brancaster, but I was not born a lady.'

'You're as much a lady as any I've met,' the housekeeper said. 'I know it isn't right, but if I'm to call you Sarah—would you call me Dorothy, in private like?'

'I should be delighted to,' Sarah told her. 'Honestly, I've no wish to be put on a pedestal simply because Father left me some money. I am a very ordinary person.'

'Respect is what you're due, miss, and respect is what you'll get—or I'll want to know the reason why. I was honoured when you told me your story. It's understandable you should run away for a while if that man was making himself unpleasant.'

Sarah had not identified the man who had pursued her so relentlessly, giving the housekeeper just the bare bones of her story. She could not cast aspersions on a man's character, even though Sir Roger made her squirm every time he visited the house and did his best to ingratiate himself in her favour.

'Well, you may ask me for help whenever you need it.'

'I was wondering what we should do about the flowers, miss? You'll need more than usual, for the ladies' bedrooms and all the parlours.'

'Yes, we shall. Leave it to me. That is something I can do with pleasure.'

Sarah had spoken to the gardeners herself, requesting more flowers than normal for the house, and on the morning the guests were to arrive she was up early so that she could have them properly arranged. Rupert came into the front downstairs parlour while she was putting the last touches to a large vase she had placed on a table by the window.

'Very pretty,' he approved. 'I've certainly noticed a difference of late. It must be your influence, Sarah.'

'Oh, no, I do very little,' she said, her gaze going over him. She hoped that she was managing to hide the hot sweep of longing that had surged through her. He was so very attractive in those tight-fitting riding breeches. 'Did you take your horse for a gallop?'

'Yes. I like to ride early, before most people are about. I think you have not been riding much of late?'

'We went out twice while you were away,' Sarah replied. 'There doesn't seem to be time for the moment. Mrs Brancaster has been so busy that I've tried to help where I could.'

'It isn't your job to care for the house. We have plenty of maids for that, I think.'

'Yes, of course. I didn't mean it that way...' Sarah

blushed as his gaze narrowed. Impossible to explain that a house that was to receive guests for the first time in an age needed a lot of attention. The maids had been working hard and Sarah had merely advised on what furniture should be moved to more advantageous positions, chosen silver and porcelain, inspected linen and checked that the guestrooms were all as they ought to be. Mrs Brancaster was efficient, but she liked her work to be noted and approved, and Sarah had been playing the part of the mistress of the house for the past four days in the flurry to prepare everything to the highest possible standard.

'This is your home, Sarah, for as long as you choose to stay,' Rupert said, giving her a brooding look that made her toes tingle. 'You are my guest and you must join the company while they are here. I do not want you to hover like a spectre at the feast.'

'I'm sure I should do no such thing!'

He smiled at her spark of defiance. 'I meant that I wanted you to enjoy our guests and feel a part of things.'

'Yes, my lord. I shall of course enjoy having guests.'

'Back to that, are we?' His eyes gleamed. 'One of these days I'm going to make you so sorry for this, Sarah. Why do you find it so impossible to say my name?'

Because she needed to keep her distance, lest she fall into a heap at his feet? Her knees were decidedly unreliable and she felt a need to put her arms about him, kiss that wonderfully soft yet firm mouth and run her fingers through his dark hair. What else she might wish to do was completely out of the question for a respectable unmarried lady and brought a hot flush to her cheeks.

She fought the need, forcing herself to speak coolly and ignore the heat coursing through her entire body.

'Forgive me, Rupert. I do find it difficult sometimes.' Especially when he looked at her with dark eyes that seemed to burn into her soul. His breeches moulded to powerful thighs, his shoulders were broad and seemed almost to strain the seams of his immaculate coat—just right for a woman to lean on in times of trouble....

Was she mad? Sarah was suddenly amused by her wandering thoughts. She had never dreamed that she, Sarah Hardcastle, would ever meet a man she would lust after to such an extent that her wits were scattered every time he came close.

'Just what is going on in that beautiful head?' Rupert's voice had dropped, become intimate and husky. Sarah tingled with anticipation as he moved closer. He was going to kiss her and she would simply melt into a puddle. 'I could almost think—'

'My lord, a carriage has drawn up in the courtyard.' One of the footmen entered the room and Rupert moved away with a muffled snarl of frustration.

'Thank you, Hodges. I shall come at once. We shall continue this interesting conversation at another time, Sarah.'

'Yes, sir.' Sarah dropped her gaze, her cheeks warm, but her heart was pounding. Had she given herself away? She rather thought she might have. The question was: would he take advantage? 'I must find Francesca. She will want to meet your guests.'

She hurried after him from the parlour, hearing him greeting someone called Freddie as she ran quickly up the stairs. Francesca was just emerging from her bedchamber. As Sarah had anticipated, she looked nervous at the prospect of meeting people she did not know.

'What shall I say to them?' she asked, her eyes on Sarah's face. 'I'm not sure what I ought to do….'

'Just be yourself, Francesca,' Sarah said. 'People will not expect you to be witty or clever, so there is no need to try to think of something interesting to say. Just greet everyone—as you would the friends you know—and tell them you are pleased to have them here, welcome them to Cavendish. When everyone has settled in we shall meet and conversations will begin. Make your contribution if you have something to say—but always think before you say anything controversial.'

'I haven't forgotten what Rupert said to me at dinner that night.' Francesca smiled and reached for her hand. 'I'm so glad you're here, Sarah. I should have been terrified if I'd been alone.'

'Everyone will love you, as I do, dearest.'

Francesca nodded and linked arms with her. 'I feel much better now.'

'Good. Remember this is an experience to enjoy, not one to dread. Just because these people have come down from London, it doesn't mean they will be different from your neighbours. I am sure they will all be delighted to meet you.'

The shadows had lifted from Francesca's face. She looked beautiful and happy, and Sarah's own mood lightened. For the next few days she would forget her problems and do her best to see that all the guests were content.

'I am not sure I understand your position here.' Lady Foxton looked down her long nose at Sarah. 'You are

Francesca's companion—but you are also the daughter of a wealthy mill owner. Is that correct?'

'Yes, ma'am.' Sarah's head went up slightly as she met the look of disapproval in the older woman's eyes. Lady Foxton had a lovely daughter of a similar age to Francesca and the two had become friends immediately. The girl was open and charming, radiating friendliness to everyone she met, but her mother was another matter. 'I came here to be with Francesca—and I have helped her with her studies.'

'What are you—a governess or a companion?'

'Sarah is a friend,' Rupert said, coming up to them. 'Are you quite comfortable there, Lady Foxton? Would you permit me to show you the long gallery before dinner?'

'How delightful,' the lady cooed, bestowing a warm smile on him. She got up as he offered his arm and walked away without another glance in Sarah's direction.

Sarah was unruffled by the lady's interrogation. It was not the first time she'd come up against barely concealed hostility when mixing in society. Lady Foxton was one of the haughtiest she'd met, but others had been even ruder, if not to her face then behind her back. She was well aware that while the gentlemen seemed ready to accept her for what she was and even to admire her, some ladies found her company not to their taste. As a young girl staying at the home of one of her friends from school, Sarah had come up against prejudice and she no longer allowed it to disturb her. She had friends enough amongst the lower echelons of society and the daughters of rich merchants. To imagine she would ever be universally welcome in the drawing rooms of London would be to deceive herself—and Sarah was not her father's daughter for nothing.

'I say, was that old trout giving you the third degree?' Sir Freddie Holloway came up to her. A man of about Rupert's age, he was not exactly handsome, but he had a nice smile and Sarah liked him. 'Take no notice of her, Miss Hardcastle—she's buried three husbands and they say they were all glad to go.'

'Oh, no,' Sarah said and laughed. 'You really must not, you know. I don't mind at all. I'm not Lady Foxton's equal and I would not presume to think it.'

'A damn sight better, if you ask me, m'dear,' he said. He sipped his wine. 'One thing about Merrivale, he keeps a good cellar. Pity he couldn't be here, but I suppose the place has too many memories.'

'Yes, I dare say. Francesca and John have missed his company, but it is better now that they have Lord Myers.'

'Myers is a good fellow. Bit of a dasher with the ladies, don't you know. He manages to find the sweetest little fillies…but I ought not to say. Reformed character, he tells me.'

'I dare say Lord Myers is no different from most gentlemen,' Sarah said and smiled, though her heart caught with pain.

'Has more luck than most,' Freddie said. 'I remember when we were both after the same charmer—an opera dancer, she was. Thought I was in with a chance, but as soon as he looked her way…' He rolled his eyes and laughed. 'Wouldn't say this to Francesca, of course, but you're a lady of sense. She's a beauty, ain't she?' He sighed and looked across the room at the two young girls laughing together. 'I'd make a stab at fixing my interest with her—but I need an heiress. Pockets to let, don't you know. Suppose you wouldn't be interested in taking pity on me, Miss Hardcastle?'

'I believe you are teasing, Sir Freddie.'

Sarah wondered if Rupert had invited him for her benefit. He was a personable man and she liked him. She thought they might become friends in time—but would she be able to trust him with the management of her empire? He seemed the perfect fop, a man of fashion without a serious thought in his head—but of course she did not know him well enough to judge.

'Of course, m'dear. What else is there for a man to do? Life is boring enough as it is—not when in delightful company, of course.'

'Do you have no ambition, sir?' Sarah looked at him in amusement. He was pleasant company, but such an attitude would drive her mad in a week. She was accustomed to hard work and would expect it of the man she married.

'Ambition?' He raised his brows in mock horror. 'Terrible word that, Miss Hardcastle. I had it once, I think, but somehow it just drifted away like mist on a summer morn. Should I take up poetry, do you think? I dare say it would serve me as well as that Byron fellow.'

'I imagine Lord Byron works hard at his poems. They are very clever, you know.'

'Another avenue closed.' Sir Freddie laughed. 'Yes, dear lady. I know I am incorrigible. Excuse me, I must talk to Morrison. He has a filly I'm interested in—of the equine variety.' He winked at her and strolled off.

Sarah's gaze passed over the assembled company. Mr Norris was only a year or two older than Francesca and seemed pleasant. Lord Phillips was a little older than Rupert and of a serious disposition; Captain Francis was a dashing fellow and talked endlessly of the *regiment*. Mr Stevens and Sir Andrew were both in their early twenties and looked handsome, pleasant young men—the kind that might become suitors for Francesca. The other two ladies were Mrs Carter and her daughter Helena. It was Helena who came to Sarah and took a seat beside her next.

'Lord Myers told me that he was thinking of giving a small dance while we're here—nothing grand, just an impromptu affair. He said he was going to send out invitations to his neighbours. I prefer the balls in London, because country affairs can be so boring, do you not think so? There are never enough personable men to go round.'

Sarah hesitated. She knew exactly what the young girl meant, for quite often at home the assemblies were very thin of presentable gentlemen, most being older and married or the kind that trod on your feet and exuded sweaty odours—and there were usually more unmarried girls than eligible gentlemen.

'We do have some presentable neighbours,' Sarah said with a twinkle in her eye. 'Besides, some of our guests are rather attractive, Miss Carter.'

'Yes, I know—but Mama says I must look higher than a mere knight and she would not consider a plain Mr anything, even if he is rich.' She sighed deeply. 'This looking for a husband is so frustrating, is it not? I suppose you do not bother over such things? You can afford to be independent and not worry about catching a husband.'

'No, I do not bother over such trifles,' Sarah agreed, managing not to laugh at the girl's clumsiness in describing her as an old maid and past such things—which perhaps she was. Even Sir Freddie had treated her as he might a favourite aunt or an older lady with whom it was safe to flirt. 'I am much too old to worry about marriage.'

'Oh…' Helena flushed. 'I did not mean it to sound like that—but I heard Mama say you were rich and could buy yourself a husband if you chose.' Her colour deepened, as if she realised she had plunged deeper into the morass.

'Please do not worry,' Sarah said kindly. 'I am not in the least offended.'

'I did not intend—'

'Sir Roger Grey and Mr James Monks….'

'Oh…' Helena flushed as the names were announced. 'I did not know that Sir Roger was staying in the country.'

The painful expression in her eyes told Sarah that the gentleman had made an impression on her, though she could not be sure whether it was favourable or otherwise.

'Helena, come here, my dear,' Mrs Carter called and the girl rose obediently and went to her mama.

Sarah saw that Rupert had returned with Lady Foxton. Immediately, he made every other man in the room look less impressive. There was something so very masculine about him…so powerful. His long legs looked strong and muscular in his tight-fitting breeches, his shoulders broad without being massive, and his countenance noble—like a beautiful marble statue from ancient Rome, only vital and very much alive.

'Sarah.' Sir Roger bowed his head to her. 'We did

not realise you had guests staying. I trust we do not intrude?'

'How could you, sir? I am sure Lord Myers must welcome all his uncle's neighbours.'

'May I sit beside you for a moment?' He fluffed out his coat-tails and sat without waiting for her answer. 'You look very well, Sarah. That gown becomes you.'

Sarah knew that he'd been puzzled by the plain gown she'd worn when he called at the house for the first time since her arrival. She was now wearing one of her own.

'Thank you, sir. You are most kind,' Sarah said. 'I believe that was the gong for nuncheon. I am sure you will be welcome to stay.'

'Oh, no, we shall not intrude further,' Sir Roger said. 'I am returning home in a few days—when may I call on you? I should like to speak with you in private.'

'I fail to see what you can have to say to me, sir. I have told you before that you are wasting your time.'

'A matter has been drawn to my attention. I think you would be wise to hear what I have to say—unless you wish to be ostracised by all your new friends?' The look in his eyes was so menacing!

Sarah went cold all over. 'What on earth can you mean?'

'I see you are listening now. A pity this is neither the time nor the place. I shall call in the morning at about ten. Please be prepared to see me. I should be loath to threaten you, Sarah.'

With that he got up and walked away, leaving her to stare after him in dismay. As she joined the general exodus to the dining room, Sarah's thoughts were in a whirl. Whatever could he have meant? Surely he was not referring to her masquerade as a governess. While that might make some of the guests frown, it was hardly likely to ruin her.

He was bluffing. She had done nothing of which she ought to be ashamed and she would not allow him to intimidate her.

'Is something wrong?' Rupert asked when he found her alone in the small parlour later that day. 'Why are you not with the others?'

'I wanted a moment to be quiet. I shall join them for tea.'

'Did Lady Foxton upset you? Her bark is worse than her bite, Sarah. She will become accustomed to you in time.'

'Will she?' Sarah frowned. 'I wasn't upset by what she said. I've met ladies of her kind before and they do not bother me particularly.'

'Something has distressed you—was it Sir Roger?'

'It isn't important. Shall we join the others for tea?'

'He has disturbed you. Please tell me. If he has made himself unpleasant I'll thrash him for you.'

'No, please do not. He did make a threat, but I shall not regard it.'

'What kind of a threat?

'He said that a matter had come to his attention— one that, if revealed, would mean that my new friends, as he called them, would no longer wish to know me.'

'That is nonsense! You haven't done anything improper or illegal, have you?'

She lifted her head. 'You shouldn't need to ask. I told you the truth about myself. You must know I did.'

'Yes…' He nodded. 'He must have something up his

sleeve. Leave him to me, Sarah. I shall sort the rogue out for you.'

'No, I will deal with it. I have done nothing wrong so he can have no reason for his blackmail.'

'You think he hopes to blackmail you into accepting his offer?'

'He might. I have made it clear I shall not accept him.' She shook her head. 'Please do not trouble yourself, Rupert. He can do nothing to harm me.'

'He's a sly rogue,' Rupert replied and looked thoughtful. 'Forget him for now, Sarah. Whatever he has to say to you, we'll sort him between us.'

'Yes, of course,' she agreed, but a cold shiver ran down her spine.

What could Sir Roger know that might make her an outcast from society?

Sarah spent a restless night, tossing on her pillows. She had painted a smile on her face the previous evening, but felt as if a shadow hung over her. The look in Sir Roger's eyes had been menacing and triumphant. Clearly, he believed he had found a way to coerce her into doing what he wanted—what could it be?

Surely there was nothing in her past that he could learn to her disadvantage? She had tried to dismiss her fears as nonsense, as Rupert clearly felt them to be. Her father was the owner of several mills and her mother had been the daughter of a clergyman. Sarah Richards was the granddaughter of a baronet, of good birth if no fortune. Sarah had been named for her and she remembered her mother as a quiet gentle lady who had always been respectable and had taught her daughter to be the same.

How could Sir Roger know something that would make the people gathered in this house turn against her?

Of course he could not. It was an empty threat intended to force her into accepting his offer. He would quite possibly invent a lie, but she must simply deny it and hope that others believed her—particularly Rupert.

With that in mind, she turned over and finally fell into a restless sleep in which she dreamed that she was on an island in the mist and all alone.

Sarah dressed in a plain but stylish grey gown. She went downstairs to the kitchen and told Mrs Brancaster that Sir Roger might call that morning.

'I shall be in the back parlour if he does,' she said. 'I believe he wants to speak with me in private on some matter—if you will kindly have him shown there.'

'Yes, of course.' The housekeeper looked at her oddly, but made no comment as to the wisdom of her decision.

Standing looking out at the garden, Sarah heard the footsteps and turned as someone entered. Sir Roger had dressed smartly, obviously intending to impress.

'Ah, Sarah,' he said and gave her the false smile she disliked so much. 'I am delighted you granted me this interview. You know, of course, that I wish to renew my offer of marriage. You are the woman I adore and it would make me the happiest of men if you were to become my wife.'

'Forgive me, sir. I have told you before that I shall never marry you.' Sarah looked at him coldly. 'If that is all you have to say, I shall leave you.'

'You would be well advised to stay,' he said and

moved to block her path. 'I had hoped you might be sensible—but as you force me to tell you, I have no choice....' He paused for effect as Sarah dug her nails into her palms. Why did he look so pleased with himself?

'Nothing you can say will harm me. I have good friends...'

'Lord Myers, I presume?' Sir Roger sneered. 'How long do you imagine he will harbour you in his house when he discovers you are an impostor?'

'What do you mean?'

'You believe yourself to be the daughter of Sarah Richards and Hardcastle, do you not?'

'Yes, I am.' Sarah's mouth was suddenly dry, her heart racing. 'Please be plain, sir. I do not know what you mean.'

'Have you really no idea, Sarah? Did you never wonder why you were the only child of the marriage?' He looked horribly confident and sure as he added, 'Your mother could not give Hardcastle children. He went to a prostitute and lay with her, kept her in seclusion and gave her money to stay away from other men. When she gave birth to you, he took you home with him and his wife accepted you as her own. You have no claim to gentle blood at all—you are, in fact, the daughter of a woman of low birth who made her living on her back.'

Sarah gasped and stepped back, feeling as if he had thrown cold water over her. 'No, it is not true,' she gasped. 'You are lying. Father would have told me... my mother loved me...'

'Your father never told anyone, but someone knew his secret. Your true mother came looking for you before she died. You might wish to know that she died of

the whore's disease and your father refused to let her
see you even though he knew she was dying.'

'No…' Sarah put her hands to her face. 'You are a
wicked, evil man to say such things. My father would
not have been so cruel.'

'If you do not believe me, ask your uncle. He told
me the truth—which is why he has agreed that you
should marry me without delay. Who else would want
you now?'

'You are lying. This is just a wicked tale to discredit
me and force me to sell my father's business. I suppose
that offer came from you?'

'I would buy the mills if I could, but I want you to
marry me, Sarah.'

'Even though you say my mother was a whore?' Sarah's eyes flashed with temper.

'I don't care whose daughter you are. I am willing
to overlook your birth. You have the money and that's
all I'm interested in. If you want to know, I shall be
ruined if you don't marry me. My creditors have hung
on because they thought I had prospects, but if they
learn you have other ideas…'

'Your money problems are not my concern,' Sarah
said coldly. 'This is the final time I shall tell you. If you
persist, I shall speak to Lord Myers. Please leave and do
not return. I have no wish to speak to you ever again.'

Sir Roger glared at her, disbelief in his eyes. He had
been so certain she would crumble when he revealed
her terrible secret.

'You'll pay for this, Miss High and Mighty Hardcastle,' he said and lurched towards her in a fury. 'I shall
give you twenty-four hours to reconsider and then I'll
start spreading the tale. If you imagine your friends

will wish to know you, then you are mistaken. Think about it carefully before you ruin yourself for good—and don't think your fine friends will save you. If they should manage to avert a scandal, I'll kill you. One way or the other I'll have my revenge on you.'

Sarah stood absolutely still as he stalked out of the room. His threat to kill her had not sunk in as yet. She was numb, but the pain had started deep inside her. Her mother was not her mother, even though she'd always loved her as if they were related by blood. Her father had gone to a prostitute to get himself an heir….

'How could you?' Sarah whispered as her throat began to close. 'How could you die without telling me the truth?'

Hot tears burned behind her eyes. She struggled to hold them back but her throat was closing and she felt so much pain that it was all she could do to stay on her feet.

'Mama…' Sarah brushed away the tears that squeezed from the corner of her eye and ran down her cheek. She felt sweeping loneliness as she realised that her whole life had been based on a lie.

Sarah had always known that she could not hope to mix in the upper echelons of society, but her mother was of gentle birth and that had been sufficient. It did not matter that her father was a rough northern man with an abrasive tongue and a sharp business brain. He'd been honest and kind to her, giving her all the love she could want—except that it had all been a lie.

How could he have left her to discover the terrible truth for herself? He must have been certain his secret was safe, believed that no one knew she was not his wife's daughter.

The knowledge that her mother was not truly her

birth mother was so painful that Sarah hardly knew how to hold her tears inside. Yet she knew she must go on, she must put on a brave face and pretend that everything was as it should be. There were a few more hours before Sir Roger would carry out his threat.

Chapter Eleven

What was she to do? Sarah's problem lingered on her mind as she consulted with Mrs Brancaster on the menus, changed flowers and then waited for the guests to come down. Some of the gentlemen and most of the ladies did not rise until just before noon and were down in time for nuncheon. Until that time Sarah was free to attend her chores, to walk in the gardens if she chose, or, had she wished, to go riding. However, she knew that Rupert had ordered she was to be accompanied by two grooms whenever she rode out, whether or not in the company of Francesca. To put them to so much trouble just for her pleasure seemed wrong. Besides, walking was a favourite pastime and she decided on a walk to the lake.

The fresh air cleared her head a little. She was still Miss Sarah Hardcastle, still wealthy and she still had friends—but for how long once the spiteful Sir Roger had carried out his threat? Some might not care a fig for his revelations, but the kind of society hostesses that would welcome Francesca would not wish to know Sarah once the rumours began to circulate.

She was determined not to allow him to frighten her into submission. Nothing would make her agree to his proposal now. If it were only she who would suffer, she would remain where she was and accept the consequences—but could she inflict her shame on Francesca? The girl was so looking forward to her come out and to Sarah being her chaperon, but if the scandal became common knowledge that would be at an end. No one would invite the daughter of a low-born whore to their social evenings—at least none of the important hostesses—and that meant Francesca would be tarnished by Sarah's shame. Also, the very fact that she had bad blood in her would cast doubts on how she had conducted herself while living under the marquess's roof. It only needed someone to say she had come there under a false name and she would be finished.

Her throat was tight with pain and she could scarcely control her desire to weep. To leave the girl she had come to love—and Lord Rupert—would slay her. The way he had looked at her the previous day…she'd hoped that he truly cared for her. Yet Sir Roger had said he'd shut Arkwright up—so did he know the truth?

No, she shook her head. Had he known he would have requested her to leave. He would have been aware of the scandal it would cause if her secret became known.

Sarah could not hold back her tears. They trickled silently down her cheeks as she stood by the lake, watching the swans swim gracefully across the still waters. Normally the sight would have been a pleasure, but all she could think was that she was seeing it for the last time. She would have to leave…and she could not tell anyone why.

Brushing away her tears, Sarah raised her head. She

would leave a letter for Francesca, assuring her of her love and apologising for having to leave. She would tell Rupert that she had discovered something that made it impossible for her to take up his kind offer to stay with them in London.

Having made up her mind, she turned as she heard a voice hail her. She saw it was Monsieur Dupree and forced a smile as she walked to meet him.

'Forgive me, my so-dear *mademoiselle*—' Andre began just as the shot rang out. Sarah felt it strike her left shoulder, gave a cry of distress and fell to the ground in a heap.

'*Mademoiselle*… Mademoiselle Sarah…' The Frenchman sounded distraught as he bent over her to discover the extent of the damage. She was barely conscious as he exclaimed and clucked over her, but then, as he gathered her into his arms and began to stride away in the direction of the house, she fainted.

'What happened?' Rupert demanded. He had seen them from the house and went out immediately to meet them. 'Good grief! She has been shot.'

'She was by the lake,' Andre said. 'I had seen her walking there and she seemed distressed. I was told she had a visitor this morning—that so-dreadful Sir Roger. I do not why she wept for he is nothing but a scoundrel.'

'He has been trying to force her to marry him, which was why she came here as a governess.'

'He is the one who so upset my Sarah?' The Frenchman's eyes flashed with anger. 'I, with my bare hands, will kill him.'

'I would have been there before you, but I need to know who did this to her.' He held out his arms. 'Give her to me, Dupree. You've carried her far enough. Alert Mrs Brancaster that we need someone to fetch the doctor and help Sarah undress.'

'*Oui,* my lord. This I shall do at once.'

Rupert frowned as he carried Sarah into the house. She moaned slightly and he thanked God she was still alive. Pain assailed him as he realised he might have lost her—lost her before he'd even had time to be sure of his intentions for the future or to tell her of his feelings.

Who could have done such a wicked thing? Had Sir Roger taken a spiteful revenge on her for refusing him—or was her uncle playing a double game? He was, after all, her heir, though Sarah could change things if she made a new will.

He felt the frustration and anger burn inside him as he looked down at her pale face. If ever he discovered who had done this wicked thing, he would thrash him to an inch of his life—and he would see the culprit hanged. A fraction of an inch closer to her heart and Sarah would have died. The thought shook him to the core. What would he have done if she had been killed? The pain of it was almost overwhelming as he realised that he would find her loss unbearable. She had intrigued him from the start, but much warmer feelings had been gradually growing within him.

God damn it, he was in love with her. He'd found her amusing, contrary and at times irritating, but this feeling had been growing inside him for a while now. It wasn't just lust he felt for her, but something much deeper—something he'd never expected that he would feel. Indeed, until this moment he had doubted that the romantic love of the poets truly existed, but now he knew exactly how those tortured knights felt when their love was lost to them.

Rupert's wariness had made him hold back from giving more of himself than he had. Having been burned and scorned by Madeline as a young man, he had held a part of himself aloof, never giving his heart, always keeping a part of himself in reserve. He'd enjoyed pleasant relationships with his various mistresses, but, he acknowledged now, none of them had meant even a tiny part of what he felt for Sarah.

She must not die! He would seek out the rogue who had done this to her, but for the moment the answers must wait. He had given orders that she was to be accompanied by grooms if she rode out beyond the estate, but he had not dreamed she might be in danger here. The keepers must be doubled, but that would do later. All that mattered for the moment was that she should be made as comfortable as possible—and that she should not die of her wound.

Rupert knew only too well how painful these wounds were and how easily they turned septic, resulting in blood poisoning or a fever that killed. He'd seen too many strong men succumb to fevers after being tended by the surgeons.

Pray God she did not die. He would never forgive himself. He should have protected her better! The wild thoughts churned endlessly in his mind as he strode towards the staircase.

'My lord…' Mrs Brancaster had been alerted and came running at him as he reached the bottom of the stairs. 'Oh, poor Sarah. Who could have wanted to harm her? She's such a lovely lady.'

'Yes, she is,' he agreed grimly. 'Rest assured that

when I discover the culprit he will be punished. If I do not kill him myself, I shall see him hang.'

'He certainly deserves it, sir.' Mrs Brancaster hesitated. 'Do you think it was that man...Sir Roger? He called to see her this morning and one of the footmen said they had words. Jennings did not hear what was said, but he heard raised voices and he thought she sounded upset for he was in two minds to go in, and then Sir Roger came out with a face as black as thunder and pushed past him in a right temper. Sarah went straight up to her room and looked as if she was crying.'

'Indeed. If that is the case it may explain why she was out at the lake alone, when I'd told her...' Rupert shook her head. 'It does not matter. Draw back the sheets, Mrs Brancaster. We need someone to undress her and sit with her until the doctor comes. I would stay myself—but I have guests to see to.'

'Yes, of course, sir. Besides, that would not be fitting.'

'You are perfectly right, Mrs Brancaster. If I may, I shall call to see how she goes on after the doctor has been. You will make sure that someone stays with her all the time—at least until we are certain she is out of danger.'

'Yes, of course, sir. I'll come in as much as I can myself. I don't mind telling you I've become quite fond of the lady. When she first came I wasn't sure—but of course she is a lady, not a governess.'

'Thank you.'

Rupert placed Sarah gently amongst the soft linen sheets, stood looking at her for a moment and then turned away. His eyes were dark and angry as he left the room. He wanted to inflict vengeance on the devil who had hurt her. He wanted it to be him who had been shot in her place, to take away the pain he knew she must suffer. If he had only himself to think of he would not have stirred from her side, but it would be impossible in the circumstances. Besides, he must tell Francesca and John, both of whom would be distressed.

'Sarah has been shot?' Francesca looked at him in dismay. 'Then that shot *was* meant for her when we were out riding. She dismissed the idea as nonsense, but John said he saw the man take aim directly at her.'

'Yes, I know. He could not describe the man's appearance, unfortunately, except to say he wore the clothes a gamekeeper or poacher might wear—a large grey coat over dark breeches, a muffler about his neck, which hid his chin, and a black hat pulled down over his eyes. The description is accurate, I think, but of little use in finding the rogue.'

'How is she?' Francesca asked. 'Is she in terrible pain?'

'I imagine she will be when she recovers her senses. The doctor has been sent for and one of the maids is caring for her until then. Mrs Brancaster will send for me if I am needed.'

'May I visit her, please?'

'I think you should wait until the doctor has been, Francesca. She is being looked after and will be better once her wound is tended and she has been given something to help the pain—either laudanum or some brandy, I think.'

'Poor Sarah. I do not like to think of her in pain. She has been as a sister to me, Uncle Rupert—I cannot tell you the difference she made to our lives here.'

'Sarah has her own charm,' Rupert agreed and frowned. 'We should all miss her if she left us.'

'She wouldn't leave us!'

'She might wish to go away somewhere once she feels better—perhaps to France or Italy where she could recover in peace and quiet.'

'It is peaceful at Cavendish. I need Sarah here with me,' Francesca protested.

'Yet her life may be in danger if she stays here. She may have to travel for her own safety.'

'If she does, I shall go with her.' Francesca set her mouth stubbornly. 'I have no wish for a London Season if Sarah cannot be with me.'

'She would feel guilty for taking you away from it, Francesca. I am not sure what she will wish to do. She has been shot at twice now and in a place where she had every reason to feel safe. I cannot think what might have happened had Monsieur Dupree not chanced to be walking by the lake.'

'He did not happen to be there. He followed her,' Francesca said. 'I think he is in love with Sarah. He told me he would give his life for her.'

'I see.' Rupert frowned, for he had not realised the dancing master's intentions were so serious. Had Sarah encouraged him to think of her? He felt a sharp slash of jealousy, but quashed it. His feelings were not important. Only Sarah mattered now. 'Shall you tell John about her injury or would you prefer I did?'

'I'll tell him. I suppose you will have to inform the guests.'

'Yes, I imagine they have the right to know, if only to warn them a dangerous man is in the vicinity.'

'You don't think he will shoot anyone else?'

'I think not, but I shall be asking the keepers to patrol the grounds frequently just in case.'

Francesca shuddered. 'It is so horrid, just as we're having such a lovely time. Poor Sarah. Who could want to harm her?'

'I do not know—unless it was Sir Roger?'

Francesca's brows rose. 'Why would he do such a thing? I thought he liked her.'

'He wants to marry her for her money and she does not wish to oblige him. I gather he has been quite unpleasant on more than one occasion. She told you why she came here—did she not tell you about him?'

'Not his name, though I did notice she seemed to avoid Sir Roger if she could. To think I asked him to stay to nuncheon! Sarah should have warned me.'

'I dare say she thought he would accept her answer in time—and we cannot know who did this to her. We can surmise, but we have no proof.'

'Well, I shall tell Mrs Brancaster that I do not wish him admitted again.'

'That would be the height of rudeness and might harm you. We have no proof of his guilt. However, should he come again make sure you are never alone with him—and make sure someone is with Sarah. I shall speak to the man myself if he dares to show his face here.'

'I think I shall just pop up and see if the doctor has arrived. I shall not go in if he is with her, of course.'

'You must not forget your guests,' Rupert reminded her. 'Sarah will be properly cared for and you may visit her when you can.'

'Yes, I understand. She would tell me the same,

but...' Francesca's face creased. 'I should be so upset if anything... If she should die...'

'She will not die,' Rupert said, his expression grim. His fists balled at his sides. Sarah's death was unthinkable. He could not bear to speak of it, even to the girl who loved her. 'I shall not allow it. She is to be attended at all times and the doctor will be sent for if she shows the slightest sign of taking a turn for the worse.'

'You care about her, too, don't you?' Francesca said. 'I'm glad. I thought once you didn't like her, but I was wrong. You do not show your feelings openly—but you care.'

'And you, miss, see far too much—or imagine that you do,' Rupert said and smiled. 'Run along and try not to worry overly. I am sure she will recover. Sarah is far too strong to die over a little thing like this.'

Francesca nodded and left him, walking quickly from the room. His expression hardened after she left. He wished he was as confident as he'd made out to Francesca.

If Sarah should die or become a permanent invalid because of this, he would kill the man who shot her if it took him the rest of his life to find the devil! And to hell with the law. What would his life be to him if she were dead? When the rogue was caught he would wish he had never been born!

Sarah moaned and opened her eyes. The room was lit by one small candle and she was aware of someone sitting by her bed in the semi-darkness.

'Mother...' she whimpered. 'Mother...' She could feel the dampness on her cheeks and was aware of both the pain in her left shoulder and her heart. 'I was walking and...'

'It's all right, Sarah, I am here,' Francesca said and came to the bed. 'Rupert told me I should leave your nursing to the maids, but I sent Agnes to bed and said I would sit with you for an hour. She was falling asleep when I came in and I didn't trust her to look after you. Mrs Brancaster will be here soon. Are you in terrible pain?'

'My shoulder hurts,' Sarah said. 'You should go to bed, Francesca. Rupert was right. There are plenty of maids to nurse me. It is not fitting that you should wait on me.'

'Would you like a drink? Or some of the mixture the doctor left for you?' Francesca placed a hand on her forehead. 'You do not seem to have taken a fever. I think that is what has been worrying them all. The doctor said it was just the laudanum that made you sleep so long, but everyone has been so anxious. All our guests have been asking after you—especially Sir Freddie and Lord Phillips.'

'How very kind,' Sarah said and reached for her hand. 'How long is it since I was shot?'

'Yesterday morning. You fainted and then the doctor gave you a strong dose of the medicine—and you have been given more since so that you did not feel too much pain.'

'Has anything happened? Have you heard anything?'

'Rupert has the keepers out looking for strangers. Monsieur Dupree found you and the description he gave of your attacker was the same as John's, when he described the rogue who fired at us when we were out riding. This time he met with more success. Rupert is furious. He has taken on more keepers and has them patrolling the grounds at all hours.'

'Oh, no, what a nuisance for him,' Sarah said, pushing herself up against the pillows. The movement was tentative, because her shoulder hurt rather a lot and she did not wish to make it worse, but the room seemed stuffy and her mouth was dry. 'Do you think I could have some water, please?'

'Of course.' Francesca went over to the washstand and poured some of the cold water into a glass, bringing it to her. 'Would you like me to hold it for you, dearest?'

'I think I can manage.' Sarah took the glass, sipped and swallowed a few times and then handed it back, groaning a little as she felt the ache start up again.

'You are in pain. Shall I get you something to ease it?'

'If you mean laudanum, no, thank you. I would rather put up with this than become addicted to that stuff. I know Mama was taking too much towards the end...' Sarah caught her breath as a far worse pain struck her. 'Francesca...' She reached out to touch the girl's hand. 'If you should hear something about me—something unpleasant—you will not hate me. Believe me, I did not know. I should never have come here had I known the truth, if it is the truth....' She shook her head. 'I'm not rambling. There is something I must tell you all, but I think I should tell Rupert first. Depending on his advice...I may have to leave you...'

'Rupert said something...' Francesca faltered. 'I don't want you to leave me, Sarah. Rupert said you might have to travel abroad for a while for your own sake. Would you not let me accompany you? I don't care about a silly Season. I dare say we should meet lots of gentlemen I might like.'

'Oh, my love—did he truly say that to you?' Sarah felt a pain stab at her heart. So Sir Roger had already carried out his threat to betray her terrible secret to the world. It meant that all her plans for the spring would have to be forgotten. At home, Sarah would not care that people thought ill of her, but she could not have her shame blight Francesca's future. That would be selfish and unkind—though leaving her would be like losing the sister she'd never had. 'What else did he say?'

'He said he would thrash the devil that had hurt you if he caught him and…he said that I must be polite to Sir Roger despite what he did and he would deal with the matter. I don't even want to speak to him.' Francesca's expression was indignant. 'I hate him for hurting you.'

Any doubt that Sir Roger had begun to spread the word of her lowly birth was crushed. Francesca had dismissed it, of course, as Sarah had known she would; the affection between them was too strong. She was not quite sure what was in Rupert's mind—oh, he had asked her to call him that, but that was before he knew her secret.

What would he make of her now? He could not allow the plans for Sarah to be Francesca's chaperon to go ahead in town the following spring. He had a duty to the girl and so did Sarah. Francesca must be protected from scandal at all costs.

'I think I shall sleep now,' Sarah said, though it was far from the truth. 'Go to bed and rest, Francesca. I do not need to be watched now. I am out of danger.'

'I am so glad. I should have been devastated had you come to harm. I do truly love you, Sarah.'

'I love you, too, as if you were my sister. If I must leave you, it will be with a heavy heart—but I shall always write to you, until you tell me to stop, and perhaps we may meet again one day.'

'Yes, of course we shall. You are my friend. We shall be together sometime when this stupid business is over.'

'Yes. Kiss me, dearest, and then leave me to sleep.'

Francesca bent and kissed her cheek, then went softly from the room. Sarah lay back against her pillows, the tears running unheeded down her cheeks. She was hardly aware of them.

It hurt so much to know that her darling mama was not her true mother. She had loved her so much, been so happy and secure in the knowledge that she was Sarah Hardcastle's daughter, proud to carry her name. Now she knew that it was not true. The shocking revelation was hard enough for her to bear, but it must not be allowed to reflect on Francesca—or on Rupert.

He was a man and might take the news in his stride. He might find a way to hush the scandal up and deflect the mud that would inevitably be thrown at them, but Sarah could imagine the whispers.

'I did wonder at her living there with him...a confirmed rake...with no proper chaperon.'

'Well, my dear, you know how these things are. She is no better than her mother...blood will out.'

Everyone would think she'd been Lord Myers's mistress while sharing a roof with Francesca. She'd come there under false pretences and if that got out her fate would be sealed. If she dared to visit London with the girl, she would be shunned, ostracised by the proud hostesses who ruled society. Francesca's chances would be ruined. She might find a man who would love her enough to marry her, but her Season would be overshadowed by the scandal.

No, try as she might, Sarah could see no way she could carry out her promise. Indeed, the longer she stayed here, the worse it would be. If she could raise the energy she would dress, pack a small bag and leave now. Her things could be sent on later. She tried putting her legs over the side of the bed and immediately felt dizzy. Her departure must wait for another day. If Sir Roger had spread his lies, the damage was already done. She would go as soon as she was able to dress herself. In the meantime, she would write to her uncle and ask him to confirm or deny the truth of her birth, but she had little hope that the story was a lie. Why should anyone invent such a pitiful tale?

Lying back against her pillows, Sarah tried to make sense of what she had been told. Her father was a hard man in business, but she had always thought him decent. Would he really have paid a whore to have his child and then refused to allow her to see her child when she was dying?

That poor woman! What must she have suffered? For the first time Sarah thought properly about the woman who had given her birth. Even if she were a whore, forced to make her living on her back, that did not make her a bad person. Sarah had no means of knowing her story. Suddenly, she knew that it was important to her to know the truth. Her birth mother's blood flowed in Sarah's veins and even though society might reject her because of it, her mother had loved her enough to want to see her when she knew she was dying.

If only she had not died. Sarah would have sought her out, found a home for her and got to know the poor lady.

Tears trickled down her cheeks again. She dashed them away. She was turning into a watering pot. One thing remained constant. She was her father's daughter and strong enough to overcome this hurt and the scandal. If Sir Roger imagined she would spend the rest of her life in hibernation, he was wrong. Her friends at home would not desert her simply because she was not her mother's daughter—but whatever happened she must know the truth.

Sarah was feeling much better the next morning. She managed to wash herself without help and to brush her hair, but was still a little unsteady on her feet. However, the maids had been very kind, bringing her books as well as all manner of treats that Mrs Brancaster had prepared for her.

'It is so kind of Mrs Brancaster to spoil me this way. Thank her for it, Agnes. I know she is very busy with the guests.'

'We're all concerned for you, miss. Lord Myers is looking for the wicked villain wot done this—and I wouldn't like to be in his shoes when they catches him.'

'I was wondering whether Lord Myers had time to see me,' Sarah said, holding her sigh inside. She'd had no reason to expect him to visit her room, but she missed him—which was very silly. In a couple of days she would be on her way home and he would forget her as the unusual governess he had for a short time been tempted to seduce.

'I don't know, miss. I could pass the message on, but he's been out riding most days—what with searching for that rogue and entertaining the guests. I should think he's too busy. 'Sides, it wouldn't be proper, miss.

Him being a single gentleman and you a lady and not married. He did carry you up here, mind. Told us all that we had to look after you or he'd want to know the reason why.'

'Well, that was kind of him.' Sarah's heart eased a little, but she still longed to see Rupert, just for a moment. Surely he could not imagine her reputation mattered now? She had none left to speak of. He had not bothered to visit her and that must mean he did not wish to speak to her alone—perhaps he was afraid she would weep all over him and beg him to help her. 'Thank you, Agnes. I have all I need.'

But she didn't, of course. She wanted to be her mother's daughter and she wanted to be loved, passionately without reserve.

Sarah faced the truth. She loved a man who was far beyond her in station. He might have considered having an affair with her when he thought her a respectable governess, but now he was not even interested in making her his mistress.

She refused to cry. Sarah was feeling much better. In the morning she would get up and go downstairs. She would request that a post-chaise be sent for and then she would come back to her room, pack a bag, write a letter of farewell to Rupert and another to Francesca and perhaps also one to John. Then she would leave Cavendish Park.

Chapter Twelve

'My lord, a moment if you will…' Mrs Brancaster stopped Rupert as he came in from another wasted ride. For days sightings of strangers had been coming in and he'd investigated them all, but so far there was no sign of the rogue that had shot Sarah. He was beginning to think the fellow had left the district, as he would be well advised to do. He was but a pawn in the game anyway; the problem was—who had paid him to kill Sarah? Rupert would give a fortune to know.

'Yes…' He was aware that he sounded impatient. 'What may I do for you?'

'Miss Hardcastle wondered if you could spare her a few moments, sir?'

Rupert frowned. He had visited Sarah's room twice when she'd first been ill, but had made himself leave her to the care of the servants for the sake of her reputation. Lady Rowton had a vicious tongue and the merest hint of scandal would have given her some ammunition to use against Sarah. He'd already heard her wondering aloud why someone would wish to shoot Miss Hardcastle and her tone had implied criticism of Sarah. Mindful of the damage a woman like that could do, he'd curbed his feelings and contented himself with almost hourly updates on her condition. Fortunately, the woman was due to leave the next day. After that he would be able to let down his guard a little—and he'd made a decision to call off the hunt for the rogue and set a couple of Bow Street Runners on the case. It would mean a trip to London, but he had other business and on his return Sarah would be well enough for him to discuss the business that was burning at the back of his mind.

'You will please ask Miss Hardcastle to forgive me,' he said. 'Convey my sincere apologies, please. Tell her I am delighted she is so much better and say that my duties as a host have kept me from visiting her. I shall make it a priority tomorrow.'

'Yes, my lord—only she did seem anxious to talk to you.'

Rupert hesitated. Ought he to cast convention to the winds and follow his inclinations? No, that would be foolish. Such a thoughtless act on his part might result in Sarah being compromised. He would not wish her to be forced to accept him as a husband simply because she would otherwise lose her good name.

'I dare say another few hours will not matter. You did have the roses I asked for sent to her room?'

'Yes, my lord. She said they were beautiful.'

Rupert nodded. 'Please excuse me. I have planned an excursion for our visitors' last day. We are to take a picnic and visit the Abbey ruins this afternoon. I really must change or I shall keep everyone waiting.'

It had been such a long day. Francesca had popped in for a while during the morning. She'd told Sarah that Rupert was out riding.

'He goes out most mornings,' she said. 'This afternoon we're going to the ruins of an Abbey. It's about ten miles from here and they say it's haunted.' She laughed. 'I do so wish you could come with us.'

'I am sorry to have missed the treat. I dare say I shall feel better soon.'

'I just think things are more fun when you're there.'

'Are you not enjoying your guests? Is there no one amongst them that you feel attracted to?'

'I like Miss Rowton, though not her mama very much. I like Mr James Monks, but he hasn't visited for a couple of days. I believe Sir Roger has gone home—good riddance to him. I suppose I like Sir Freddie as much as anyone. He makes me laugh.'

'Yes, he is amusing,' Sarah agreed. 'I liked him. He was kind enough to send me a new novel he purchased by Mrs Burney.'

'Yes, he told me he thought you might like it.' Francesca's cheeks flushed. 'I can't quite decide…but, no, I shouldn't say. He hasn't shown any preference; indeed, I think he likes you more than me.'

'Are we speaking of Sir Freddie or Mr Monks?'

'Sir Freddie. I like him very well, Sarah—but Mr Monks is so flattering. He says I'm beautiful and that his heart stops when he sees me. He compared me to a rose in a poem.'

'Did he, indeed? I wonder if it was one of Mr Shakespeare's sonnets?'

'Well, I did think he might have borrowed pieces of it from someone else.' Francesca giggled. 'Some gentlemen say foolish things just to amuse one, do they not?'

'They do indeed.' Sarah's brow wrinkled. 'Are your feelings for either of the gentlemen likely to be serious?'

'I'm not sure. They might be for one…' Francesca shook her head. 'No, I am foolish. It is much too soon. I should not imagine myself in love with anyone. Love takes time to grow, does it not?'

'Yes, perhaps,' Sarah said, though she was not sure of the truth. Perhaps sometimes love came suddenly like a blinding light.

'I suppose I must go down and mingle,' Francesca said and kissed her cheek. 'I shall tell you all about it when I return.'

Sarah had smiled and nodded. She'd hoped for a visit from Rupert, but supposed that he was with his guests. Unfortunately, Mrs Brancaster came up later to tell her that he had sent a message to say he was too busy and would see her the next day.

'Yes, of course, it does not matter,' she said, swallowing her disappointment. She was the last thing on his mind, of course. 'Tomorrow I'll be fine.'

Rising, she went over to her desk and wrote the letters she needed to write. She was much better now and the sooner she began to make her preparations, the better.

To Rupert she wrote a brief note.

Dear Sir, I know you are aware of what happened or, if you are not yet, you soon will be. Sir Roger has threatened to ruin me with a scandal I knew nothing of until he informed me of it. I had hoped I might save you this scandal. Had I been able to travel I should have left before this, but I trust you will find my short notice acceptable. I realise now what a terrible thing I did by coming here as Hester Goodrum and I beg you to forgive me. I am sure you will easily replace me with someone far more suitable.

Yours truly, Sarah Hardcastle

The letter to Francesca was much harder.

My dearest friend. I cannot regret meeting you for I have come to love you as my sister and I hope with all my heart that you will forgive me for leaving you this way. I do so hope that you will understand that it is for your sake. I shall bring scandal on you if I stay and my hopes of being there at your come out in London are useless. Should I carry on, as I know you would wish, I should ruin you, my dearest one. For your sake I shall not see you in public again, though it is my hope that we may one day meet privately and, if you will honour me by accepting my letters, I shall write to you. Leaving you breaks my heart. Forgive me for causing you pain.

Your sincere and loving friend, Sarah Hardcastle

Satisfied that she could do no better, she wrote a brief note to John and enclosed five guineas for him as spending money when he went to his college at Christmas.

Her letters written, Sarah packed a small bag. She placed a few of her more personal items in it and left the rest to be sent on to her home. Mrs Brancaster would see to her trunks for her and she would take her leave of her in the morning, quite early.

Even the small amount of movement involved in packing a bag had aggravated her shoulder and made her feel tired. She decided to lie down and was soon sleeping.

Sarah was awakened by the sound of loud voices and footsteps outside her room. The next moment the door was flung open and Lord Myers entered, looking wild and angry. She pushed herself up against the pillows and met his furious gaze, wondering what on earth had caused him to burst in on her this way.

'My lord—is something the matter?'

'Where is she?' he demanded. 'I know she tells you everything. Is that what you wanted to tell me this morning? Why the hell did you not say it was urgent?'

'Because it was not,' Sarah said and frowned. 'Are you speaking of Francesca? What is wrong?'

'She has run off with that Monks fellow—eloped. I blame you for encouraging her.'

'No, she has not run away with anyone,' Sarah said, ignoring his last remark. 'Please tell me exactly what happened?'

'You sound very sure.' He glared at her. 'She told us she was going for a little walk to the other side of the ruins. Miss Rowton went with her. She says that they were looking at a particularly fine wild rose, which had grown through the fallen stones. Francesca had wandered a little apart from her when Mr Monks came up to her. They spoke urgently. Francesca hesitated and then went off with him. They got into a chaise and drove off at speed. Now tell me she has not run away.'

'I have no idea where she went, but I imagine she was tricked,' Sarah said. 'Francesca spoke about her feelings this morning and I am quite certain she would not have chosen to run away—with Mr Monks at least.'

'What do you mean?'

'I think she loves someone else. She is not sure that he cares for her and Monks has been flattering her, but she would not have gone off with him.'

'Who does she imagine herself in love with?'

'I'm not sure I should say.'

'I need to know. This is important—it isn't that scoundrel Sir Roger?'

'Good gracious, no. She dislikes him. You must not breathe a word—but I rather think she hoped for an offer from Sir Freddie.'

'Good grief.' Rupert looked stunned. 'I had no idea. He's perfectly suitable if he would offer for her—but why did she go with Monks? Miss Rowton said she was not abducted.'

'Do you not think she may have been tricked?'

'Tricked…' Rupert's expression grew darker. 'He made her think something was wrong…good grief! Do you suppose he told her you had been taken for the worse? She would have gone with him then without a thought for herself.'

'Oh, no, I do hope it was not that.' Sarah was stricken. 'Yes, I believe you may be right. How wicked he is—but why would he do such a thing?'

'Monks is deep in debt. Sir Freddie warned me of it the other day, felt I should be on my guard. No doubt the scoundrel knew his chances of getting her to marry him were nil so he decided to snatch her, but did so by a trick rather than risk her screaming and bringing me down on him.'

'You must find her, Rupert,' Sarah said, jumping up

from the bed. 'If you are quick all may not be lost. If you wish, I will pretend to be ill and you can say that she came here to me—but you must go now, without delay.'

'I have already lost time. I thought you would know.'

'Believe that she has not gone willingly.'

'I'll kill him,' Rupert growled. 'If he touches her, I'll tear him limb from limb.'

'Go quickly, please. I shall remain in my room in case we need the excuse, but I shall be anxious.'

Rupert turned, saw the letters she'd written on the desk and picked up the one addressed to him. He turned to her, accusation in his eyes.

'What is this?' Without waiting for an answer he broke the seal and scanned it. 'Damn you, Sarah! Were you planning to leave without a word? What scandal is Grey supposed to have revealed to me?'

'He has not done so?' For a moment relief flooded through her, but she knew it was a mere respite. If Sir Roger had not yet spoken, he was waiting for the right moment.

'He has threatened to ruin me by revealing a scandal I knew nothing of—something from my mother's past,' she said, unable to meet his eyes. 'Please, do not bother with this now. Francesca needs you. I give you my word I shall not go until she is safe back where she belongs. I am not worthy of your notice. Francesca is all that matters here.'

'For the moment that is true,' he said. 'But if you break your word I shall hunt you down and you will be sorry. Have the decency to tell me when you are ready to leave and I shall arrange for you to be taken wherever you wish to go.'

'Yes, thank you. I could not bear to leave now while Francesca is in such danger. I pray you are in time.'

'Amen to that,' he said and was gone. She heard him shouting at one of the footmen and she went to the window in time to see him leave the house. As she watched, another gentleman went out to him. They spoke for a moment and then went off toward the stables together.

Sir Freddie must have offered his help. Sarah felt a choking sensation in her throat. It seemed as if that kind gentleman cared enough to join in the search. She could only hope that the two of them would be able to catch up with Mr Monks and stop him carrying out his wicked plan to force Francesca to marry him because she was compromised.

All her thoughts now were for the girl she loved, the scandal that had threatened her forgotten as she felt fear for Francesca.

She regretted the impulse that had made her write the letters. Crossing to the desk, she tore Francesca's into little shreds. The situation was changed. Francesca would need her now and her own reputation might be stained beyond redemption.

Rupert would not allow her to marry that odious rogue, would he? She knew that marriages had been forced on an unwilling girl for less, but surely he would not condemn her to a marriage that could never give her happiness?

She supposed that Mr Monks believed Francesca would inherit a small fortune from her grandfather and that might well be the case. He had other relatives, of course, but John and Francesca were the children of his only daughter and must surely be his favourites. It was the reason she had been abducted of course.

Sarah was anxious for the girl she loved. Rupert's fury on discovering her letter would have had her shaking in her shoes at another time, but for now she could only worry about Francesca. Where had Monks taken her—and what was she doing now? She must have been so frightened when she discovered that she'd been abducted....

'I demand that you take me home,' Francesca said, raising her head in a way she imagined Sarah would approve. She had been told about men like this and if he thought she was going to weep all over him and beg him to marry her, he was wrong. 'You lied to me. I thought I liked you. I might even had agreed to marry you, had you asked—but to tell me Sarah was dying and then to drive off with me to goodness knows where is outrageous! I shall not marry you now if you keep me here for a month.'

James Monks glared at her. 'Damn you, Fran, I thought you would find it amusing to be abducted. Sir Roger put me up to it. He was thinking of abducting Miss Hardcastle, but then he asked her instead and what she said...well, he gave up. Told me she wasn't worth the effort and he would find another heiress. He mentioned you and I told him he'd have you over my dead body. Why won't you let me take you to Gretna? I know you'd like me if you gave me a chance.'

Francesca stared at him. He was almost begging her. She'd been frightened at first, but now she saw he was weak. He wouldn't dare to harm her because of what her relatives might do to him.

'Abduction is a hanging offence, you know.'

He stared at her, his eyes popping. 'It was an elopement. You know it was, Francesca. You didn't really believe Miss Hardcastle was dying. She's been fine for days....'

'You frightened me and I shan't forgive you for that,' Francesca said. 'I love Sarah—she means a lot to me and I really did think something might have happened to her. Now, please, take me home.'

'I can't,' he said, sounding desperate. 'I have to keep you here until someone comes. Your family will send someone to look for you—and we shall be forced to marry to save your reputation. I'll be good to you, Fran. I promise.'

'Do not call me Fran,' Francesca said. 'My name is Francesca. Indeed, I would prefer to be called by my father's name, if you please—because our friendship is at an end. I do not wish to speak to you again and I shall never marry you. You may keep me here for a month, but it makes no difference. I don't like you and I will not be your wife.'

'I could force you,' he said and his tone was suddenly ugly. 'I could seduce you. You would be ruined. I dare say you would marry me soon enough then.'

'I care nothing for my reputation. I would rather never enter society again and live in obscurity with a man I love rather than marry a rogue like you, sir.'

'I suppose that's what she taught you,' Monks said, scowling. 'Sir Roger tried to blackmail her into taking him, but she faced him down, told him to go to the devil. I thought you would give in....' He sat down, putting his head into hands, then lifted it to stare at her in desperation. 'I shall be ruined if you do not marry me. They will throw me into the debtors' prison and throw the key away.'

'I am sorry for you. If you had spoken to Lord Myers, he might have arranged a loan for you, perhaps.'

'Couldn't do that…one gentleman to another.' He stood up and raked his fingers through his hair, his cheeks flushed. 'What the hell do I do now?'

'I suggest you take me home,' Francesca replied haughtily. 'If you do that immediately, I shall tell everyone I was needed urgently at home, but we had an accident and the chaise overturned. We shall pretend that you were unconscious and I had to wait until you recovered….'

'Would you do that?' He looked at her hopefully. 'I've made a mess of this, haven't I? It is all Sir Roger's fault for putting the idea into my head.'

'What did he say to Sarah? What did he think she had done that he could blackmail her over?'

'I have no idea.' Monks shrugged gloomily. 'He was in a temper and went off without finishing his tale—just said she was a stubborn wench and he would get even somehow.'

'Then he must have been the one who shot her.'

'It might have been him, but I thought he'd left the district.'

'Take me home. I have to tell Rupert—and the sooner we get back the better. You'd better wrap your cravat about your head if you don't want my friends to kill you. Rupert wouldn't have made me marry you, you know. He would just challenge you to a duel and send me abroad with Sarah until the scandal died down.'

'In that case we'd better leave now,' he said. 'I don't suppose you could forgive me and…? No, I didn't think so. I can only say I'm sorry.'

* * *

It was almost dusk. Sarah was standing at her bedroom window when she saw the chaise draw up outside. Her heart started to race and she leaned forwards as she saw the man get down and help the girl out of the carriage.

'Francesca! Thank God—oh, thank God,' she whispered and went quickly out of the room.

She had reached the top of the stairs when Francesca burst in. She looked up, screamed Sarah's name and raced up the stairs to her. Sarah opened her arms to receive her.

'I thought you were worse,' she sobbed against her neck. 'I thought you were dying.'

'What happened, dearest? As you see I am fine now, even though I had a little headache this morning. Mr Monks exaggerated the situation—is that what happened, my love?'

Francesca looked at her, took a deep breath and nodded. 'Yes,' she said in a voice that carried to the people gathering in the hall below. 'I asked to be brought here to you quickly. Mr Monks was kind enough to oblige. We went at such a pace that the chaise overturned. He was thrown and hit his head and lay unconscious for more than two hours. By the time someone came and helped us, half the day had gone. That is why we are so late....'

'You have had a terrible experience. Mr Monks is at fault for driving so carelessly. Are you hurt, dearest? Is there anything else you should tell me—in private, if you wish?'

'Nothing at all. Mr Monks was good enough to bring me back, though he has a terrible headache.'

'Where is he now?'

'I left him outside. I could not wait to see if you were well.'

'As you see, I am back to normal. Come into my room, dearest. I shall send for some tea and Mrs Brancaster will bring you some sandwiches.'

Francesca opened her mouth and shut it again. 'Thank you,' she said meekly. She turned to look at the people in the hall. 'I am sorry if anyone was worried. It was all a mistake.'

Sarah could feel the girl trembling as she drew her inside her room. She led her to the bed, sat her down, then looked at her. 'Now tell me the truth, my love.'

'He told me you were dying and abducted me. He thought Uncle Rupert would make me marry him for the sake of my reputation. I told him I would rather be ruined and I would go abroad with you—and if this causes a scandal I shall. You wouldn't desert me for a little scandal, would you?'

'No...' Sarah looked at her and, seeing the girl's determined pride, she laughed. 'No, my dearest, that would be foolish. We shall neither of us let the gossips hurt us. I am not going to run away as if I've done something terrible and neither are you. We shall carry on as we are and those who do not wish to know us may do the other thing.'

'You haven't done anything wrong, have you?'

'I learned something recently—something that I did not know when I came here. My mother was not the lady of gentle birth who loved me and married my father. She loved me as her own until the day she died, but she was not my birth mother.'

'That is sad, but it just shows how kind she was to take you in. Who was your mother?'

'I am told she was a prostitute my father paid to have his child,' Sarah replied. 'I am told she died of a disease women of her profession sometimes get in later life....'

'Oh, how awful for her—and for you to be told that,' Francesca said and hugged her. 'I was told Sir Roger threatened to blackmail you, but you faced him down. He gave Mr Monks the idea, you see. How horrible some men can be.'

'Yes, they can,' Sarah agreed. 'But others are very different. Both Sir Freddie and Rupert have gone to search for you. Rupert swears he will kill Mr Monks, but when we tell him there is no scandal he might be prepared just to land him a facer... I believe that is the word gentlemen use for knocking someone down.'

'Yes, it is.' Francesca giggled. 'I've heard them say it when they think one is not listening. He deserves it—but he did bring me back. He could have refused. He could have forced me...'

'Had you been another sort of woman he might have,' Sarah said and smiled. 'He thought you a silly girl, but you're not. You are a young woman and perfectly able to stand up to a rogue like him.'

'Yes, I am,' Francesca said and smiled. 'I wasn't until you came. I should probably have run off with him for real—but you taught me about truth and honesty and thinking before doing something silly.'

'Oh, my love, you make me want to cry,' Sarah said and blinked hard. 'I am so very glad you are back and unharmed.'

'So am I. In future I shall think carefully before I get into a gentleman's chaise alone.'

'Had he been a proper gentleman it would not have happened—there lies the difference. You might travel anywhere with Sir Freddie and he would not lift a finger to harm you.'

'If only he liked me enough to…' Francesca sighed. 'You did say he was helping to search for me?'

'Yes, he is. I'm not sure when they will be back. I think we should ring for our refreshments and then I'll ask Mrs Brancaster to tuck you up in bed, my love.'

'I ate some sandwiches at the inn he took me to. I am not hungry.'

'I couldn't eat a thing all day for worrying,' Sarah said and smiled. 'We'll have a light supper and you will be all the better for it. Do not argue, Francesca—in this case I know best.'

Francesca laughed. 'You win. Are we truly going to London together?'

'Yes, if Lord Myers agrees. I must, of course, tell him the truth—though I think Sir Roger may have done so already.'

'No, I don't think so. Mr Monks said he left in a temper without telling him the rest of it. So if he didn't tell him, I doubt he told anyone. I think he realised that it was a waste of time. Who would care when we all love you so much?'

'Dearest Francesca…' Sarah was thoughtful. 'I wonder why Rupert did not come to see me? I thought it was because he knew that I was the child of…' She caught her breath because it still hurt so much.

'It was because he was concerned that he might compromise you, of course,' Francesca said. 'He did visit twice late at night, because I saw him leave when I came to sit with you. Agnes said he gave her a guinea not to mention it to anyone.'

'Oh…' Sarah's heart lifted a little. 'It was good of him to be concerned for me.'

'He likes you. I've told you before.'

'Perhaps…' Sarah shook her head. 'It isn't important. For the moment I want you to eat your supper and be tucked up safe in your bed—and then we can all sleep soundly.'

Chapter Thirteen

Sarah was in her dressing robe and on the point of going to bed when she heard footsteps outside her door. Someone knocked and she rose from her stool, going to open it. Rupert stood there, his hair windblown and his look frustrated rather than angry.

'Is it true that she got that scoundrel to bring her home?'

'Yes, perfectly true.' Sarah hesitated, then stood back. 'You had better come in—oh, do not look so worried. We must discuss this in private if you want to save Francesca's reputation.'

Rupert followed her in. He nodded as she locked the door. 'You do not wish to be disturbed—tell me the worst. Did he violate her?'

'Not at all. He did lie to her and make off with her, but only to an inn some twenty miles or so distant. It was his plan to keep her there until you arrived to force him to marry her.'

'He was far off there. She would have been a widow before she was a bride.'

'Fortunately, Francesca managed to keep her head.

She told him that she would not marry him whatever he did and that you would kill him unless he brought her home. It seems he did not have the courage to force her, and after begging her to marry him without success, he brought her home and left again as swiftly as he could.'

'I'll thrash him when I catch up with him.'

'Not if you care for Francesca's good name. He brought her home because I was suddenly taken ill and their chaise met with an accident. He was thrown and rendered unconscious and it was some hours before he recovered enough to bring her home. That is her story and, if you do nothing to convince the gossips it is a lie, I think we shall brush through well enough. Besides, if Sir Freddie cares enough I believe her future is settled.'

'Do you indeed? Are you her guardian now?'

Sarah flinched at the sarcasm in his tone. 'No, I am not—and if you feel I have overstepped the mark I can…' Her words died away, for she could not simply leave. She had promised Francesca she would stay.

His gaze narrowed, nostrils flared as if in temper. 'Going to run off and leave us again, are you?'

'Perhaps if you would calm down a little I might explain why I felt it necessary to leave.'

'It had better be good.' He glared at her and then sat down in her chair. 'I'm listening.'

Sarah told him the tale Sir Roger had told her in his effort to blackmail her, leaving no sordid detail to his imagination. Then she paused and looked at him.

'I thought that I might ruin Francesca's chances. She has begged me to stay with her until and during her Season. I have, of course, told her the chance we take, but she says she does not care. You must be the judge of the situation, Lord Myers. I am prepared to risk it, but if you feel Francesca may suffer too much I shall withdraw.'

'And do what? Run away and hide?'

'No, not at all. I am determined that Sir Roger shall not win. I shall go home for a time—and then I may take a house in London for the Season.'

'Francesca would want to know you. No…' He frowned and Sarah's heart sank—he meant to forbid her. 'I have a better solution. You will become engaged and then in time you will marry me.'

Sarah gasped, feeling the colour drain from her face. It was the last thing she'd expected. Her heart leaped with joy, but the feeling was quickly followed by one of doubt. She would be a fool to think that his proposal meant that he loved her. Yet he was prepared to do so much to save her from public scorn—why?

'But you can't… I do not see why you should make such a sacrifice for my sake.'

'Who said it was for your sake?' His eyebrows rose imperiously and her heart sank. His offer had nothing to do with love or affection, but was intended to deflect more scandal from Francesca. The pain struck deep into her heart. 'I have reached the age where I need an heir, Sarah. You cannot be unaware that I find you attractive. I have already taken steps to protect you from unscrupulous men who might wish to force you to sell your mills—which in the minds of most people adds up to an interest on my part. It will solve everything neatly, do you not think?'

'Perhaps…yes, I mean, no.' Sarah's mind was reeling from the shock and she hardly knew what she said. If he'd spoken of love, she would have been so happy, for then a marriage between them would have been all she could wish for. 'Do you really want to marry the daughter of a low-born whore?'

Her mind was in a whirl. Sometimes she'd felt he was interested in her as a woman he would like to make his mistress, but she'd sensed that he held a part of himself in reserve. She'd wondered if perhaps he'd suffered some reverse or heartbreak in the past. Was that why he was willing to make a marriage of convenience to save them all from scandal? Had he been so hurt that it was impossible for him to love? The thought pained her and made her want to take the hurt from him, because whatever he felt she loved him with all her heart—so much that she did not think she could bear to lose him.

'You are a woman of sense, Sarah. I think we should do well together—and it will suit me to marry. This tale of Sir Roger's—do you mean to simply accept it as the truth? For my part I think him a liar and a knave. Had it not been for his prompting Monks would never have thought of abducting Francesca.'

'You think he might be lying? He said my uncle told him. I have written and hope to hear the truth from his hand.' She caught her breath, her heart taking a dizzying somersault as she thought what it might be like to marry Rupert. She knew it would bring her happiness to be his wife and bear his children, even if she could never truly have his love.

'I do not care if it is the truth,' Rupert said flatly. 'I've met whores who were more of a lady than some who call themselves by the name.' His gaze narrowed. 'Would it be so very hard to be my wife and bear my children, Sarah?'

'No…of course not,' she said, her breath expelling nervously. She must not betray herself for he would not want a clinging vine. She must remain the cool Miss Hardcastle despite the clamouring of her heart. 'You know I need a husband I can trust and—and I like you very well. Are you sure you wish to? I am stubborn and can be quite difficult at times, I'm told.'

'I imagine you can.' He laughed softly in his throat. 'I dare say I can manage you if I try. I should not want a woman who gave me all my own way. I need an equal, Sarah, and I believe you would match me in many ways.'

'What of Francesca? You know I must see her safe and happy…'

'Sir Freddie told me he has hopes of her. No doubt he will pet her and spoil her—and I dare say she will twist him round her little finger. That kind of relationship would not do for me. I want a woman of sense I can talk to about business as well as pleasure.'

Sarah was silent. What he was offering her was not love, but affection, passion, at least for a time, and companionship. Well, she'd known that he did not particularly like or admire young women of his own class. Perhaps he had learned to distrust them for reasons of his own. Because of his past hurts, he'd decided that a woman of Sarah's class might prove more trustworthy. He liked her, even desired her, but his emotions were not deeply involved. He would be her husband, give her children and a home and protect her from men like Sir Roger. She supposed it was enough. If she refused, she did not think she would have the chance of happiness again.

'I thank you for your very kind offer…Rupert,' she said and a shy smile hovered on her lips. 'If you are perfectly content with the idea, I shall accept with pleasure.'

'At these times one is supposed to declare undying love, but I shall not bore you with that nonsense,' Rupert said, a mocking twist to his mouth. 'We'll announce it in the morning. Then I'll leave you for a while...' He laughed as she looked startled. 'I am not prepared to let the rogue who shot at you get away with his crime, Sarah. You might have died—and that means he must pay. Also, I intend to have it out with Sir Roger—make him apologise—and then I shall set private agents on to discovering the truth of your conception. If your mother truly was a whore, something caused her to be that way. I think you would like to know her story—and if you have another family somewhere. My agents are already working on your behalf and I dare say the mystery is halfway to being solved before we ask.'

'You would do that for me?'

'Once we are married, you will discover just how much I am prepared to do for the lady who honours me by becoming my wife.'

Sarah nodded, her throat too tight to speak for a moment. He was such a fine honourable gentleman. 'If what you discover is too terrible...'

He touched his fingers to her lips and then hesitated before bending to kiss her lips. It was a very soft, sweet kiss, but it left her feeling weak at the knees.

'You will not say foolish things. I am a man, not a boy, Sarah. I know what I want, believe me.'

'Yes...I have thought you wanted me...' She could feel the heat in her cheeks as she met his eyes. 'Your... kind feelings were returned.'

He flicked her cheek with his fingertips. 'I rather

thought they might be or I should not have spoken. We shall do very well together. Now I should leave. If someone sees me coming from your room, you will have to put up with odd looks from the ladies and the occasional wink from the men. We shall announce our engagement tomorrow.'

'Very well, Rupert,' she said, her heart racing despite her controlled speech and steady manner. 'As you wish.'

'We must arrange something for Francesca while we are away on our wedding trip, which need only be a few days to buy you a wardrobe in Paris. Perhaps Merrivale will come down—or Sir Freddie may take her off to stay with his mother.'

'We must also think of John.'

'He seems to like Dupree. He may take over as his tutor until he leaves for school—and of course the boy can live with us until he leaves home. I am sure you would always welcome him during the holidays.'

'You seem to have worked everything out. What if I had refused?'

'Then I should have been devastated,' he said and gave her a mocking smile. 'Fortunately, I was able to persuade you it was for your own good.'

Sarah's expression altered, took fire. 'You sound like my father when I did something that pleased him.'

'Ah, I have struck a spark.' His eyes gleamed. 'Good. I like it when you fight back, Sarah. It would be a mistake to let me have my own way all the time.'

'I have no intention of it.'

'I am very pleased to hear it, and now, my dearest Sarah, I must leave you—or I shall be tempted to sweep you up into my arms and carry you to that tempting bed…'

Sarah gasped. Before she could recover her breath, he had opened the door, let himself out and closed it behind him. She locked it immediately and heard him laugh.

He was an arrogant rogue and altogether too sure of himself. His plans were so neat that she thought he must have been plotting them for a while.

Yet he might have his pick of the young ladies looking for husbands. He was handsome, rich in his own right and charming—why should he choose her?

He wanted an heir and he wasn't interested in a girl straight out of the schoolroom. He clearly had an aversion to women of his class. Rupert clearly felt a marriage of convenience to a woman he could trust would suit him well—and Sarah would be a fool to regret her bargain. He'd given her so much already and she could only think that being his wife would bring its own rewards. He might break her heart one day, but that was a chance worth taking.

Smiling to herself, Sarah removed her robe and slipped into bed. Before long she was sound asleep.

Rupert savoured his brandy and reflected on the future. He had gained part of his objective, but there was more to achieve. Sarah seemed content to accept his plans and he had much to do, much to sort out before he could relax and reveal all of them to the woman he intended to be his wife.

Had he truly considered making her his mistress? Only for a short time at the start; it had not taken him long to see her true worth or the potential of a match between them. Sarah might not like the idea of selling her father's property at the start, but if the right buyer could be found it would be the best solution. Her fortune could be joined with his and used for the benefit of them all. As yet he had not spoken to Merrivale about Cavendish Park. It would one day be John's inheritance, of course, but that was a long way off and the marquess was far from able to care for it, as it ought to be cared for. If Rupert did not take permanent charge it would dwindle into nothing by the time the lad was grown.

Of course he would need Sarah's agreement to his plan, but he thought she might be willing to listen. He would bring the subject up once their engagement was public knowledge and she had become used to the idea.

Sipping his brandy, he lay back against the pillows and smiled. Yes, it was all going his way, but he had to sort out this business of whoever had taken a shot at Sarah—and settle with Sir Roger. Not a pleasant business, but it had to be done. Either the rogue would take his punishment like a man—or he would have to be killed in a duel.

Either way, he must protect the woman he loved.

Sarah dressed and went down to breakfast. Some of the gentlemen were at table and rose with alacrity as she entered, making her welcome and enquiring after her health with such sincerity that she was overwhelmed by their kindness.

'We were all so sorry to learn of your setback,' Lord Phillips said. 'Such an upset—with Miss Francesca being involved in an accident. I dare say you found that distressing?'

'Yes, I did,' Sarah agreed and smiled at him. 'However, she was just a little shaken by her experience and will, I am sure, be herself today.'

'I was mightily relieved to hear it,' Sir Freddie said. 'If no one minds I've decided to stay on for a couple of days…talk to Rupert when I see him. I believe he went riding early this morning, had some important business, I understand.'

'Did he?' Sarah's cheeks were warm, as she wondered whether Rupert had said anything to his guests about their engagement, but as neither gentleman mentioned it she thought perhaps he intended it later. 'When do you leave, Lord Phillips? Or have you decided to stay on, too?'

'I wish that I might, Miss Hardcastle.' The look he gave her was so warm and admiring that Sarah's heart jolted. She had thought he might like her quite well at the start and he had sent messages of goodwill and flowers while she was ill. 'Had it not been such a difficult time—but you have been ill. I must keep another engagement, but I hope we shall meet again soon—should you visit London or perhaps Bath.'

'I do not think there is any intention of it as yet,' Sarah replied. 'We are here until Christmas, I believe—but we shall certainly be in London next year.'

'Then I may call on you before Christmas,' Lord Phillips replied, looking oddly shy. 'Sometimes one wishes one did not have so many engagements.'

He was a gentleman and it restored Sarah's pride to know that any feelings he might have had for her were not motivated by her wealth. He liked her for herself.

Sarah smiled and murmured something appropriate. She was not sure if he was hinting that he would like to make her an offer if the circumstances were more auspicious. Clearly, he felt she was not well enough to deal with a matter of that nature now.

Rupert had not let such notions weigh with him. He'd made his intentions very clear and, perhaps in something of an emotional state, she'd accepted his offer. A night of rest and reflection had not changed her mind, though she was aware that her position was not ideal.

She would be a fool to demand too much. Her ideas of loving and being loved were perhaps the dreams a young girl might cherish, but did not apply to a woman who was past five and twenty. No, she must accept passion and companionship and not look for romantic love.

Lord Phillips rose to his feet, having finished his breakfast. He bowed his head to Sarah and said he hoped they would meet again soon, took his leave of Sir Freddie and went out. She heard his voice addressing someone and thought he was asking for his trunk to be brought down.

'Now we are alone, Miss Hardcastle…' Sir Freddie looked at her a little uncertainly across the breakfast table. He cleared his throat. 'I was thinking… I mean, I should very much like to speak to Miss Francesca this morning. Do you think she is well enough to see me?'

'Yes, I am very sure she will be,' Sarah said and smiled at him. 'Indeed, I think your failure to do so might be more distressing than anything else that has happened to her.'

He looked struck, then his eyes lit up. 'Do you say so? By Jove! Then there's hope for me?'

'You must ask Francesca,' Sarah replied with a smile. 'But I think everything may be as we should all wish.'

'You are an angel. She told me how wonderful you were…' He got to his feet. 'I think I'll go up and change. Want to look my best, you know.'

'I'll speak to Francesca. Shall we say half-past the hour of ten in the small back parlour?'

'Thank you. Thank you...' He bowed to her and hurried off and Sarah heard him speak to someone in the hall. The next moment the door of the breakfast parlour opened and Rupert entered. He had been riding and, as she looked at him, she saw a small cut at the side of his mouth. It had stopped bleeding, but swollen a little.

'Rupert...' She got to her feet and went to him. 'Are you all right? Did you have a fall?'

'No, I called on James Monks. We had a fight. I think you could say that he came off worst. It was my intention to thrash him and I did—but he threw a lucky punch.'

'I cannot pretend to be sorry that you gave him a good hiding,' Sarah said. 'But I think your lip may be sore for a while.'

'It was better than calling him out—besides, that honour is reserved for gentlemen and he does not deserve the name. I do not imagine he will bother you or Francesca again.'

'No, I should imagine not,' Sarah said and laughed. 'Well, since you are no worse, I shall go up and speak to Francesca. Sir Freddie intends to speak to her this morning.'

'Yes, he told me. I warned him that Merrivale will not think of allowing the marriage before she's had a Season—but there's no reason they shouldn't have an understanding, is there?'

'None, as far as I am concerned. The marquess would not forbid her—would he?'

'Oh, I think Sir Freddie is eminently suitable. He actually knows Merrivale quite well. I imagine there can be no objection. He will have to be told and I expect he will come down. The engagement might be announced at Christmas.'

'I think that should make them both content. She is still young in years, though as sensible as girls much older.'

'Your influence, I imagine?' His eyebrows rose.

'Oh, in part, I dare say. She has a lovely nature and might have been taken advantage of by that rogue had I not been here.'

'Then I dare say Merrivale will forgive the small deception.'

'I suppose he must know?'

'He will need to be informed, but I shall vouch for you, Sarah.' Rupert's tone was teasing. 'Do not look so anxious, my love. I shall tell him of our engagement when I write—and that reminds me, I must give you a ring. You will, of course, have your pick of the family heirlooms when we are married, but I am not sure of your preference—emeralds, rubies or sapphires for your ring? Or do you prefer plain diamonds?'

'I've never worn rings, though I have Mama's,' Sarah said with a frown. 'I think something fairly simple would suit me—perhaps diamonds in the shape of a daisy. I think it is possible to purchase such a ring, is it not?'

'Perfectly possible. I shall send to my jeweller in London. In the meantime, perhaps you would care to wear this?' He took a small box from his pocket, in which, when it was opened, nestled a plain gold band set with one rather fine diamond. 'This was my mother's wedding ring. She stopped wearing it before she died, because her finger became too thin. You must have your own rings—but for the moment…'

There was a question in his voice. Sarah held out her hand and let him slip it on to the third finger of her left hand, where it fit perfectly.

'It is so beautiful. Do you think we might use it as our wedding ring?'

'If you wish.' He looked pleased. 'Wear it for now and I will buy you a ring of your own when I am in town.'

'Are you leaving us?' Her heart sank for she had hoped that they would have a period of quiet time when they could get to know one another better.

'Only for as long as it takes, Sarah.' Rupert smiled and it was a caress, making her heart leap. 'I have to settle certain matters. Someone almost killed you. We've searched for the villain, but I believe he must have left the district. I need to know who is behind this business.'

'I thought Sir Roger…'

'Yes, I think it likely he tried to take his revenge on you for refusing him.'

'I have always disliked him, but I did not think he would go that far. How could he benefit from my death?'

'I have no idea. It is one of the matters I mean to investigate.'

'When must you leave?'

'I shall not go until I know the outcome between Francesca and Sir Freddie. If that goes as we think, I shall ask him to remain here until I return—and, as I said, I think Merrivale will come down.'

'We shall have company, but—you don't think I am still in danger?'

'I hope that the danger is past, but I intend to make

certain if I can. It would distress me greatly if you were to be shot at again. I find it outrageous that a lady in my care should be treated so shamefully.'

Sarah thanked him. His words at one moment seemed to indicate his care for her and at another his outrage that any woman should be subjected to such treatment. He certainly gave her no cause to think that he loved her. He had spoken of passion when he proposed, but that, of course was a different thing.

After they had parted company, Sarah ran up to Francesca to warn her to be ready to receive Sir Freddie. The girl stared at her with a mixture of delight and apprehension in her eyes.

'Do you think he means to ask me to be his wife?'

'I should not be at all surprised, my love. Is that not what you want?'

'Oh, yes, with all my heart. It's just that…what do I say? How do I answer? I mean, should I smile and tell him I should be pleased—should I let him kiss me?'

'I do not think there is a set rule for these things, my love. You must answer from the heart. I think he will tell you he loves you, perhaps in words stronger than mine—and you might tell him his feelings are reciprocated, if you wish. If he offers to kiss you, I see no reason for you to refuse.'

'Oh…' Francesca went pink with excitement. 'I am so lucky. I cannot believe he truly wants me. I thought he might like Miss Rowton better—or you, Sarah.'

'He is a kind gentleman and polite to everyone, but I am sure he thinks only of you. Besides, I do not think Rupert will mind if I tell you. He has asked me to marry him and I have accepted.'

'Oh, Sarah, that is wonderful,' Francesca said and hugged her. 'We shall be related and you will visit me and I shall visit you. Nothing could be better. I am so glad he asked you. I thought he liked you rather a lot, but you cannot always tell with Uncle Rupert.'

'No, you can't,' Sarah agreed. 'What shall you wear, Francesca? What about the jonquil silk—or would you prefer one of your white-muslin gowns?'

'I think the jonquil,' Francesca said and looked nervous. 'I want to look my best, after all, and the white morning gowns are very simple. Yes, I like my yellow silk. Will you help me to change? It is almost half-past nine already. I do not want to keep Sir Freddie waiting.'

'He won't change his mind, dearest,' Sarah teased, but smiled at the girl's obvious pleasure. 'You do know your grandfather will need to give his permission and he might insist you wait for a while—but Rupert agrees that there is no reason you may not have an understanding.'

'I know Grandfather must be consulted because he has been so good to us—but I am sure he would not disagree. He must approve of Sir Freddie, mustn't he?'

'Yes, I'm certain he will,' Sarah said. 'Turn around and let me unfasten your gown. You can send for Agnes in a minute to dress your hair as you would like it.'

'I'm so happy. Yesterday, I thought everything might be ruined, but now it is all coming right.'

'Yes, it is,' Sarah said and smiled at her. 'I'm glad you're happy. We were all concerned when it was thought you might have eloped—or been abducted.'

'I was, but no one needs to know that,' Francesca said, her face aglow. 'I must be the luckiest girl in the world.'

* * *

'Weak fool!' Sir Roger looked at the younger man sitting opposite him in the inn with scorn. 'You had the girl. Why let her talk you into taking her home and concocting that stupid story to save her reputation? You should have seduced her and made sure of her. If you're ruined, it's your own fault. There's no use in coming to me for help. Unless I can pay my creditors by the end of the month I shall have to leave England.'

'I'm thinking of it,' James Monks said gloomily. 'What's a fellow to do when his pockets are to let and the girl of his dreams doesn't want to know?'

'You had your chance. Now you must take the consequences.'

'You're one to talk. If you venture back to London without a penny to your name, you'll end in the Fleet.'

'Damn you! Do you imagine I don't know that? It's why I've hung around here after… That damned woman seems indestructible. She won't listen to threats of exposure, tells me to go ahead and tell her story—and twice she's been shot at. The idiot who missed her the first time has been dealt with. He won't talk now.'

'You mean…you killed him?' James Monks was shocked.

'He could have betrayed me and I've no wish to hang.' Sir Roger glared at him. 'I had her uncle eating out of my hand. He told me how valuable those mills are. If I could have gotten her to marry me, I could have taken control and my troubles would have vanished. I even made her an offer for them because I thought she might think of marriage if they were off her hands.'

'You couldn't have paid for them.'

'No, but by the time she realised that they would

have been mine through the marriage. If she caused too much trouble, I'd have found a way to be rid of her soon enough.'

'You're an unscrupulous devil. If Myers knew what you'd done, he'd kill you.'

'What's it to him?'

'According to something I heard, she's agreed to marry Rupert Myers.'

Sir Roger swore ferociously. 'I feared that might happen, but if I'm quick there may still be time to act.'

'But what are you going to do?'

'Exactly the same as you, but I shan't let her go when I have her. She may resist, but I know ways of bringing a woman to her knees. I shall rather enjoy teaching Miss High and Mighty Hardcastle her lessons—and she will learn to beg on her knees before I've finished with her.'

James Monks touched his sore nose gingerly. 'He will come after you if you lay a finger on her—and he'll kill you. I thought he was going to kill me....'

'Well, he may have a go, but I'm a pretty good shot. I would have had her the other day if someone hadn't come. I saw him from the corner of my eye and it spoiled my aim.'

'Well, rather you than me.' James pulled a wry face. 'I shan't be around, so don't ask me for help. I'm driving down to my uncle's for a visit. He's asked me to call. If he comes up with the dubs I'll be in town next Season—if not, I'm off to the Americas.'

'Coward.' Sir Roger's lip lifted in a snarl. 'I can manage without your help. Fat lot of use you'd be. You couldn't even manage a teenage girl.'

'Fran has a lot of sense,' James replied. 'I rather liked

her. If she'd married me, I'd have been good to her. I might even have settled down.'

'Violets and roses.' Sir Roger's tone was one of disgust. 'I have no such feelings for that uptight Hardcastle. I'm going to enjoy making her crawl at my feet.'

'I must go. I have some packing to do,' James murmured and rose from the table.

He was thoughtful as he left the inn and mounted his horse. Sir Roger was eaten up with bitterness, his anger against the woman who had refused him so white-hot that he was surely a little mad. He didn't really intend to harm Sarah Hardcastle, did he? An abduction that forced her to either pay him money or marry him was one thing…but there was something distinctly unpleasant about the look in his eyes.

It was only as James dismounted in the courtyard of his family home that the idea came to him. He had been feeling disgruntled because of the beating Lord Myers had given him—but Sarah Hardcastle didn't deserve the fate Sir Roger had planned for her.

What could he do? He didn't dare risk getting involved—but he might send a note warning of Sir Roger's intentions, leaving it unsigned, of course. Yes, he rather thought that might serve. He would warn her that Sir Roger meant to abduct her—and that he was a vindictive man who meant her harm. He might also give her a hint that Sir Roger was the one who had shot her.

He might have made a mistake in associating with a man like that and he rather thought he owed the family some sort of an apology for what he'd done. An anonymous letter to Lord Myers would be a perfect way of warning him of the danger without getting too involved. Lord Myers would know what to do.

Chapter Fourteen

'I've heard from Merrivale,' Rupert said the next morning. 'I had intended to leave today, as you know, but I think my business must wait. I've written to my agents and they may do some searching on my behalf.'

'Oh…' Sarah's heart caught, her pleasure marred because he stayed for his uncle's sake rather than hers. 'I am glad that you need not leave us yet.'

Rupert looked down at her, his gaze narrowed. 'You know I would not wish to leave you at all if it were not that my business is important?'

'Yes, I know.' Her heart raced as she looked up at him. The heat in his eyes made her wonder if perhaps she'd misjudged his reasons for marrying her. 'I'm glad you are staying. I was afraid the marquess might be angry with me for coming here under false pretences.'

'I fear he may—which is one of the reasons I decided to wait and leave my work to an agent.'

'Thank you…' Her breath caught in her throat and for a moment she thought he would kiss her, but then Sir Freddie walked into the breakfast room and the moment was lost.

'I was thinking of shooting a few pigeons,' Rupert said. 'Do you care to take the guns out for an hour or so?'

Sarah left them to their talk of sport and went upstairs to Francesca's room. The girl was just having her hair done and she waited until the maid had left, before telling her that her grandfather was coming down and would arrive later that day.

'Rupert has delayed his trip to be here,' she said and saw a look of relief in Francesca's eyes. 'Are you anxious about something?'

'Only that I am not sure Grandfather will permit us to become engaged at Christmas—and I do so want to, Sarah.'

'Well, you must give him a little time, but I am sure that he will agree, dearest. Once he sees how happy you are.'

'I hope he will not be angry with you, Sarah.'

'Well, I dare say he may a little, but Rupert is here— he will talk to him and I must hope to be forgiven.'

'Good afternoon, Miss Hardcastle.' Merrivale's eyes narrowed as he looked at her later that day. 'My nephew has nothing but good to say of you, and it is clear how much better my girl is for your influence—but what have you to say to me? You came here under a false banner.'

'Yes, sir, I did,' Sarah said, meeting his gaze honestly. 'It was very wrong of me, but I was not thinking clearly at the time. I am truly sorry for deceiving you by pretending to be the new governess.'

'You ought not to have done it.'

'I know and I do beg your pardon, sir.'

'Well, all's well that ends well,' he said, beaming at her. 'I can feel the difference your presence has made to this house—it hasn't been so alive since before my girl married that scoundrel.'

'That is a very great compliment, sir. I am flattered.'

'I was too old to have the care of a couple of children when she died,' he said heavily. 'I didn't know what to do with them and I fear I left them to a succession of governesses and tutors who let them down.'

'They were certainly bored and lonely, but someone had managed to teach them some lessons.' Sarah smiled at him. 'What they needed was company—and Lord Myers provided a role model for John.'

'Yes. It was a stroke of luck that he agreed to come down for a while. I've no idea why. He isn't being pursued by creditors—I know that for a fact. I dare say he fell out with his current lady-love. I thought he might be interested in getting married, but it came to nothing. Dare say he wanted a little time to lick his wounds, what?'

Sarah inclined her head, but said nothing. Had Rupert lost the woman he loved shortly before he came down—and was that why he was willing to settle for second best?

The thought made her throat tighten, but she drove it away. She'd thought as they spoke that morning before he went shooting with Sir Freddie that he might care for her, but it must have been wishful thinking on her part.

The marquess was looking at her intently. 'What do you think of this match between Francesca and Sir Freddie, then? Bit old for her?'

'There is a difference in years, but I think they are in love.'

'Are they indeed?' His bushy brows met. 'In my day we did not allow sentimentality to enter the equation. However, I can't have my girl breaking her heart so I suppose the match will have to be—but there's no rush. I've decided on an engagement at Christmas and the wedding next year, perhaps in the summer.'

'Yes, sir. Lord Myers rather thought you might be of that opinion and I have warned Francesca that she must be content to wait, because she is still very young.'

'Kick up rough, did she?'

'No, not at all. I think she just feels very fortunate to have found someone she can love—and to know he loves her.'

'Sir Freddie wants to take her to meet his mother and sister. Suggested I go, too—and you, m'dear. Seems my girl cannot be parted from you. I told him I wasn't ready for another journey just yet. He'll have to be patient for a few days. Too much junketing around isn't good for my health.'

'You must take care of yourself—' Sarah broke off as one of the footmen entered bearing a silver salver with a letter on it. 'Good morning, Sims. Is the letter for the marquess?'

'No, Miss Hardcastle. It is for you.'

'For me?' Sarah picked it up. 'Thank you. I shall read it later.'

'The boy said he was to wait for a reply, miss.'

'Oh?' Sarah tore it open and read the brief message. It said that her uncle had been taken ill and she was to come at once if she wished to know the truth about her mother. 'No...'

The Marquess of Merrivale looked at her face. 'Is something troubling you, Miss Hardcastle?'

'I am told my uncle is very ill and asks for me to come immediately.'

'Then of course you must go, my dear. I shall send you in my own carriage with a maid and groom to accompany you.'

'I'm not sure…' Sarah was doubtful. 'I promised Francesca I would stay and, besides, I do not know who has sent this. It is unsigned.'

'Unsigned?' Merrivale's brows met. 'That is a trifle unusual, what?'

'Yes, it is.' Sarah decided she must explain. 'I was shot at and injured some days ago. I have recovered, as you see—but this might be a trap. I had a letter only three days ago and my uncle was perfectly well then.'

'In that case you are wise to think twice. How sensible you are, Miss Hardcastle. Most young women would have gone rushing off in a panic.'

'I believe that is what I was meant to do. If you will forgive me, I shall write a letter and ask one of the footmen to send it for me.'

'Write your letter. We'll send a groom with it to discover the truth—unless you wish to go yourself. I could send an armed escort with you.'

Sarah thought for a moment and then shook her head. 'Thank you, sir, but I believe this is a trap. My enemy wishes to draw me out because I have stayed close to the house. I shall write and if a groom could deliver it and bring back a message I should be grateful.'

'Write your letter, m'dear, and I'll see to the rest. We don't want some rogue shooting at you again, do we?'

She thanked him, took her leave and went up to her room to write the letter. Her instincts were telling her that the letter was false and that meant she was still in danger from whoever hated her.

Sarah's letter had been sent and she'd asked the marquess if it might remain their secret, as she did not wish for anything to overshadow Francesca's happiness. Sir Freddie had given his love a ring, but for the moment she was wearing it on chain beneath her gown. Their engagement would not be announced just yet, even though they were to pay a visit to Sir Freddie's mother in the near future.

Sarah had not allowed her suspicions to cloud her pleasure in the company and walked in the gardens, but always in the company of her friends. Sometimes Rupert, Francesca, Sir Freddie and John, together with the dancing master, made up the little group, and on occasion the marquess joined them for refreshments outdoors.

Sarah noticed that there was usually a gardener hanging about when they spent time walking amongst the roses and various flowerbeds. The weather kept fine obligingly and they played croquet on the lawns, drank tea in the shade of some fine trees and walked, enjoying each other's conversation. Each day followed the last in a haze of perfect contentment and Sarah's feeling of alarm began to fade. Rupert was always pleasant to her, always considerate, and sometimes the look in his eyes sent her pulses haywire, but he had said nothing further to make her think that he was marrying her for any other reason than convenience.

She was determined that he should not guess she felt more than he did and her smiles for him were no more intimate than for anyone else. If he wished for a comfortable wife, it was what she would be, undemanding and good-tempered.

She'd told Rupert of her letter and her belief that it was a ruse to trap her into leaving the safety of his protection.

'You must remain here,' he had told her sternly. 'Your uncle will write to you if it is necessary—though if you are anxious I could escort you.'

Sarah had shaken her head. 'I do not think my uncle would have sent such a letter. I am content to wait until we hear from him.'

She was returning with her friends from one of their outings some days later when a coach drew up at the front of the house. As she watched, the door opened and a man got out. Surprise and pleasure made her start forwards with a glad cry.

'Uncle William! What are you doing here?'

He turned to look at her with a frown. 'I wanted to make sure these people were treating you properly. Were you mad to run off like that, Sarah? What in heaven's name made you change places with a governess?'

'It was just a whim, Uncle. I am so glad to see you are not at death's door.'

'I dare say that was that rogue who wheedled your mother's story out of me,' her uncle said. 'I'm sorry for telling him, girl. He has a smooth tongue and I trusted him, thought he cared for you. From what Lord Myers told me in his letter, Sir Roger is a sly snake and not to be trusted.'

'Rupert wrote to you?' Sarah glanced at Rupert, for he'd said nothing to her. He was laughing with Sir Freddie and did not notice her glance.

'It's the reason I came,' her uncle replied. He looked

about him, seeing the little group of curious onlookers. 'Sorry to turn up out of the blue, but I wanted to tell you the whole truth. I gather that serpent twisted the story into something ugly.'

'Wasn't it?'

'Far from it. Can we talk in private?'

'I must introduce you to the others, then we'll go to the back parlour. I am very pleased you have come, Uncle, though a letter would have been sufficient.'

'I thought I should apologise in person. It may be because of me that all this unpleasantness has happened.'

Sarah took his arm and led him towards her friends. She watched as he shook hands with Rupert, greeting him as a friend, and then introduced him to her friends.

'You must come in, Uncle. We are about to have tea.'

'This is a bit above my touch, girl. I was never one for mixing in society, you know—at least, not on this level.'

'Everyone is very friendly. I am sure the marquess will say you must stay for a day or two.'

'I couldn't do that, Sarah. I know my place and it isn't here. I'll take myself off to the inn, though I'll call on you again tomorrow. You may have been brought up to be a lady, but I came from the lower ranks, as your father did. It was because of your mother that he had you educated as a lady.'

Sarah nodded, because she already knew what had been in her father's mind. Francesca said she would have some refreshments sent into the back parlour so they could be private and Sarah took her uncle there.

'Please sit down, sir.'

'I'll stand, if you don't mind.' He looked at her awkwardly. 'Is it right that you're to marry Lord Myers?'

'Yes, Uncle. He asked me and I said yes.'

'I suppose you know what you're doing—not always a good idea to mix the classes, but if it makes you happy…'

'It does. Why did you come all this way?'

'You've been told you were not the child of your father's wife?'

'Yes, I have. Was it a lie?'

'Your mama couldn't have children. She tried, but it almost killed her and your father wouldn't let her go through it again—but they both wanted a child.' He cleared his throat. 'Your father asked her permission to have an affair with a view to getting himself an heir. It cost her pain, but she gave it…' He paused and Sarah frowned.

'So that much is true?'

'Yes, Sarah. Your father chose a respectable widow who lived in poverty with one child. He gave her money and a house and she promised to give you up when you were born, but…and this is the part that hurts…when the time came she wept and clung to you and he had to force you from her arms.'

Sarah gave a little cry of stress. 'Oh, but that was cruel.'

'What was he to do? Your mama longed for a child and you were his. He loved his wife beyond reason and so he took you and gave you to your mama. He adopted you legally and made you his heir. Your mama never knew that he had forced your mother to give you up.'

'I see…' Sarah's eyes felt wet with tears. 'It is such a sad story. Is it true that my mother came looking for me when she was dying?'

'She came once to ask if she might see you, but your

father refused. He thought she might try to steal you from him. He sent her away and he heard later that she had died of consumption.'

'Why didn't he tell me?'

'I think he thought you might despise him for what he did. He wasn't a bad man, Sarah—he simply loved your mama too much.'

'Yes, I see that.' Sarah blew her nose on a lace handkerchief. 'Thank you for telling me. It is easier to accept than the story Sir Roger told me—though the truth remains. I was not born in wedlock and my mother was not a lady.'

'Oh, but she was, Sarah, the equal of your mother—and her husband was also a gentleman, but a terrible gambler. He left her with nothing when he died.'

'I see… How terrible that must have been for his wife. I think I understand why she agreed to the bargain.'

'Can you forgive your father—and me for telling that scoundrel? I thought he would make you a good husband, Sarah.'

'I would never have married him even had he not tried to blackmail me—but I wish I had known the truth.'

'Would it have made a difference? You could not have been more loved, Sarah. Your mama's life was so much richer for having you.'

'Yes, and I loved her—but what of my true mother? It hurts me to think Father sent her away.'

'He gave her money. She had enough to live decently for the rest of her life.'

'But she had lost a child. I think that must have been hard for her to bear.'

'Well, it cannot be changed now.'

'No, it cannot…' Sarah looked up as the door opened and a maid entered carrying a tray, which she set down close to Sarah. 'Thank you, Rose.'

'Is there anything else, miss?'

'No, I believe we have all we need.' She looked at her uncle as the maid went out. 'Will you have tea or some Madeira wine, Uncle?'

'I believe the wine,' her uncle said, looking relieved that the awkward business had gone off better than he might have hoped. 'You're such a sensible girl, Sarah.'

'I have tried to be, particularly since my father died—but I am thinking of selling the mills if Lord Myers can find a suitable buyer.'

'I made a mistake there as well,' her uncle said with a look of apology. 'I thought you'd be better without the burden of those mills—but I should have left it to you decide when you were ready.'

'I believe I may be ready now—if a trustworthy buyer can be found.'

'I reckon as Lord Myers will find you a buyer who can be trusted. Your workers won't suffer and you'll be the richer for it. That young fellow has a good head on his shoulders even if he is an aristocrat.'

Sarah laughed. 'I am glad to hear it.'

'He says you're to be married within the month. Your aunt and cousins are invited—so that will mean an expense with all the new gowns.' Her uncle sighed. 'But if he's right for you, it's worth it.'

Sarah was a little shocked, for Rupert had not told her that he intended the marriage so soon, but she merely smiled.

'I hope you will give me away, Uncle?'

'Well, if it's what you truly want...' He looked pleased, then shook his head. 'I hope this other business can soon be sorted out. Sir Roger is an evil man and he needs to be brought to justice.'

'He was wicked to tell me those lies. I do not know what he hoped to gain by spreading a false scandal.'

'Mud sticks, girl—especially when you're not out of the top drawer. No, do not look like that, Sarah. You know some of those top-lofty dames in London society will look down their noses at you, even if you are Lady Myers. They will never forget that your father made his money from trade.'

'It was a decent, honourable business and I am not ashamed of what Father did for a living—but I think he treated my birth mother ill.'

'Well, you must make up your own mind on that—but try not to hate him.'

'No, how could I? He loved me and I loved him—but I wish he had let her at least see me sometimes.'

At that moment a discreet knock at the door heralded Merrivale's arrival. He greeted Sarah's uncle with every sign of friendship, shook his hands, insisted he must stay and took him off to speak with the housekeeper about his accommodation.

Sarah was left to the contemplation of her thoughts. She was conscious of a deep ache inside. The knowledge that her mother had been a respectable woman who had given her child to a childless woman but at the last had been grieved to part with her was painful. She wished with all her heart that she might have known her, spent a little time with her.

She needed to talk to Rupert, but knew that he would be with the others. Besides, as kind as he was, she could not expect him to understand her hurt over her mother's distress and pain.

'I do not love you the less, Mama,' she whispered. 'It's just that I would have liked to know her, too.'

Feeling an unexpected sweep of loneliness, Sarah left the parlour by the French doors and went out into the sunshine. She knew it was almost time for tea, but she needed a few moments alone to sort out her thoughts. It was difficult to reconcile what her father had done and yet she understood. Mama had always been delicate, but so sweet and gentle. Sarah and her father had both done everything they could to please her and make her life easy and gentle. They had both mourned her desperately.

Her feelings for her mama and her father had not changed, she discovered as she walked in the direction of the rose arbour. However, there was an empty space inside her, a feeling of terrible loss.

Sarah had been wandering for some minutes lost in thought when she became aware of the rustling sounds. She stiffened, glancing over her shoulder just as a man lurched towards her. He had a thick blanket in his hands and she guessed that he had been about to pounce on her. Sir Roger had somehow found his way inside the grounds and was intent on causing her harm.

'Stay back or I shall scream.'

'You are far enough from the house for it not to matter,' he snarled. 'I've plotted and planned for this, Miss Hoity-Toity, and I've waited day after day for you to venture out alone. I was about to give up and go back to town—and now here you are.'

Sarah swallowed hard. He was right. She was far enough from the house for her screams not to be heard. Normally there were gardeners about, but she could see none. She had nothing that she could hit him with and only her wits to hold him off.

'Whatever you do, I shall not marry you.'

'If you prove stubborn, I may have to kill you.'

'What good would that do you?'

'If I can't have you and your money, I'll make certain no one else can.'

Sarah gasped. Was he mad or just driven to desperation by his debts?

'Why do you hate me so?' He had clearly lost his mind and she must play for time, try to think of a way to escape him.

Sarah heard the twig snap behind her. She thought that he must have heard it, too, but he was lost in his grievances, both real and imaginary, his eyes taking on a strange glazed look.

'I do not hate you. I love you—you must know that you encouraged me at the start.'

'That is a lie. I never encouraged you—never wished to be your wife….'

'Then I might as well kill you now.'

He dropped the blanket and suddenly there was a pistol in his hand. Even as he lifted his arm to fire, two shots rang out simultaneously and he fell to the ground where he lay, twitching horribly.

Sarah's scream brought three men running from the shrubbery, two from behind Sir Roger and one from closer to her. She saw that one of them was a man she had thought a gardener, Monsieur Dupree and the other was the man she needed most.

'Rupert,' she said, took a step towards him and fainted. He was there to catch her before she hit the ground.

Chapter Fifteen

Rupert bent down by her side, looking at her anxiously. It was merely a faint rather than serious injury. Pray God they had been in time thanks to the dancing master's timely warning. Rupert had but dismounted from his chaise when Dupree came rushing at him, shouting that he was sure he had seen Sir Roger lurking in the bushes.

'I saw Miss Sarah walking alone, but she looked in some distress and so I did not join her—but then I spotted this rogue lurking and came to find help.'

Summoning one of the men he had hired to protect Sarah whenever she went beyond the boundaries of the estate, Rupert had felt for his pistol and smiled because it was already loaded and ready for use. He'd had men searching everywhere for Sir Roger without success, but now it seemed he had come to them. His satisfaction as he pulled the trigger and saw it hit home flared triumphantly through him. The devil had paid for his misdeeds and she was safe.

He felt a rush of tears as he knelt by her side, running

his fingers over her face, looking for signs that she was hurt. God help him if he'd been too late.

Rupert lifted Sarah into his arms. She moaned a little, her eyelids fluttering, and he knew a rush of relief. She was alive. Thank God, thank God! His darling girl was alive.

'Hush, my love. You're safe now,' he said and glanced coldly at Sir Roger's body, which had stopped twitching. 'Dead?'

'*Oui,* of a certainty,' Monsieur Dupree said. 'He was shot twice, in the back and the head. Both shots might have killed him.'

'Good. The rogue deserved to die. Take him to one of the annexes and send for a doctor—and the magistrate. This business is messy and must be cleared up as swiftly as possible if we are to avert a scandal.'

'Yes, cap'n.' The old soldier saluted and then bent down to haul Sir Roger's body over his shoulder. 'I'll see to 'im if the Frenchie sees to the rest.'

Rupert nodded grimly, but made no reply as he strode towards the house carrying his precious burden. As he approached several people came out to meet him, Francesca running towards him, Sir Freddie close behind and the two older men standing on the steps watching.

'Is Sarah all right? We heard two shots.'

'We found her in time. Sir Roger was about to kill her—he's dead. I think the man was entirely mad.'

'It was my fault,' William Hardcastle said. 'I told him her story.'

'No, he knew it before he even met her. He was bent on getting her fortune, but when she proved too stubborn he decided to settle for revenge.'

'Good grief. Because she wouldn't marry him?'

'There's a lot more to the story. Explanations another day, if you please, gentlemen. Sarah's comfort comes first.'

'Of course, of course.'

'Take her to the salon and put her on the daybed.'

'No, take her up to her room,' Francesca said. 'She will want to be private for a while. You should stay with her until she feels better, Uncle Rupert.'

'Good girl, go up and pull the covers back.'

Francesca was ahead of him as he carried Sarah carefully up the stairs. He knew she was stirring, but she merely buried her head against his shoulder, not saying anything until he had placed her gently on her own bed.

'Please do not be cross with me, Rupert,' she said and her eyelids flickered. She sighed and then looked up at him. 'I know it was foolish to go there alone, but I had something on my mind.'

'My foolish love,' he said and bent to brush his lips over hers. 'Why should I be cross with you? I might be annoyed with your uncle, for I suppose he told you the truth, and I am furious with that devil that tried to murder you—but I could never be angry with you. I love you far too much. If anything, I am angry with myself. There was a letter on my desk warning of an attempt on your life from James Monks, but some papers of mine had covered it and I missed it. If you had died, I should never have forgiven myself.'

Sarah inched her way up against the pillows, looking at him, her lovely eyes wide open as if in surprise. 'You love me? You truly love me? I thought, but I…'

Francesca discreetly closed the door behind her as she went out. She shook her head at the small group gathered there. 'No need to worry,' she said. 'Rupert will take care of her. She will be quite safe with him.'

Inside the room, Rupert smiled down at the woman who looked at him with such dawning wonder in her eyes. 'Come, Sarah. This is not like you. Surely you knew I was in love with you? I could barely keep from carrying you off to my bed and ravishing you.'

A smile lit her face, making her look beautiful. 'I thought you might want to lie with me—but lust does not always mean love, does it? Your uncle said something about you once losing a woman you cared for?'

'Years ago when I was wet behind the ears,' he said and smiled, his fingers brushing her cheek tenderly. 'For too long I have felt little inside—transitory lust for a beautiful woman, yes, but true feelings, no, they have eluded me, until you came.'

'Why?'

'Why did I feel nothing?' Rupert frowned. 'My parents were not particularly happy together—an arranged marriage—and I asked a lady to marry me. She laughed and called me a boy, which I was at the time. I joined the army because there was a war...' His smile faded, his eyes, had he known it, wintry and bleak. 'I saw too many friends die in terrible circumstances, Sarah. A man can only take so much. I carried my best friend Harry from the field. For two days he lingered in terrible pain and then he died in my arms, begging me not to forget him and to take his things to his family, which of course I did. Some of my friends blamed me for my decision to attack the enemy position that day. Lives were lost, though we gained our objective, but some of my friends blamed me for those lost.

'After that, I shut all feelings out. When I resigned

my commission I gave myself up to a life of pleasure, taking a woman if I felt like it, but giving nothing. I think that would not have changed had not a most unusual governess walked into my life.'

'Oh, Rupert, my dearest one,' Sarah whispered and held out her hand to him. He took it and pressed it to his cheek, then kissed the fingertips. 'I am sorry about your friends. I know nothing can change what happened or give you back what you lost—but when we have children of our own they may help to fill the empty places inside you.'

'You have already done that,' he said and bent to kiss her, this time a long, lingering kiss that made her sigh and cling to him. 'If you cling to me that way, I might just get in that bed with you.'

Sarah laughed, the laugh that had melted the ice and set warm blood flowing through his veins. 'If I did not think that everyone was waiting for us to go down to tea, I should invite you to keep your word. You may consider it an open invitation.'

'Shameless hussy,' he murmured and nibbled at the side of her neck. 'You taste so good, my love. I can hardly wait for our wedding night.'

Sarah touched his cheek. 'I do love you so very much.'

He caught her hand and kissed the palm. 'Do you? I was afraid you couldn't possibly love me as much as I love you. I have not exactly courted you, have I? For a long time I could not trust my feelings. I feared to be hurt or disillusioned and it was not until you were shot the first time that I began to understand how much you meant to me. Even then I was not sure that I could truly give my heart, but then I realised that my life would be nothing without you.'

Sarah smiled and caught his hand, holding it to her cheek. 'I have no need of flattery. I want you with all your faults and all your virtues. I do not think that any other man could content me.'

'That is just as well, Miss Hardcastle, because I cannot kill all your unwanted suitors.' He saw the light fade from her lovely eyes and cursed himself for a fool. 'Forgive me. It was but a jest. Sir Roger has gone now, Sarah. Nothing can harm you now. I have a special licence in my pocket and we shall marry just as soon as you are ready.'

'Tomorrow?' Sarah said, laughing up at him. 'No, no, my aunt is looking forward to the wedding. We must wait the three weeks, I think—but I do not see why we should wait in other ways....' Her cheeks turned pink and he laughed in delight.

'Wanton jade. How much I am going to enjoy being married to you, Sarah. You will set all the old tabbies by the ears when I take you to town. They will not know what to make of you.'

'I fear they may cut us.'

'Nonsense. They may be shocked by your story, but their curiosity will bring them flocking and, when they meet you, they cannot fail to appreciate that you are a true lady. Your mother was one after all.'

'I believe her married name was Harlow,' Sarah said, her brow wrinkling. 'Her husband was killed in a foolish duel, leaving her penniless—but my uncle must have told you.'

'My agents uncovered the story, dearest. I have many agents working on this business and we knew that Sir

Roger had returned to the area.' He took her hand and kissed it. 'I fear I cannot give you the news you would wish for. Your mother died, just as your father was told. However, there is something…'

She gazed up at him, enquiring. 'You have discovered something else?'

'You have a brother called Harry. I had the information just this morning and intended to tell you when we had a moment to be private—which has been devilishly few and far of late, my love.'

'A brother?' Sarah stared at him, some of the pain of her mother's death draining from her. 'I truly have a brother?'

'A half-brother to be precise,' Rupert said. 'He is an officer in the army. I had thought you might wish him present at our wedding?'

'Oh, yes, I should love that. Does he know about me?'

'I think he is aware he has a sister somewhere, but not the details. I shall leave that to you, Sarah. We can make arrangements for you to meet—or you could invite him here so we might get to know him a bit before we wed.'

'Do you think of everything?'

'I am used to being in command. If I am too authoritative, you must tell me and I shall try to change.'

'I would not change you for the world,' she said and the sparkle was back. 'At least…perhaps little things…'

'And what may they be, minx?'

'You do not kiss me enough,' she whispered. 'I dare say I may find other things—'

She got no further for he decided to supply the lack immediately.

* * *

'So it is all arranged,' Francesca said and hugged her arm as they walked together in the gardens a few days later. It seemed to Sarah that her life was free of a dark shadow and the sun shone brighter than ever before, the birds singing sweeter than of late. 'You are to be married in three weeks. When you leave on your honeymoon I shall leave with Grandfather and Freddie to stay with his mama—and when I return you will be here again.'

'Yes, that is what Rupert suggested. I know I promised to come with you, but you have your grandfather and John—and, of course, Sir Freddie, who loves you dearly.'

'I shall still miss you, but you must have your trip to Paris,' Francesca said. 'I have all the rest of this year and next spring to be with you, dearest Sarah. It is wonderful that Rupert says you will make your home here with us until I am married. I cannot thank you enough for all you've done for me.'

'It was a happy chance for us both that I came here,' Sarah said and squeezed her arm. 'We have both found happiness—and I have found a brother. I have written to invite him to stay and attend our wedding. Your grandfather is to spend more time with us, and, if he can bear it, may make his home here once more.'

'Freddie says he can live with us if he chooses—or we will live here some of the time. I am sure that there is no need for him to be so lonely again.'

'I believe he knows that,' Sarah said and bent to smell a rose, picking the delicate pink bud and tucking it into her gown. 'Everything has turned out so well for us.'

'Everything is perfect.' Francesca said. 'Oh, here is Freddie. Shall we join him?'

Sarah let her go. 'Go on, dearest. I want to pick one or two more roses.'

'So you are happy, Sarah?' Rupert asked as they walked in the moonlight that night. He stopped and drew her closer, brushing his lips over hers. 'Can you look forward to our wedding without any shadows?'

'I shall always be sorry that I never knew my mother, but perhaps my brother will tell me about her.'

'I am certain he will,' Rupert said and touched her cheek. 'You have the rest of your lives to get to know one another. We shall begin at the wedding and, if it pleases you, I would like to settle some money on him for the future, for when he retires from the military.'

'Should I not do that?'

'You will allow me the pleasure,' Rupert said. 'Your money is your own, but I shall do what I can to further your brother's career and set him up with an estate when he is ready.'

'Would you do so much for my sake?'

'I would do more,' he promised and kissed her.

'I think my mother would be happy that her children were reunited as family.'

'Then you are truly happy?'

'So happy,' Sarah said and gazed up at him. 'Of course, one thing could be better. You could kiss me more....'

She gurgled with laughter as he crushed her to him and she felt the burn of his urgent desire.

'Shall I take you to bed, Sarah? I am tempted, but with a house filled with friends and relatives I fear it could not remain our secret—and I would not have anyone think less of you.'

'Then take me to the summerhouse,' Sarah said. 'There are cushions and blankets and we could make ourselves a bed.'

'You wicked wanton girl,' he murmured huskily. 'I might have known you would think of a way.'

Sarah turned on her side, raising her body to look down at Rupert as he lay with his eyes closed, the moonlight playing over his features. She reached up to trace the proud line of his neck and moved across his sensitive mouth—the mouth that had kissed her nearly senseless. He caught her finger with his white teeth and she laughed.

'I thought you were sleeping?'

'Just content,' he said and opened his eyes to look at her. 'You are such a warm, wonderful woman, my Sarah. I do not know what I have done to deserve you.'

'Oh, I can think of a few things,' she murmured and bent her head to nibble at his neck. 'Rather a lot of things actually. It might take a long time to tell you—and I think we ought to get back.'

'Not just yet,' he growled and rolled her beneath him into the bed of cushions and blankets. His hand stroked the satin arch of her back, his hands cupping her neat bottom and pressing her closer. She could feel the burn of his arousal and a spiral of desire curled through her. The hot, sweet liquid ran between her thighs and she knew she was ready for him again, longing to be lost in that wild passion that had overtaken them when they threw off their clothes and loved for the first time.

'I do adore you, Rupert.'

'I adore you, my darling, he whispered. 'I didn't believe I could ever love like this, but you captured my heart and refused to let go. You know I want you again, don't you?'

'Yes.' She tangled her hands in his hair. 'I want you, too. I'm yours—as often and as much as you wish.'

'I mustn't again yet because you will be so sore,' he said huskily. 'But I can pleasure us both in another way—if you wish?'

'I am yours….' She looked up at him with such trust and love that he moaned low in his throat, then bent his head and began to kiss her. His tongue stroked and caressed her, licking delicately at the hollow in her throat. His hand stroked as he cupped her breasts, gently kneading and caressing until she was arching and moaning beneath him, begging him to enter her again. Instead he bent his head lower, his tongue travelling down her navel to that soft, moist centre of herself that he had pleasured earlier. As his tongue began to weave its magic, she screamed and cried his name. Her fingers dug into his shoulder as the sensation became almost too much to bear before she exploded into flames and lay quivering in his arms as he stroked her until she came back from the heavens. 'Rupert…oh, Rupert…' she whispered and the tears ran down her cheeks.

'My hair has come down,' Sarah said and buried her face in his shoulder. 'I must hope I can escape to my room without being seen.' She laughed and sat up as he rolled away. 'I do not care. I do not care if everyone knows. I am not ashamed to let them see how much we love each other. Besides, I do not think they will care—except that it may set a bad example for Francesca.'

'I dare say that young lady has ideas of her own,'

Rupert said. 'It may be as well if Merrivale allows an engagement now and a wedding at Christmas. I shall see what I can do for them. She can still go to London after all.'

'I know she is impatient and wishes her wedding was sooner,' Sarah said. 'Perhaps when we return from Paris…'

'Yes.' Rupert stood and began to dress. 'Allow me to act as your maid, my love. I dare say we can make you look respectable if we try.'

'I suppose you are proficient as a lady's maid.'

He arched his brow. 'Jealous? There is no need. None of my former ladies meant anything to me.'

'I know,' she said and smiled. 'You've told me. I but tease you, dearest, as you tease me.'

'Then continue, my lady,' he replied. 'I would not have you change.'

'I do not think I can put my hair back up without my combs and brushes,' she said. 'It will have to hang loose and everyone must make of it what they will.'

'Come,' he said and took her by the hand. 'We must go in or I shall want you again.'

Sarah had once thought her wedding day would never happen, but suddenly it was upon them. The sun was shining and she rose that morning feeling on top of the world. She smiled throughout the church ceremony and the reception. It was wonderful, graced by the presence of so many friends and relatives that Sarah lost count. She could not remember all their names, but would know their faces. Some of them had come down before the wedding and so she'd had a chance to meet the most intimate members of Rupert's family and some of his close friends—all of them soldiers who had served with him and experienced the same hardships.

Now at last they were alone, not at the Merrivale estate, but at a small house that had belonged to one of Rupert's aunts and was quite close by. He had not wanted to take her away from her friends too soon, but in the end they had dashed for their carriage and been showered with rose petals and dried violets for the second time that day. Sarah could see some in her hair as she looked in the dressing mirror. She was trying to pick them out when the door opened and Rupert entered from the dressing room.

'Tired?' he asked as he came to stand behind her and look down at her reflection in the exquisite marquetry mirror. 'Let me do that for you.' He took her hairbrush and began to stroke it over her long hair, untangling the long silken strands. 'I think the knots all gone now.'

'That was lovely,' she said and then stood up, turning to face him. She lifted her face for his kiss. 'I believe it all went well, did it not? Everyone was amazingly kind.'

'Why shouldn't they be? You've made me happy. I'm a changed man, Sarah. My family and friends would love you for that—and my sister is dying to have you stay with her so she can wheedle all the little details out of you.'

Sarah laughed. 'You wrong her. I thought her sweet.'

'Don't be fooled. She'll twist you round her finger if she can—as she does me. Jane has been trying to find me a bride for years, but I was not of much help, because I kept refusing to meet her candidates.'

'Fortunately for me,' Sarah said and leaned forwards to kiss him. 'It would have been terrible had you been taken.'

'There was never any chance of it. I was waiting for you, my love.'

He lowered his head and kissed her, then bent to sweep her up in his arms and carry her to their bed. She lay looking up at him, a smile on her mouth.

'I am so very glad,' she murmured. 'For otherwise I should have had to be your mistress.'

'Now she tells me,' he said in a mocking tone. 'I might have been spared all the expense of the reception. I thought they would never stop eating and drinking.'

'Oh, Rupert…' Sarah laughed as he threw off his robe and revealed that he was wearing nothing and was fully aroused '…never stop loving me.'

'Never,' he vowed and then he joined her on the bed. They moved together as one, lips meeting in a burning kiss. Flesh to flesh they held one another, looking into each other's faces, and for a long, long time there was no need of words.

* * * * *

CLAIMING THE
CHAPERON'S HEART

Prologue

'If you do this for me I shall be yours and all that I own will be at your disposal,' the woman said. Her pale olive-toned skin looked smooth and soft in the candle-light, her black velvet eyes as dark as night, but lit from within by a silver flame. She was a beautiful woman, sure of her power, and she sensed that he wanted her so badly that he could almost taste his need. The perfume she wore was heavy and had the exotic tang of musk and ambergris, and the jewels around her neck were worth a king's ransom. She was the daughter of an Indian prince and the granddaughter of an English earl, proud, haughty and vengeful—and the hatred of the man who had spurned her burned deep within her breast. 'He used me cruelly and deserted me—I want him dead. Only his death will assuage the wrong he has done me…'

She leaned closer to the man, allowing him to inhale the scent of her body, knowing that she had the power to drive men to near madness in their desire for her.

She could have had almost any man she wanted and yet one had eluded her and it was he alone she wanted. He had refused her offer to lie with her, to wed her and live in her palace, had told her that he did not love her—and she felt the bitter pain of his rejection like a snake's sting. He would learn that he could not walk away from her! In her anger she was lost to all sense of reason. She would make certain that he died a painful death for deserting her.

This poor fool who looked at her like a starving man was not the only one she had promised her favours, but the other was unlikely to do her bidding, though he loved her. This one had his own reasons for giving her the revenge she craved; she had picked him carefully and she knew that he would do whatever she asked for the promise of rich rewards. He was greedy, this one, and as desirous of vengeance as she was herself.

'He wronged you as he wronged me,' she hissed at him. 'Go to England. Follow him and do as I have asked you—and when you return you shall have all you desire and more…'

'Yes, I shall do your bidding, sweet lady, for I have business that takes me there. When it is complete and I have done as you ask, I shall return to claim my reward.'

A cruel smile touched her lips. He would have more than he desired for she would keep him only for as long as it pleased her…her heart was as cold as ice now, for *he* had broken it and she hated him.

The fool knelt before her and kissed the hem of her costly robes. 'I vow that I shall bring your enemy and mine to justice,' he said. 'Either he or I shall lie dead when this is over…but he is unsuspecting and I know him for the trusting fool he is. He will never know what is afoot until I take his life.'

She felt a trickle of fear slide down her spine and for a moment she wanted to take back all the hateful words. She loved the man who had refused her and his death could bring her no real satisfaction, and in that moment she knew that revenge could only bring her grief—and yet he had humbled her pride and he must pay. Anger and pride fought against softer emotions and won. She stared at the fool kneeling before her and knew he was not fit to kiss the feet of the man she loved, but her pain and grief was too deep and must be assuaged by blood.

After he had gone she was possessed by a wild restlessness that had her pacing until she realised that even revenge could not assuage the pain in her heart. Indeed, the thought of *his* death brought even more agony. Sinking to her knees, she wept until the storm of anger and despair had left her and then she knew that she had betrayed her own heart. She did not want the man she loved dead, but here with her, a smile of love on his face.

She must recall the fool who did her bidding so easily and tell him that she no longer wished him to kill for her.

Then, as she saw the sun had risen in the sky, she knew it was too late. His ship was already on its way and because he wanted the rewards she had promised he would do her bidding… *His* death would be her sin.

Giving a cry of terrible despair, she fell senseless to the ground.

Chapter One

'Ah, letters,' Viscount Salisbury said and looked at his elder sister Jane as she entered the room carrying a satisfying bundle. 'Any for me, Sis?'

'Yes, I think three,' Jane replied with a twitch of her lips. 'One of them smells of Miss Bellingham's perfume... Now, what would a young lady of sense be doing writing to you, I wonder?'

'None of your business, madam,' her brother said and snatched at the envelopes she held tantalisingly out of his reach. Lady Jane March laughed delightedly and withheld the letters for a second longer before releasing them to the younger brother she adored. She was an elegant lady, tall and slender, something about her making her instantly light up any room she entered, though her beauty could not disguise the sadness in those wonderful eyes.

Jane had chosen to make her home with the brother she'd always favoured, after her husband's untimely demise on the field at Wellington's side. Harry had been one of the Iron Duke's aides and so handsome it took her breath away, and his tragic death two years previously had broken her heart. The head of the family, John, Earl Sutherland, her half-brother, and his wife Gussie had offered Jane a home with them but she'd chosen to come here to William, her junior by just one year, because, as she said, *Will* was the only one who wouldn't either treat her with kid gloves or bully her.

'You will no doubt wish me the other side of the world within a month,' she'd told Will when he greeted her on her arrival at what had been their father's smaller country estate and was now his, John having inherited the main seat, of course. 'But Gussie would have driven me mad—and you know what John is…'

'I do indeed,' Will said ruefully. 'He's such an old stickler. Poor dear Mama used to go in fear of him until she married Porky…'

'God bless the Duke of Roshithe,' Jane said with a wry smile. Their mother had become a much loved and spoiled second wife, outliving her first husband by some years. Indeed, she had remarried after Jane's marriage because, she said, her dearest William did not need her help to find a wife. He had the fortune his maternal grandfather had left him, as well as the small estate from his father, consisting of a town house, a shooting box in Scotland and acres of land somewhere in Yorkshire. He was probably wealthier than his elder brother and never asked John to pay his debts, but that didn't stop the earl giving him advice on how to manage his fortune on every possible occasion.

'With your face and fortune, your problem will be in

fending off the ladies rather than finding a bride,' his mama had said before departing to the Continent with her doting second husband in tow for an extended wedding trip. Porky, as his friends and family persisted in calling him, despite his old and respected title, had been led by petticoat strings ever since Mama had taken him in hand and was blissfully happy to serve and adore her. He'd loved her all his life and been dismayed that her father had preferred the earl as a son-in-law; of course, Porky had never been expected to inherit the dukedom, and it was only after a string of unfortunate relatives met their deaths that he reluctantly came into it.

'I'm damned if I want that mouldering old house of Roshithe's,' he'd said on hearing the news. 'Of what use is the title and country seat to me? I never go near the place, never have and never will.'

'You will accept it to please me,' his lady said. 'I shall take precedence over John's wife—and that will not suit her consequence...'

To give him his due, Porky hadn't uttered another word of protest. If it suited his lady to become the Duchess of Roshithe it would suit him—and he understood perfectly the veiled hints and slights she had suffered at the hands of the earl's wife. Instead of complaining further, he'd given a grand ball, to which he'd invited anyone of consequence and it had afforded him a quiet amusement to see the countess having to curtsey to her mama-in-law, something she'd refused to do once her husband became the earl.

Jane and Will had watched their darling mama's success in society with barely held mirth, for she did so enjoy it. As a young bride, married for consequence and money, Helen had suffered at her pompous husband's hands as well as at the hands of his equally pompous eldest son, the child of his first wife—a lady of far greater family but less fortune. Helen had brought her husband a large dowry, but her father had been wise enough to tie most of it up so that it remained with her and her children after her husband died. Not that she needed it now for Porky was richer than any of them, perhaps one of the richest men in England—and he had little to do with his wealth but spend it on his bride and her children, Will and Jane. John, of course, was deemed to have enough of his own, though whether he would have agreed if asked was doubtful. He was far too polite to mention it, of course, though he frowned over the vast sums squandered on his stepmother's vanity—as he called it.

Immersed in her letters, Jane became aware that Will was hovering. She looked up and smiled, because she knew her dearest one so well.

'You want something,' she said. 'Come on, what is it?'

'Dearest Jane,' Will murmured, his blue eyes sparkling with mischief. 'You know me so well... It's Melia Bellingham. Her aunt has taken sick at the last minute and she won't be able to come to London next month... unless you will be her chaperon, Jane? Please say you will. She's been looking forward to this visit for so long...'

'Amelia Bellingham shouldn't have written to you,

Will. Her aunt must write to me if she wishes me to chaperon her niece.'

'I'm sure Mrs Bellingham's letter is in your pile,' he said. 'You had such a lot. Why do you always get piles and piles of letters? I never get more than two or three and most of them are just bills…'

'Perhaps because I write lots of letters,' Jane said, her mouth quirking at the corners. 'It is my chief occupation most of the time—unless we go up to London to visit Mama and then it's just non-stop balls and dinners and all the rest…'

'Mama loves to entertain, and she has so many friends.'

'Of course she does,' Jane said drily. 'They queue for the lavish dinners Porky puts on. It beats me how Mama can be exposed to all that rich food day in and day out and never put on so much as a pound.'

'Because she eats like a bird and always did,' Will said. 'You're just like her, Jane, and will never put on weight. You will invite Melia to stay with us, won't you?'

'Of course, if you wish it,' Jane agreed. 'It's your house, my dearest. I'm your guest and I dare say you may invite whomever you wish…'

'You know I couldn't invite Miss Bellingham,' Will said. 'She must have a chaperon—and you've known her all her life, practically grew up together.'

'Her elder sister was my friend,' Jane said and a sigh escaped, because her friendship with Beth Bellingham brought back memories of Harry. Beth had been in love with him, as had most of the young girls that season…but he'd only had eyes for Jane, and she missed him so much, so very much. Sometimes in the night the ache was like a sword thrust in her chest. 'I like Melia, Will—and I'll be glad to invite her.' She shuffled through her letters and opened the one from Melia's aunt, nodding as she rose to pen an immediate answer. That done, she rang the bell and gave her letter to the footman. 'Have that one sent immediately please, Flowers.'

'Yes, my lady,' the footman said, inclining his head correctly. Only the very observant might have seen the look of devotion in the man's eyes as he bowed and left the room. Will knew that all the servants adored Jane. It wouldn't make things easy for his wife when he married, because Jane was undoubtedly the mistress here— and he'd been glad of it until he began to realise that he was actually thinking of marriage.

'So?' Jane asked as she rose from her elegant chair and closed the writing desk she'd brought with her on her return from France. 'Am I to wish you happy quite soon?'

'Well, if Melia is of the same mind when she's had her season, yes,' Will said. 'You do wish me happy, Jane? I know it makes things awkward for you…'

'Nonsense,' she said. 'I've taken advantage of your good nature for too long. I have a perfectly good house of my own a few miles from John and Gussie and I shall probably take a house in Bath once I decide to settle. I should have done it a year ago, when I put off my blacks.'

'But how can you live alone?' her brother asked. 'I

know you don't want to live with John, but Gussie isn't too bad—or Mama…'

'I wouldn't dream of treading on her toes,' Jane said, laughing softly. 'And you know Gussie would drive me mad within a fortnight…'

'You could stay on here. Melia likes you so much…'

'And I like her and I want it to stay that way,' Jane said gently. 'No, my dearest brother, I shall not make your wife's life difficult. It's quite simple; I must find a companion…'

'Well, I suppose—but who is there that you could put up with? You're not the most patient of women, Jane.'

'I am not in the least patient,' she said. 'But—do you remember Cousin Sarah? You might not recall her because you were away at school when she came to stay. It was shortly before Papa died…'

'I seem to remember her at the funeral. She was tall and thin and plain…and her mother was always demanding things, making her life hell.'

'Yes, well, Aunt Seraphina died last month and Cousin Sarah wrote to me asking if I knew of a position that would suit her. I was thinking of asking her on a visit to see how we got on—and, if we can bear each other, I shall set up house with her in Bath.'

'But can you imagine what John would say to such a suggestion? Sarah Winters could never be a chaperon for you, Jane. She isn't old enough and she has no consequence.'

'And needs none in my house. I was married for a year before Harry died,' Jane said, her face pale. 'I am Lady March, a widow of independent means, and that is exactly how I intend to live…' She arched her fine dark brows as he stared at her. 'After the freedom of marriage and then living here with you—do you really think I could live with John and his wife?'

Will stared at her for a few minutes and then nodded. 'Of course you couldn't, Jane—but they will all be against it, even Mama.'

'Mama wants me to marry again, Will. If I went to stay with her she would present me to all the eligible men she knows, and keep on doing it until I gave in. I married for love and would never marry for any other reason—indeed, I value my independence.'

'You don't think it might be a better arrangement to marry someone you could admire if not love? You would have a large house and a husband to help you…'

'I couldn't even think of it yet,' Jane replied and her throat tightened. 'I know it's a year since I came out of blacks, but I still grieve; I still think of him all the time and wish…'

'Of course you do and I'm a brute to suggest anything that upsets you, love. Please forgive me.'

Will was sincere in his apology and his sister was pleased to tell him there was nothing to forgive. They parted on good terms, Jane to write to Cousin Sarah, and Will to ride his new young horse that he had great pleasure in schooling. It had taken him a while to tame the brute, but it could go like the wind and he'd a mind to race the young stallion, riding him himself, of course. He was whistling as he strolled down to the stables, content with his world, which looked like continuing in the same happy-go-lucky way it always had.

Will was lucky. Everyone said so and he saw no reason why his luck shouldn't continue. Melia would marry him and be content to live in the country, apart from a few visits to town, which was exactly the way he wished to live...

'Oh, look, dear Aunt—' Melia Bellingham opened her letter from Lady March and her deep blue eyes lit with excitement as she showed the very fine calligraphy to the lady, who had now recovered enough from her illness to sit in a chair but was still far too fragile to contemplate taking a lively young woman to London. 'You will not mind my leaving you here alone? Please say I may go—for I am sure I am of little use to you. You always say I make your head ache, Aunt Margaret.'

The older woman sighed and sniffed the lace kerchief soaked in lily of the valley perfume. 'You have so much energy, Amelia. It's no wonder I find your company tiring, especially when I feel a little fragile. However, I should not wish to disappoint you in this matter, and of course you may go to Lady March. I would have preferred you to be in your sister's care, but poor dear Beth is increasing and cannot entertain you. You must write a pretty letter to Lady March and thank her.'

'She says she will send her carriage to bring me to her at home in the country, and then we may travel to London together. I must write my reply at once because otherwise she will not get my letter in time...'

'Child, you are always in such a hurry,' her aunt said and waved the heavily scented kerchief at her. 'Please go away now and send Miss Beech to me. I need quiet companionship.'

Melia skipped away, only too happy to be set free of her duty to her aunt. Aunt Margaret had been good to her and Beth, though Beth had not needed much from their long-suffering aunt for she'd been eighteen when their parents were lost at sea on what was meant to be a pleasure trip to Papa's estates in Ireland. Such a storm had blown up that the yacht had been buffeted on to the rocks far off its course on the wild Cornish coast and both crew and passengers drowned in the terrible storm.

Grieving and not knowing what to do, the sisters had been taken in by their kindly aunt, for they had little choice but to leave their home. Papa's estates were naturally entailed and fell to a distant cousin they had never met and who presently resided in India. The girls both had small dowries, put aside by their father, and two thousand pounds each left to them by their maternal grandfather. Had it not been for the kindness of Aunt Margaret Bellingham, they would have been forced to live in a small house in a village somewhere—or so the very formal solicitor had informed them soon after the funeral.

However, six months later, when they had both removed from their home and Beth was already married, a letter had come to say that they might remain at the house for as long as they wished. It seemed that their father's cousin had no intention of returning from India at present and even when he did so would not wish to deprive the sisters of their home. He had written to an agent who would look after the estate and would let them know when the new owner was thinking of returning to England.

It had been too late for Beth and Amelia. Beth had married and was happily living at her husband's estate, and Melia was living rather less happily with her aunt. Aunt Margaret was not in the least unkind, nor did she make unreasonable demands of her niece, but she was too old to attend many parties and those she did were very dull. She'd promised Melia a season in London when she was eighteen, but a nasty bout of gastro-enteritis had laid her low and then, just as she was recovering, she'd caught a chill. Her doctor said that London was out of the question, and Melia had almost resigned herself to giving up all idea of going to town until Beth was over the birth of her child and had finished nursing the babe.

'I shall be on the shelf by then,' Melia had told her friend Jacqui as they walked together through the grounds of Aunt Margaret's house. 'I shall die of boredom before I ever have a chance to fall in love and be married.'

'What about Viscount Salisbury?' her friend asked slyly. 'I thought you and he swore undying love when you stayed at Beth's house in the country?'

'Yes, we did,' Melia said, her eyes dancing with merriment. 'Shall I tell you a secret?' She laughed as Jacqui nodded eagerly. 'Well, he has been in the district visiting friends twice since then and we walked and rode together—and he has written to me and I to him...'

'You could not!' her friend cried, shocked. 'That is

so forward of you, Melia. Whatever would your aunt say if she knew?'

'Well, she does not know for Bess gets the letters from the receiving house and brings them to me without her seeing them.'

'She would be so angry if she knew you had deceived her.' Jacqui was in awe and yet a little censorious. 'Mama would shut me in my room for a month on bread and water if I did such a thing.'

'Well, you wouldn't,' Melia replied and hugged her arm. 'I dare say I should not had Mama lived. She would have invited young people to the house for me and I might have been engaged by now.'

'Has the viscount asked you?'

'No, but he will if I wish it.' Melia's eyes sparkled wickedly. 'I am not yet sure if I wish to marry him, but I do want to find out. If we were to go to London, I should have the chance to meet so many pleasant young men…'

'Well, you must get your aunt to write to Lady March and ask if she would be kind enough to have you as her guest when she goes up to town. I know for a fact that she has chaperoned other young girls since she was widowed, for one was my cousin. As you know her brother, Viscount Salisbury, I dare say he would prevail upon her to invite you.'

Melia had thought her friend's suggestion a good one, for the families had been close before Jane and Beth were married, but, to make certain of a favourable answer, she'd written of her aunt's illness to the viscount. The letter had clearly done its work and now she was to visit London, as she'd hoped—and, if she could achieve it, she would be engaged before the end of her visit, either to Viscount Salisbury or another...

Having finished her letter, Melia rang the bell for Bess. The maidservant had come to her aunt's house with her and was devoted to her. Bess would not mind walking down to the village to see the letter went as soon as the next post bag was sent off to London. However, when she answered the bell, Bess was carrying a silver salver on which resided a letter addressed to Melia.

'Thank you,' she said and smiled at the woman who had nursed her from a babe and now looked after her clothes and tended her hair. 'I want this letter to go off straight away. I'm going to visit Lady March and she is taking me to London—and you'll be coming with us, Bess. You will enjoy that, won't you?'

'Well, miss, I know you will and I don't mind anything if you're happy.'

'You are the best friend I ever had,' Melia said and pounced on the plump, kind woman, arms about her waist as she kissed her cheek. 'I do love you, Bess.'

'Get on with you, Miss Melia,' Bess said but her face was pink and smiling. 'I'll take your letter for you, no need for flattery...'

'I wonder who could be writing to me,' Melia said as she looked at the seal and then frowned, for it was a family crest. 'Good gracious! Can this possibly be from...?' She broke the wax seal and glanced at the letter.

Scanning the first few lines, Melia discovered that it was from someone calling himself her Cousin Paul.

Papa's cousin, not hers, Melia thought with a little frown. A look of annoyance settled over her pretty face as she continued to read the contents of her surprising letter.

I was concerned to learn that you had been asked to leave your home. It was against my wishes and I do most sincerely apologise for it. My hope is that you will forgive the mistake and return to your home. Clearly you cannot live there alone, though on my return from India in early June I shall be living at my house in London and will pay only brief visits to Willow House.

However, it is my intention that you shall be introduced into Society under the aegis of a friend of my mother's, Lady Moira Fairhaven. Lady Moira, widowed these eighteen months past, is preparing to take her place in Society again this year, and will live with you at Willow House until you come up to London. She will be with you by the end of May and you may become accustomed to each other before coming to the house I shall take for you in town.
Yours sincerely,
Paul Frant

Well, really! Melia could not see why he should write her such a letter—as if the fact that he had inherited Papa's estate made him her guardian. He was no such thing and she had no intention of doing as he asked. She would keep to her intention of being Lady March's guest, though, had she not already arranged things to her liking, she supposed she might have been grateful to her father's cousin for his offer.

Aunt Margaret must not know that she'd received this letter. If she read the contents she would say that Melia must remain here to meet her chaperon and do as her distant cousin asked. Putting her letter carefully away in the secret drawer of her writing slope, Melia wondered uncomfortably if perhaps her father's will had given this distant cousin power over her. Yet surely Papa would never do such a thing? Neither she nor Beth had ever met the gentleman. She knew nothing about him, and she did not wish to. It was most disobliging of him to return to England now, just when Melia had everything in hand. She knew that if she wished to marry a suitable gentleman, her aunt would be only too willing to oblige her—but this stranger might have other ideas…

Chapter Two

'This is being too kind, Adam,' Paul Frant said. 'I never expected you to accompany me to London, my dear fellow. Your help on the ship was invaluable, for I must confess that I have never felt quite as ill in my life as I did when that fever struck. However, I am on the mend now and you might have gone to your own estates after we docked at Portsmouth. I know you must have business to attend.'

'I've never before known you to have a day's illness,' Adam, once Captain of His Majesty's Own Guards, serving with the Indian troops, and now, newly, Viscount Hargreaves, said with a faint twist of his mouth. 'It was not like you, for you fought on the Peninsula in Spain and came through, despite being wounded twice. I was concerned, my dear fellow. You still look a trifle weary.'

'I feel less than my normal healthy self,' Paul replied truthfully. 'It pains me to say it, but for a while there I believed it was the end. I must have been carrying the fever with me, for some of my colleagues had it at the Company offices before I left. Poor Mainwaring died of it, leaving a widow and two young sons in England. His death was a part of the reason I decided to come home. Before he died, he asked me to make sure that his family received his pension and all that was due to him. I think he'd hoped to make his fortune out there, but unfortunately he was not good at business.'

'Unlike you,' Adam said with a wry twist of his lips. 'You must be as rich as Croesus, Frant.'

'I haven't done too badly out of the Company,' Paul said modestly. 'Enough to give that poor child of Bellingham's a decent dowry. I inherited the charge of her along with the title, for which I have not the slightest use, but I must accept it, I suppose, if I choose to live here. I'm not sure yet whether I shall do so. I may return to India when I've seen to things in England. I'm not certain I could settle to the life of an English gentleman.'

'Find it a trifle dull after fighting the wild tribesmen of the hills, eh?' Adam gave him an odd look. 'Or is it the lure of a beautiful woman that calls you back, my friend?'

'I had little time for ladies of any description; I left that to you and the rest of the Army,' Paul mocked him gently. 'Annamarie was beautiful; I give you that— but she was not to be trifled with. Only if I'd decided to marry her would I have thought of trying to capture her heart. If indeed she has one; I found her charming but with little real warmth.' Paul had thought there was something hard and cold about the woman so many men admired.

'She is a proud beauty,' Adam said. 'I admired her. It must be hard to be of mixed birth as she is, Paul. Her father was an Indian prince, her mother an English lady. Annamarie says that her father was married to her mother by a Christian priest; his other wives went into purdah after he died but Princess Helena was allowed to leave the palace and bring up her daughter as she pleased in a palace of her own. One might almost say that she'd been cast out by her royal relatives. Because of her marriage, which was not in the Indian way, some of her husband's people think her a concubine rather than a wife.'

'Yes, that is unfortunate. Princess Helena sent her daughter to the school for the daughters of English gentlemen,' Paul said. 'Annamarie was brought up to believe she was legitimate and, since her maternal grandfather still lives in Shropshire and is an earl, she has been accepted by some of the officer's ladies…but not all. If it had not been for Colonel Bollingsworth's wife, she might have found herself ostracised, but most followed her lead and accepted Annamarie into their company.'

'Out there, some of the ladies allow a little leeway.' Adam nodded to himself. 'You know as well as I do why her mother does not send Annamarie to school in England. She would not be accepted into the top echelons of Society here, I think.'

'Then Society is a fool,' Paul said angrily. 'She has every right to be accepted here, but it is the same in

India—her father's people treat her as an outcast. I believe she and her mother might do better to come home to England. I am sure such beauty as Annamarie's would find many admirers and, if she were taken up by the Regent's set, might do well enough.'

'Yes, perhaps…' Adam eased his long legs as the carriage drew to a halt. 'Ah, I believe we are here. This is your house, Paul?'

'It was my father's but now mine,' Paul replied with a twist of his lips. He was a good strong man, with fine legs and broad shoulders. Seen in company with Adam, he might not be thought handsome, but there was nothing coarse or ugly in his features. His chin was square and forthright, his eyes clear, his gaze sometimes piercing, but his mouth was softer than the rest of his features, a clue to the warmth of his heart. He had warm brown eyes and light brown hair, but not the pure blond of his companion's locks. Adam's profile was almost beautiful, his hair short but softly curled about perfect features, his eyes a blue some called cerulean and his mouth sensuous. His body had all the proportions of a Greek god and his skin the natural tan that came from being accustomed to a life outdoors in a warm climate.

'Ah yes, your father.' Adam frowned, uncertain now. 'As I recall, you did not exactly see eye to eye with Lord Frant?'

'No, and never could after the way he treated my mother and I…'

Paul's eyes narrowed in anger. The row with his father after his mother died had split them apart. Paul had left his home vowing never to return while his father lived, and he'd kept his word. He'd made his own way, rising first to the rank of Major with Wellington at Salamanca and then, after a wound to his leg from which he recovered well, gave up the Army that would have bound him to an administrative position and used his share of the prize money to go out to India and invest with the Company. Some shrewd business moves had made him richer than he'd expected, and a fortunate encounter with a rich Maharaja had resulted in him being made an honorary son and given lands and palaces. If he chose to return to India, he could live like a prince and marry almost anyone he chose.

Paul knew that Annamarie had hoped he would ask her to be his wife. Because he'd once saved the life of a prince, Paul had a unique position in the region. It would have suited the daughter of an English lady and an Indian prince to marry a man who had both English rank and Indian favour. Together they might have been second in importance to the present Maharaja in the district. She'd made it quite clear that she hoped for a proposal of marriage before he left for England, but Paul had not been sure what he wanted.

In England he had inherited his father's title and estates, but he knew that his younger brother—the son of his father's second wife, although still only in his teens, would have been delighted to step into his shoes. Paul had no need of his family estates in England—and in particular he had not needed the bother of the small estate that had come to him through a distant cousin. The young girls who were made his wards by Bellingham's will were a part of Paul's reason for returning. Although he'd been told the older girl had married well, that still left the younger one—at eighteen, she was ready for marriage if a husband could be found for her. To that end, Paul had written to an old friend of his mother who had recently been widowed, asking her if she would be kind enough to chaperon the young girl. She had graciously given her consent, though the exchange of letters had taken months to complete. It was imperative that the girl be chaperoned, for Paul was unmarried and could therefore not fulfil his task of guardian without female assistance.

Some years had passed since Paul had met Lady Moira. He'd been seventeen then and it had been just before his mother died of grief over her husband's infidelity, and the terrible quarrel that caused him to leave home and become an officer in the Guards. Fortunately, he'd had some small fortune left him by his maternal grandmother and when his own father cut him off without a penny was able to survive on his pay as an officer and his allowance from the inheritance. Later, he'd won prize money and honours and life had become much easier when an uncle left him a small fortune.

Paul knew that his father had bequeathed everything that was not entailed to his half-brother. He minded that not at all, and would have been glad to pass the rest of it over had he been sure he did not wish to live in England, but some small perverse part of him clung to what his father had been forced to leave him. How it must have gone against the grain with Lord Frant to know that the son of the wife he'd married for her dowry would have his title.

Paul would have freely admitted that the woman his father had taken in his mother's place was beautiful. Goodness knew, his own mother had been far from a beauty, but she had a beautiful nature, gentle and loving—and her heart had been broken by her husband's cold indifference.

Watching his mother fade, become frailer and sadder, had broken the young Paul's heart and after her death he'd railed at his father for his cruelty.

'I never loved her,' his father had told him bluntly. 'I needed her money to restore my estates—but it was not the fortune I'd been led to believe. A paltry twenty thousand…'

'Twenty thousand would have been a fortune to many,' Paul said. 'If you'd put it to good use instead of wasting it on gambling and women…'

'Your mother came from trade and it has not yet been bred out of you,' his father sneered. 'Had I known I should get no more when the old man died I'd never have taken the silly bitch.'

Paul had tried to knock him down then, but his father was a strong bull of a man and he'd sent the youth flying. Even so, Paul had tried again and again, until his face was cut and bleeding and he could not rise.

'Well, you can take yourself off where you came from,' his father said. 'Go back to the mills and dens of the North and stay where you belong…'

His taunt was a cheap one, for though his maternal grandfather's wealth had come from the mills of the North, they had been sold two generations back and the money invested in land. However, the Martins were better mill owners than farmers and much of their former wealth had been badly invested. Paul had received a bequest of ten thousand pounds on his grandfather's death, and was the owner of several hundred acres of farmland, but had the family still owned the mills they would have been worth more.

Lord Frant had inherited the ten thousand that would have come to his wife on her father's death, but thought nothing of the sum and promptly lost it in a week of frantic gambling at the tables.

Paul had known nothing of this or his own inheritance for some years, by which time he was well on the way to making his own fortune. Now, on the verge of entering the house that had been his father's, he felt chilled. Standing in the dark, unwelcoming hall, he thought of turning tail and finding accommodation in a hotel, but pride would not let him.

'Welcome home, my lord. It's good to see you back.'

Paul looked hard at the black-clothed footman who had opened the door to them and his brow wrinkled in concentration. 'Is it Matthews?' he asked at last and saw the smile on the man's face.

'Yes, my lord,' he said. 'I worked as a boot boy when you were a lad, sir, then as a man of all work. I was made up to footman six years back.'

'Were you now?' Paul nodded, looking him over. He glanced about him. 'I seem to remember this hall looked different when I last stayed here.'

The smile left Matthews's face. 'Yes, sir. I regret to say that his late lordship sold much of the furniture and the paintings last year.'

'In debt again, I suppose,' Paul said and sighed. 'Has he left me anything worth having?'

'Not much, my lord,' the footman replied. 'The bedrooms are mostly the same but the silver, pictures and some porcelain pieces have been sold. Your mother's rooms were stripped bare years ago…' Matthews looked awkward. 'Thought you should know, sir.'

'Well, what are a few bits and pieces?' Paul said and laughed ruefully as he turned to his companion. 'I'm sorry to bring you to such a place, Adam—but I dare say we've a bed to offer and, I hope, some food.'

'Oh, yes, sir. Your instructions have been followed. A new housekeeper and cook were hired and the rooms opened up and cleaned. Mrs Brooks says she's made one room look proper for you, sir; it used to be her ladyship's sitting room…that is to say your mother's room, my lord. I believe a fire has been lit there for you…'

'Thank goodness someone has some sense,' Paul said as he led the way through to a room he knew well. Matthews was directing two other footmen to carry his bags upstairs, and a woman had appeared from the room at the far end of the hall. She hurried forward, seeming flustered.

'We were not sure when to expect you, sir.'

'I think we should like some wine and a light meal in the green room, Mrs Brooks.'

'Yes, my lord. I understood it was the room you favoured as a lad—and the other room usable is what was known as the library, sir.'

'Don't tell me the books have been sold?'

'Some of them, sir. However, it is quite comfort-

able—until your lordship decides what to do about re-
furbishing the other rooms...'

Paul gave a wry laugh. The Frant library had contained some rare books and the loss of those meant
more to him than any silver or paintings, but he could
not do anything about that loss. His father had sold everything he could without actually breaking the entail,
and he supposed he ought to have expected it. Had he
come home with only a few guineas in his pocket he
would have been in trouble, but as it was he could afford
to smile at the pettiness of the man he'd called Father.

At least his mother's room was comfortable, though
not as he'd remembered it. Nothing of hers remained,
but everything decent in the house must have been
placed here and the comfortable wing chairs by the fire
were more than adequate, as was the mahogany desk
and elbow chair, the large settee and the sideboard on
which some fine glasses and decanters stood waiting.

'At least it seems I have some wine to offer you,'
Paul said, casting an eye over the contents. 'Brandy,
Madeira or Burgundy?'

'A glass of Madeira, please,' Adam said and stretched
out in one of the chairs. 'Well, you'll be busy now, my
friend, though I do not envy you the task. Buying furnishings is not my idea of amusement.'

'Nor mine,' Paul said and laughed. 'I imagine I can
find someone to do it for me.'

'Know what you need?'

'No. What?' Paul asked with his lazy smile.

'What you need, my friend, is a wife,' Adam said, a
faint challenge in his eyes. 'Just the thing for making

a man's house look comfortable. I'm thinking of getting one myself now I've given up adventuring—and if I were you I should do the same...'

'It's odd that you should say it,' Paul said thoughtfully. 'I have been wondering if perhaps I ought not to offer her marriage—Bellingham's girl, you know. I'm damned if I wanted her father's estate, but perhaps I ought to offer her a home. I could only do that if I married her...'

'I should think about it for a while if I were you,' Adam advised. 'You haven't seen her yet—and she is a little young for you, is she not?'

'You are quite right, which is why my words were mere idle speculation. No, I shall not marry unless I find the right woman...'

'You at least do not need to look for a fortune,' Adam said and there was the faintest trace of envy in his voice. 'You have more than enough for any man.'

'Yes, I have been lucky,' Paul agreed, 'but it was honestly earned—and I have not yet decided where to settle...'

'You won't return to India?'

'I do not know.' Paul sighed. 'It has been my home for several years—I am not sure there is anything to keep me here. You came home to settle your affairs, Adam—shall you return after you have done so?'

'I am in two minds,' Adam said and his eyes stared at a point beyond Paul's shoulder. 'It depends on many things. Not least whether I have sufficient funds to live decently here...'

'Surely your father has not left anything away from you? You were his only son.'

'No, but the question is—has he actually left me anything but debts?' Adam asked wryly. 'I did not earn a fortune out there as you did, Paul—and, for all I know, I may be a pauper...'

Chapter Three

'This is so very kind of you,' Melia cried, looking round the pretty bedroom with delight. 'My aunt is very good to me, but, poor dear, she could hardly be expected to bring me to town. Such a delightful room...'

'My brother was concerned that you should have the best guest room, Miss Bellingham,' Jane said, smiling at the girl's pleasure. 'It is a lovely room. I have stayed here myself many times in the past.'

'Oh, you should not have given me your room,' Melia said. 'I do not wish to put you out, dear Lady March.'

'No, you have not,' Jane said, shaking her head. 'This was my room as a girl, but now I have a permanent suite of three rooms at the other side of the house. At least, it has been mine since...for a while now. Of course, when my brother marries I shall take a house of my own. I am thinking of making my home in Bath.'

'You will not desert the viscount?' Melia cried involuntarily. 'I know he is so fond of you, relies on you for advice in almost everything.'

'He will turn to the lady he marries once he becomes a devoted husband and I should not wish to interfere with her way of running the household.'

'Oh, but perhaps she would rather leave it to you.' Melia's face was an open book. Jane held back her smile because it was obvious that the young woman had no interest in the duties of a chatelaine, but thought only of the amusement of being a bride and being spoiled by a devoted husband. 'If his wife is young and knows little of household management. I hate dealing with servants; they are always so superior if they think you don't know—don't you find?'

Jane's merriment left her and she answered seriously. 'It is important that one does know what one wants. The first rule is to make your people respect you. It is good if they also like you—but a calm, firm manner when giving instructions is always best. You must have observed it in your aunt's house.'

'Oh, no,' Melia said ingenuously. 'Aunt is so lazy. Her butler rules the household and arranges everything as she likes it. He has been with her since she was a girl and treats her as if he were a benevolent uncle. She never seems to give orders. Benson just does everything without needing to be told.'

'How fortunate is Mrs Bellingham to have such a devoted man in her service.'

'She is always complaining about things, but never to Benson, of course. She might have everything as she likes if she stirred herself, but she can never be bothered and just leaves it all to him—and then she grumbles if the meals are not quite what she wanted.'

'Well, at least you know how not to conduct your household,' Jane said, amused by this description of the indolent Mrs Bellingham. 'Now, my dear, I want you to settle in first and come down when you are ready. I shall order some tea in half an hour in my sitting room downstairs, but you may have a tray brought up if you wish to rest.'

'I am not in the least tired,' Melia declared. 'I shall come down and join you... Do you mean that very pleasant sunny room at the back of the house?'

'Yes, it was Mama's until she remarried,' Jane said. 'Now, of course, she has a dozen pretty rooms she may choose from, and if she wants anything different she has only to ask Porky.'

'Is that what you call the duke?' Melia's eyes sparkled with mischief as Jane nodded and laughed. 'Oh, it does suit him—but it is a terrible thing to call such a lovely man. He was so kind to me when I attended the wedding as one of your mama's bridesmaids—and he gave me a beautiful gold bracelet as a gift.'

'Roshithe is a lovely man, and so kind to us all,' Jane said. 'I assure you, the name was given him years ago and stuck. He does not regard it, because he knows it is used with affection. His enemies are more likely to call him Roshithe in a supercilious manner, and that he does resent—though you should probably address him as sir, unless he gives you permission to use the name.'

'I would not dare. I shall probably address him as Your Grace...'

'He cannot abide that sort of toad-eating, as he calls

it, Miss Bellingham. Much better just to use the simple sir.'

'I'll try to remember,' Melia promised and gave Jane a small shy smile. 'Will you not call me Melia?'

'Yes, of course, if you wish it—and you must reciprocate. I am Jane to my family and friends.'

'Yes, I know. Viscount Salisbury always speaks of you that way. He is very fond of you, Jane.'

'We have always been close,' Jane said. 'I shall leave you to change if you wish.'

She left the bedchamber, which was indeed the prettiest in the house, its curtains pink and white striped silk, which matched the décor of pinks, cream and a deep crimson. Jane had ordered some pink roses to be placed on the dressing stand to complete the welcome offered to a lady who might, if she chose, become the next mistress here.

It would mean a big change in Jane's life, she thought as she made her way down to the sitting room she favoured. She would miss playing hostess for her brother and it would be an upheaval making the move to Bath, but she intended to make way for her brother's wife, despite Melia's hints that she would be welcome to stay on to run the house for her. No, that would eventually lead to resentment and perhaps unkind words between them; Melia might need help at first but once she found her own confidence she would not wish for another woman in her home.

Jane had already begun to make inquiries about a house in Bath. She was unsure whether she wished to rent a place while she looked about her or buy something immediately. If she bought she would need to furnish it, and she intended to look for suitable items while she was in town this time. Even if her brother Will was not successful in securing his bride immediately, it would happen, and Jane had no wish to live in the country house left to her by her husband.

'It's a bit dull and quite lonely,' Harry had told her the day he took her to see his small country house. 'I know we can make it nice, Jane—and with servants and children it will soon become a home. I dare say we'll make friends soon enough. There's plenty of time before we have to retire to a country life, because I want to rise in the Army. We can live in London when we're home on leave—and in time you will find a way to make this place into a home.'

Jane had assured him gaily that she would enjoy it, but that future had seemed so far away as not to be of much interest. Before they settled down to living off the land, they had so much fun to have—travelling overseas, putting up at the most frightful billets had all seemed amusing to the young couple in love. Her friends were Harry's friends, the ladies she met officers' wives, all living their nomad existence with a smile on their faces and secret fear in their hearts. Yet, even so, Jane had not thought it could all end so abruptly. She'd thought of her life as being married to Harry for years and years, but in fact she'd had only a year of happiness.

She would not think of that! Jane told herself severely that she must begin to look to the future. She had already written to her cousin. Sarah's reply had not arrived before they left for London, but Will's servants would send on any letters and, if Sarah wished, Jane would invite her to join them in town.

She would make a few inquiries about whom to consult on the matter of furnishing a house, but perhaps it might be better to hire a furnished house for a start, though Jane had some of her personal things at her brother's country house. She had intended to set up her own home long ago but living in Will's home had proved so pleasant for them both that she'd let her own plans drift.

'It is lovely to have you here again, ma'am,' Mrs Yates, Will's London housekeeper, came up to her as she reached the hall. 'There are quite a few letters waiting for you in the parlour, Lady March. I dare say your ladyship's friends knew of your intention and most of them look like invitations.'

'Yes, I dare say,' Jane replied with a faint twist of her lips. 'Mama knew we were coming, of course, and I imagine she has informed most of her friends—and that includes everyone who gives decent parties...'

Jane laughed softly as she saw an answering gleam in the housekeeper's eyes, because Mama was well known in this house. She picked up the large pile of letters and cards awaiting her and flicked through them. Three were in her mother's hand, each of them speaking of some party she really must attend or an exhibition she must see. Her mother intended to visit her the day after she arrived and she was to come to dinner that evening and bring the delightful young woman she'd invited as her guest.

Laying aside her mother's letters, Jane opened some

of the others. Most, as her housekeeper had guessed, were invitations to dances, masques, picnics, dinner and a grand ball. If she tried to attend them all, and this was the tip of the iceberg because as soon as it was known she was in town the invitations would pour in, she would need to attend three affairs in an evening so as not to offend the eager hostesses.

Picking up a neat cream-coloured envelope addressed to Lady March in a hand she did not recognise, Jane slit the seal and took out the piece of paper inside. She frowned as she read the few lines written on the single sheet.

Madam, Lady March,
Forgive me for writing when you do not know
me, but I have been informed that my ward, Miss
Amelia Bellingham, is to stay with you in town. I
would ask that you let me know when it is conve-
nient to call on you both.
Yours sincerely,
Paul Frant.

Brief and to the point, not particularly friendly, Jane thought as she scanned the lines again. She had not been aware that there was any other guardian than Mrs Bellingham. As Melia's father's widowed sister-in-law, she would surely be the proper person to have charge of the girl, Jane thought, but obviously Lord Frant—whoever he might be—thought differently.

It was slightly concerning, because the tone of the letter was distinctly cool. In fact, she would say that he'd been annoyed when he wrote the letter—only yesterday. She wondered if Melia knew of the gentleman and decided to ask when she came down for tea. Meanwhile, she continued to open her letters, discovering two more invitations for balls and one to the theatre from a close friend of her mother's.

Major Harte was some years older than Jane, but he had taken a fancy to her the last time she was in London and she'd received more than one proposal from him. As she knew he was a widower with two daughters under fifteen and needed a wife to keep them in order, Jane understood his persistence, but always gave him the same answer. She was not yet ready to remarry...

She had just finished sorting her letters into piles, those needing replies in one pile and the others in another, when the door opened to admit the housekeeper carrying a tray. Melia followed her in and tea was poured.

'I thought we would dine at home this evening,' Jane told her. 'It is the only night we shall be at home, because we are invited out almost every night for our entire stay, and will go from one to the other like bees gathering pollen from flowers.'

Melia laughed and looked delighted. 'Could we visit the duchess this afternoon? I do so like your mama, Jane.'

'She informed me that she would be out but would visit us tomorrow afternoon and expected us to dine at night. What we might do is visit my dressmaker and milliner, Melia. I think you might like some new clothes. Your own are pretty, but not quite as stylish as the fashions in town.'

'My aunt gave me fifty pounds, but I'm not sure how many clothes that will buy...' she said doubtfully and Jane smiled.

'Your aunt told me to have your dressmaking bills sent to her, my love. She would not expect you to spend your pin money on clothes. No, we shall have your measurements taken, and see if there is anything already made up that might fit you with some alteration.'

'Do you think there will be?' Melia looked anxious. 'At home it takes ages to have dresses made up.'

'Oh, I am sure Madame François will be able to accommodate us sooner than that,' Jane assured her. 'She has many girls working under her and takes no more than a day or so to complete a simple gown— and often there is a half-finished dress from a cancellation that we may have finished to your specification if you care for it.'

'Oh, good,' Melia said, excitement rising. 'How soon may we go?'

'We shall have our tea and some of these delightful sandwiches and biscuits Mrs Yates has brought us, and then we may fetch our bonnets. I shall have the carriage sent for in one hour...' She got up to ring the bell, then remembered the annoying letter.

'Do you know of a Paul Frant?' she asked. 'Is that the person who inherited your father's estate?'

'Lord Frant, yes...' Melia looked wary, her hand suspended as she was about to eat a tiny cucumber sandwich. 'He is in India I think...'

'According to the letter I received this morning, he must be in England as he has learned that you were coming to stay with me here—he has asked to meet us both at our earliest convenience. Did you know he was returning?'

'I didn't know when,' Melia said a little guiltily. 'He sent a letter but it was vague. I did not see why it should interfere with my plans...'

'No,' Jane replied, but she wasn't sure. Melia was underage and if her guardian had chosen to withhold permission for this visit he might have done so: Melia had clearly chosen to ignore his letter. 'What did he ask you to do?'

'Oh, he spoke of my returning to my father's estate and said that he would provide a chaperon for me,' Melia said with a shrug of her pretty shoulders. 'However, his meaning was vague, and I had already arranged this visit. If he wishes me to live at Willow House with a chaperon he must arrange it with my aunt—that is the proper way, do you not agree? After all, I know nothing of Lord Frant—or this lady he wishes to foist on me.'

'It would certainly be best for him to speak to both you and your aunt, to ascertain what your wishes are,' Jane agreed, but she felt slightly anxious on her young friend's behalf, for she surely did not wish to antagonise the man who might do something for her if he chose. Not that a dowry would signify if she took Will, because he could well afford to provide for his wife.

'Oh, well, I shall write this evening,' Jane said, dismissing the matter. 'Finish your meal, Melia, and then we'll change and visit my dressmaker. I wrote her that we might so she will be expecting us...'

'Oh, what a pretty little thing it is that you bring me to dress...' Madame Françoise cooed over Melia's trim figure. 'She ees perfection, no?'

'Yes, I believe Melia will take very well,' Jane said. 'Particularly, I think, if she is seen first in Society wearing one of your creations, *Madame*. Do you have anything at all that she could wear almost immediately?'

'Yes, I believe perhaps...there is the blue silk, Michelle—and the yellow net... Fetch them quickly!' Madame Françoise clapped her hands and the seamstress hurried to obey.

In all, four half-finished gowns were produced. They were orders that had been cancelled or changed after the work had begun and Madame was delighted to do the small amount of work needed to finish them to Miss Bellingham's liking. Melia was charmed with what she saw and easily pleased, agreeing to the four gowns and agonising over a wealth of materials, styles and trimmings until Jane declared it was enough for one day and assured Madame Françoise that she would receive more visits until an adequate wardrobe had been supplied.

Riding home in the carriage with Jane later that afternoon, Melia was excited and talked endlessly of the gowns they had ordered until at last she grew a little quiet, and then looked at her hostess anxiously.

'You do not think I have been too extravagant?' she asked in a small voice. 'I have very little money of my own and my aunt has already been generous...'

'Mrs Bellingham is not a poor woman,' Jane said. 'She assured me that she wanted you turned out in fine style, Melia. I should not worry if I were you. I shall pay for everything, and your aunt will reimburse me in good time.'

'You are both very good to me,' Melia said with the shy smile which Will's sister thought was probably what had drawn him to her. She had taken to the young girl and thought that if he did marry Melia he would most likely be very happy, for she had a sunny nature—even if she did bend the truth a little now and then.

It was as they approached Will's town house that they saw a man leaving it. He paused for a moment in the sunshine, looking about him in a manner that Jane could only describe as impatient, and then strode off in the opposite direction. She did not have long to wonder who it might have been for they encountered Will coming down the stairs as they entered and he exclaimed at once.

'Ah, there you both are! Lord Frant called in the hope of seeing you, Melia. At first he was quite put out at finding you both out—and seemed surprised that you should be staying here in my house. I had to explain that Jane lives with me and that you were her very good friend…'

'I do not see why he should be put out.' Jane frowned at him. 'I had his letter and intended writing to make an appointment for one morning this week. If he must call without one, he must not expect us to be sitting in waiting for him.'

Will looked a little surprised at her tone, for she did

not often speak so sharply. 'I wasn't aware that you knew him, Jane?'

'I do not,' she replied and laughed. 'His letter rubbed me up the wrong way. You had gone to your club, Will—and we decided to visit the dressmaker to have some new gowns made up for Melia. Had he said he would call this afternoon I would have put it off until to-morrow—though how Melia can be expected to appear in public without some decent clothes I do not know…'

'I dare say you've already taken care of all that,' Will said and grinned at her. 'Besides, Melia looks very pretty in what she's wearing.'

Since Melia was wearing a simple yellow gown of muslin over a thin petticoat with a charming bonnet of straw trimmed with matching ribbons, there was truth in his words, but only the silk shawl that Jane had lent her had given the ensemble a touch of town bronze. Since he saw his beloved through rose-tinted spectacles, he could not be expected to realise that—though, had his sister ever appeared in town in such a simple robe, he might have raised his eyebrows at her.

'Well, I shall write to Lord Frant and explain,' Jane said. 'Will, please ring for some tea for us all while I see to my letter—Melia will keep you company. Unless she has something more urgent pressing?'

Melia dimpled prettily and shook her head. She and Will walked into the front parlour, talking together animatedly. Jane thought the very ease of their manner together boded well for the future, but she was not certain that her young guest's mind was as firmly fixed on marriage as was her brother's.

She went into the smaller parlour that was her own when in town and sat down to pen a polite letter, explaining that she had taken Melia out to order some of the wardrobe she would need for the season. She apologised for wasting his time; had she known of his intention to call she would have waited in but, since they had arrived only that morning, Melia had been anxious to see a little of the town.

Feeling pleased with a letter that matched his in coolness, but was far politer, she sealed it with her own wax, mauve in colour, and pressed Harry's ring into it. Lord Frant should see that he was dealing with the widow of Lord March and not some little *nobody* he could order about as he pleased! She had informed him that she would be at home any morning that week from ten-thirty until twelve and he would be welcome to call in those hours, but at other times he might find them all out.

Paul frowned over the letter that had been brought to his house just as he was changing for the evening. He and Adam had been invited to dine at a gentleman's house and to play cards in the evening. Since the gentleman was an officer they'd known when serving with Wellington, both were delighted to accept.

Paul was not sure what to make of the letter. The paper smelled delightfully of a perfume that pleased the senses, but which he could not have named for it was subtler than the heavy perfumes he'd been used to in India. The writing was beautifully formed, but the message seemed glacial to him. What could he have done to deserve such excessive politeness? He'd seen middle-aged ladies giving the cold shoulder to some junior officers before this, but he himself had never been on the receiving end.

Lady March was probably some old trout with an acid tongue, he thought and grimaced. It was regrettable that he must call on her during the hours she'd set, for he normally steered well clear of those very haughty dames. However, since his ward had chosen to ignore his invitation to take up residence in her own home and await her chaperon and his ideas for her future, he had no choice. Had he been married, he would have had no hesitation in commanding Miss Bellingham to do as he bid her, but, as a single man of no more than one and thirty, he must be circumspect in his dealings with the young lady—and therefore he must try to get on to terms with the old biddy who had brought her to London. He had never met the Viscount Salisbury or any member of his family, but he'd been told by Mrs Bellingham that they were respectable people and rich. He'd thought Lady March a younger woman, but the tone of this letter made him think he'd been mistaken.

Well, he would forget it for this evening. Paul had already set things in motion regarding the furnishing of his house. Lady Moira had returned to town after discovering that her charge was not in residence at Paul's country house and, discovering that he was camping out in two rooms, promised to arrange for him to meet a very good man who would furnish his house in the latest style.

He'd thanked her, for although he had his own ideas

on what he wanted, he really had no idea where to start. Lady Moira knew all the best shops and the silk merchants—because, she said, when she called, all the drapes in the house needed refurbishment too.

Adam had told him he needed a wife, and a certain unease at the back of Paul's mind warned him that Lady Moira was thinking of herself as filling the position, which meant he would be reluctant to ask for her help furnishing his house. She was actually five years older, but because she dressed in the first style, was intelligent and up to date in her thinking, she seemed younger. Many men seemed to prefer a slightly older woman, and there was something very sensual about Lady Moira. Although Paul did not care for the perfume she wore; it was too heavy and reminded him of some that the ladies of easy virtue who pleasured the Army officers had a habit of wearing. Indeed, Lady Moira reminded him of a beautiful courtesan he'd been offered by the Indian Prince he'd saved from death.

'I owe you my life, *sahib*,' the young Prince told him. 'Selima is of royal blood and she is yours for the taking. She is trained to please men and she will show you tricks you never dreamed of, my dear lord and saviour.'

Paul had held his laughter inside for he knew the young man believed he was bestowing a great honour by giving him the services of the beautiful concubine, but he'd refused as politely as he could. A certain gleam in the woman's eyes had spoken of a sly nature and she'd held no appeal for him. However, to refuse point-blank would have been considered an insult, so Paul was forced to fabricate an excuse. He'd been preparing himself for marriage with his English bride, he'd said, and must forswear the pleasures of the flesh until his wedding so that he could do his bride justice.

This had found favour with the young Prince, who clapped his hands and said very seriously that he thought the *sahib* was wise not to waste his strength on a courtesan when he could have a sweet young bride. Selima would be waiting for him when he returned to India, his heir already born or on its way.

Everyone had felt certain that Paul would return. Why would he wish to live in a cold, wet climate when he could have a life of ease in the heat and splendour of palaces made cool by tinkling fountains and little pools, with lilies and beautiful courtesans to play in them and await the attentions of their master? A wife was necessary for sons, who could inherit his wealth, but after one had sons there was so much more to enjoy.

Paul did not truly know what he wished for. Since his return, almost two weeks since, he'd taken a trip into the country to look at various estates, hoping to find Miss Bellingham where he'd expected her to be. Failing that, he'd visited her aunt and finally returned to London in a less than contented mood. He was still not quite back to his full strength and felt the extra journey had been wasted. Finding that his ward was out when he'd called that afternoon had seemed the outside of enough, and now this letter... For two pins he would sell his estates here and return to India. There seemed little reason for him to stay and he had almost made up his mind to book a passage next month, leaving the winding up of his various estates to his agents and lawyers.

* * *

Jane had just come downstairs the next morning and was about to write some letters in her parlour when she heard the door knocker sound in a manner that was no less than imperious. She hesitated as the footman looked at her, inclined her head and said, 'I'll be in my parlour if it is for me, John.'

Going into her parlour, Jane sat at her desk and dipped her pen in the ink. She had just begun her first reply to an invitation when a tap at her door heralded the arrival of the impatient guest. She waited as the door opened and the man she was expecting was announced. Getting slowly to her feet, Jane looked at the man that entered, her heart suddenly beating faster. He was at least a head taller than she, and she was a tall woman. Harry had been slightly shorter but that had never mattered because they were so much in love, but this man could look down on her. Her first thought was that he had a harsh face, but was otherwise unremarkable, and then she looked at his eyes—fierce, and wild, she thought with a little shock, untamed.

'I have come to speak with Lady March and my ward, Miss Amelia Bellingham. Would you have the goodness to ask them to come down, ma'am?'

'I am Lady March, and I will certainly ask Melia to come down shortly, but perhaps it might be wise if we spoke first alone?'

'You—but you're far too young…' he said, looking astonished.

'What have you been told?' Jane felt a laugh escape her, try as she might to control it. 'Forgive me, sir, but

I believe you are Lord Frant—and I am certainly Lady March. My brother, the Viscount Salisbury, will verify that if you wish.'

'Of course not…forgive me,' he said and his eyes glinted, though she was not sure whether it was anger or something else she saw in them. 'I presumed from… but no matter. I hope I do not inconvenience you but you did say any morning at this hour?'

'So I did,' Jane replied. 'Melia is trying on some gowns that were delivered this morning, but I will send for her in a moment. When we have established why it is so very urgent that you see both of us.'

'I merely wished to make her acquaintance,' he said, looking as if the wind had been taken out of his sails. 'Without my consent or knowledge, her father made both Amelia and Elizabeth my wards. The elder girl is married but I thought…' He paused, as though he was not sure what he wanted to say. 'It was never my wish that they should be turned from their home and I wanted to make sure that they—Miss Amelia in particular— had all she needed for her comfort and happiness…'

'Ah, then we are in agreement,' Jane said and smiled at him. He stared at her as though he did not quite know what had hit him. 'Melia is my friend and—although it is not certain, she may one day be my sister. I believe my brother is fond of her and, if they find they suit, he intends to make her an offer of marriage….'

'Indeed…' Lord Frant went on staring at her. She thought he looked shocked and felt quite sorry for him. Jane suspected that he had come spoiling for a fight, and something—she had no idea what—had pricked the bubble of anger, leaving him drained like an empty balloon. 'I am glad to hear she has prospects. It was—and still is—my intention to settle five thousand pounds on her. I intend to do the same for her sister. Ten thousand pounds is more or less the sum I shall receive once I sell the Bellingham estate, and I have no wish to profit from any of it.'

'It is your intention to sell then?' Jane appraised him with her clear eyes. 'I had thought perhaps you had come home to live?'

'Yes, perhaps I have,' he said, seeming to come back to himself all at once. He smiled and she saw that his mouth was soft and sensual, not at all hard or harsh as she'd first thought. 'I have not decided; it will depend on various things...'

'Well, I see we have reached a happy agreement,' Jane said, realising she had quite misjudged him. 'I shall send Melia down to you so that you may talk in private.'

'Oh, no,' he said quickly. 'Pray send your servant to fetch her, ma'am. There is nothing I wish to say that you may not hear...'

Chapter Four

'We have an engagement for the theatre tomorrow evening,' Paul told Adam when they met at the boxing club that afternoon. 'Please keep the evening free, dear fellow. I want you to escort my ward, while I entertain her chaperon.'

'Do you mean Lady Moira?' Adam asked, reluctant, for he had not liked the lady Paul had chosen for the task when she called at the house.

'Oh, no, that is all changed,' Paul informed him in a blithe tone that made him arch his brows. 'Lady March will be accompanying us. Melia is happy with her and there seems no point in taking her away from where she is settled. Besides, it was all arranged on the spur of the moment. I did ask Viscount Salisbury—Lady March's brother—to accompany us, but he was engaged to play cards that evening.'

'So you thought I would oblige?' Adam gave him a clear look. 'I suppose Miss Bellingham looks like a horse?'

Paul gave a shout of laughter. 'I think her quite pretty. Of course she cannot hold a candle to Lady March... She is lovely, Adam. Truly lovely...'

'Good grief, if I did not know better I would think you smitten,' Adam said and his eyebrows rose higher as he saw the expression on Paul's face. 'Are you? Is she more beautiful than Annamarie?'

'Completely different and utterly wonderful...' Paul shook his head as he saw the astonishment in his friend's eyes. 'Yes, you may stare. Such a letter she wrote me! I thought she must be some old trout and went there prepared to put her down—but one look from those eyes and I was floored. I just stood there and couldn't speak for some minutes. I have never experienced anything like it, my dear fellow. She took my breath away when she smiled.'

'You have got it bad,' Adam said drily, still hardly believing that he was hearing those words from Paul's mouth. 'In India you could have had any woman you wanted...including the daughter of an earl, but you barely spared any of them a look.'

'Wait until you see her,' Paul said. He grinned at his friend. 'If you value your life, please do not fall in love with her. She's mine...'

'Prepared to fight to the death for her, are you?' Adam teased, thinking he was merely jesting, and then caught his breath as he saw the answer in Paul's face. 'What is so special about Lady March?'

Paul stared at him for a full minute in silence and then shook his head. 'I'm damned if I know, Adam. She is beautiful, but it isn't that...the laughter in her eyes, perhaps, and yet it isn't just that. To be honest, I have no idea why I feel this way; it just came out of the blue. I was angry, prepared to come the injured party and demand my rights, but then…it was just so sudden. One minute I wanted to strangle her, and the next it took me all my resolve not to take her in my arms and kiss her until she surrendered.'

'I should not advise that you do any such thing,' Adam warned. 'I met her brother this morning at my club and he told me that Jane is still grieving for her husband. He has only been dead just over two years.'

'Jane…her name is Jane? Sweet Jane, my love,' Paul said and sighed. 'Yes, I was told she was recently a widow but I didn't realise…I thought her older. She is the woman for me. If she will not have me then I shall never marry.'

'Nonsense,' Adam chided. 'You do not know her yet. Supposing she turns out to have a vicious temper and a sharp tongue?'

Paul looked rueful. 'She may have, for all I know. She certainly wrote me a cool letter but perhaps I deserved it, for mine to her was curt and I was angry when I left the viscount's house.'

'Be careful, my friend. You do not know this lady yet. Take your time, for if you plunge straight in one of two things will happen…' Paul looked enquiring and he smiled. 'Either she is on the catch for a husband and she will take you for your money—or she truly loved her husband and will break your heart by turning you down instantly.'

'I do not think there is a lack of money there,' Paul

said. 'Nor do I think she is on the catch for a husband—but she would very likely turn me down flat. No, you are right, Adam. I must play a long game—but I could not help sharing my feelings with you. You are the only other person I care for in the world. Had I had you for a brother I should have counted myself fortunate.'

'Speaking of brothers, have you heard from that lad—your stepbrother?'

'Mark? No, I have not and I do not expect to. He must be at Harrow or Eton by now—and I heard that his mother had remarried to a rich man. I believe she thought my father wealthy and must have been disappointed when she discovered that he was far from it, and a gambler to boot. He would have spent all she had, I dare say, leaving her only with her widow's settlement.'

'You are not thinking of settling money on her, I hope?'

'Certainly not,' Paul said and his expression hardened. 'She and her brat may go to the devil for all I care. She was already carrying her son when they married. I believe the affair had gone on for a while before my mother died of a broken heart.'

'Well, I am glad of your decision,' Adam said frankly. 'You have one weakness—a soft heart for those in trouble. Do not let your family take advantage of you—and make certain this widow is what you think her before you offer marriage.'

'I would go down on bended knee and beg her to marry me today if I thought she would say yes,' Paul told him and smiled wryly. 'Do not worry, my friend.

I shall exercise all the caution you advise in other matters—but where Jane is concerned...'

Adam shook his head and gave up, grinning from ear to ear. 'I never thought to hear those words from your lips, but if you feel that way, Paul, I can only wish you joy.'

'Save your good wishes until she takes me,' Paul said. 'You will come to the theatre?'

'Wild horses would not keep me away now,' Adam replied with a twist of his mouth. 'I am curious about Miss Bellingham—and even more interested in meeting Lady March...'

'I wish you had not agreed to go to the theatre with that fellow,' Will said to his sister that afternoon at tea. 'I would not have minded if I could accompany you—but we hardly know him, and I do not trust him near Melia...'

'I believe him to be a gentleman.' Jane smiled and placed a gentle hand on his arm. 'Do not concern yourself, dearest. Lord Frant has no interest in Melia other than as his ward. I think he found the whole business troublesome and was glad to leave her in my care once he understood that we were respectable. He is to settle five thousand on her, which is a decent sum. Not that you care one iota for a dowry, but others might.'

'It does not matter what others think,' Will said loftily. 'Melia is already sure of her future...should she wish it.'

Jane looked at him intently. 'Melia is very young, my love. I think her sweet and gentle and I am sure she would make you happy—but you must not be too certain of her yet. Bringing her to London may not prove to have the result you hoped for.'

'You think she might fall in love with someone else?'

Will looked so hurt that Jane felt terrible. Yet she had to make him aware of what she sensed. They had only been in company twice so far, but on both occasions Melia had been introduced to attractive, wealthy men, and she'd shown her pleasure in the attention paid her.

'I do not know, my love. I only felt that you should be a little wary. Melia has not given you her promise—has she?'

'No, but she knows how I feel. I spoke frankly the last time I visited near her home. She said that she needed to know me better and that's when the visit to London was first discussed…'

'Yes, I see.' Jane was thoughtful. If Melia had been a schemer she might have suspected her brother had been used, but she did not think it. Perhaps not always truthful, and sometimes careless of others' feelings, Melia might hurt Will but not intentionally. She liked him, considered him her friend and thought that she might like to marry him, but that did not mean she'd given her heart and, until she did, she might well bestow it on another. Jane hoped she would not, but Melia had to have her season; she had to have her chance, because otherwise she might do something regrettable after marriage. She was a girl who liked excitement and adventure, and Will preferred a quiet life in the country. Melia would have to be very certain that she loved him to settle for that life.

'Well, time will tell,' she said now and smiled lovingly at her brother. 'Things happen and people change…but I should not worry about us attending the theatre with Lord Frant. I do not believe you have anything to fear from him.'

In that much Jane was right, but if she wanted to safeguard her brother's interests she should have refused the invitation until Will could go with them, but perhaps even that would not have made much difference.

Melia was not sure how she felt about going to the theatre with Lord Frant. He had been kind to her, and she was grateful for the five thousand pounds he was settling on her through the family lawyer. Yet she thought him stern and was a little in awe of him, though her dear Jane seemed to like him and that must mean he was all right. However, the moment he introduced his friend, Captain, Viscount Hargreaves, Melia began to enjoy the evening.

His smile made her heart race and she thought him the most handsome man she had ever seen. Indeed, he resembled the pictures of Greek gods she'd once seen in an art book in her father's library, but was so much more impressive in the flesh. Not that she could see any flesh other than his hands and face—but after seeing that picture she could *imagine* what he might look like stripped to the waist.

How immodest she was! Her imagination did not go further than his waist, though his long legs looked powerful and strong in pale pantaloons and she thought would show to even more advantage in riding breeches.

She lamented that she had no horse in London, not realising that she had done so aloud until he at once insisted that he would hire her a good ladies' horse and take her riding in the park.

'Would you really?' Melia asked and fluttered her lashes at him. 'I have a darling mare at home. She has the softest mouth and has spirit, but is a gentle soul as a rule and would never dream of tipping me off.'

'I shall bring you a creature to rival your darling,' Adam ventured, vowing privately that he would buy such a horse if none suitable were to be hired. 'I promise you will not be disappointed. I am said to be a judge. Even Frant takes my advice on horses, though he is a marvellous judge and rider himself. We have been talking of setting up our racing stables together.'

'So Lord Frant intends to remain in England?'

'Yes, I think he does,' Adam said with a small smile and for a moment his eyes seemed to dwell on Lady March and his friend. 'Though we may keep our horses in Ireland and train them there...'

'Papa told me that the best horses came from Ireland...'

'Well, perhaps,' Adam agreed, 'but I like Spanish myself. Spanish bred and trained in Ireland—a winning combination...'

'How clever you are,' Melia said, gazing up at him. Her fingers fluttered on his arm and she felt almost faint when he smiled down at her. 'Do you intend to stay in England, Captain?'

'I dare say I shall divide my time between London and Ireland,' he told her. 'We shall race the horses here, you see—but I must visit them often. However, I prefer to live in London. It is the heart of things…but I do not mind travelling. I have had adventures enough for any man, and must find a good house where a sensible woman could be happy. I think my wife must love London, as I do, but be prepared to visit Ireland and other parts with me from time to time.'

'Oh, yes, she would surely wish to do that,' Melia said, quite carried away by such an enticing picture. 'To live in London for most of one's life must be heaven… though it is pleasant to walk in the country when the weather is good.'

'Yes, exactly,' Adam said and smiled again. 'I think we are to see a good play this evening. It is a comedy, I believe, and then we shall be entertained by a dancer. I am led to understand that she is wonderful to behold but I shall reserve judgement. I have seen a great deal of dancing in India.'

'Oh, yes, how exciting that must have been,' Melia said and her fingers curled about his arm. 'You must tell me all about it.'

'Not this evening for we must be quiet now the lights are going down,' he whispered, 'but perhaps I can take you driving in the park in the morning…'

She indicated that she would love that above all things and then was silent for the play had begun and Melia, like everyone else, was soon laughing at the scandalous romp Mr Sheridan had written for their amusement. Melia knew that it had first been acted upon the stage in 1777 and was much admired, but she had not expected to be so amused by the intrigues un-ravelling upon the stage.

When, after the performance, she and Lady March were taken for a light supper consisting mainly of ices, sweet trifles and jellies for the ladies, and bread, cold meat and cheese for the gentlemen, accompanied by wine or a cool, crisp sweet cider.

Later, after they had been escorted home in Lord Frant's very comfortable carriage, the gentlemen had said their goodbyes and they were about to depart to their own rooms, Melia asked Jane what she had thought to the play.

'Very amusing,' Jane said. 'I had seen it years ago when my mama took me, but I believe I appreciated it more this time.'

'Some of it went over my head, I must admit,' Melia said, 'but Viscount Hargreaves explained it all to me.'

'How very kind of him,' Jane said and hid her amuse-ment, for only a very innocent mind would need to have the play explained and she did not think Melia that innocent and she certainly was not stupid, and so it seemed she had enjoyed having it all explained to her. Perhaps for the purpose of inviting the viscount's whole attention? 'I am glad that you enjoyed your eve-ning, my dear.'

'Oh, yes, very much,' Melia replied, a small satisfied smile on her lips.

They parted, each to their own rooms—Melia to dream of a handsome face and a young god coming down from the heavens to bear her off with him to ce-lestial heights, and Jane to wonder if she'd served her brother a bad turn by accepting what she'd imagined a harmless invitation to the theatre.

For her it had been a pleasure. Paul Frant was an attentive host, making sure that the ladies were served with cooling drinks between the acts of the play, and taking them to a very pleasant supper in a private booth afterwards. Enjoying herself more than she had for some time, Jane had not become aware of the way Melia was flirting with Viscount Hargreaves until halfway through supper. She'd wondered then how long it had been going on—the little intimate smiles, the light touches on his arm and that ingenuous way of looking up as if in awe of his superior intelligence.

It was what every young lady on the catch for a husband learned to do, though some did it much better than others. Where some inexperienced young ladies might have seemed coy, Melia played the sweet innocent to perfection. Her aunt must have told her that gentlemen did not care for clever women or some such nonsense. Jane felt such behaviour to be deceitful, especially when the girl in question was perfectly capable of understanding and coping with most situations alone; to pretend misunderstanding or to act as if one were a weak and vulnerable female in need of a gentleman's strong arm was not something Jane would have resorted to. She believed in calling a spade a spade and taking one's life in one's own hands whenever possible, but perhaps some gentlemen did prefer the childish woman that Melia portrayed so well at times.

Knowing how firmly Melia spoke out for her own opinions in the matter of dress or other domestic matters, Jane thought her husband would soon be relieved of any such misapprehension once she was mistress of his home. Melia liked her own way and she'd heard her argue with Will over a horse he'd considered too strong for her to drive when he'd given her lessons in a light phaeton that his sister knew he'd had made especially for her. Will knew her as the wilful and sometimes headstrong girl she was and loved her, but in trying to trap the viscount with a sweet modesty that was not her own Melia was, in Jane's opinion, behaving badly.

She sighed as she unpinned her hair and her maid brushed it for her, the slightly waving length of it tumbling way past her shoulders. Jane had told Tilda not to sit up but she might as well have saved her breath, for her faithful servant had replied huffily, 'The day I can't sit up for you, my lady, you may give me my pension and send me off.'

'I couldn't possible manage without you,' Jane told her affectionately. 'You will have to go on for many years yet. I'm sorry, Tilda, but you must train a girl to care for me as you do before you think of retiring.'

Tilda had given her a dark look and muttered something that Jane could not hear and diplomatically ignored. The girl had come to her via her mother, a shy young thing of fifteen when she first worked for the family; employed in the nursery, she'd worked her way up to become Jane's maid, had gone with her to Spain and France when Harry was fighting under Wellington, and been a tower of strength when his death had almost killed Jane. Indeed, she did not know whether she could have borne it without Tilda and some other friends who had supported her in her grief.

After Tilda had wished her pleasant dreams and left her, Jane felt too restless for sleep. She looked at the portrait of her husband that she had kept by her bed since it was first given her as one of many presents from an adoring lover, for Harry had remained the ardent lover to the end. Sighing, she replaced the jewelled trinket in its place and walked to the window to look out at the night sky. Jane's heart had been broken when she lost the man she loved, and she would not wish such pain on her darling brother. If Melia's heart had been captured and her head turned by the dashing soldier, she would feel responsible—though, of course, they could have met at any time during the round of parties and dances that were about to begin.

Jane sat on the edge of the bed then lay back against a pile of soft pillows, another sigh escaping her. Was it only Will's disappointment that hung over her like a heavy cloud—or was there more?

She could not be certain. The evening had been pleasant, much of that deriving from the gentle smile and amusing conversation offered by Lord Frant. There was something about him that had made her very aware of him from their first meeting, but she could not put her feelings into words. He was direct, strong-willed and would make a bad enemy, of that she was sure—but to her he showed only courtesy, though she was certain he'd intended to quarrel with her that first morning.

What had made him change his mind? Jane puzzled over it, but could find no reason for the thunderstruck look on his face as he'd stared at her. A vainer woman might have hit upon the truth, but Jane had never thought herself either beautiful or desirable. She dressed in good clothes that suited her and were considered elegant by others, but, since she only glanced in the mirror when she dressed or changed her clothes, she was not aware that she was a striking woman with good strong features and fine eyes.

It would be vain indeed to imagine that a man like Paul Frant had fallen instantly in love with her and the thought never entered Jane's mind. He was a man of the world, obviously wealthy and experienced in business matters. She could only think that he'd been surprised—he had mentioned that he'd thought she would be older, so that must be it.

Her own feelings had shocked her, because she'd liked him despite her determination not to. His letter had been abrupt and she'd been ready to think him a villain for turning Melia and her sister from their home, but indeed that had been the lawyers, who had since been put in their place and were now doing all they could to make amends. Paul Frant was a long way from being the most handsome man she'd met; indeed, his friend Adam Hargreaves put him in the shade and was a viscount to boot rather than a mere lord. As a girl, Jane had been expected to look higher and her husband's title had not been considered one of importance. She'd married for love, with her mother's approval and her half-brother's grudging permission, and, until fate had taken everything away, she'd been very happy.

Jane did not feel it would be possible to love like

that again. Surely any other attachment she might form would pale into insignificance against the love she'd known—and, that being the case, she'd more or less made up her mind not to marry again. It was better to be a widow and independent rather than find oneself trapped into a less than perfect marriage.

Yet Jane could not deny that it was comfortable having a man to care for one's comfort, even if one was capable of arranging things for oneself. Will had never interfered in her arrangements, but she'd known he was there if she'd needed a male opinion on any matter of business. Living with her brother had suited her well, but she had her doubts about living in Bath with a female companion.

As yet there had been no reply to her letter to Cousin Sarah, which had surprised Jane a little. She'd thought the girl would be only too happy to accept the offer of becoming her companion. She'd made it clear that, though she would be accepted as family, she would be given an allowance that would make her independent and able to buy the small luxuries of life that made the difference between drudgery and content.

Perhaps the letter had been lost between Sarah's home and hers. She would wait another week or so and then write again.

Chapter Five

Having made what amends he could to the Bellingham sisters, Paul was giving some thought to disposing of their father's estate. He had paid a fleeting visit when he first came to England, expecting Melia to be living there under the guidance of Lady Moira. He had not stayed more than an hour to take some refreshment before pushing on, but he had naturally found his way to the library, and what he discovered there was pleasing. Bellingham had obviously been something of a collector and there were some books Paul would like to keep on the shelves. He'd decided he would have all the books transferred to his library in London for the time being, and gradually sort out those he ultimately wished to keep; the others could be sent elsewhere once he'd had the leisure to go through them and would in the meantime fill the large spaces in what had once been his great-grandfather's excellent collection.

Paul sighed as he looked up from the letters he was writing to his man of business. It had occurred to him that there might be some pieces of furniture at the Bellingham estate that he would like for his London home. As yet, he had purchased very little and in truth was not much inclined to it, though he knew he must furnish his town house in style before he could entertain properly—yet the prospect of searching various cabinet makers was daunting for a man who had never bothered with such things. He could leave it to an agent, of course, or— The thought that he might consult Lady March on the matter brought a smile to his lips. As his wife, she would have the freedom to purchase anything she chose, but he could not convince himself that he was making any impression on her inner calm. Perhaps if he were to beg for her help in choosing the furniture for his house it would bring them closer together—of course, she would quite likely refuse but nothing ventured, nothing gained...

He'd noted with some amusement the flirtation between Adam and the young girl who was by her father's will his ward, but as he believed the viscount to be trustworthy he had no qualms. Adam would not step beyond the line, and had already confided that he was on the lookout for a wife. Paul would have no objection, should his permission be sought, though he was not sure she was the wife he would have chosen for his friend. Paul did not intend to be critical, but her artless sighs, smiles and pouts seemed artificial to him and he wondered that Adam should be taken in by them—or perhaps he was making too much of the thing and the pair were merely enjoying a flirtation.

Had Paul thought much about his friend's state of

mind, he would have imagined that Adam had been more than a little in love with the beautiful Annamarie, though he had never said as much. The proud girl had shown her own preference for Paul, and Paul had seen her snub several of Adam's fellow officers. That would probably have been enough to prevent Adam from speaking, even if his heart were engaged, for his pride would not have taken kindly to such a snub.

Oh, well, there was no point in dwelling on something of which he had no real knowledge. Paul played with his pen for a few moments longer and then a smile touched his lips as he began to write. As yet he had not received a single invitation to an affair at which he could be sure of meeting the lady he wished to meet, but perhaps if he invited her to help him choose the new furnishings for his house, that would provide a reason for them to meet more often…

'More letters for you, Jane,' Will said and smiled as he handed them to her in her parlour that morning. 'How many more affairs are we to be invited to, I wonder?'

'Several, I imagine,' his sister said, looking at him in amusement. 'If I do not have at least four engagements each day I shall think myself abandoned. You must not grudge me my fun, Will. I come so seldom to London that my friends clamour to see me and have me attend their parties.'

'And the house is inundated with young smarts,' her brother said, a trifle put out. 'I think you were right, Jane. Melia hardly has time to pass the time of day with me of late. If she is not driving in the park with one of her admirers, she is riding, or attending an al fresco breakfast or a waltzing party in the afternoons.'

'You would not have her appear a country dowd?' Jane lifted her fine eyes to his. 'Naturally, she wishes to waltz well by the time she appears at Almack's, and Lady Sopworth's invitation to join her daughters at their waltzing lessons was a great favour that I was delighted for her to take up.'

'I do not mean to complain,' Will said with a wry smile for his sister. 'Melia is lovely and it is no wonder that she is in demand. I knew it would happen but I hope she will not forget me.'

'If she loves you this will be but a passing phase,' his sister said. 'If she does not—then I do not think you would wish to marry her?'

'Perhaps not,' Will admitted, a flash of pain in his eyes. 'But I do think the world of her, Jane—and I hoped she felt the same.'

'She is young, dearest, and must have a little time to flirt,' Jane said softly, feeling his hurt and wishing that she might help him, but there was little she could do.

'I do understand,' Will answered with a determined lift of his head. 'Take no notice of me. Have you arranged to see Mama today?'

'Mama is always engaged,' her loving daughter said. 'She did make time to call on us and we have all dined with her—but I am informed she means to give a large ball next week and we are all summoned to attend.'

Will's eyes lit with laughter. 'I should not dare to plead another engagement, and I know you would not think of it. Besides, everyone will be there. It will be the biggest crush of the season if I know anything of Mama.'

'Yes, I dare say it will...' Jane had been opening her letters. Most were invitations to various affairs, but the one she had just glanced down at made her sit up straighter. 'Cousin Sarah apologises for her tardiness in replying and asks if she may join me here on Thursday afternoon... Oh! That is the day after tomorrow. I must be at home to receive her, which means I cannot accompany Melia to Mrs Broom's for tea and a little music...' She turned beguiling eyes on her brother. 'I know it is the kind of affair you most despise, Will— but perhaps you could escort her?'

Will seemed to hesitate, then nodded. 'Of course, love. At least it will give me the chance to spend more than a few minutes in her company.'

'Yes...' Jane scanned the rest of her cousin's letter and frowned. Sarah seemed to be in a fret over something, hinting that she had a problem that she wished to discuss with her. Discarding the letter, she opened the next in her pile. 'I must make sure that one of the best guest rooms is prepared for Sarah...' A little cry of surprise left her lips as she read her next letter. 'How odd...'

'Something wrong, Sis?' Will asked.

'No, not wrong—just surprising. Lord Frant has asked if I can help him choose some suitable furnishings for his house. He says that he has been living in two rooms and that cannot continue if he wishes to entertain, which he does—and he has no idea where to start.'

'What can the fellow be thinking of?' Will frowned. 'You must say no, Jane. It is not your place to furnish the man's home.'

'No, but he does not expect that, merely some advice. He really has no idea how to start—and you know that kind of thing has always appealed to me. Mama says that if I ever lose my fortune I might make it again by advising others how to furnish their homes.'

Jane was very surprised that a man she hardly knew had suggested such a thing, but also flattered. She was aware that her good taste was often mentioned in po-lite circles and imagined he must have heard that she was famed for her style in all things. Mama was always extolling her virtues to others, particularly gentlemen.

'I suppose he has heard some sort of garbled tale about your flair for such things.' Will frowned. 'I still think you ought not to agree. There's something about him…and that friend of his. I cannot put my finger on it, but I don't like Hargreaves and if Frant insists on keeping him in his pocket it shows…'

'What does it show?' Jane enquired, believing she understood her brother's hostility. He was feeling a lit-tle jealous of the handsome gentleman for whom Melia had shown a particular liking. 'I find Lord Frant a very pleasant companion—as for Viscount Hargreaves, I hardly know him.'

'No more you know Frant,' her brother said harshly. 'I suppose he is well enough but I don't like his friend and that I tell you…' Will's face was a little red as he added, 'And it ain't just because Melia likes him either. I wouldn't trust that man further than I could throw him.'

Jane was a little surprised, for her brother was the most easy-going gentleman she knew. It was unusual for him to take such a dislike to anyone. Even allowing for Melia's attraction to the man, Jane had not expected this reaction.

'I wasn't aware that you knew much of him?'

'Well, I don't,' her brother said. 'When we first met I thought him a pleasant enough fellow, but I saw him fleece a young fool at the club one evening. I'm almost sure that he cheated, but I couldn't be certain. The youth in question was General Brent's grandson. He came into his estate when his father died last year and if he carries on at the card table in the way he did that evening, he will soon run through his fortune.'

'Oh, Will!' Jane exclaimed for she knew the general and the young man's mother quite well. 'I am shocked. Indeed, I am. Are you sure he was cheating? It is bad enough to go on playing when a young man like that is losing constantly, but to cheat him…'

'I saw him take a card from his sleeve. I almost intervened—but I could not prove anything. If he called me a liar and protested that it was only his kerchief, which he did take out to conceal the card…it would have ended in a duel. I did not wish to become embroiled in such an unbecoming brangle, Jane. He is Lord Frant's guest, his trusted friend—and it would seem as if I were trying to discredit him for my own purposes…'

'Yes, of course I do see,' Jane said, frowning. 'I am perfectly sure that Lord Frant is not aware of such behaviour. I do not believe he would count a cheat as his best friend…'

'No?' Will looked dubious but then he inclined his head. 'I dare say you are right, Jane. I know you to be a good judge of character. Please, keep your eyes and ears open as regards this man's character, as I shall. I promise you that it is not sour grapes. I trust I am man enough to accept Melia preferring another man, but I would not want to see her ruined or have her heart broken by a scoundrel.'

'Be careful you do not use such words to her—or anyone but me,' Jane warned. 'I am glad you've been frank with me, Will. I shall try to steer her away from his company gently, but to forbid her or cast a slight on his character would make her rebellious.'

'Yes, I know her temper and her heedless character,' Jane's brother said a little sadly. 'I love her for her faults as much as her good points. If she were a paragon, perhaps I should not love her half as well.'

'Oh, my dearest,' Jane said, but would not let words of sympathy tumble out. Will would resent it if she showed pity. He was a man and could fight his own battles. 'Well, we must do what we can to keep our dear friend from harm—but if I were sure of Hargreaves's unkind nature I should speak to Lord Frant of it.'

'I dare say he would not believe you,' Will said. 'However, be a little careful in your dealings with the pair of them. You've suffered enough, Jane. I would have no harm come to you either.'

'I do not think Lord Frant means me harm,' Jane said and gave him a loving smile. 'I am well able to control my life, dearest Will. You need have no fear for me— but we must certainly try to protect Melia, for she is a dear girl.' Jane might have added *despite her faults*, but refrained.

Will heard Melia in the hall and went out to join her, suggesting a walk in the park before nuncheon, something that found favour with her. Melia came in to tell her they were going out for an hour, leaving Jane to read her letters and write her answers.

Paul smiled as he read the answer to his letter, which had been sent round by hand. Lady March had suggested that they go to various merchants and emporiums that she had favoured in the past, but asked if she might be privileged to see the rooms she was advising on before they started. He immediately sat down and invited her to visit with his ward and, if he chose, her brother, any morning that week, suggesting the day after next if she had time.

Paul did not truly expect a reply to his second letter immediately because Lady March must have a score of appointments but, returning at four in the afternoon after a visit to the tailor he preferred, he discovered her letter waiting for him in the hall.

Lady March and Miss Bellingham would call at eleven on the preferred morning and be delighted to see the rooms in need of refurbishment.

Paul immediately penned a short note of thanks and assured her of his gratitude for her kindness. He was feeling more hopeful than before, because at least she did not dislike the idea of some hours spent in his company.

It was as he was drinking a small brandy and smoking a cigar in his library, his mood one of quiet reflection, that Adam walked in. He had clearly been riding and seemed in a mood as he flung down his whip on the sideboard and helped himself to a large drink.

'Something troubling you?' Paul asked, wondering at his friend's expression, of anger mixed with something more—was it fear or anxiety?

'Oh, nothing,' Adam said, but it was obvious that he was disturbed. 'I had thought to be out this evening—a card party with three friends, but it has been cancelled.'

'Is that all?' Paul asked, looking at him closely. 'I can offer you my company for I am dining at my club—but I sense something more. Can you not tell me?'

Adam hesitated, as if wondering whether to unburden himself, and then shook his head. 'I may have to leave you sooner than I'd thought,' he said. 'I'd hoped—but matters have gone too far and I may have no choice.'

'You visited your father's lawyers this morning,' Paul probed deeper. 'Are things not as you'd hoped in the matter of his estate?'

Adam snorted with disgust and threw himself down in the wing chair opposite. 'The damned fools have made a mess of things, if you ask me. They say I must sell…house, land, horses and carriages. Everything my father left me is owed to the bank and more. They tell me I am not responsible for more than his estate is worth, but they cannot tell me how I am to live— or who will loan me money for the scheme we had in mind. I do not have three thousand to put up, Paul, nor yet half as much…'

'I am sorry for it.' Paul frowned over the news. 'Are you certain everything must go?'

'It appears my father ran on the bank for years. Nothing is left after the bank is paid—so I must either marry an obliging heiress quickly or return to soldiering. Yet without the allowance my father made me I am not certain I could support myself in the manner expected of an officer.'

'I could put my lawyers on to it,' Paul offered. 'We might get a better offer than these fellows have told you. Why not let me see what I can do—if I can save enough for our venture, would that suffice?'

'Yes, for I should make my home in Ireland and visit London only occasionally.' Adam looked slightly odd. 'I am in funds for the moment because I won five hundred guineas the other night. I had hoped for similar luck this evening but...' He sighed and shrugged.

'Better to keep what you have for the moment,' Paul said. 'That sum would buy you a decent house in Ireland—and if I buy the land we need to train our horses, we shall be halfway there...'

'I do not care to hang upon your sleeve, Paul.'

'Nonsense. I intend to go ahead with the scheme and at the very least would offer you a partnership, even had you no money to contribute. I told you before, I think of you as my brother, Adam—and your friendship, horsemanship and sheer good sense would make me want you as my partner and manager. Whether or not we can salvage something from your estate is immaterial to me, though not of course to you.' He smiled warmly at the man who had nursed him through a debilitating fever on the ship from India. 'Come, Adam, do not refuse me.'

'You make it impossible for me,' Adam said and looked half angry, half rueful. 'You're too good, Paul. I don't deserve such consideration.'

'Nonsense,' Paul replied carelessly. 'You've been a good friend to me, Adam. Without your care and attention, I think I might have died on that ship—and I am grateful to be alive and recovering my health. I could not run my stable as I wish without your assistance, my friend, so let's have no more of this nonsense. You will remain my guest until my lawyers can sort out your affairs and then we shall go to Ireland and buy what we need.'

Adam shrugged his eloquent shoulders. 'Since you insist on being grateful for a mere kindness, what can I say?'

He tossed off his brandy and stood up. 'I must write some letters, and one to permit your lawyers to investigate my father's affairs.'

Paul watched him leave, puzzling over something he'd noticed for the first time…though it might have been there before but not as strongly. There was a slight resentment in Adam's manner of late, almost as if he disliked receiving favours from a friend. Yet why should he feel like that? They had been friends in India…or had Adam been a little resentful then, because of Annamarie?

Paul would have dismissed the idea as mere fantasy had he not seen that smouldering look in Adam's eyes when he'd told him he would give him a partnership even had he no money to put into the scheme. On the ship Paul had been totally reliant on his friend and nothing could have exceeded Adam's care for him. The ship's doctor had been busy, for more than twenty others had taken the virulent fever and nine of them had died. Paul believed that he owed his existence to Adam and would willingly have settled the sum of ten thousand pounds on him had he thought it would be accepted, but he believed that to flaunt his wealth in such a way must spoil what he had thought a perfect friendship.

It was difficult when one had rather too much good fortune and the other had none, Paul reflected. He could not give such a sum to Adam without giving offence but perhaps…yes, perhaps there was a way that it might seem to be a stroke of luck and not charity…

Jane was pleased when she saw the two gentlemen enter the ballroom that evening. She had not seen either of them at a fashionable affair like this one and had decided that Lord Frant must dislike social events of this kind. However, both he and Viscount Hargreaves looked very elegant this evening, immaculately dressed in their black evening clothes with frilled white shirts. One slightly taller and heavier, the other an Adonis. Jane was amused to see almost every feminine eye follow their progress through the room. Two newcomers were always of interest, but these men were both striking—and one at least was reputed to be wealthy. Of the other's estate she had no knowledge and would not have given it another thought had she not seen Melia's immediate reaction.

Her face lit up and Jane sensed the suppressed excitement in her. She was clearly waiting for the man she admired to come to her. He did not do so immediately, but joined a group of gentlemen who were laughing and talking excitedly, possibly about a horse race. Several of the gentlemen had been talking about a particular race that evening. Not one of the usual meetings at Newmarket or another of the racecourses but a private affair between two gentlemen, who had placed a large bet on the outcome at White's. Lord Bedford and Captain Marchant had been a trifle the worse for wear when the bet was placed, it seemed, but now everyone was placing odds, mostly for Captain Marchant's grey, which was held to be the better horse, but, since the race would take place on a private estate, only those invited would be privileged to see the outcome. Everyone else would have to wait until the news reached town.

'Lady March, I trust I am in time to secure a dance with you?' Lord Frant's voice behind her made Jane turn in surprise. 'I should like a waltz—and the dance before supper so that I may claim the privilege of taking you in.'

'Why, yes, I see no reason to refuse you since my card is still untouched.'

'I cannot believe that,' Paul said and took her card from her to write his name in two spaces. Two dances were the permitted number allowed before one was thought to show an attachment. 'There, I did not expect to have my choice and can only think that Someone Above thinks kindly of me.'

Jane smiled, looking up at him with a mixture of amusement and an odd shyness. She had come to the ball prepared to act as Melia's chaperon, but there was really no reason why she should not dance—although it was the first time since she'd become a widow that she had even thought of it. For a moment grief and regret smote her. Was it right that she should dance and be happy when her dearest Harry no longer shared such pleasures?

'Perhaps He does,' she replied, but the sparkle had gone from her eyes. 'However, I must admit to curiosity about your request, sir. Have you no other lady to oblige you?'

'None I cared to ask,' Paul replied with an innocent air. 'I have noted your perfect taste, in all you do and wear—and your mama told me that you have a flair for knowing what will look well.'

'You have met Mama?'

'Yes. I happened to meet Roshithe at my club and he was very interested in the situation in India. He asked me to dine and I accepted. Your mama was a kind hostess and talked to me about you later that evening...'

'Oh, dear,' Jane said and sighed. It was as she'd half expected: Mama had been meddling again. 'I fear my darling mother may have exceeded what is necessary or proper in extolling my virtues—you see, she wants to find me a second husband. I have disappointed her in refusing all her suggestions.'

'You wrong her sadly,' Paul said, mouth twitching. 'I found your mama delightful company and enjoyed my evening. Since I believe I have made a friend in her husband, I look forward to many more such affairs—when perhaps I may also have the pleasure of your company.'

'Did Mama tell you I should be here this evening?' Jane asked, half annoyed that her mother should try to throw her in the gentleman's way. She toyed with the idea of refusing his request for help but decided that would be churlish after she had first accepted.

'Everyone is here this evening, are they not?' Paul remarked, waving his hand to indicate the rapidly filling reception rooms. 'Shall we make our way to the floor? I believe our dance is starting now…'

Jane placed her hand lightly on his arm, marvelling that he seemed to have the knack of making his way easily through the crowd—a word, a look, a smile and the thing was done. When he placed one hand at the small of her back and then took hers in the other, Jane felt a small tremor run through her. She looked up at him a little uncertainly but he merely smiled and swept her out into the throng of dancers.

He was so light on his feet for a large man. Jane was immediately aware that she need have no care for her feet; she had only to follow his lead and let herself flow with the music. Dancing with this man was sheer delight and a pleasure Jane had seldom known. As a young girl she'd been popular enough, but too often gentlemen had either trodden on her toes or been stiff and awkward when dancing. Harry, of course, had danced well, but then, he did everything well. However, he preferred hunting to dancing and once they were married he had avoided attending a ball unless it was a regimental one and he was ordered to attend.

She had learned that Wellington expected all his young officers to dance well and enjoyed entertaining the ladies who accompanied the Army; wives and daughters were made much of and always treated with respect. Indeed, the worst thing any officer could do was to flirt with or compromise a brother officer's wife or daughter. It was an unwritten law and Jane had been treated scrupulously by Harry's friends.

'May I share them?' Paul said, making her aware that she had not spoken for a while. 'Your thoughts—or are they too personal?'

'I was thinking that I had not enjoyed a dance so much for a long time,' Jane said. 'I have not danced since my husband was killed...but before that I did not have much opportunity. It is rare to find anyone so perfectly in tune with oneself on the dance floor, sir.'

'I have never danced with anyone who gave me so much pleasure,' Paul said. 'But I learned when I was with Wellington, of course—as all his officers do. If they have no skills before they become staff officers they are obliged to learn quickly, and well.'

'Yes, indeed. When I was with Harry in France all his friends danced well...' Jane caught her breath but discovered she could continue without tears. 'However, I could not say that any of them were quite your equal, sir.'

'Now you have put me to the blush, for you will think me a vain creature seeking compliments,' Paul said, but his eyes smiled at her. They lapsed into a pleasant silence, each enjoying the sensation of the dance and the magic of the music as they swept about the floor.

It was some time before Jane noticed that many of the dancers had drawn back to the edge of the dance floor, seemingly to watch them as they moved fluently across the floor and back again. She laughed, caught with sudden excitement and reckless as she twirled round and round, never thinking for a moment beyond the moment the dance must end. Yet end it did at last and there was a little buzz of spontaneous applause, which only then Jane realised was for them. It brought a flush to her cheeks and she felt warm with embarrassment. Had she been able, she might have escaped to the veranda to take a little air, but immediately Paul escorted her from the floor, Jane was surrounded by young gentlemen clamouring for a dance with her.

'I was not sure you would dance.' A man she recognised as one of Harry's closest friends asked for her card and wrote his name in two spaces, each of them waltzes. 'Had I known you were in town I should have called.'

'Captain Forlan,' Jane said. 'How nice to see you this evening—the last I heard was that you were wounded in Bonaparte's last battle.'

'Yes, but it was merely a scratch,' he replied with a smile.

Jane nodded, knowing that every young officer spoke of the most appalling wounds as just a scratch. As he walked away from her, she noticed a slight limp and understood that he did not wish to speak of his wounds, especially at a ball. He was a charming young man; Jane remembered him from those dreadful days after Harry was killed, when his friends had been so kind. She'd been in such grief, dazed and shocked, unbelieving that the man she'd adored could have been taken from her so cruelly. His friends had seen her on to a ship; some of their wives had been dispatched to stay

with her until she was home with her family. She recalled Captain Forlan begging her to send for him if
she were ever in need of a friend, which of course had
not been the case. Mama had fussed over her, and then
Will had carried her off to his home and simply been
there, neither fussing nor ignoring her, but ready to do
whatever she required.

However, this was not the time to be thinking of such
things. Now that Jane had been seen willing to dance,
she was not permitted to sit out. At supper she was once
again surrounded by young officers, though Paul had
secured their table and had the waiters bring a selection
of all manner of trifles to tempt a lady's small appetite.
However, this did not stop the gentlemen from wandering over to offer a glass of champagne or anything else
Lady March desired. Jane might have preferred a little
time to engage her companion in private conversation,
but she was not granted the time, and consoled herself
that she would certainly have time the next day since
she was to visit his house.

'We shall talk tomorrow,' she said in a low voice
when it became apparent that they were not to be
granted a moment of peace. 'I had not expected to have
so many friends around us at supper...'

'I shall look forward to it and give you to your admirers with a good grace, ma'am.'

The smile in his eyes brought an answering one to
hers. He could not know it, but she had little interest
in all the flattery that was bestowed on her that evening. She almost wished she had not danced, for that
seemed to have opened the floodgates, but she could

not wish away the two wonderful dances with Paul, one that magical waltz and the other a more sedate two-step before supper.

She had only time to go upstairs to make herself comfortable before being claimed once more. A few times Jane had felt the prick of conscience and looked for Melia, but every time she was seen to be dancing with various young gentlemen, clearly enjoying herself. However, she did not sit in Viscount Hargreaves's pocket and so Jane felt there was nothing to concern her in the young girl's behaviour.

It had been a very pleasant evening, and quite unexpected. Jane had many female friends but until this evening she'd had few admirers other than those her mama placed before her, who were inevitably rich, older and too often boring for Jane's liking.

Mama had not been present this evening, because Porky was feeling a bit under the weather, but she was bound to hear of Jane's success, and it was sure to bring a visit.

It was not until she was alone in bed that Jane examined her feelings. For a while that evening she had been swept away by the excitement of an evening spent in good company—but now she was alone and the familiar ache and longing for Harry returned.

It seemed almost a betrayal of her love to have been so happy. Jane liked Lord Frant because he was charming and good company—but it could never be more than liking, of course. Jane's heart had been given to Harry and she could never love again.

Chapter Six

Leaving her brother's house at a quarter to eleven the next morning, Jane was driven in her carriage with Melia the short distance to Lord Frant's home. They were admitted by a footman in what looked to be a smart new uniform; he was smiling and seemed very interested in his master's guests, telling them they were most welcome and must ask him for anything they desired. He had been instructed to take them to a pretty parlour, where they found Lord Frant standing by the window looking out at the gardens through an open French window. He turned instantly, his eyes lighting up as he saw Jane.

'Lady March, Miss Bellingham,' he said, coming forward to take Jane's hand. 'I am delighted you have come, though ashamed of my poor house. It has been treated ill and I must make changes quickly. However, my people are loyal and I have secured the services of an excellent chef. May I offer you some refreshment, ladies?'

'Could we have a small tour of the rooms you wish refurbished first?' Jane asked, looking about her with interest. She had almost sent to say that she had changed her mind, but now she was glad that she had not been so foolish. All that was required of her was a little advice and surely that was little enough. The room had nice proportions and was furnished properly, but might have been better, in her opinion, since some of the furniture was of too large proportions. 'This has a pleasant aspect, sir—and those windows let in plenty of light.'

'This and my library house the only decent pieces left to me. My father was forced to pass on the title and the entail, but he left nothing that he believed was his own to dispose of, I think.' And some things that ought to have been passed to him had been sold, but Paul did not mention this circumstance.

'Yes, I thought something of the sort must have happened. This room should have fine delicate pieces that do not overcrowd it, perhaps—and some of these things might be transferred to another room. Unless you prefer what you have here?'

'Oh, no, my housekeeper did what she could with an almost empty house. You may have remarked that we have no pictures or silver, nor yet any important porcelain.'

'Yes, I have noticed,' Jane said, believing that frankness was best. 'Do you wish to make this your principle home, sir?'

'When I am in London, yes. The structure is sound and of course I do have my own estate in the country—not my father's, which I believe he somehow contrived to leave to his younger son, but one left me by my mother's father.'

'Yes, I see.' Jane looked about her again. 'But you do intend to spend much of your time here?'

'As much as any gentleman of fortune,' Paul replied. 'I was left a certain amount through my mother's family and an uncle…but I was able to make my personal fortune in India. As yet, I have not disposed of much of my land and property out there, for I was not certain of remaining here when I left—but the Company will sell it for me. I do not have many calls on my purse for I am single and I suppose I might support a wife in luxury— if I were to find a lady who could love me for myself.'

'You are very frank, sir, for which I am glad. I shall not scruple to advise you to purchase only the best. Cheap furnishings are always a false economy.'

'Oh, you need not bother to count the pennies; Frant has more than enough to purchase a houseful of furniture,' Adam said from the doorway. 'Miss Bellingham, might I show you the garden? There is little to see in the house at the moment.'

Melia dimpled at him and after a nod to her guardian took Adam's arm and went out to look at the pretty gardens to the rear. Jane frowned over it for a moment, but decided that there could be little harm in a stroll round the garden on a pleasant morning; they would be in sight of the house at all times, for the gardens were not extensive.

'You may trust Adam, you know,' Paul said, obviously picking up her doubts. 'Have you any reason to doubt his behaviour towards my ward?'

'No, none—other than the foolish girl may give her heart where it is not truly wanted.'

'Yes, that is possible,' Paul agreed and cast a glance after them. 'I know that Melia's fortune would not recommend her to him.'

'Perhaps he requires a larger portion,' Jane said, her gaze very direct. 'I have not tried to forbid her because it would be useless—but I shall hint her away from him, and you might do the same.'

'I am very sure he would do nothing to disoblige me,' Paul replied but was thoughtful as he led Jane through the various rooms that contained only the occasional piece of furniture: a very large cabinet that was a fixture and could not easily be moved, and some built-in shelves in an alcove that were rather attractive and had swags of ribbons carved into the wood beneath. Occasional tables, chairs, all small objects that made a house a home, had been removed and there were faded patches on the walls where a mirror or a picture had hung. 'As you can see, we are in a sad case—but I have found someone to repaper the worst of the rooms. I am told it may be done while I am away at the Newmarket races.'

'That would be excellent,' Jane agreed. 'Nothing is more disagreeable than having workmen in when one is in residence. If we ordered the furniture you require and some mirrors, some candlesticks of silver and a few pieces of porcelain, you may buy your pictures at your leisure. I think they should be chosen when one finds something that appeals—furnishing pictures are not to be admired.'

'Yes, I agree. I hear there is an exhibition of new young artists due to start in three weeks. I might find one or two there, though anything of real merit must come through an auction, I think.'

'Yes, I believe that would be best,' Jane said. 'If one hears of a country house to be auctioned with all its contents, some fine things may be purchased that way.' She stopped to admire an exquisite ceiling and a run of long windows. 'I am glad to see that you do not cover those with drapes, sir. It is a lovely view out to the garden and must be pleasant in here during the summer.'

'Yes, and damned draughty in the winter,' Paul said and laughed softly. 'We only ever used this room to entertain; it soon warms up if there are enough guests—but I always preferred my mother's parlour and the library for comfortable evenings...'

'The rooms we saw first,' Jane said and nodded. 'I should certainly prefer your mother's parlour if it were furnished well—either in the French fashion or that set by Mr Adam, I think. That large Chippendale cabinet would do much better in here, I believe—against that far wall. You should have two settees here, facing each other, and an occasional table to the side. Behind this one you might have an elegant sofa table—indeed, why not order a pair with some important candelabra to set them off? Over there by the window I think a desk of good proportions, a chair to match the sofas at the desk—and at that end of the room a pier table with a shaped mirror above. We might have two areas, one at either end, of a small table and comfortable chairs set conversationally: a pair of fine cabinets against the long wall, flanked by a set of good single chairs, and some display tables between the windows at the back...'

'You make a fine start,' Paul said and scribbled some notes on the pad he'd brought with him for the purpose.

'You will need things like candle stands, torchieres and a reading frame, but perhaps not too many in here. The cabinet makers I have used in the past will send things we like and if we do not find a place for them, they will take them back.'

'I am enthused by your ideas,' Paul told her. 'When may we begin?'

'Tomorrow I must wait at home because a young cousin is coming to stay with me and I must be there to greet her,' Jane said. 'However, we might make an appointment for Friday morning. Some of what you require will need to be made up for you, and therefore the sooner we start the better...'

'You must not let me take up too much of your time...'

'Oh, I do not often bother with morning engagements,' Jane said. 'Melia may be charmed by an alfresco breakfast but I prefer to rise later, do a little shopping, perhaps visit a few friends in the afternoon and then prepare for the evening, for then, you know, we might have three engagements—dinner, a soirée and perhaps a supper and dancing elsewhere...'

'I wish I knew which events you favour,' Paul said without thinking. 'I cannot always rely on your mama to tell me.'

Jane stared at him, a little surprised and wary too. She was prepared for friendship, but was Lord Frant flirting with her?

'I am very sure that some of the events I attend would

not amuse you. I dare say you are invited to more than you can attend?'

'I have my fair share of invitations, but some of them hold little interest… Last evening was the first I have managed to meet you in company.'

Jane's spine tingled, a little unease creeping into her mind at the exquisite compliment. He was flirting and because of that she made her tone cool as she replied, 'I cannot think your evening wasted if you do not see me, sir.'

'No, perhaps not,' he said, recovering his mistake. 'It was just so pleasant to dance with you. I should not wish to miss a chance to repeat it.'

'Then you must accept all the invitations to balls and dances you receive,' Jane said and smiled because she could not quite resist.

'Yes, I shall of course be certain of meeting you sometimes then,' Paul said. 'In the meantime, perhaps your brother, Melia and yourself would join me for an evening of pleasure at Vauxhall Gardens—unless you have already been invited to such an event?'

'Will has promised to take us one evening,' Jane replied, 'but I am sure he would be happy to make up a party with you, sir. You must speak to him. However, I must warn you…' Jane stopped, her cheeks warm. She had been about to tell him of her brother's feelings of distrust regarding his friend, but realised that she could not confide such a thing to him. At times she felt he was a friend and to be relied on, but she hardly knew him and must exercise caution for the moment.

'No matter…I am sure my brother would be happy to see *you* at any time, sir.'

His eyes narrowed and she wondered if she had stressed the word *you* too much, for she did not wish to give offence and Paul Frant was an intelligent man who would not need things spelled out to him. They had returned to the parlour they began with just as Melia and her escort returned from taking the air and therefore no further conversation of an intimate nature took place. She suspected that he might have questioned her on her meaning had they still been alone, but was unable to in the presence of the others.

Refreshments were brought and they talked of the ball they had all attended and of future engagements, many of which Melia had mentioned to Viscount Hargreaves and which he seemed eager to attend. Jane had noticed that her young friend had seemed a little flushed when they first returned to the parlour, but she gave no sign of distress and seemed in high spirits when they left in Jane's carriage.

'Adam told me that Lord Frant's father behaved shamefully to him,' Melia said, chattering, her eyes very bright. 'That is why he has to refurbish the house completely—but of course he is very wealthy and can afford to do so.'

'I had understood something of the kind,' Jane said in a repressive tone. She did not think it seemly of Paul's friend to have discussed his personal circumstances with a young girl, but felt it unwise to speak against the gentleman to a girl who was clearly enamoured. 'It is hardly our business to speculate, Melia. I hope you will not speak of this to anyone else. To discuss another person's wealth is unseemly.'

'Of course I would not.' Melia flushed and looked uncomfortable. 'Adam was explaining that he is to go into business with Lord Frant, though he is not wealthy himself for his own estate is but small.'

'Ah, I see.' Jane gave her a direct look. 'You speak of the viscount as Adam. Do I take it that he asked you to do so?'

'Yes, of course.' Melia smiled saucily at her. 'Oh, I know better than to do so in Society, but privately we are Adam and Melia.'

'I do not wish to criticise your behaviour,' Jane said. 'Yet I am your chaperon and I would not wish you to be hurt...or to be thought fast. It might be prudent to be a little careful, Melia. Viscount Hargreaves is charming, but we know so little of him or his affairs.'

Melia's face flushed stubbornly and for a moment she looked as if she would argue, but then she inclined her head. 'I would never do anything you felt shameful, Lady March. Surely you cannot think it? I am grateful to you for bringing me to London for I am sure you did not want the bother of a young girl.'

'You could never be a bother to me,' Jane said. 'Indeed, if you think me harsh I am sorry for I did not mean to scold—I think only of your future, my dear. Both Will and I are very fond of you.'

'Yes, I know.' Melia looked a little ashamed. 'Pray forgive me, Jane. I did not mean to sound petulant but... the viscount is so flattering and it is nice to have a gentleman say pretty things...'

'Yes, of course,' Jane said. 'However, some gentlemen say more than they mean. I do not think it of Viscount Hargreaves necessarily, but a little care in one's dealings with a gentleman one hardly knows...'

'Do you not like him?' Melia asked, looking bewildered.

'I have formed no opinion,' Jane said truthfully. 'However, I do like Lord Frant and I would suppose any friend of his to be a gentleman—but for your own sake, Melia, take your time.'

'Yes, I shall.' Melia sparkled at her suddenly. 'He is not the only gentleman to pay me exquisite compliments. I might have had my head turned a dozen times at the ball if I were a foolish child.'

Jane smiled, the look in the girl's eyes making her wonder if perhaps Melia was not well able to take care of herself. Perhaps she too was merely flirting and would not lose her heart to a rogue...

Now why had she thought of Viscount Hargreaves as a rogue? It was not because of her brother's hints about his card playing... No, more a certain note in his voice when he'd spoken of Paul Frant as having plenty of money to buy a houseful of furniture. Something in his tone and his face had made Jane suspect that underneath the smiles and the assumption of friendship for his host there lay a simmering jealousy.

Melia felt a flicker of guilt as she went upstairs to put off her bonnet before nuncheon. She had lied to Jane about her feelings and her intentions, allowing her to think that she was interested in a score of admirers who had paid her such pretty compliments at the ball, when in truth the only one that made her heart flutter was Adam.

He had pressed her hand to his lips in the garden, gazing ardently into her eyes as he told her that she was the loveliest girl he'd seen in England and he was rapidly falling under her spell.

'I am so unworthy of you, my dear Miss Bellingham...'

'No, no, do not say so,' Melia had begged him. 'You must call me Melia; everyone I like does...'

'In private, perhaps,' he'd said in a voice husky with passion. 'I am Adam to you, and you are Melia in my heart—but I can never presume to hope for more than friendship, sweet lady. I have little to offer and, though Frant and I are to go into partnership in the matter of our racing stable, my estate is unable to support the wife I would wish for. In time, perhaps, I shall have my own houses in Ireland, London and perhaps Leicestershire for the hunting—but that may be some years away, and I could not ask any lady to wait for me...'

Melia's heart had swelled with a mixture of love and grief. How noble he was in renouncing her because he could not afford to give her the things she deserved. The portion Lord Frant had given her no longer seemed enough, for though it increased her fortune to seven thousand pounds in all, it was not enough to buy her a husband who needed the means to support a wife and live in comfort in the way he described.

How could Papa have left his whole estate away from his daughters? Melia supposed it must have been worth some twenty thousand pounds or more—which meant she ought to have had ten thousand pounds, not the measly five that Lord Frant had granted her.

She stared at herself in the dressing mirror, her mouth pulled down in discontent. It was not Adam's fault that his own father had wasted his inheritance to almost nothing. He'd told her that Lord Frant's father had done much the same to him.

'It is all right for Paul,' he'd said and she'd seen his rueful look of regret. 'He has the luck of the devil. In India we rescued a young prince from a pack of vengeful tribesmen from the hills—but it was he that received the gratitude and rewards from the Prince's father. I received almost nothing…'

Melia had been given the impression that Adam had been the principle rescuer and Lord Frant had taken the credit, which had resulted in him becoming the owner of palaces and lands out there in India.

'You should have spoken out,' Melia had said, outraged on his behalf. 'Lord Frant should share the rewards with you.'

'He was the one who snatched the Prince from a burning building,' Adam had said. 'My men and I made it possible by fighting off the tribesmen, but of course the Prince called Frant his saviour. I did not wish to push myself forward—and the Maharaja sent wine, food and one hundred gold coins, which I shared out amongst my men.'

'Yes, I do see it would be impossible for you to push your claim,' Melia had said, her heart won by his self-lessness in sharing the small reward he'd received with his men. 'Yet I still think Lord Frant should have given you half of the rewards he received.'

'I should not wish you to think ill of him,' Adam had told her. 'You must not speak of this to anyone, Melia—it was merely that I wished you to understand why I cannot offer marriage to any lady, even if it breaks my heart. I must earn my fortune by hard work and skill.'

Melia changed into an afternoon gown, for she was going out with Viscount Salisbury after luncheon. She was aware that she had once given a careless promise to him, but she'd never said that she loved him or that she would marry him, merely that she would wish to get to know him better before answering his question.

Melia did like both Jane and Will very much; they were her friends and she would not shame them or hurt them for the world—but she'd discovered a new and exciting world here in London and meant to make the most of her chances while she was here.

Her heart was given to Adam, but he was set against marriage until he could earn enough to keep his wife in style. Only if Melia could persuade her guardian to give her a larger portion might she be able to persuade him to think better of his noble sacrifice. A man who would not speak out when he was cheated of a fortune would not marry just for money—and yet she believed that he'd been telling her he loved her. If she had ten thousand, perhaps he would marry her...

Jane was about to change for the evening when she heard the rattle of carriage wheels outside the house; the sounds of postilions shouting and a loud rapping at the door made her throw on a silk wrap and hurry to the top of the stairs. Hearing a commotion in the hall and then the sound of a young woman's voice, she gave a glad cry and looked down. Cousin Sarah had arrived some hours early and her arrival had thrown the servants into disarray.

'Come up to me, Sarah,' she called down. 'I am changing and may not come down, but please do come up to me. You were expected tomorrow but your room is prepared and we shall have some tea in my sitting room while they carry up your bags.'

'Jane…' A tall girl with dark eyes and a pale complexion started up the stairs towards her. 'I am sorry to throw your arrangements out, but I had the offer of a carriage part way and it brought me here some hours earlier than I'd expected.'

'It doesn't matter in the least,' Jane said, meeting her with outstretched hands. They kissed cheeks warmly, Jane looking intently into her face. 'You look pale, Sarah. I was so sorry when your dear mama passed away.'

'It has been a terrible time,' Sarah confessed, her voice catching. 'My father left us with little to live on and poor Mama was living in fear of being turned from the house. I do believe it was that…' She shook her head and forced a smile. 'I am determined not to cry all over you, Jane. It was so good of you to offer me a home and saved me from…but that will keep for later. You are dressing for the evening, I think?'

'Yes. Melia and I are engaged for an evening of music and supper, also perhaps a little dancing later. I do not wish to disappoint Melia, but I should not like to leave you alone, Sarah.'

'You must not concern yourself,' Sarah said and sighed. 'To own the truth, a little light supper in my room and I shall be very well for this evening. Please, Jane, I should feel so awkward if I kept you here when all I wish for is to rest.'

'Very well, I shall instruct my housekeeper to bring you your supper on a tray—and I will take you to your rooms, my dear cousin. Tomorrow we shall have a long talk and you may tell me all your news.'

'Thank you for your kindness,' Sarah said, and again there was a break in her voice. 'I was near desperate when I wrote to you and for a while I did not think I could escape my fate...'

Jane looked at her enquiringly, but she shook her head. Realising that Sarah was indeed exhausted, Jane led the way to the large and pleasant chamber she'd had prepared for her.

'Oh, what a lovely room—two rooms,' Sarah said, realising that she had both bedchamber and sitting room of her own. 'This is sheer luxury, Jane. I cannot thank you enough.'

'We shall discuss my plans and yours tomorrow,' Jane promised her, kissed her cheek and left her to the maids who had come up to attend to her unpacking.

After giving the housekeeper instructions for her cousin's comfort, Jane left her and returned to her bedroom to finish changing. Had she not been entertaining Melia she might have cancelled her engagements for the evening, but she did not wish to disappoint the girl—and Sarah's story would wait for the morning.

Chapter Seven

Paul picked up the invitation from Lady Featherstone and read it once more. He thought it most likely that it would be an insipid affair and would normally have rejected it in favour of an evening playing cards with some friends at his club. However, Melia had told Adam that she and Jane would be guests of Lady Featherstone this evening, and that meant it would not be a complete waste of time—and yet was it too soon? He did not wish Jane to feel that she was being pursued, for he sensed that although she was intrigued and interested in the project he had invited her to oversee, her feelings towards him were, as yet, merely those of a casual acquaintance. She was quite clearly still grieving for her husband, even though she'd put off her blacks. Had he not been Melia's guardian, he doubted that she would have obliged him in the matter of furnishing his house.

Paul looked at himself ruefully in the mirror. His natural impatience made him long to make her an offer of his heart, his name and his fortune, in that order, but he believed that she would become embarrassed and turn him down. Had he seen any sign of anything warmer than what he thought was the beginning of liking, he would have shown his feelings for it was not in his nature to be secretive.

Paul remembered the day he had snatched the young Prince Kumal from the building in which his captors had imprisoned him. When the preparations for an assault on their camp was noticed, one of them had set fire to the wooden hut and the youth's terrified screams had caused Paul to rush straight to his rescue. The tribesmen had been caught by surprise but that did not prevent them from shooting at him as he rode up to the small building and dismounted, attacking the door with an axe until it gave. Rushing into the fire against the shouted orders to wait from the captain in charge of the soldiers that day, Paul had carried the now almost unconscious lad from the building, sustaining burns to his back and one of his legs. He'd covered the Prince and his own head with a blanket, thus preventing much of the harm that might have been done; his scars were hidden and he never spoke of them.

Prince Kumal had suffered only minor burns to his hands, incurred in trying to pull away burning wood from across the door before Paul's arrival. He and his father had been overwhelmingly grateful, for his quick actions had undoubtedly saved the Prince's life.

'You must also thank the soldiers who helped drive off the tribesmen,' Paul told the grateful father. 'I could not have done it alone.'

'I have been told it was your quick thinking that

saved my son. Your soldiers and their captain were interested only in subduing the tribesmen. It was you who insisted they go in at once—and indeed they could only follow once you led the way. Kumal told me that he thought he would die until you started hacking down the door. He heard no shots until after you plunged in to rescue him.'

There had been none for Adam had been waiting to assess how many rebels there were before committing to the attack. He and his men had been sent to subdue the tribesmen, who had been causing a deal of trouble in the area, but Paul's reason for being one of the party was the suspicion that it was these particular renegades who had kidnapped the young Prince.

He knew that Adam and his men had received two thousand gold pieces as the Maharaja's reward for helping to save his son. His reward had been more personal: a pink-walled palace, lands—and the offer of a half-royal bride who would come with a rich dowry, besides many other gifts. His son had offered one of his own concubines for Paul's pleasure, but the Maharaja had offered him a prestigious wedding that would have brought both power and wealth.

'The Princess Helena's daughter is beautiful and carries the blood of my uncle,' the Maharaja said, smiling on him. 'It would honour her to become your wife— and it would honour us if you would make your home amongst us and share our lands.'

He had been tempted for a moment or two because Annamarie was very lovely, and any man might be happy to live like a prince. Paul's fortune had come through his own endeavours, but the lands and palace he'd been given were worth what many would think a small fortune in themselves—and Annamarie had a rich dowry settled on her by her father before he died. Adam had thought Paul a fool to turn down the offer and he'd had to be very careful for he did not wish to give offence, either to the Maharaja or Annamarie herself.

Perhaps if that letter from his distant cousin's lawyers had not arrived when it did he might have stayed and taken Annamarie as his wife—and what a terrible mistake that would have been. The proud beauty would soon have guessed that he did not love her, and she would not have been happy at being part of a bargain made by her uncle. She no longer lived in the palace and thought herself a free agent, bound to do only her mother's bidding.

Pushing all thought of India and the past from his mind, Paul finished his preparations for the evening. He was fortunate that his face had not been scarred as his back was, and one of his legs. He'd never been as handsome as Adam, but sometimes he wondered if any woman would put up with the scarring on his back… yet a nightshirt would cover it and the old scars never pained him now.

It was strange but he'd never thought he would ever fall in love—so deeply in love that nothing else mattered—but one look at Jane, one smile from those lovely eyes, and he could think of nothing else. He had for one fleeting moment considered wedding his ward, but that thought had been forgotten the moment he'd looked into Jane's eyes.

Deciding that he was ready, Paul picked up his hat, cloak and cane. Adam had decided that he would prefer an evening of cards amongst his friends and excused himself.

'You do not need me,' he'd told Paul, an odd look in his eyes. 'I shall visit a club I've been told of with some new acquaintances.'

Paul had wanted to warn him about trusting new friends and new gambling establishments, but the advice might have caused offence and would not have been heeded.

In India they had been friends, though not often in each other's company since Adam was a part of the Army that protected the Company and the district from various warring tribes. On the ship coming over, Paul's illness had formed a bond between them and he had sincerely wished that Adam was his brother—but, since then, Adam's behaviour had planted a small seed of doubt in his mind.

Paul was not a gambler. He was willing to play a hand or two with friends at his club for reasonable stakes and usually rose with either a small loss or an equally small gain. However, he believed that Adam was playing for high stakes and hoping to win enough to repair his fortunes. Adam's father had been a reckless gambler, which was why he'd lost most of his estate, and it seemed that it was in the blood. Paul feared for his friend because of it, but he could not interfere.

His lawyers were looking into Adam's affairs and the outcome of that might be the only way that this madness could be brought to a close. If Adam discovered that after all there was a reasonable sum left from his father's estate, perhaps he would be happy to go off to Ireland as they'd planned and put aside this reckless gambling.

Sighing, Paul put his friend's problems from his mind. The fever he'd suffered on the ship had dragged him down but he was at last feeling more like himself again. He would have to visit the country to sort out his various estates soon—and he wanted to visit Newmarket for the races. If he saw any young horses he liked the look of he would purchase them at Tattersalls. Perhaps if he could carry Adam off with him to Ireland, he might settle down and forget his foolish dreams of winning back all that his father had lost...

Jane was conscious of a feeling of pleasure when she saw that Lord Frant had come that evening. It was to be a simple evening of a little music and some cards for those who wished for it. Many of the gentlemen had accompanied wives, daughters and young cousins, and would disappear into the card room as soon as the music began. However, when she found a seat for herself and Melia where they might sit and listen but not be too close, it was not long before Lord Frant came to stand near them.

'Good evening, Melia, Lady March,' Paul said. 'I believe Madame Meloria is a fine soloist and we are in for a treat this evening.'

'Yes, so I have heard,' Jane said and smiled at him. 'Are you comfortable there? I believe there is a chair just behind that you might fetch to sit beside us if you wished.'

'Yes, I see it,' Paul said and moved away to pick up the single chair and place it next to Jane as she sat on the small sofa beside Melia. 'That will be more comfortable if the music continues for a while.'

Melia leaned forward in her seat. 'Is Viscount Hargreaves not with you this evening, sir?'

'No. I believe he had another appointment,' Paul said and frowned.

'Is something wrong?' Jane asked but he shook his head and assured her that all was well.

They spent a very pleasant evening listening to the music, taking supper together and talking. Melia had seen some friends and was carried off by one young lady to join her and her brother and his friends in a light-hearted and very noisy and amusing card game. No money was wagered by the young people but there was a great deal of rivalry and Melia's laughter was heard on several occasions.

'Your brother did not accompany you this evening?' Paul asked towards the end. 'I had thought he might have done so.'

'It was his intention, I believe, but Mama summoned him to attend her to the theatre. It seems the duke was indisposed and suggested that Will took her instead, which of course he was delighted to do. We are both very fond of her.'

'Yes, I dare say you are,' Paul said and laughed softly. 'I imagine not many can resist the duchess's charm?'

'Oh, it has not always been so,' Jane assured him.

'Mama was very young when her father arranged the marriage to my father and it was not a happy one. Papa was too critical for poor Mama, but Porky adores her. I do believe he has remained faithful all his life.'

Paul looked thoughtful. 'Marriage should always be for love or at the very least where liking and respect are sufficient. For myself, nothing but love would content me. If I were to ask a lady to be my wife she would know that I should never look elsewhere and make it my purpose in life to see that she was happy.'

'Yes, I believe that you would,' Jane said, her interest caught. 'For myself, I could never marry unless I loved. I was very much in love when I married Harry March.'

'Yes, I believe your husband was a brilliant soldier. You were unlucky to have lost him so soon, ma'am.' His eyes dwelled on her with a warm sympathy that made Jane's heart catch, for in that moment she felt that she could find comfort against his broad shoulder.

'Yes, it was ill luck—but Harry was never one to sit at the rear and send his men forward. He led the charge and was shot down…' Jane's throat caught and for a moment she felt close to tears, but held them back. 'I was devastated when they told me. I have begun to accept and move forward—but it is the only source of discord between myself and Mama. She cannot see why I say I shall not marry again…'

'You think it would not be possible to find such happiness again?'

'I do not think I could settle for second best,' Jane admitted candidly. 'Only if I felt another person necessary to my very life would I think of taking another husband.'

'I can only say that the man you chose would be fortunate—and since I think it a shame you should live alone I must hope you find him one day.' Something in his words touched her in a way that other expressions of sympathy had not and she almost wished that he would put his arms about her and hold her safe.

'I shall not be alone,' Jane said with her sweet smile that, unknown to her, clutched at his heart. 'My cousin Sarah has come up to town to bear me company. When Melia's visit is done I may think of taking a house in Bath. If my brother were to marry I could not continue as his hostess because it would be unfair to his wife— whoever she might be.'

'Yes, I see…' His expression did not change, but Jane knew that he was thinking about what she'd told him. 'Would I be wrong in thinking that your brother still has hopes of her?'

Jane glanced towards the group of young people and sighed. 'I believe he thought she returned his feelings, but now he is not sure. She is young and pretty and it is only right that she should have her chance to shine in Society—and to make her choice. I do not wish for Will to be unhappy, but I would not have Melia feel constrained to marry where her heart did not follow.'

'You think her head has been turned by gentlemen paying her compliments—or by one gentleman in particular?'

'It is not easy to be certain,' Jane admitted. 'Melia likes flattery and attention—who does not? She seems happy this evening, and yet I believe she was disappointed that Viscount Hargreaves did not come.'

'Adam is not truly in a position to take a wife—unless she has a fortune and is willing to bestow it on him. Melia's portion would not be enough for him, Jane. I think he would marry only if he were to find an heiress—or a rich widow, you see. You might hint at his lack of real fortune if you think it would save her pain. He is not penniless; I would not have you think that— but not rich enough to support the lifestyle he enjoys and a wife and family.'

'Yes, I had supposed something of the sort,' Jane said. 'However, I think it unwise to try and influence her. Melia must decide for herself what she wants of life.'

'You are very wise,' he said and once again that thoughtful look was in his eyes. 'It is seldom wise to meddle in the lives of our friends, unless they ask us— and even then too often they will not thank us for it...'

'I fear you are right,' Jane said. She rose to her feet and offered her hand. 'It has been a most pleasant evening and I am reluctant to leave, but I think I ought. I have neglected Sarah long enough and must go home and enquire how she is.'

'Ah yes.' He glanced at Melia. 'My ward will not take kindly to being asked to leave, I think. She is still intent on her game—and winning, by the sound of it.'

'Even so, I must take her away.'

'Unless you thought I might bring her home safely in—say another hour?'

'Oh...' Jane was about to say she did not think it a

good idea, but then remembered that he was Melia's guardian and might, if he'd wished, have insisted that she live with him and a chaperon. 'Yes, I think that might suit—if she likes the idea.'

Melia hesitated and then agreed. She said she hoped that Jane found her cousin well and she would not disturb her when she came in but go straight to her room.

'I prefer that you say goodnight. I shall not be asleep by then and indeed I could not unless I knew you were safely home.'

'Oh, if you wish it.' Melia gave a shrug of her pretty shoulders. 'But Lord Frant is my guardian—and far too old to be of any consequence…'

Jane gave her a puzzled look, wondering how she could speak of a man who had done so much for her. Five thousand pounds was a considerable gift and, properly invested, would bring in enough to keep the girl in comfort until she married. Living with her aunt, as she did, she would have no need to spend the interest on anything but trifles she fancied.

Having taken her leave of her charge, Jane had her carriage brought round and was driven home. A sigh escaped her as she settled back against the squabs, for she half wished that she had stayed another hour. She had seldom passed a more pleasant evening and could only thank Lord Frant for that since he had been attentive and an interesting conversationalist, telling her some tales of life in India that she found fascinating.

She spoke to her housekeeper, who told her that Miss Sarah had settled for the night and had drunk a tisane she'd given her.

'She had a headache, my lady, and I gave her the special mixture I used to make for your dear mama. It will make her sleep through to the morning, never fear.'

'Then I shall not disturb her,' Jane said. 'I should like some hot milk and sweet biscuits, if you please—and I will sit up in my dressing room until Lord Frant brings his ward home. Please let me know the moment she is in the house.'

'Of course, my lady.'

Jane went up to her own apartments and allowed her maid to undress her and brush her hair. It seemed that she'd left the company early for no good reason, but she had not liked to think of Sarah sitting alone in her room, despite her declaration that she was perfectly content to go to bed and rest.

After she had dismissed her maid, Jane tried to read a book in the comfort of a large wing chair, but her mind kept returning to Lord Frant and his smile. His years in India had caused him to have lines at his eyes, caused perhaps by the relentless sun and the need to screw up the eyes against it at times. She did not find it unattractive that his face should have a slightly craggy look, for it showed that he had lived—and, if she were not mistaken, suffered in some manner.

Something about him had caught her interest. Jane could not have said what, but at each meeting she discovered more about the man and his character, and she liked what she'd learned. Paul Frant was a man to be trusted and relied upon, Jane thought, and there was something honest and straightforward in his manner of address that appealed to her.

* * *

'I am glad to have this time alone with you,' Melia said when she was sitting in Paul's carriage on the opposite seat facing him. 'I wanted to talk to you about Viscount Hargreaves…of the predicament he finds himself in, which makes it impossible for him to marry where he will…'

'Indeed?' Paul's eyes narrowed but Melia ignored the warning sign. 'Do you think it quite proper for you to speak this of a man you hardly know?'

'Not when it affects my whole happiness, for you must know that I am in love with him and if he cannot wed me for lack of fortune I shall break my heart.'

Paul was silent for a moment, then, 'Has Hargreaves spoken to you of marriage? He should properly have asked my permission for you are under the age of consent and, even had you reached that age, mere politeness makes it imperative that he do so.'

'Oh, pooh, as if I should care for such things if I were of age and had a suitable fortune. Had Papa only lived I am certain he would have given me at least ten thousand pounds on my marriage.'

'I very much doubt your father could have found such a sum,' Paul told her. 'To do so he must have sold the estate, which, as you know, was entailed.'

Melia stared at him, a rebellious look on her pretty face. For a moment she was silenced, but then began the second prong of her attack. 'Do you not think you owe the viscount something for what he did when that young prince was rescued? You received a large reward while he had nothing but a few gold pieces, which he shared with his men.'

'Did Hargreaves tell you that?'

Melia hesitated, as though realising that she'd been not only rude but unguarded. 'Can you deny it is true?'

'The truth of the matter is my affair and no other's,' Paul replied in a measured tone that hid the anger he felt inside.

Her accusations were unfair and he could not be sure how much of it was due to her resentment against him and how much Adam had said to her. Did the man he'd thought of as a true friend feel resentment because Paul had received so many gifts from the Maharaja? His part in driving the tribesmen off had indeed been heroic and vital, but it would all have been too late had Paul not done what he had—and the Prince's father felt that the soldiers had merely done their duty to protect the province, for which service he'd already paid handsomely. His generous gift of two thousand gold coins was not something to be dismissed as paltry, even when shared with Adam's men.

'I do not think two thousand gold coins an unfair reward for a man doing his job. The Army is paid to keep the tribesmen in control and two thousand was a generous gift.'

'It was nowhere near as much! Surely...'

'I assure you that was the sum given to Hargreaves and his men, together with wine and food.'

'Even so—why should you have so much more?' Melia asked, looking sulky, but she stared in disbelief and he realised Adam must have mentioned a different sum.

Paul might have told her why he'd been so favoured, but he held his tongue. 'You speak of things you do not understand,' he said in a mild tone. 'I think you should reflect a little longer before you speak to me on this subject again. If you knew the truth…' He sighed. 'No matter—you are in love and young. You believe that only your wishes are important. Until you grow up a little and learn to think of others, I should not give my permission for your marriage even if Hargreaves had asked and had the fortune to keep you as you expect.'

'I hate you and I wish my father had not named you in his will.'

'I dare say he meant my father to be your guardian,' Paul said. 'They were friends, I believe—but my father died and yours just before him. It is unfortunate. I dare say my father's wife might have brought you out, but I can assure you he would not have given you five thousand pounds. You should try to be content with your lot, Melia. Sulking does not become you.'

Melia glared at him but did not reply, and, since they had arrived at Viscount Salisbury's house, Paul got out, giving her his hand to help her down from the carriage and see her to the door.

'Will you not wish me goodnight, Melia? It will be better for us to remain on good terms, I think.'

'Oh, goodnight then,' she said ungraciously. 'But I think you might help Viscount Hargreaves, so that we can marry.'

'I know you do,' he said with a faint smile. 'Try to

be patient, Melia; things often have a way of working themselves out. One day you may be glad I did not do as you asked.'

The door opened and she was admitted. Paul returned to his carriage. He was thoughtful as he was driven home. Melia had no doubt been spun a tale that led her to believe Adam had played the leading part in the Prince's rescue; it was the only possible reason for her attitude. He did not care for her character and could only be pleased that he had not been too hasty in the matter of offering her marriage; they would not suit, even had she agreed.

Was Adam as resentful of him as Melia's unguarded words seemed to indicate? If she believed that he'd taken all the honours and rewards for himself—rewards that rightfully belonged to Adam—it was possible that he thought much the same.

Paul felt a slight unease. He'd been so grateful for Adam's attentions on the ship that he'd fallen into the habit of thinking him a great friend—but in India they had not been close. He recalled that he'd once thought the young Army officer was in love with Annamarie. Now that he was remembering, Annamarie had only begun to show her preference for Paul when he'd recovered from his injuries. Her mother had visited him several times when he was suffering from the burns to his back and leg, and she'd invited him to visit them when he was able to resume his normal life. It was then that the beautiful young girl had made it clear she thought him worthy to be her husband.

A wry smile touched Paul's mouth; he'd become a

hero overnight in the small community, and Annamarie was not the only girl to throw him encouraging smiles. Glad to be well again and wishing only that people would forget his actions and not make so much fuss over what had, after all, been instinctive, Paul had taken little notice. He'd been aware of Annamarie's marked interest because she'd been offered to him as a wife—but before that…before the night that was only a blur in his mind and the weeks of pain, had Adam believed she might favour him?

Paul sought in his mind for a scene he only partially recalled. It was at a regimental ball. He'd been invited as an ex-officer and an influential businessman—but Adam had been there, dressed in his uniform, new to the post and looking very handsome. Was he imagining it, or had he seen the pair go out to the veranda, returning some thirty minutes later looking flushed and excited?

It was an image Paul had long forgotten. Of no importance to anyone but the girl and her mother who she chose to spend her time with…but now it made him wonder.

Was it possible that Adam held a grudge against him because Annamarie had transferred her attention to Paul after the dramatic rescue? Had he been hoping that she would marry him? Annamarie had quite a large dowry and a man with no fortune and, in peacetime, little hope of earning prize money, would never have been considered a suitable husband?

Paul would have supposed she might be married off to an Indian prince, unless her mother intended to bring her to England and find a husband amongst her own people for the girl. It was not his concern. He shrugged his shoulders as he entered the house. As he intended to make his home in England and would never marry the beautiful girl who had been offered to him by a grateful father, he had no interest in the matter—but it did affect his relationship with Adam.

He'd looked forward to running the racing stables with his friend, but if Adam was harbouring resentment perhaps it was not such a good idea… Paul put it from his mind. Melia clearly resented her father's will and perhaps she'd misunderstood what Adam said to her. Paul could only hope that had been the case…but he would keep an open mind.

Chapter Eight

'Mama was left almost penniless,' Sarah confessed over the coffee she and Jane were drinking in Jane's parlour that morning. 'When she discovered that Papa had been getting further and further in debt for years, it was a terrible blow to her.'

'Yes, I imagine it would be,' Jane said. 'Why did you not come to me at once? I should have done what I could to help. You might both have lived in my house. I would gladly have given you a home.'

'We did not want to ask for charity from anyone. Mama's brother sold what was left of Papa's estate and loaned us a cottage on his estate, which is where we've been living. We had enough to live respectably, but when Mama died my uncle told me he did not think it right for me to live alone there—and his wife does not like me…' Sarah hesitated. 'He suggested that I should marry and brought two gentlemen to my attention—Sir Jonathan, a pleasant gentleman of some sixty years, and Colonel Brush. He is a widower and needs a mother for his six children. Since his wife died because she was simply worn out with childbearing I did not care to take her place. Sir Jonathan was kind and told me that he needed only a gentle companion but...'

'Oh, my dear,' Jane cried and sat forward to catch her hand. 'Your uncle was most unfair to impose such conditions. Of course you should not marry either of those gentlemen.'

'Well, I considered taking Sir Jonathan's offer just to satisfy my uncle—but then I thought of you, Jane, and wrote my letter more in desperation than in hope.'

'I'm so pleased you did,' Jane said, giving her a frank look. 'If Will marries I must set up my own house. I think I shall take up residence in Bath—though I may spend some time in the country. Naturally, I must have a female companion, and your letter made me think of you. We might be very happy living in Bath together, Sarah. Visits to London and the country, and my brother occasionally, of course, but mostly in a pleasant location in Bath—what do you think of that?'

'It sounds like heaven,' Sarah said and sighed. 'Do you not think of remarrying?'

'No, I do not think so...' Jane hesitated. 'I had made up my mind to remain Harry's widow, but now I must admit that it might happen one day. However, you too may meet someone you wish to wed, and if that happened I should wish you well, dear Sarah. If I did marry before you, you would always have a home with me.'

'You are so kind,' Sarah said. 'I do not wish to be a burden...'

'Nor will you,' Jane said at once. 'I should have to

employ someone to bear me company, and I would so much rather you were my guest for as long as we both wish it. Melia is staying with me now, but she—she is a young lady of strong opinions and this was only intended to be a visit for the duration of our stay in London. Will had hopes of her, but I think her head may have been turned. I hope it is her head and not her heart, for I cannot like the man she favours…'

'Surely she cannot prefer another man when she has the offer of…' Sarah's cheeks flushed as she halted. 'The viscount is so very kind and thoughtful, Jane. When I came down this morning…nothing could have been more pleasant in the way he welcomed me to his home.'

'Yes, I am fond of Will and I shall be upset if Melia hurts him—but I hope that he will find his own way. Either she is the girl he loves or she is not…but I speak out of turn. Melia has not told me what she feels and I must not presume to know her mind or Will's.'

'As a sister you think of him first,' Sarah said. 'I longed for a brother or sister when I was a child, but now that I know of Papa's behaviour… I am glad there was no one else to be hurt by it.'

'I know how you feel. My father was a stern man, though he did not waste his fortune. Instead, he dictated to his family and made all our lives difficult—most of all for poor Mama.'

'But she is happy now? She sent me a most delightful letter and told me she would help me to buy some pretty clothes when I came to you—and…' Sarah blushed delicately. 'She suggested that she could find me a husband from her many acquaintances...'

'Poor Sarah,' Jane said with a wry laugh. 'Mama has almost given up trying to find me a husband so now she will turn her attention to you. I shall tell her to leave you in peace.'

'Oh, no, for she means well, I am sure. She promised not to bully me but to introduce me to lovely gentlemen who would make me happy if I let them...'

'Mama has paraded so many handsome and rich men for me to see,' Jane said, smiling at the memory. 'But for some reason she seems to have given me up this time. I dare say it will amuse her to introduce you to her friends—and if it does not upset you, there is no harm done.'

'It will not upset me,' Sarah told her. 'The duchess is to call for me at ten this morning and she insists on taking me to her dressmaker.'

'In that I shall not interfere,' Jane said. 'Mama has perfect taste and will know just what suits you. I had intended to offer you a dress allowance and I shall, but you must let Mama spoil you a little—Porky gives her far more than she can spend on herself and she enjoys spending it on those she cares for. She will inundate Will's wife and children with gifts once he is married, I have no doubt.'

'Why should she not?' Sarah said and laughed softly. 'It is surely what money is for—to spend on those one cares for.'

'Yes, indeed, which is why you must let us spoil you, Sarah. This trip to London was meant to be enjoyed and, like Mama, I enjoy giving presents.' Jane touched her hand once more. 'I have an errand to run this morning—unless you would like my support?'

'No, not at all; I adore the duchess,' Sarah said. 'You must not let me interfere in any way with your plans, Jane.'

'I had none for this morning, other than to make you welcome. This afternoon I shall take you visiting and this evening there is a small dance, to which we are all invited. Will intends to accompany us so it will be all the family together. Tomorrow I shall be visiting some furniture warehouses and emporiums with Lord Frant. I am sure you could come if you wish.'

'I shall be quite content here. Perhaps there is something I could do for you, Jane—flower arranging or keeping your correspondence in order. I did those things for Mama.'

'Oh, the flowers perhaps, if you choose,' Jane said, 'but you are here to enjoy yourself, Sarah. You will soon make friends, and of course your name will be included on all my invitations once it is known you are in town.'

'I must go up and fetch my shawl,' Sarah said. 'The duchess will be here at any moment and I must not keep her waiting.'

Jane nodded and let her go. She wandered over to her desk but she had hardly settled to her letters when a small commotion in the hall told her that her mother had arrived. The next moment the door was flung wide and the duchess walked in; she was a delicate, pretty woman with good bone structure and hair that was still the colour of spun natural silk or white blonde as some called it. Dressed in the height of fashion, she contrived to look half her age and she had often been taken for Jane's sister by strangers.

'My darling Jane.' Mama embraced her lovingly in a cloud of expensive perfume. 'How is poor little Sarah? Such a terrible time she has had...'

'Sarah is very well, I think,' Jane said. 'A little sad still, I believe, but ready to come out of mourning and be dressed by you, dearest. I think she would not wish to wear bright colours yet, but I know you will do the thing perfectly.'

'Of course I shall,' the duchess said. 'No one has ever doubted my taste in such matters, Jane. She shall wear what suits her, but nothing loud or distasteful in a girl so recently bereaved—it is only a month since dear Seraphina died, is it not?'

'Yes, it is,' Jane agreed. 'Sarah is just such a person as I can set up my own home with, Mama. We shall agree very well and I think our tastes are not dissimilar.'

'Well, that's as maybe,' Mama said, a little smile playing about her lips. 'Yet who knows? I may find husbands for you both long before then...'

'Mama, no!' Jane warned her but with a smile. 'Please no schemes for me—and do not put pressure on poor Sarah. She has had enough of that from her uncle.'

'Yes, indeed, I know it,' Mama agreed. 'I would not press her for the world—but if she should meet someone, perhaps who loves her but of little fortune, my dearest Porky will see her right. He would do anything to oblige me, you know.'

'I know, dearest one,' Jane said and laughed. 'You have him wrapped about your little finger, do you not?'

'Jane, it is no such thing,' the duchess said, her eyes alight with mischief. 'Porky likes to be generous. How could he spend a tenth of his fortune if I did not show him how? He has never been happier than now and tells me so every night and first thing in the morning.'

'Yes, I know that to be true,' Jane agreed. 'And you are truly happy, Mama?'

'Of course. Porky adores me, and that is rather lovely, Jane. I am very fond of him and I like to look after him. He needs me, you see; he was so lost and lonely before we married.'

Jane smiled inwardly for the duke had a vast crowd of friends and legions of faithful servants to care for his every need—but perhaps, in adoring his pretty and mischievous wife, he'd found his happiness.

Sarah came back downstairs and Jane went to the door to see them off in Mama's smart carriage, with its cream leather cushions and shiny black paint. She returned to her parlour just as Melia came downstairs, dressed for walking.

'Are you going out, Melia?'

'Yes, with Miss Anne Smythe and her brother Captain Smythe,' Melia said. 'It was arranged at the party last evening. Do you not recall my telling you last night when I returned?'

Jane was certain the girl had merely poked her head in to ask if she was well and then gone off to her own room. Looking at her closely, Jane thought she looked a trifle pale and heavy-eyed, not as fresh and lovely as when they had come to London.

'Is something upsetting you?' she asked, thinking that Melia looked as if she'd been crying.

'No, I am perfectly all right,' Melia said but did not look comfortable. 'I must go. My maid is waiting and I am to meet the others at half past eleven. I shall not be home for nuncheon, but I am not hungry.'

Jane let her go. Melia was her guest but she was not her guardian and it was not for her to speak of propriety—at least not yet. Providing the girl took a maid with her, there was no reason why she should not meet her friends in the park.

Sighing, Jane continued to look through the invitations that had arrived that morning. Most evenings they had their choice of at least three and quite often made an appearance at all three, though on the evening of an important ball or a private visit to the theatre she wrote apologies for her absence at some affair or other.

Jane had been standing at the window lost in thought for a while when she heard a sound behind her and turned to see her brother enter. He looked so handsome and so dear that her heart caught; if Melia broke his heart she did not think she could forgive the girl.

'All alone, Jane?' he asked, seeming concerned.

'Yes, for the moment. Mama has taken Sarah shopping and Melia has gone walking with Captain Smythe and his sister.'

'Not out with Viscount Hargreaves today then?'

'No, I think she was a little annoyed because she

particularly told him where we would be last night and he chose to go elsewhere.'

'Oh, I see… Yes, that would not please her.' Will smiled at her. 'It will be just the two of us for luncheon then.'

'Yes, just like at home,' Jane said and moved towards him. 'Are you enjoying your visit, my dearest?'

'Yes, I always enjoy the chance to visit friends, entertain them and purchase a few clothes. I have ordered three pairs of boots and two new coats—the last from Weston. I believe his style will suit me in the country.'

'If you marry, your wife may wish to be in London more often, Will. Melia seems to love it in town.'

'Yes, she does quite clearly,' Will said, seeming thoughtful. 'Well, we shall cross that bridge when we come to it. I hope you've given up this nonsense of living alone?'

'Oh, I never intended to be alone,' she said mildly. 'Sarah will make an ideal companion—do you not agree?'

'She seems a pleasant girl to me,' he replied and laughed. 'It is wrong to call her that, for she is the same age as you, Jane—and very much a woman.'

'Yes. I imagine she has had to be. It seems she and her mother have had a hard time of it since her father died—and Sarah has had a worse one since then. Did she tell you her story?'

'Yes, a little, but it was easy enough to read between the lines. I admit to feeling sympathy for her, Jane. You must make sure that she knows she is welcome to live with us for as long as she wishes—though she is too attractive to be unmarried for long.'

'She has no portion, Will.' Jane smiled inwardly for her brother had changed his tune concerning her cousin, whom he'd thought plain at the start.

'Yet her good nature will attract suitors—and I would be glad to settle a dowry on her, if she would accept it.'

'As would I,' Jane agreed. 'Mama would adore to have Sarah live with her, for she is much taken with her—but, as you say, I do not think it need be long before our cousin weds.'

'A second cousin only,' Will reminded her. 'Sarah is Mama's cousin, though we have been used to call her such…'

'Yes, of course…our second cousin,' Jane said and wondered why her brother had stressed the more distant relationship.

'You have perfect taste,' Paul said when they had completed their tour of the furnishing emporium and made several choices. He led her out to his waiting carriage, helping her inside and then climbing in after. 'I liked everything you picked and shall be happy with them, I know.'

'We have accomplished but a third of your needs,' Jane said and laughed as she saw his look. 'Yes, I know. Gentlemen often consider such purchases as slow work, but it must be done if you are to be comfortable again.'

'Yes, I know it,' Paul said and laughed wryly. 'I am

forever in your debt, Lady March. I should not have known where to begin had you not lent me your aid.'

'You are most welcome, my lord,' she replied demurely but with a wicked twinkle in her eyes. 'I have enjoyed myself a great deal this morning and shall look forward to visiting your house once the furnishings are installed.'

'Naturally, I shall offer you the chance before anyone else,' he said. 'However, I must tell you that I am about to leave town for a few days. We attend the races at Newmarket and in my absence I hope that most of the redecorating will be done…'

'Ah, yes, that is best,' Jane agreed. 'A house is not your own when invaded by builders.'

'Very true,' he said ruefully. 'I confess it is the first time I've attempted it. I've never owned a house in England before—and in my palace in India all was done before I saw it…'

'Your palace?' Jane stared in surprise. 'Do you own such a thing, my lord?'

'It was given to me by the father of the Prince I rescued—a small palace by his estimation, but a palace all the same, with pleasant gardens, cool tinkling pools and trees to shade you from the heat of too hot a sun…'

'India sounds fascinating,' Jane said. 'I have sometimes thought I should like to travel again…'

'You travelled to France or Spain with your husband, I dare say?'

'Yes. Harry warned me it would be hard at times, and it was—but I would not have changed it for the world. I loved my husband and that time was precious; it mattered not to me that we sometimes lived in cramped and draughty quarters.'

'I think I envy Lord March,' Paul said softly, but Jane hardly caught the words and blushed at what she thought she heard.

'So when do you hope to return?' she asked. 'Would it be of use to you, sir, if I visited some other warehouses alone and asked them to send certain items on approval? You may view them at your leisure and reject anything you dislike.'

'If you choose as you have today, items of quality and taste, then I am certain I shall not need to return them,' Paul said. He hesitated and then went on, 'I am always in your debt. You must tell me if I can do anything to please you, my lady.'

'Then I shall use the time to good purpose,' she promised. 'I enjoy shopping and will perhaps find some items I shall need when I set up my house in Bath. My cousin has arrived in town and she seems happy to make her home with us—until she marries, of course.'

'I shall look forward to making her acquaintance.' Paul took her hand and kissed it as his carriage halted before her door. 'And now I must thank you again and leave you, for I have things to attend before I leave.'

'I enjoyed your company,' Jane said. 'Have a pleasant visit and enjoy the races, Lord Frant.'

Paul smiled and helped her down, escorting her to her door, which was opened as she reached it. Returning to his carriage, he was thoughtful. Jane's taste matched his own perfectly, and his feeling that she was the only woman he would ever wish to marry had grown steadily throughout the morning they had spent together.

He had fortune enough to please any woman, and his birth was good—though her father had been of higher rank. Yet there was nothing to stand in the way of a match between them in that regard—but could he turn her heart towards him? Jane was pleasant, friendly and he believed that she enjoyed his company—but would she ever trust her heart to him?

He was a man who faced reality and he had to admit that not once had she shown any warmer feelings towards him than that of a pleasant acquaintance. Perhaps it was hardly surprising. She had loved once and lost tragically. Could she let go of the past and give herself in marriage again…had she even thought of it, or of him, in such terms?

Paul was rueful as he reviewed her manner and words in his mind, but nothing she had said or done could convince him that he was more to her than an acquaintance.

How could he make her fall in love with him? He was not sure it was possible. He'd tried compliments and that had seemed to cause her to draw back. She was not a vain woman and flattery would be useless. He sighed as he realised that love either happened or it did not…

Sighing, Paul turned his thoughts. He had an appointment with his man of business. Spencer had investigated the affairs of the late Viscount Hargreaves, and would tell him if anything could be salvaged—and if not they must discover a way of making it seem to be so…

* * *

Jane found Melia and Sarah sitting in the front parlour together when she had taken off her pelisse and bonnet. Sarah was reading and Melia was sitting at a table with a pack of cards, playing patience, but without much evidence of being in that mood, for she threw them down with a sound of disgust.

'I cannot make them come out,' she cried. 'It is a useless game. I am glad you are back, Jane, for Sarah said we should not ring for tea until you came.'

'It is a little past our time,' Jane said. 'Forgive me. We were longer than I'd imagined—but it was so pleasant that I quite forgot the time...'

'I do not know how you can find choosing furniture for that man pleasant,' Melia said with a sulky look. 'He but uses you, Jane. You should not allow it.'

'Oh, I do not think myself used,' Jane replied, determined not to lose her patience with the girl, even though she found herself resenting Melia's tone concerning Lord Frant. How could the girl be so ungrateful after what he'd done for her? 'Like many gentlemen he does not care to spend his time choosing furnishings and I am happy to do it for him—besides, I have seen a few pieces that I should like for my own house when my brother marries.'

Jane saw a guilty flush in Melia's cheeks and suspected that she no longer wished to be Will's wife.

'Is the viscount to marry?' Sarah looked up from her book.

'Oh, in time,' Jane said and glanced at Melia. 'I do

not think it is imminent, though I had thought it might be...'

Melia's cheeks grew red. She got up and went over to the window, looking out at the street below. 'Did you know that Lord Frant and Viscount Hargreaves go to Newmarket?'

'Yes, Lord Frant has just this minute told me. You had it from Viscount Hargreaves, I dare say?'

'Yes...' Melia avoided her eyes. 'He mentioned that he might be leaving town soon.'

'They leave tomorrow for Newmarket...for the races, I think. Afterwards, they will buy young horses for the stables they intend to set up.'

'Yes, so I believe,' Melia said and sighed. 'I understand they will buy land together in Ireland...'

'Ah, I did not know that,' Jane said. 'It appears you have been privy to more information than I...' She rang the bell and when a maid appeared asked for tea to be served. 'We must prepare for this evening...just music and cards. We do not dance until Mama's ball next week...'

Of its own volition, a sigh left Jane's lips. She had hoped that Lord Frant would attend the duchess's ball, but if he were in Newmarket—or even Ireland—he would miss it...and that meant the prospect of dancing, of being held close to a man's chest, held little appeal for Jane.

Chapter Nine

'It seems that I have the means to pay for my share of the stables,' Adam announced from the doorway of the inn chamber. 'The letter arrived this morning. I shall have five thousand clear when everything is settled—enough for the three thousand needed and a decent house in Ireland, should I wish it.'

'With your winnings these past two days you have enough to live on for a while,' Paul said and smiled. 'It seems your fortunes have changed, my friend.'

'Yes, thank God!' Adam looked elated. 'When I placed that bet of a hundred guineas it was my last, leaving me barely enough to settle my score here had I lost it.'

'You are braver than I.' Paul chuckled. 'I do not think I could have placed such a bet.'

'You are not a gambler,' Adam said wryly. 'You have courage, Frant—but you would not gamble your life on the fate of a horse. If it had lost, I fear there would have been nothing left but to put a ball through my head.'

'Then I thank the fates for making your horse win,' Paul said, his brows rising. 'I should not want to lose a friend on such an account…'

'Well, it seems that for the moment I am saved.' Adam grinned at him. 'We should take a look in at Tattersalls today, Frant. We may be able to purchase some decent stock.'

'Young horses with good bloodlines that we can rear ourselves,' Paul said. 'But we need also a good mare to breed from—and one or two horses that show promise of good form in the near future.'

'Will you race that beautiful horse of yours? The one the Prince gave you and you brought with you on the ship.'

'I fear my poor Suleima fared worse than I did on the journey,' Paul replied. 'One day I hope to race him, but it may be that I shall simply keep him for stud purposes.'

'None other could match him in the race you rode in India…'

'No, that is true,' Paul said. 'I was offered riches to sell him, but I wanted to bring him home to England…'

'You intend to settle here then?'

'Yes, I have made up my mind to it,' Paul said. 'I shall keep some of my horses here at my estate in the country, but the young ones can go to Ireland with you.'

'We have but one more day at the races,' Adam reminded him. 'Do you wish to take ship for Ireland immediately?'

'No, for I am engaged to the Duchess of Roshithe for her ball in two days hence,' Paul said. 'I shall return this evening, after the meeting—and we will talk of a trip to Ireland, perhaps next week.'

'Yes, of course, you would not wish to miss the duchess's ball,' Adam murmured softly. 'Shall we to the races then and see if we can find another winner?'

'Win or lose, I bet modestly,' Paul said. 'You would do well to do the same, Adam.'

'Of course,' Adam said but the gleam in his eyes sent a shiver of apprehension down Paul's spine. If Adam bet recklessly, he could easily lose all he had won and more besides...

'You look lovely,' Jane said to her friends as they came down to the parlour where she and Will were waiting for them. 'Melia, that gown suits you so well—and Sarah, I think I have not seen you look as beautiful before.'

'Oh, I am not beautiful,' Sarah denied with a blush and a shake of her head. 'You look wonderful yourself—is that a new gown, cousin?'

'No, one I have worn once before,' Jane said. She did not add that she had forgone her new gown in order to see both Melia and Sarah supplied with the beautiful creations they were wearing. Madame Françoise had been inundated with requests for new gowns for one of the most important balls of the season, but Jane had waited patiently. She did not expect Lord Frant to attend, therefore it hardly mattered that she was wearing a gown she'd worn before, though Mama had scolded her for it.

'Jane, you are too unselfish,' she said. 'You should

have put yourself before Melia. She has already had two new ball gowns.'

'But she is young and this is her first season. It is more important that both she and Sarah should look well.'

'And why is that, Jane?' Mama demanded. 'I would have my daughter look well—and perhaps find herself another husband...'

'Mama, please do not...' Jane sighed. 'I have told you before that I do not wish to marry the Marquis Vermont—or Lord Hamilton's nephew or...'

'No, of course not. Why should you when a much better match presents itself? He is not a marquis, but fortune and good nature are more important and Lord Frant has these qualities in abundance.'

'Mama!' Jane's cheeks burned. 'Please do not suggest such a thing...'

'I merely point out that the man is there...and is already halfway in love with you, Jane. If you were to give him a hint, I dare say he would propose to you in an instant...'

Jane felt hot and uncomfortable. Yet her mother was only suggesting what she had suspected once or twice, but immediately dismissed. Sometimes there was a look in Paul Frant's eyes that seemed to suggest that his feelings for her were more than mere liking.

'Oh, no, I couldn't...' Jane looked away from her mother's too bright gaze. She tried to dismiss the idea, as she had others—but this time she could not quite manage it. Was it possible that Lord Frant's regard was something deeper than friendship? And what would she feel about it if that were true, fantastic as it seemed? No, no, it was ridiculous because they had known each other such a short time…

Jane found that the idea was not as distasteful to her as she'd thought it might be and if she were to think of marriage—but of course that was ridiculous. She had no wish to marry again, even to a gentleman as generous and good-natured as Lord Frant…and he'd given no indication that his affections had turned towards her, except now and then there was that look in his eyes. Jane did not wish to believe it. She was not ready to feel love again; it would be a betrayal of Harry. Besides, she did not think it true: it was merely Mama being a matchmaker again, of course.

'I do hope that Viscount Hargreaves will come this evening,' Melia said. 'He thought that he might be in Ireland, but perhaps…' She stopped, aware that Jane was staring at her. 'What have I said?'

'I wish you will not set your heart on that gentleman,' Jane said gently. 'I believe he has little fortune and though that would not necessarily prevent the marriage there are other considerations…'

Jane halted once more, because she knew she could not tell Melia what she feared. She must simply let the girl make up her own mind and hope that she came to her senses in time.

'If he'd been given what he was owed…' Melia blurted out but then stopped, her face turning red. 'No matter…' She turned away in some confusion. 'Yes, I dare say you are right, Jane.'

Jane would have pressed her to finish what she'd

been saying, but they were on the point of leaving for the duchess's ball and she did not want to spoil the evening for anyone. An argument with Melia would cast a shadow over what should have been a happy evening.

Smiling brightly, she walked to the door, which was opened promptly by her footman. Outside, the carriage was drawn up and another footman stood ready to assist the ladies into the carriage. The viscount came last, sauntering down the stairs as if there was all the time in the world.

'Will, dearest, do hurry,' Jane told him with a warm smile. 'Mama shall not be pleased if we are late.'

'Oh, I tremble in my boots at the thought of it,' Will said and laughed. Their mother was dearly loved by both but had never made the least attempt to keep either of them in check.

'No, do not be wicked, dearest,' Jane said and poked him in the ribs. 'Move up and do not squash my gown.'

'That would never do,' Will murmured mischievously. 'I should not wish to be in your black books, Jane.'

'How can anyone do anything with him?' Jane appealed to Sarah, who laughed but looked as if she had enjoyed the banter.

'I think the viscount but means to tease you,' Sarah said, her eyes resting warmly on the young man, who had moved over to the corner to give his sister room to spread her gown.

So they travelled to the duchess's grand home in the west of town, three of them chattering and laughing and only Melia silent in her corner. She was subdued and thoughtful and Jane was relieved that she had not scolded her, for the girl's spirits were already lower than they had been when she first came to town. It was a pity if she'd given her heart to a man who did not deserve her, Jane reflected, but then they were arriving and one of the duke's flunkeys was opening their carriage door so that the ladies could descend from it to the red carpet spread out to keep their dainty shoes clean, for even outside such a house as this the streets might be stained with dirt.

Then they were inside the magnificent and lofty entrance hall with its floor of shining marble and the magnificent wide staircase leading up to the first floor, where the duchess was standing to receive her visitors.

Jane led the way up the stairs and was graciously welcomed by her mother. Curtsying, Jane waited until the others had greeted the duchess and then remained with her for a few moments while her brother led the two young ladies along the landing to the first reception room.

'I am delighted to see you looking so well, my dear,' the duchess said warmly as Jane kissed her cheek.

'Thank you, dearest Mama.' Jane smiled at her. Seeing some of her mother's friends arriving, she inclined her head. 'I shall leave you to greet your guests and we shall talk later…'

The reception rooms were overflowing with happy, smiling people. Porky was circulating, as was the duty of the host, but when he saw Jane he nodded to his companion and left him, coming to meet her with hands outstretched.

'My very dear Jane,' he boomed at her and kissed both her hands in turn. 'How delightful you always look—charming and pretty, just like your mama.'

'I thank you, sir…' she said and dipped a slight curtsy.

'Now, none of that nonsense,' he chided and patted her cheek. 'I am your dear Porky and father, I hope?'

'You are a dearer one to me than I ever had,' Jane said and kissed his cheek, which made him blush with pleasure. 'I hope you know that, Porky?'

'You make me proud indeed,' he said. 'The duchess looks beautiful this evening, did you not think so?'

'Mama is always beautiful,' Jane said, 'but I think that rather lovely diamond tiara is new?'

'Ah, yes, a little bauble it pleased me to buy for her,' he said. 'Off with you to the ballroom, Jane. Do not waste your time talking to an old fellow like me— there are many fine young ones waiting to greet you, my dear.'

'But I enjoy talking to you,' Jane said, and accepted a glass of champagne from one of the footmen circulating, and then saw that Melia, Sarah and Will had been waylaid by friends and had not yet reached the ballroom either. Taking a few sips of her wine, her eyes searched the room but the tall figure of Lord Frant was nowhere to be seen and she was aware of disappointment briefly, before finding herself surrounded by several gentlemen clamouring for dances. She handed over her card, smiling particularly at two officers who had been Harry's friends.

'Major Harding, Lieutenant Brandt…' she said. 'How pleasant to see you again. Are you both on leave?'

'Yes, there is very little true soldiering to do at the moment,' Major Harding replied with a smile. 'We have been with Wellington in Vienna but now we are officially on leave. I intend to sell my commission shortly—and George here is wavering on the brink.'

'Trouble is, my father won't let me help with the estate,' the young man with melting brown eyes said and grinned at her. 'What is a fellow to do but spend his time in town, drinking and gambling—and that don't please his lordship either.'

'Find some employment, George,' Major Harding chivvied him. 'It is my intention to import wine—and to set up a breeding stable for thoroughbreds...'

'Oh, you should talk to Lord Frant,' Jane said impulsively. 'I believe he means to race horses...'

'Are you speaking of Captain Frant?' The major's eyes gleamed. 'We were great friends in the old days, but then he sold out and went to India.'

'I was not aware that Lord Frant had served as captain,' Jane said, liking the honest, open manner of the officer. 'Not when...when Harry and I were with you, I think?'

'No, a few years previously. He was my first commanding officer on the Peninsula...'

'Ah...' Jane nodded. 'He had intended to attend this evening, but I am not sure—he may have left for...' The words faded as her eyes were drawn across the room and she saw the very man entering. Yet something was wrong and she heard murmuring around her, not realising at once what it meant—and then she saw that he was wearing a sling on one arm and there was a dressing applied to his forehead. 'No...excuse me, please...'

Jane made her way through the room, unaware that people turned their heads to watch her or of the whispers and smiles, quickly hidden behind a hand or a kerchief. She reached the newcomer and stood staring up at him, searching his face and seeing that it bore small scratches as well as a binding on the forehead.

'Lord Frant, you have been hurt...' she croaked, her lips barely able to move for the shock of seeing him thus.

A rueful smile lit his eyes and he reached out with his right hand to touch hers. 'A mere accident, Lady March. I was advised to rest for a few days, but I could not forgo the pleasure of seeing...of the duchess's ball...'

Jane felt warmth flood through her as his smile seemed to caress and she knew what he had meant to say. It was the pleasure of seeing her this evening that had made him come, despite his injuries. Oh, no! How vain she was to think it.

'What happened, sir?'

'Oh, the merest incident,' he declared, dismissing his sling as if it were nothing. 'A toss from my horse, no more...'

Jane was certain there was more behind the accident as he described the fall, but it was clear he would say nothing, at least this evening.

'I am happy to see you,' Jane said. She suddenly realised that everything had become brighter, although until that moment she had not been aware of missing him. Now she realised that had he not come the evening would have seemed less for it. 'Though I do not think you will be able to dance this evening, sir.'

'No, perhaps not,' he said ruefully. 'I had looked forward to our dances, my lady, but they must wait for another time. Perhaps you will sit with me and take a glass of wine—or walk out on the balcony...'

'Yes, of course,' she said. 'I had reserved two dances for you...'

'I am glad you remembered that I asked for them,' he murmured throatily and Jane's heart jerked and then raced in a manner it had not done for some years. For a moment as she looked into his eyes it was as if her heart reached out to his and her breath came faster, making her aware of something she had not felt for a long time—a desire to be kissed by a man other than her late husband. Yet in an instant the desire was replaced by regret. She could never...must never let herself love again: that way lay too much pain and hurt. It was safer to remain where she was, in her own little bubble.

'Yet should you truly be here?' she asked as she realised she had been silent too long.

'If one always did what one ought it would be a dull life,' Paul said and laughed as her brows rose. 'I have often taken risks, as this gentleman may tell you...'

Jane saw that Major Harding had come up to them and was giving Paul a quizzical look. 'What mad escapade brought you to this, Captain Frant?'

'That is fine talk, coming from the wildest fellow I ever had under my command.' Paul laughed and offered his right hand, which was gripped and held. 'Jack Harding—how are you? A Major now, I hear?'

'Yes, but unlikely to go further now that Boney is safely tucked up out of harm,' Major Harding said, grinning. 'I am thinking of setting up a stable—and Lady March told me you have a similar idea. We must dine together one evening and talk of this…'

'Yes, indeed. I should enjoy that,' Paul told him. 'Perhaps tomorrow at my club—at eight?'

It was agreed and then Major Harding left them to claim a partner for the next dance.

'This was one of your dances,' Jane told Paul. 'Would you care for a turn on the balcony, sir?'

'Only if you stop calling me sir,' he said. 'Frant if you must, though I prefer Paul. I believed we were friends, Jane?'

'You know we are,' she said as he offered his arm and they made their way through the crowds to one of the long doors that stood open to admit fresh air and passage to the various small balconies. Her heart had opened to him earlier but now she had herself under control and was the polite society lady again. 'Now, tell me the truth—what happened to you?'

'My horse was spooked by a stray ball as I rode home from Newmarket yesterday.'

'You were shot at?' Jane felt severely distressed by the very idea and it must have shown in her face for Paul squeezed her arm against his side comfortingly.

'No, I fancy it was a poacher or some such thing—unless he was a poor shot. Unfortunately, my horse was not trained to the sound and reared up, sending me crashing to the ground—though I held on to the reins, luckily, and Adam was there to help me up…'

'Viscount Hargreaves was with you?'

'Yes, thankfully. He helped me to mount and got me to the nearest inn, where I was seen by the local doctor. A good man, who informed me that I had no broken bones and would live but must take it easy for a day or so.'

'Thank God someone was with you…' Jane was shocked to discover how much the idea that he could have lain hurt…particularly if the shot had wounded him.

'It was fortunate, but it is not the first time Adam has come to my aid,' Paul told her. 'I suffered from a fever on the ship returning from India and I believe I should have died had Adam not cared for my needs.'

'I did not realise that he had been such a good friend to you.'

'No, he does not speak of it, but he is a decent fellow,' Paul said and smiled as they took a turn on the small balcony and looked out at the pretty gardens, which were enhanced by fairy lights strung in the trees and bushes. 'It was a successful meeting for both of us and we leave for Ireland next week to buy land for our young horses—of which we now have six.'

'So it is definite that you will set up your stables in Ireland together?'

'Yes, I see no reason for it not to go ahead now,' Paul said softly, speaking almost to himself. 'I believe Adam intends to purchase a house there, where he will live for some part of the year, though he enjoys Society too much to bury himself there for ever.'

'Did he not come with you this evening? Melia thought it was his intention…'

'I believe he has another engagement, one more to his taste…' Paul frowned but shook his head, apparently wishing to leave the subject of his friend there. 'I was determined to keep my word and come—though I fear I present a sorry appearance. We must hope the sight of me does not distress the ladies…'

'There is nothing unpleasant in your appearance,' Jane assured him. 'I am glad to see you, Paul, though I am sorry if you are in pain.'

'Sweet Jane,' he said and gazed into her eyes for a moment before moving his hand to her cheek and caressing it lightly with the tips of his fingers. For a moment her breath caught and she almost swayed towards him as the need to feel his arm about her swept over her, but in an instant she had conquered the foolish desire. She must not let her longing for Harry confuse her; she did not know this man well enough to care for him—surely she could not be so inconstant. Only a few weeks ago she'd believed that she would never feel love or desire again. And now? Now she was not sure how she felt. 'You look beautiful, as always.'

'You flatter,' Jane said and laughed, but the look in his eyes was having a disturbing effect on her. She felt young and excited again, like a girl at her first ball. 'But it is most pleasant…and the evening would not have been the same if you had not come.' She felt her cheeks flush as he smiled down at her and for a moment it was as if they were the only two people in the world. For a moment then Jane thought that if he had held her and kissed her she might have given herself to him…and then another couple came out onto the balcony and the lady called out to them, breaking the spell.

'Is it not warm this evening, Lord Frant? I swear I thought I should melt if I did not catch the air…'

Paul moved back, turned and inclined his head towards her. 'You are very right, Lady Catherine. It is the reason Lady March and I came out. Yet after a while it seems cool…do you not think so, Lady March?'

'You are very right.' Jane took her cue. Besides, it would be safer in the ballroom, for her emotions had almost betrayed her. 'Take care you do not stay too long, Lady Catherine. We should go in, Lord Frant.'

'Oh, but I wanted to hear what happened to you,' Lady Catherine said, placing a hand on Paul's arm to delay him. 'Everyone is whispering different tales—is it true that someone tried to kill you and that they might have succeeded had Viscount Hargreaves not ridden up with your groom?'

'Exaggeration,' Paul said and smiled at her eagerness. 'It was merely a little tumble from my horse. Excuse us, please, Lady March grows cool…'

Giving Jane his arm, he swept her back into the ballroom. Jane was aware of the pretty young lady staring after them. The daughter of an earl, she was betrothed to a marquis, but there were whispers that her father was desperate to get her married to curb her wildness. Some gentlemen spoke of her being no better than she ought, but as yet the remarks had not come to the lady's ears or those of her father or betrothed.

'I believe Lady Catherine came out in order to corner you, my lord,' Jane said with a teasing look. 'She enjoys excitement I understand...'

'That young woman is the bane of her father's life,' Paul replied with an amused smile. 'I knew her father years ago and his wife was a flighty one—unfaithful to him for years, though he believes that his first two sons are his own.'

'You think Lady Catherine takes after her mother?'

'I would not besmirch a young woman's reputation, though others are less circumspect,' Paul said. 'I have heard tales but, gossip being what it is, I am inclined to discount most of it.'

'I think she likes you,' Jane teased but he shook his head.

'No, I think her more interested in Adam. He has escorted her to some function or other on more than one occasion, for their families were friends...but I do not think the earl would countenance a union between them...'

'You think Viscount Hargreaves might wish for it?'

'As I believe I mentioned once before, he needs to marry money—but Lady Catherine's father wants more for her.'

'She is engaged to the Marquis of Barnchester.'

'A man old enough to be her father,' Paul said and frowned in disapproval.

'Yes, that is a sad thing,' Jane agreed. 'I do not agree with such marriages, for they can bring little joy to either partner, I think.'

'Barnchester needs an heir,' Paul murmured. 'After that, I dare say she will do much as she pleases...'

'Yes, perhaps,' Jane said but could not help feeling sorry for the lovely young woman who was so full of life. How must she feel about being married off to a man so many years older? Jane would never have agreed to such an arrangement. 'Does she have money of her own—or is she in need of a fortune?'

'Oh, her family is rich enough, but her father believes in keeping the coffers filled. The earl is full of juice, they say, but he wants a title and fortune for his daughter so if he has his way the match will go ahead.'

Jane nodded, and then turned her head to look up at him. 'My next partner comes to claim me, but I shall see you for the dance before supper.'

'How ridiculous these customs are,' Paul said. 'If I could dance I should want to keep you to myself and dance the whole night long…' He raised her hand to his lips and kissed it, and there was something in his eyes then that set her heart racing once more. 'Yet I am not too selfish to keep you from the pleasure of dancing, Jane. Go to Brandt and enjoy yourself. He waltzes well, as do all Wellington's aides…'

Jane moved from his side reluctantly, though she greeted her partner with a smile and went willingly with him to the dance floor. She enjoyed dancing and soon discovered that the man was an excellent dancer. Their dance was soon over, and though she looked for Paul she did not see him to speak to again as she went from one dance to the next with a succession of partners. When she caught the occasional glance it was to see him engaged in conversation with the Prince Regent and some political gentlemen.

However, Paul did not forget their second dance and came to claim her. The touch of his hand on her arm set her pulses racing and she wished that they might dance the beautiful waltz that was about to begin for she would have liked to be in his arms, swaying to the music.

Once again they went out to the balcony to take some air, before moving into the supper room. For some moments they strolled in the peace of the cool evening air, but others had the same idea and they were never alone. Jane looked at Paul and saw the slight frustration in his eyes, as if he too wanted some time alone with her, but then he asked if she was ready to go into supper and the moment passed. Here they were joined by various gentlemen, friends of Paul's, Melia, Sarah and Jane's brother.

'Have you enjoyed your first ball in town?' Jane asked of Sarah and was greeted with a bright smile.

'Oh, yes, it is lovely to dance—and your brother dances so well, Jane. He has danced with me twice and introduced me to his friends; I have sat out no more than three dances—and on two occasions I spoke with Lord Frant. He is such a pleasant gentleman, Jane. I know he likes you very much, for he spoke of you in the warmest terms.'

Jane refrained from asking what Paul had said about her, but she saw that his eyes were upon her and her heart began to race. Until this evening she had not truly understood how much she had come to like the quiet gentleman—and how much she enjoyed his company.

All too soon the last dance was over and people began to drift away as the sound of the music ended.

Paul remained until the last and came to her as she and her friends were preparing to leave.

'I hope you will call when I return from Ireland, to see how my house improves,' he said and held her hand for a moment longer than necessary. 'Bring Melia and your cousin—and your brother, if he cares to visit.'

'I cannot vouch for Will, because he always seems to have so many engagements,' Jane replied and looked up at him. 'Sarah and Melia will be delighted to accompany me, I know. Your ward must take an interest, for perhaps one day—when you have taken a wife—she may reside within the walls of your home.'

'Yes, perhaps she may,' he said and there was a hint of laughter in his eyes. 'I shall hope to see you—the day after tomorrow, perhaps?'

'Yes, in the morning,' Jane said. 'We shall look forward to it.'

'Goodnight, sweet Jane,' he said and his eyes spoke more.

'Goodnight, Frant,' she said and smiled up at him.

They went out to the carriage together. Will handed his sister, Sarah and Melia inside and then climbed in after. Jane caught a glimpse of Paul's face as he turned away. She thought he looked tired and sad and her heart caught. She wished that she did not have to leave him... For a short time on the balcony that evening she had almost believed that she was ready to love again.

Alone in the darkness, Jane wrestled with her thoughts. How could she even think of caring for another man when she had loved Harry so much? She knew very little of Paul Frant and, from the way Lady

Catherine had looked at him, Jane knew that he was a man who drew women to him—how could she be certain that he wasn't simply flirting with her?

In truth, she knew nothing of him. His past was a closed book to her and he might be an adventurer or a rogue for all she knew—she had sensed that he was not telling her the truth when he'd spoken of his injury, so what was he hiding?

Paul's arm was aching as he entered the house, handing his cane, hat, gloves and cloak to his manservant with a sigh of weariness. That country doctor had known what he was talking about when he'd told him to rest for a few days. He felt weary after standing for hours, talking, smiling, catching up with old friends—and all the time his eyes followed Jane, his mind could not quite shut out the ugly suspicions.

Whoever had shot at him from behind a tree had meant to wound, for he had fired a second time before taking flight as Adam and the groom came riding up and Adam had instantly taken a pot-shot into the darkness.

He must have an enemy, but he had no idea of who it might be—or what he had done to bring on such hatred. Why would anyone wish to kill him?

He'd been puzzling over it since the incident the previous evening, just as dusk was falling. Had the villain aimed only a little straighter, Paul might have been badly wounded or even dead.

His first thought was that his half-brother wasn't old enough to conceive such a plot—nor would the boy or his mother know that he would be on the road from Newmarket to London that evening. Very few could know that, because he had not decided until the last moment…unless he was being followed by someone who was waiting for such an opportunity.

Yet who could hate him that much? Adam had suggested it might be his stepmother. Perhaps she believed that if he were dead her son would become Lord Frant. Yet the boy was already heir to everything of worth left in their father's possession at his death. Paul was the one who might have borne a grudge but did not. So why would the dowager Lady Frant want him dead?

It made no sense. Indeed, if anything, she'd seemed apologetic when Paul had paid her a fleeting visit out of courtesy. She'd made it plain that she made no claim on him and he'd told her that he bore her and the boy no malice. Whatever his father had done, he had done, and that ended with his death.

Having lived so many years abroad, Paul could not think that any of the friends he'd made in the Army— or since his return—would want to harm him.

Was it something to do with India? Paul thought he might have made enemies there. He'd risen fast and gained a fortune, much of it by hard work but some because of what he'd done to help the young Prince escape his captors. Could it be something to do with that— perhaps one of the soldiers Adam had commanded had resented that Paul should receive so much more in reward than he or anyone else? Perhaps there was some truth in that point of view, though they had merely done their job, while he had risked his life with no thought of reward.

Paul had broken down the door of that burning hut and rescued the Prince at some cost to his person—but the soldiers had fought the tribesmen and some had been wounded. They should have received a reward for it and Paul was not certain how much of the two thousand gold coins paid to their captain had gone to the soldiers...

He frowned as his manservant eased him out of the tight coat he'd worn to the duchess's ball. The bandage beneath showed a few spots of blood and the wound stung. Paul had lied when he said he was injured in the fall; he had taken the ball in his arm and the force had knocked him from the horse. Had the ball pierced his chest...but he would not dwell on such thoughts.

The assassin, for such he must have been, had not taken enough care with his aim and so Paul lived. Yet next time he might not be as lucky. He knew he must do something to protect himself—and he must employ an agent to discover the reason for the attack.

He felt the frustration of not being able to devote his mind to the woman who dominated his thoughts. Jane had looked so lovely and for a moment on the balcony he'd felt she'd invited his kiss—and then that woman, Lady Catherine, had intruded and the mood had been shattered. The spoiled beauty was a nuisance and had tried to pique his interest on more than one occasion but, like others of her ilk, she had failed—something that would displease her if she guessed it. Yet perhaps she'd done him an unwitting favour.

If Paul's life were truly at risk, it meant he could not ask Jane to be his wife. She had suffered a terrible loss once; Paul would not wish her to suffer another. He would continue to be friendly, but a proposal of marriage was not to be thought of until he had discovered his enemy and could take the precautions necessary.

He was about to retire when someone knocked at his door.

'It's Adam. May I speak to you?'

'Yes, of course. Come in,' Paul said and picked up the glass of whisky his valet had poured for him.

'I could not retire without enquiring how you were,' Adam said, standing in the doorway, his golden locks dishevelled and in his shirtsleeves. 'It was foolish to risk the wound opening again by dancing...'

'I did not try to dance, but I saw Jane—and met some good friends. I do not think you know Major Harding? He served with me many years ago...before we met in India.'

'I am glad you met friends,' Adam said and hesitated, then, 'but have a care, Paul. Someone meant to kill you last evening. You have an enemy, my friend—and it might be anyone...'

'Yes, I've realised that,' Paul said. He was about to confide his plans but thought better of it. 'I cannot imagine who...but I am sure that ball was meant to wound or kill me.'

'Had we not come along when we did...' Adam shuddered. 'We delayed to help a lady whose coachman had lost his way, and if we had been but a moment longer...I am certain he meant to finish you off as you lay there, but at the sight of us he made off into the trees.'

'Yes, that was fortunate,' Paul said and frowned. 'What have I done that someone should wish to kill me, Adam?'

'Men have many reasons to kill,' Adam muttered and something in his eyes at that moment made Paul wonder if he still harboured resentment against him because of Annamarie. 'Jealousy, anger…even resentment over a slighting word has been known to move a man to murder.'

'Yes, I suppose, but I do not think my half-brother or his mother hate me that much… If he were older, but…'

'An assassin works for a few coins in the hand,' Adam said. 'Do not look for reasons; accept that you are hated and watch your back, my friend.'

'Yes, I shall.' Paul grimaced and eased his shoulder. 'Was your evening a good one?'

Adam laughed ruefully. 'I think my luck resides in the turf rather than the tables. I lost five hundred guineas this evening, but I still have the funds we need for our venture. The day after tomorrow we leave for Ireland and I shall not gamble again before then so stand in no danger of losing what I have.'

'You have not yet received the money from your lawyer, I think?'

'No, but that will buy land and perhaps a house,' Adam said. 'I shall have that, whatever happens at the tables, Paul—for I shall not risk my land or the share in the future we plan together.'

'I am glad of that,' Paul replied with a lazy smile.

'I should not like to lose my partner. Now, if you will excuse me, I'm for my bed.'

Adam laughed softly and went out, leaving Paul to his thoughts, which were neither clear nor pleasant as he crawled into bed and closed his eyes.

Chapter Ten

Jane knew better than to visit her mama too early the next morning, but in the afternoon she drove to her house to take tea with her and found that several other ladies and gentlemen had formed the same intention. It was impossible to have a private word with Mama, but both Melia and Sarah found friends there and Melia seemed happier than she had the previous evening, when Captain Smythe and his sister Anne asked her to go walking with them in the park the following day.

Sarah also seemed lost in her thoughts as they drove home, though she answered when Jane spoke to her and discussed their plans for the evening, which were to dine quietly at home before joining a few friends for a trip to the theatre in the evening.

Jane enjoyed her evening, and when in the interval Major Harding entered their box she greeted him with a smile. His invitation to go riding the next day was accepted with pleasure and he spent the whole of the interval at her side.

Will had accompanied them that evening and he sat between Melia and Sarah, entertaining them both and providing ices and drinks in the various intervals for their pleasure. Melia was more talkative than she had been for a few days and Jane heard her agree to go riding with Will the next afternoon.

Jane watched her brother's face as he turned from Melia to Sarah and asked her if she would like to ride with them. Sarah hesitated, and then said she would very much like it if a horse could be found for her. Will promised that he would see her mounted properly and Sarah smiled, and then the lights dimmed for the last act. Just before the lights lowered, Jane noticed that someone was watching them from below in the pits through a small pair of opera glasses.

For a moment she wondered who the gentleman was and why he stared so intently, but then he seemed to become aware that she had noticed and inclined his head, turning his attention to the stage. Jane was soon drawn into the performance and forgot him, though later that evening, before she retired, she mentioned it to her brother.

'Did you notice that gentleman in the pits?' she asked. 'He seemed to be very interested in us…I suppose you did not notice him?'

'No, I cannot say I did,' Will said and smiled. 'You are a lovely young woman still, Jane. I am sure a great many gentlemen stare at you, dearest—and it might have been Sarah or Melia who was attracting his attention.'

'Yes, very likely,' Jane said, but she was still uneasy.

The man had been staring at her—and something in his manner had struck her as being odd. Yet perhaps Will was right and she was making too much of it.

Jane was soon asleep and no dreams came to disturb her rest. In the morning she decided she would visit one or two of the furniture makers' warehouses and see if she could find the missing items needed for Lord Frant's house. Both Melia and Sarah were engaged to friends so she would go alone...

As she left the second of the two cabinet makers' establishments feeling pleased with the purchase of several pieces, Jane stood for a moment in the side street and took stock. A cab had brought her here and she would need to find one to take her home. Had she realised the warehouse was as secluded as this, she would have brought her own carriage, but she'd expected it would be within easy reach of the showrooms. She believed that Lord Frant would be well pleased with the items she had purchased on his behalf, and there was no need for her to look further for the moment.

Ready to go home, she decided that she would return to the warehouse and ask if someone could summon a cab for her. As she turned, Jane was suddenly accosted by a man she'd never seen in her life. He was dressed in a brown coat and breeches with a dark hat pulled down low over his brow and the hand he placed on her arm was not quite clean about the fingernails.

'I reckon yer be the one I be lookin' for,' he grunted and thrust his face closer so that she could smell the sour odour of his breath. 'I've been told to warn yer that my mistress will have a reckoning if you continue your pursuit of her man. If you know what's good for yer, yer'll go home and forget him…'

'What are you taking about?' Jane suppressed the trickle of fear that ran through her. 'I have no idea who your mistress is—or her man…'

The brute pressed his face closer to Jane's. 'I reckon yer knows, all right. It ain't no use playin' the innocent with Pyke. I'm warnin' yer, and if yer ignore me warnin' yer'll be sorry.'

Jane wrested her arm from his grasp but he grabbed at her again and threatened her with his fist.

'Hey, you!' a man's voice cried. 'What do you think you're doing? Unhand that lady at once or I'll make you sorry you were born…'

Instantly, the man ran off down the street and she turned to find herself face to face with the gentleman she'd seen watching her from the pits at the theatre the previous evening.

'Sir,' Jane said, breathing deeply to steady her nerves, 'I must thank you for scaring off that brute.'

'Was he after money?' he asked and looked at her in a puzzled manner. 'You are Lady March, are you not? A friend pointed you out to me last evening at the theatre…'

'You were staring at me through your opera glasses,' Jane said after a moment. Her fright had subsided now and she was angry. 'Did you arrange this incident…to gain my favour?'

'You wrong me,' he said and smiled oddly. 'I was not privy to your intention to visit the warehouses of

Master Morrison. I came only to complete a purchase myself.' He tipped his hat. 'Excuse me; I shall not impose on you a moment longer…'

'No, please, stay,' Jane said, realising that she had been rude. 'I was shocked by that rogue's attack—and it seemed so odd that you should stare at me last evening…'

He laughed softly, his teeth gleaming against skin that had obviously been exposed to the sun often. 'Does it surprise you that beauty such as yours should attract attention? Yet you asked me to tarry—may I be of some assistance?'

'I came here by cab and need to summon another but I am not sure where to find one…'

'You will not find one here, my lady,' he said and inclined his head. 'Captain Richard Hershaw at your service. My carriage waits for me. I shall instruct my driver to take you home…'

'Oh, no, I could not impose on you,' Jane said at once. 'The warehouse manager will know where to hire a cab for me. I should have retained the last one but was not sure how long my business would take me.'

'I would have thought it safer for a lady of your standing to come accompanied by your servants in your own carriage,' Captain Hershaw said, a smile flickering in his eyes. 'Yet I know that some ladies are of an independent mind and I understand that sometimes you may wish to be alone. Please, take my carriage. I am well able to find my own way home.'

Jane hesitated for a moment and then thanked him. 'You are kind, sir—and I have not been polite…'

'Give me your address and I shall instruct my man,' he said and walked over to the carriage. Jane followed and was helped inside. Captain Hershaw doffed his hat to her and the carriage moved off.

She watched from the window and saw her rescuer walk into the warehouse. Leaning back against the squabs of the comfortable carriage, Jane closed her eyes for a moment. The small incident had alarmed her, but she would have been foolish to refuse the offer of a man who was obviously a gentleman.

For a few moments wild ideas that he might have been trying to kidnap her ran through her mind and she wondered if she had been a fool to step willingly into his carriage, but they vanished as swiftly as they came. Some half an hour later, when the carriage stopped outside her brother's house, Jane realised that she had indeed mistaken Captain Hershaw's intentions.

Of course he had not planned to rescue her from that brute or yet to kidnap her. It was, as he said, a coincidence that he had happened along at the right moment... and yet something lingered at the back of her mind, a suspicion that she was being duped in some way. She could not fathom the purpose if it had all been arranged, for had he wished to abduct her the opportunity had been his—so why did she feel it would be foolish to trust Captain Hershaw too much?

Caught up in the busy social whirl, Jane forgot the unpleasant incident at the warehouse over the next few days. She told no one that she'd been threatened, nor did she say anything of Captain Hershaw. When she found his calling card with the others in the hall, Jane made no mention of it. However, when her brother told her that he'd added the captain's name to the list of guests they had invited to a musical evening, she asked him who the gentleman was and how Will came to know him.

'Hershaw?' Will wrinkled his brow. 'He was introduced to me by a friend last evening at my club. I won five hundred guineas from him, Jane—so I thought the least I could do was invite him to dinner to make up for it.'

'I did not think you gambled for high stakes?'

'I do not often. It was a game of piquet. Although I seldom play for more than a few guineas, Hershaw suggested the stakes and I felt obliged to agree.'

'I should not make a habit of it,' Jane advised.

'Have you heard something against the man? I did not think you knew him.'

'We have met but once somewhere,' Jane said. 'I know nothing ill of him—but I would not trust him too far, Will.'

'I am not a gambler, my love,' Will said, 'but I must offer the man a chance to regain his losses—it is a matter of honour, dearest one.'

'Yes, I know…' Jane sighed for she knew her words would fall on deaf ears. She feared that Captain Hershaw meant them no good but could not put her fears into words, for there was no reason behind her distrust—and Will would laugh if she said it was her womanly instinct.

Jane wished that Lord Frant was in London. She could have asked him for his opinion and knew he would take her concerns seriously. How long did he intend to stay in Ireland? she wondered, and wished that she'd asked him, but their last meeting had been brief and she had not liked to press him. Jane had no claim on Lord Frant…but she would feel so much happier when he was home again.

Melia had taken to going out with Miss Anne Smythe and her brother Captain Smythe, the godson of Sir Henry Clarke. They called for her in the mornings to go riding or shopping, and in the afternoon she was invited to tea at their house. Jane, her brother, Sarah and Melia were invited to dine for cards and music, and during the evening Lady Clarke spoke to Jane about her ward.

'I believe you are dear Melia's chaperon. You know her guardian well I understand?'

'Yes, I know Lord Frant—and her aunt, Mrs Bellingham.'

'I was wondering if she had a dowry?' the lady said frankly. 'My husband's godson and heir is quite taken with her and I believe her to be of good family.'

'I know nothing ill of her family,' Jane said. 'I understand her guardian settled a sum of money on her, but I am not at liberty to disclose it…'

'No, of course not. I should not dream of asking. Of course my godson thinks it of no concern—but we like to do our best for our dear ones, do we not?'

'Yes, certainly,' Jane said. 'Has Melia shown a particular interest in your godson?'

'Has she said nothing of it to you?' The lady sounded surprised. 'They are forever in each other's company. I thought you would have remarked it.'

Jane shook her head. She'd seen Melia departing with her new friends but had given little thought to it, but if the girl had thoughts of marriage…surely she could not be so changeable? It was only a matter of weeks since she'd declared herself madly in love with Viscount Hargreaves. Had she given up all thought of him since he'd neglected to keep his promise and attend the duchess's ball?

Jane turned the conversation. She was not Melia's guardian, merely her chaperon for a short time—and she almost wished that she had never agreed to bring the girl to town. Will would be hurt if she turned her attentions to the young captain. He must be feeling that Melia preferred almost anyone rather than he, and that must be hard to bear.

Jane did not feel able to remonstrate with her guest. She did not wish to tell Melia where to bestow her affections. Indeed, if she were so shallow, it might be best if she married someone else. Will would be hurt but he would recover—if she married him and then turned her affections elsewhere it must be far worse. Better that his eyes should be opened to her failings now.

Although she said nothing to Melia, Jane spoke to her brother the next morning. She had come down to breakfast early, as she often did, and found him already in the parlour. From his dress, he had been riding and returned with a good appetite.

'Ah, I see you have been out already. I have agreed to go riding with Major Harding later—and I believe Sarah has promised Mama that she will call on her. I am not sure of Melia's intentions…'

'I understand she goes for a drive and then takes luncheon at the house of Sir Henry and Lady Clarke. Sir Henry is Captain Smythe's godfather...'

'We dined there last evening... It seems a little excessive to spend so much time in their company.'

'I dare say Melia has her reasons...'

'Will, dearest,' Jane said, looking at him in concern. 'His godmother asked me about her prospects last night...'

'Am I to wish her happy then?' A flicker of regret showed in his eyes. 'I suspected as much when I saw the way he looked at her—he is besotted with her and, since he has his own fortune, I doubt his godmother will sway him against her.'

'I am not sure she wished to—and it matters very little to me. It is you I am concerned for,' Jane said. 'I think Melia unkind to treat you so ill...'

'She is in love with Hargreaves,' Will said bleakly. 'I asked her and she confessed it was so—but he will not marry her because she does not have enough fortune...'

'Your fortune is surely large enough to satisfy her?'

'You are wrong, Melia,' Will said. 'She told me that she was sorry but she could not offer me her heart and so would not marry me...because she likes me too well. I think she intends to marry John Smythe because he adores her and will not question her. Yet if Hargreaves were to offer, she would abandon all others...'

'I am so sorry for your pain,' Jane said and went to him, touching his hand. 'I know you loved her.'

'Yes. Perhaps I still do in a way, but the blinkers have fallen from my eyes, Jane, and I see her for the heartless creature she truly is.' Will sighed. 'Better now than if we had married… John Smythe is welcome if he can get her. I shall not envy him.'

'Truly?'

'Truly,' he said and smiled at her. 'I shall recover, Jane—and next time I shall make sure that the woman I give my heart to is worthy of it and can love me in return.'

'You will feel easier in time…'

'Do not think I suffer as you did when you lost Harry,' Will said and kissed her cheek. He looked long into her eyes. 'You have not seemed as happy as you were, dearest—is it Frant's absence?'

'Perhaps…yes,' she admitted. 'I did not think I could care deeply again, Will, but I think…' She sighed and shook her head. 'Oh, I am not sure. Perhaps I am foolish to hope that I might find love again. We are friends but he has given no sign of more.'

'You think not? From what I have observed, I believe he truly cares for you,' Will said and frowned. 'Does he stay in Ireland much longer?'

'He did not tell me of his plans—but I thought it was his intention to return, leaving the viscount there to oversee the young horses.'

'He told me he will have his stables at his estate in Cambridgeshire. I think he hopes to race one of his horses at the autumn races.'

'Then surely he will return soon,' Jane said. 'Now, before I go out I must speak with your housekeeper, Will, and make the arrangements for this evening.'

'Yes, I would have everything as it ought to be, but

I know I can leave that to you,' Will said. 'I shall leave you now and go up to change. I have business this morning—and this afternoon I have promised to take Sarah for a drive in the park...'

Jane watched her brother leave the parlour and was thoughtful. Will had taken the news of Melia's desertion more calmly than she'd believed possible. Could Sarah's arrival in town have something to do with that—or was she being fanciful?

'I saw Frant this morning as I came to collect you,' Major Harding said when they had been for a brisk canter about the park. 'We acknowledged each other in passing but did not stop to speak. I shall call on him later and discover his plans—when he means to go down to the country.'

'I did not know he had returned,' Jane said and her heart skipped a beat. Paul was in town once more—and yet he had not sent word. Perhaps his smiles and soft words had been merely flirtation? Yes, she had been foolish to imagine more. They had such short acquaintance and love did not happen that way, did it? Jane had known Harry most of her life and loved him long before he asked her to marry him. 'Had I known, I would have sent an invitation for this evening...'

'I dare say he will call on you soon,' Major Harding said and smiled. 'I believe my old friend is much taken with you, Lady March. I have tried to steal a march on him while he was away, but I think I have not made much progress.'

Jane lifted her clear gaze to him. 'Your friendship gives me pleasure, sir.'

'But your heart belongs to another,' he replied and the look in his eyes was warm with affection. 'Paul is my friend and I would not come between you for the world—but, should he let you down, know that I would stand in his stead and it would make me happy to have you for my wife.'

'I think that is the nicest thing anyone has ever said to me,' Jane said. 'Know that I value your friendship and would have it continue.'

'I shall always wish to be of service—to you both...'

Jane could only thank him. She liked and respected the major, who was an honourable man, but she loved Paul Frant. His absence had revealed the truth to her and she could not wait to see him again.

However, he did not call on her that afternoon, and in the evening Major Harding told her that he had spoken briefly with Lord Frant, who had told him that he would be in town only for a few days before he left for the country to set things in order at his estate.

'Oh, I had thought he would be in town longer...' Jane could not keep the disappointment from her voice, though she schooled herself not to show it in her expression. She must have been mistaken in him. The doubts had set in now and she scolded herself for having been a fool.

'He will come.' Major Harding pressed her hand and then frowned as he glanced across the room at a newcomer. 'Hershaw here? I should not have expected to see that man at your house, Lady March.'

'My brother invited him because he won a substantial sum from him the other evening.'

'Then warn your brother to make sure he does not lose far more the next time they play...'

'You do not trust him?'

'I served with him in France for a time,' Major Harding said. 'He was accused of cheating at the tables by another officer and they were to fight a duel—but someone told the commander and Hershaw was sent off on a mission. I heard later that he had been sent to India...'

'To India?' Jane was suddenly alert. 'What became of him there?'

'I have no idea, but I believe he is still in the service, though why he has returned to England I do not know.'

'I am glad you warned me. I did not trust him but could not give a reason to my brother—now I shall warn him at the first opportunity, but not this evening. Captain Hershaw is our guest and must be shown respect, but I would rather he was not invited again.'

'Be careful of him, my lady.' Major Harding frowned. 'There was some scandal about one of the officers' wives...'

'Yes, I can believe it,' Jane said. 'He can be charming, I dare say, but he does not appeal to me.'

'I am glad to know it—and remember what I have said, Jane. If ever you need me, you have only to ask...'

Jane smiled and thanked him. She did not get another chance to speak with him in private that evening, but she was aware of Captain Hershaw's eyes following her wherever she was in the room and he kept her talking once or twice during the evening, asking her if she would permit him to take her riding one morning that week.

Jane excused herself on the grounds that she was busy and saw a gleam of annoyance in his eyes, but he accepted her excuses and told her he would ask again.

She was not sorry when the evening was over, and afterwards spoke to her brother alone.

'I should prefer it if you did not ask that man here again, Will. Meet him at your club if you must but…I cannot like him. The way he looks at me…'

'Yes, I noticed it,' Will told her. 'Be at peace, dearest. I managed to lose six hundred guineas to him at cards this evening and so the debt is paid. I doubt I shall have much to do with the man in future.'

'I am so glad,' Jane said and kissed his cheek. 'Did you not think Sarah splendid this evening? She kept Lady Clarke and Mrs Holbein amused for ages after dinner.'

'Sarah makes a good hostess and friend,' Will said and looked more like his old self as he grinned. 'Cease your matchmaking, sister. It is not necessary. I am perfectly able to make my own plans for the future.'

'Will…' she breathed and looked at him expectantly, but he laughed and shook his head.

'Go to bed, Jane, and stop worrying. I have made up my mind to nothing—and you shall know my thoughts as soon as I know them myself…'

Jane was smiling as she went up the stairs. Lord Frant was home, Will did not need his sister to watch over him and there was nothing to worry her…

Chapter Eleven

Jane waited at home the following morning and her patience was rewarded when Lord Frant came to call on her just before luncheon. She was in her parlour at the back of the house and welcomed him with both hands outstretched. He took them and kissed her on both cheeks.

'I am so glad you are home. Is your injury recovered?'

'Perfectly,' Paul said and held her hands a moment longer. For one fleeting glorious moment he seemed to drink her in, as if his eyes could not have their fill of her. Jane longed for him to give her a sign that he felt as she did but there was nothing except that look of longing in his eyes. 'I have been impatient to see you, Lady March. I wanted to thank you for making my house into a home.'

'So you are happy with everything?'

'It is all quite perfect—but it leaves me with no excuse left to visit you.'

If he cared for her he would not need an excuse!

'You may always call on me as a friend—surely you know it?'

'I have hoped it,' Paul said. 'Indeed, I have hoped for more—but certain things prevent me from speaking of what lies in my heart.'

'What things?' Jane asked, puzzled, as she looked into his face and saw that his eyes were veiled, holding secrets. Why could he not speak openly if he cared for her? He spoke of his hopes and yet she sensed a withdrawal in him that had not been there at the start. 'Yet I should not ask—I have no right…'

'I would give you every right,' he said huskily. 'May I ask you to be patient with me for a time, Jane? I have business that will keep me from you—and there are some situations best dealt with before I can come to you with an honest heart.'

'Of course,' she said shyly, and her heart beat faster as she saw the look in his eyes. Surely his eyes did not lie when they spoke to her of love and need and wanting? She felt herself melting in the heat of that gaze and longed for him to take her in his arms and kiss her until there was no need for words—but it did not happen. 'Yet if I understand your words it would seem that I do have the right to ask what keeps you from speaking plainly.'

'Will you trust me, Jane? Will you believe me when I say it is as much for your sake that I do not speak now as anything else? I do not wish to involve you in…' He shook his head, an expression of frustration in his eyes. 'No, you must trust me because I cannot have you exposed to this…'

'I shall trust you if you ask it,' she said. 'Yet I do not understand why you may not be open with me.'

'For the moment I am not free to speak of what is in my heart concerning you, Jane.'

'Then I must wait until you are free…'

'I came to tell you that I leave for Cambridgeshire tomorrow,' Paul said. 'Major Harding is to accompany me. I asked him if he would bear me company for a few days while I set much needed work in train—and then I shall return to town. I hope to make up a party to dine one evening and a trip to Vauxhall gardens another…'

'Then I shall look forward to your return,' Jane said and restrained the urge to tell him that she did not want him to leave again so soon. How provoking his air of mystery was. She was not a tattle tongue and he might have told her whatever worried him in confidence. 'I had hoped you might come to the theatre with us this week, but your business is urgent, I dare say.'

'I fear it presses,' he said and looked regretful, because she had not been able to hide her feelings: he asked her to trust him and yet he did not trust her enough to speak of what was bothering him. How could he care for her if he could not tell her what was in his heart and mind? 'You do not know how much I wish that I might stay in town—but we have purchased horses to be trained and must make sure they have a roof over their heads.'

'Viscount Hargreaves remains in Ireland?'

'Yes, it is better for him. In town he becomes reckless. In Ireland he will attend to business, as he must.

Perhaps one day he will be rich enough to repair his family estates and then he may marry.'

'Yes, as you say, it is for the best,' Jane agreed. 'It will give Melia time to heal her broken heart, I think.'

'My ward has been in real distress?' Paul looked concerned.

'No, not truly,' Jane said. 'I believe she loved the viscount in her way but she finds amusement to heal her hurts.'

'Ah, I thought as much,' Paul said. 'If I believed it was a true match between them I should consider whether I could do more than I have so far.'

'I am sure you have been generous enough.'

'Perhaps—but I would not have either of them languish of a broken heart.'

'Well, Melia does not languish. She is out with her friends now.'

'Then I shall wait and see what happens,' he said and smiled. 'I had hoped there would be time for you to see my house—but when I am ready to entertain will be time enough, I dare say.'

'Yes, of course,' Jane agreed, though she'd hoped to see it privately long before he entertained others.

'Well, I must leave you,' he murmured reluctantly. 'Please forgive the briefness of this visit. I have business to attend before I leave and my lawyer awaits me now.'

'Of course…' Jane said and offered her hand. He took it, held it and smiled and then he went from the room, leaving her to stare after him in frustration and disappointment.

She had hoped for so much when he returned from

Ireland and now he had left her for the country and nothing had changed between them. For a fleeting moment his eyes had spoken to her heart of love, and his words had seemed to suggest he truly cared for her, but he had not spoken plainly of love or marriage and Jane could not be certain that what she hoped was true.

Hearing voices in the hall, Jane realised that Melia had returned and dashed a hand across her face lest any foolish tears should be upon it. As she went out into the hall, she realised that Melia was not alone and frowned as she saw that Captain Hershaw was with her.

'Richard brought me home,' Melia said with a dimple. 'I was caught in a rain shower when he saw me standing in the doorway and offered to bring me here.'

'I did not realise it had been raining,' Jane said truthfully.

'Oh, it was nothing much and stopped before we were home,' Melia said, blushing. 'However, it was so nice not to walk…'

'I thought you were shopping with Miss Smythe?'

'I was, but she wanted to go to the library and I did not so I thought I might as well take advantage of Richard's offer.' She darted a roguish look at the man, who smiled and bent to kiss her hand. 'He must stay and take nuncheon with us—please say he is welcome, Jane…'

Jane hesitated, reluctant to say the words that would give the impression she was happy for the man to come informally to her brother's house, and in that instant Captain Hershaw relieved her of the necessity.

'I have an appointment I must keep,' he said. 'It was delightful to have your company, Miss Melia—perhaps you and Lady March would honour me by being my guests at the theatre one evening…your cousin also, of course,' he added as Sarah entered the house.

'You are kind,' Jane said. 'We must consult our diaries. We have so many engagements it is hard to find a space for new ones…'

His eyes darted a look of anger at her, but in a moment it was gone and he was smiling. 'Of course, of course. I have no doubt we shall meet everywhere, Lady March. I am given entrance by most, you will find…'

In another moment he had gone, leaving Jane with the distinct impression that she had made an enemy of him. Yet a little voice at the back of her mind told her that he had always meant her harm…or perhaps to harm her brother through her. Did he hope to fleece Will? It was unlikely her brother would be drawn in again… but if not her brother's fortune, who else did he think he might get to through Jane?

It was not until after luncheon with her family that it occurred to Jane it might possibly be because she was known to have a close friendship with Lord Frant.

Remembering the night Paul had come to the ball with a binding round his head and his arm in a sling, Jane felt a cold shiver at her nape. Paul had said there were circumstances that kept him from opening his heart to her. She'd thought it matters of business…but had the shot that sent him crashing from his horse been meant to kill him? Was he afraid to tell her of his love because she was a widow and he thought he might also be killed violently?

The thought made Jane sick with fear. She tried to

tell herself that she was jumping to conclusions, to dismiss her foolish fears, and yet they had taken root and she wondered if he was in danger. Did Paul suspect that his life might be at risk—and was that why he'd asked Major Harding to accompany him to the country?

'When did you suspect that your life was in danger?' Major Harding asked.

They had stopped at an inn for the night and were talking over a meal and wine. Paul was silent for a moment, then, 'When my horse almost ran into a wire stretched between two trees in Ireland. The first time, when someone shot at me, was inconclusive. Adam rode upon us in time and the rogue made off. I could not know if it had been an accident or an attempt to murder me.'

'Hargreaves? I know of him, but have not met the gentleman—do you trust him?'

'A few weeks ago I would have said implicitly. He saved my life on the ship coming over—and I cannot think he has reason to want me dead...'

'You're not as sure of his loyalty now, are you?'

'I do not want to believe that he could be to blame,' Paul said reluctantly. 'Yet he was one of only a few that knew my route on both occasions...and he might resent that he received only two thousand gold coins while I received much more for saving the Prince's life.' Paul had no need to explain the circumstances of the rescue because Major Harding knew it all, though not from Paul's lips.

'So you do suspect he might be behind the attempts but do not wish to believe it.'

'I have to accept that it is possible,' Paul said reluctantly. 'It would be a bitter thing to me if I should discover that beneath his friendship lies only hatred.'

'Has he said or done anything to give you pause?'

'No, not truly—except that he told someone else he had been unfairly treated in the matter of the reward…'

'Yet, even so, it would be a spiteful fool who would hold such a thing against you to the extent where he would seek to take your life.'

'Yes…' Paul frowned. 'That is what I thought but I cannot think of anyone else who would wish me harm.'

'What of Hershaw?'

'Hershaw…?' Paul sought for the memory and frowned. 'That was so long ago…surely it could not be. Why now?'

'He was suspected of cheating and it was on your recommendation that he was sent away.'

'Yes, I remember now. Colonel Forster asked me for my opinion and I told him that I did not trust the man. I forget—where was he sent?'

'To India…you did not meet him when you worked for the Company?'

'No, never to my knowledge: India is a huge country and our troops are everywhere. I had little to do with the interior, being stationed in the mountain regions, as was Adam Hargreaves.'

'I saw him the other evening at Viscount Salisbury's house and warned Lady March to be a little wary of him. She told me that she did not care for him but must treat him as her brother's guest, but would warn him to be careful.'

'I dare say he goes everywhere in Society,' Paul said. 'He was not proven a cheat but only suspected and warned in private by the colonel. His reputation was not truly sullied by the charge, though if rumours persist...'

'I think he has not long been in London,' Major Harding said and frowned. 'He may have returned because an uncle left him a small estate. If he has come for business it might have occurred to him that he could settle an old score at the same time.'

Paul smiled oddly. 'It would relieve my mind if I could think of him as my enemy rather than Adam Hargreaves.'

'Of course there is always me,' his old friend said and grinned. 'I might have accompanied you for the chance of putting a ball through your head.'

'Had it been you I should already be dead,' Paul said and chuckled. 'You need only one shot, Jack.'

'Yes, there is that,' the major said and his eyes gleamed with amusement. 'Have you taken precautions to protect your back?'

'Some, but now that you have warned me there are others I need to set in motion,' Paul said with a grimace. 'Both attempts so far have failed. I am certain there will be a third. I only wish I understood what I have done to merit them...'

Had he known the identity of his enemy, Paul would have spoken of what was in his heart to Jane. He knew that she had been confused and hurt by his ambiguous words and felt he'd made a mess of things. Perhaps he should have spoken openly and told her that he loved her deeply but feared that his enemy might succeed in his aim of murdering him. Something in him had held back, because Jane had been robbed of happiness once and if she gave her heart to him it would be broken if he were killed. He'd been on the verge of telling her that night on the balcony before they were interrupted, but it was as well he had held back. Paul knew now that his enemy was determined to harm him; he just couldn't be sure why or who...

'Are you enjoying yourself, Lady March?' The voice made the back of Jane's neck prickle and she turned to look at the man who had come up to her unnoticed. It seemed that she could go nowhere these past days without meeting him, and she had a feeling that he was following her. He'd boasted that he was welcomed everywhere and it appeared that it was no idle remark. 'I know you love good music and I think we shall be royally entertained this evening.'

'Yes, I believe Madame Justine de Rigorini is much admired,' Jane replied. 'I would have thought you more inclined to cards, sir?'

'What makes you think I prefer cards to music and the company of a beautiful woman?' he asked, his voice smooth and even but a gleam of something in his eyes that made her stomach clench. 'I am a man of many interests and tastes.'

'Yes, of course. I meant no insult,' she said. 'My brother is here but I think he chooses the card room, but my cousin Sarah and Miss Bellingham will listen to the music with me.'

'I have invited some friends to an evening party of my own,' he continued as if she had not spoken. 'Perhaps you and your brother and your guests would be gracious enough to accept my invitation?'

'It is not usual for a single gentleman to host such a party?'

'Oh, my aunt, Mrs Sargent, is to host it for me. You may be acquainted with the lady. I believe she is an acquaintance of the duchess.'

'Yes, I do know Mrs Sargent,' Jane said and inclined her head. 'You must send me a card, sir, and we shall see if we have a free evening—and now you must excuse me…'

Jane walked away, not bothering to turn her head though she knew his gaze followed her. Mrs Sargent was indeed an acquaintance of her mother's but not a lady she liked. Mama did not much like her either; she was received everywhere and to snub her would be extremely rude, but she was never invited to one of the duchess's more intimate affairs.

'Did I see you speaking with Captain Hershaw?' Melia said as Jane went to sit down with the others, who were waiting for the music to begin. 'He is such a charming man, is he not? I believe he means to invite us to his party…'

'Yes, but I do not care to accept an invitation from that gentleman,' Jane said. 'I do not care for him and it might be best if you did not welcome his company too freely.'

Melia shot her a resentful look. 'It seems that you do not care for any gentlemen I like,' she muttered beneath her breath.

Jane frowned but did not chide her. She had no wish to fall out with her charge in public, nor was it her business to prevent Melia forming a friendship with the captain. If he made her a proposal of marriage it would be for Lord Frant to decide whether or not to accept it.

Jane had begun to think recently that it would have been better had she not asked the pretty young woman to accompany them to town. She had done so because her brother wished it, believing there was an understanding between them, but it seemed that Melia bestowed her affections easily on a handsome face. First it had been Viscount Hargreaves and now Captain Hershaw. Neither was suitable, in Jane's opinion, and had the girl been her sister or ward she thought she might have immediately removed her from town. In fact, the only suitor Melia had encouraged that Jane thought suitable was Captain Smythe.

It was, in any case, almost time that she began to think of going home. They had been in town several weeks and Jane had purchased all the new gowns she needed for a while. Will had mentioned leaving towards the end of the following week and Jane thought she would go with him, though had either Sarah or Melia been courted by suitable gentlemen she might have remained longer.

No, she would tell them in the morning that they must make any last purchases they needed and return books to the lending library. She herself intended to purchase a parcel of the latest books to take home to the country. It would seem quiet after so many balls and parties, though if she removed to Bath she and Sarah would have a good deal of company there. Will entertained his close friends at home, and Jane asked their neighbours to dine once or twice a month, but it was mostly just the two of them—three with Sarah, for Melia would return to her aunt's home, unless an engagement should be announced between her and Will. Jane did not think it likely now.

Would she see Lord Frant before she returned home? Jane hoped he would call on her before then, but if not…perhaps he might one day chance to call on them in the country…

Her heart ached when she realised she might not see him for months on end, if at all. He had hinted that he cared for her, and surely she'd seen it in his eyes—but if he truly cared for her would he not have spoken of his feelings and asked her to be his wife? The fact that he had not done so had raised doubts in her mind and she wondered if perhaps it was his habit to flirt with ladies who came his way. If that were the case Jane would be very disappointed… No, she would be hurt for unwisely she had begun to care for him rather too much for her own comfort.

Chapter Twelve

Jane sat opening her letters and cards when Will walked into the parlour. He was dressed for riding, the smell of the stables still on him. He smiled at the pile of letters before her.

'Even in town you have so much correspondence,' he said. 'I wanted to tell you that I intend to go home on Friday next, Jane—but if you wish to stay in town a few weeks longer one of my friends will be pleased to escort you home. George Brandt is coming to stay for the shooting in September. He likes you, Jane, and I know he would gladly put aside all other pursuits to be of service.'

'Lieutenant Brandt is a pleasant and attractive man,' Jane said. 'I enjoy his company and so does Sarah, I believe.'

'Oh…?' Will's brow darkened and Jane laughed, her suspicions confirmed. 'I had not realised she was interested in him.'

'I meant only what I said. Sarah finds him pleasant company, as I do—but neither of us has romantic inclinations towards him.'

Will's expression did not lighten. 'Is it that fellow Frant, Jane? I thought he cared for you, but he went off to Ireland and then to the country—I am sorry if the rogue has hurt you, sister.'

'Lord Frant is not a rogue,' Jane said and made herself smile at him, even though his words echoed thoughts that continued to haunt her despite her efforts to ignore them. 'Nor has he hurt me. I knew he had business in the country that would take some time. I hope he will return to town before we leave, but I intend to return with you, Will—no matter what…'

'I'm glad, for the house seems empty without you, love. You will not take yourself and Sarah off to Bath too soon?'

'Perhaps next spring,' Jane said and her eyes quizzed him. 'Will that be long enough for you to decide, dearest one?'

'Yes, I dare say it will,' he replied and shook his head at her. 'I had hoped you might marry…for I would not spoil your plans, Jane.'

'You must think of your happiness,' she told him. 'I can find a dozen companions if I choose…'

'But I want you to be happy. Have you met no one else you would wish to marry…or is your heart given to Frant?'

'I believe it may be,' Jane confessed. 'For a long time I did not think I could love again—not as I loved my dearest Harry. Now I think perhaps I have met someone I can respect and love. It may be in a different way, for it was a wild sweet joy I knew with Harry, but I think this time it would be just as sweet, but not the same.'

'What does Mama say?' her brother asked. 'She hinted to me weeks back that she thought you would make a match of it—but then Frant went off to Ireland and I know she is anxious for you again.'

'Mama would have me marry; any decent and wealthy man would do, as long as she thought he would make me happy. Was it her suggestion that you should invite Lieutenant Brandt to stay?'

'She might have mentioned it,' Will said, 'but George is a good fellow, Jane. I like him—and he likes you very much.'

'Major Harding likes me too,' Jane said. 'Shall you invite him to stay for the shooting?'

'If you wish it. I shall also ask Frant…if he can spare the time from his business…'

'Invite all three,' Jane said impulsively, because perhaps if he thought she had suitors Paul would make up his mind to speak plainly, 'and do not let your fears for my happiness stand in the way of your own, my dearest one. I shall consider each of the gentlemen and if I can find it in my heart to marry, you shall be the first to know.'

Will laughed and made a wry face, for she'd given him his own words back again. Jane laughed too, because they were so very close and she knew that her brother would wish her to be settled before he proposed to the lady he now hoped to make his wife.

Jane could not help but be pleased that he no longer wished to marry Melia Bellingham, for she had proved herself spoiled and flighty. Once they went home, she would return to her aunt's house—unless she accepted a proposal of marriage from someone before then.

* * *

'Go home next week?' Melia looked at her in sullen disappointment. 'I thought we should stay until the end of the season at least.'

'It is almost over,' Jane said. 'Most of the important balls have been held—apart from Lady Marshall's ball next week. We shall attend that on the Wednesday evening and then prepare ourselves to leave, by visiting friends to say our farewells and any last minute errands you may have—but you have several days before that...'

'We shall miss Captain Hershaw's affair...'

'As I told you, I did not mean to accept it,' Jane said and was glad to have a valid excuse for refusing it. 'Surely it is not so important to you? You have made so many friends and been invited everywhere. You must have known it could not go on for ever?'

'Yes, but...' Melia stared at her sulkily. 'I have not yet received an offer of marriage. I hoped...' She broke off and her cheeks heated.

'I do not think either your aunt or Lord Frant would agree to a marriage between you and that gentleman,' Jane said gently. 'I thought there was someone else... Miss Smythe's brother likes you very much. Perhaps if you smiled on him...'

Melia pouted. 'I do like John and his sister Anne, but there are others I like better. You've told me neither of them is suitable and I think that is unfair of you. What right have you to tell me who I may marry?'

'I have none, of course,' Jane said. 'You mistake me if you think I mean to forbid you, Melia. I hoped to advise you, because I would wish you to be happy and

I do not think you would be happy with Captain Hershaw. I think him a gambler and perhaps not a man to be trusted with the care of a young girl's heart.'

'And Adam?' she demanded. 'Is he also not to be trusted?'

'If he had asked you, I would have been happy for you,' Jane said softly. 'I think his reasons for not doing so were honourable—he cannot afford to give you the life you deserve. Yet it was unkind of him to raise your hopes in vain.'

'I should be happy living in a cottage with him,' Melia cried and promptly burst into tears, running from the room and slamming the door behind her.

Jane watched her leave sadly. She did not wish to cause the girl pain, even though she'd given Will some heartache when he'd first realised her promises were lightly given and not to be trusted. Yet she'd spoken only the truth. Viscount Hargreaves was a man who many young girls might break their hearts over, but he needed to marry a fortune and could not afford a young lady with only seven thousand pounds to her name.

Melia apologised later that day and a wary truce was called between them. Jane did her best to mend the breach, but could not think it was so easily done. Melia wanted to live in London and to continue the round of parties and dances that would go on all year, but that would mean accepting a man who wished for the same kind of life and Jane did not think that Adam Hargreaves or Captain Smythe was interested in living permanently in town. However, there was nothing more she could say and it was up to Melia to decide what she wanted from life now.

At the card party they attended that evening, Jane was happy to see that Melia joined her friends, Miss Smythe and her brother, and appeared to spend a noisy happy time with them. She seemed in better spirits than earlier and told Jane that Captain Smythe was taking her riding the next morning. Jane nodded and smiled and they parted on good terms.

Sarah had taken the news that they were leaving for the country in much better heart. She looked pleased and made a list of everything she'd seen that she wished to purchase and went shopping with Jane that morning. They bought material, books, sewing items for embroidery, sweet bon-bons, soaps and perfumes and many small luxuries that were not available in the country.

'We shall have so many trunks that we shall need another coach to carry them all,' Sarah said and laughed. 'Oh, I have enjoyed my stay, Jane. I cannot thank you enough for all you have done and given me.'

'It gave me so much pleasure,' Jane said and then her heart caught as she saw the gentleman walking along the street towards them. It was clear that he had seen her and immediately came up with them, a smile on his face. 'Lord Frant, I am glad to see you return. I was afraid we should miss you, for we go home next week.'

'Ah, that is unfortunate,' Paul said and looked regretful. 'Business has kept me from your side too long— but perhaps I may call on you in the near future? I hope that things will be settled soon enough.'

'You are very mysterious,' Jane said and gave him

her hand. He held it to his lips briefly and her heart fluttered as she saw the fire burning deep in his eyes. He did care for her—he must! If not, he was a heartless flirt to look at her so. 'You have been sorely missed, sir.'

'As have you,' he said. He smiled as he saw all their packages. 'I see you have been busy. May I walk with you and assist in the carrying of all these trifles?'

'This is only a part of the whole,' Sarah told him. 'Many of our purchases are to be delivered. We were just about to seek an ice or some coffee, were we not, Lady March?'

'Then allow me to treat you both to an ice at Gunter's.' Paul smiled at them both, though his gaze lingered longer on Jane's face. 'Perhaps we may go to the theatre together, all of us, before you leave town?'

'We are free this evening,' Sarah told him, a hint of mischief in her voice.

'Then I shall arrange it,' Paul murmured. 'Thank you, Miss Sarah, you are very good to aid me so—theatre and supper later it shall be.'

Jane had planned to spend the evening at home because it was a rare thing in London to have no engagements, but she accepted the invitation with pleasure and her heart lifted at the thought.

Perhaps there would be a moment or two for them to speak alone…

Jane was surprised to find that Melia had brought guests to take luncheon with them for she had not mentioned her intention earlier. However, she smiled and welcomed Miss Smythe and then her brother.

'I feared we might impose on you,' Captain Smythe said, 'but Melia insisted that you should be the first to hear her news—she has done me the very great honour to say that she will become my wife...'

Jane was stunned for she could never have expected it. Surely Melia had given no indication of her intention to accept the young man's proposal? However, she recovered quickly and congratulated them both and then called the butler, sending him for champagne to celebrate.

'I know I must speak with Lord Frant,' the young man said, looking very happy and a little bemused, as if he had not quite expected this himself. 'I hope that he will think me worthy...'

Since Captain Smythe was of good family, not fabulously wealthy but rich enough to not care about his wife's dowry, Jane could not think that her guardian would have any objections. He would, no doubt, be grateful to see her well settled and happy.

'I am happy for you both,' Jane said and kissed Melia's cheek. 'I think it a good match for Melia—and I am certain her family will think the same. Lord Frant is in town, I know, for we spoke no more than twenty minutes since.'

'Then I shall take my leave and call on him,' Captain Smythe said and inclined his head.

'Will you not stay to luncheon?' Melia begged, dimpling at him.

'No, for I would have this settled. I shall return later, if I may, Lady March—and we shall settle details of our visit to my parents and your aunt. Come, sister. We must leave these good people to their luncheon and return later...'

After they had gone, Jane looked at Melia. 'It is a good match for you, Melia—but are you happy with it?'

'Yes, of course I am,' the girl replied but her eyes did not meet Jane's.

Jane said no more on the subject, but told her and then her brother when he came in a few minutes later of their arrangements for the evening.

'I shall not accompany you,' Will said, 'but you have no need of me if you are with Frant.' His eyes dwelled for a moment on Melia's flushed face. 'I must wish you happy, Melia. I am sure you will be... Captain Smythe is a decent man.'

'Will, I...' She hung her head and could not continue, but Will took her hand and smiled.

'We are still friends, Melia. You never promised to wed me, merely to consider the idea. You have broken no promise to me—and I hold no grudge against you.'

Melia laughed in relief and said, 'We should not suit, Will. I like the town too much and you prefer the country—Captain Smythe is an officer and I shall enjoy living in married quarters, for there are parties and regimental balls. For now, he is based in town, but his regiment may soon remove to Bath for some months.'

'You will enjoy a military life,' Will agreed and turned away.

After that the conversation was general. After lunch Will left them to keep an appointment with some friends and the ladies went up to their rooms to rest or write letters. Jane had changed into an afternoon gown of coral silk when Captain Smythe and his sister returned. It was clear that the news was good and they had made plans to visit their parents in the country almost immediately.

'We shall leave before the last ball of the season,' he informed them. 'I cannot wait to introduce Melia to my family, and my sister will accompany us—and we shall invite Mrs Bellingham to stay if she so wishes...'

'I am very glad everything has worked out well for you both,' Jane said. Melia's sulks had disappeared completely and she seemed perfectly happy to leave town, knowing that after her wedding she would return as the captain's wife.

'Lord Frant invited us to accompany you to the theatre this evening,' Captain Smythe went on, his enthusiasm carrying all before him. 'However, I want to take Melia to meet my grandmother and so we shall go to her house this evening...'

Jane could only smile and agree and feel relieved when sister and brother had taken their leave so that she could prepare for the evening. Her own thoughts were only for the pleasure that lay ahead and the hope she would have a little time alone with Paul Frant...

'You look beautiful this evening,' Paul said when he greeted her, presenting her with a small nosegay of red roses. 'I have missed seeing you, Jane. I hope that one day soon I shall see much more of you.'

She smiled and murmured her thanks, holding the roses delicately to her nose to smell their scent, but could not say what was in her heart and, despite his compliments and his attentions to her that evening, he did not say the words that would make it possible for her to open her heart to him.

The play was a comedy by Sheridan and well received by the audience, and the music and dancing that followed was pleasant. It was only as they were leaving the theatre after the performance that Jane's gaze was drawn to a lady and gentleman she knew: Lady Catherine and, with her as her escort, Captain Hershaw. She had no other chaperon and that seemed odd since she was engaged to be married to another gentleman.

Captain Hershaw seemed unaware of her but Lady Catherine saw her and her eyes narrowed, a look of something that could only be dislike or anger in her eyes. Jane inclined her head slightly and was given a frosty nod in return, but then Paul spoke and Jane turned to him. When she turned back the pair had gone, mingling with the crowd as the theatre emptied.

The four of them ate supper together in a discreet restaurant and enjoyed each other's company, Sarah and Will seeming to find a great deal to talk and laugh about. On being told that Melia and Captain Smythe were not to be of the party, Jane's brother had decided to accompany them after all.

'Your cousin is a pleasant girl,' Paul said softly when the other two were laughing at some jest of their own. 'Your brother seems happier than he was a few weeks ago.'

'How observant of you,' Jane replied in the same hushed tone. 'I think they like each other but it is early days yet, of course.'

'Of course.' Paul looked into her eyes with such long-

ing that her heart caught. 'Would that I was free to follow my heart, Jane. I long to speak but I may not for
the moment. Indeed, it would have been wiser had I not
come at all this evening, but I could not forgo the pleasure of being with you…forgive me if I seem reluctant
to be plain, but I may not speak openly yet.'

'You do seem to speak in riddles,' Jane said and
frowned, for she did not care for this mystery. 'If something troubles you, I would be happy to listen.'

'You are everything that is lovely and precious to
me,' Paul told her. 'Yet I have good reason to keep my
silence—but know that I care for you deeply. If I could
I would ask you to be my wife.'

What impediment could there be to his asking her to
be his wife if he really wished for it? Jane was puzzled
but, even though her honest nature would have preferred
things to be plain, she sensed that his secret was something he felt unable to share with her.

She touched his hand. 'I see that you are sorely troubled, my friend. I must tell you that I value your friendship and perhaps more, but if there is some barrier…'
She was puzzled for he seemed so strange.

'One that I hope may soon be overcome,' Paul replied and pressed her fingers. 'Now, may I order more
champagne?'

'No more for me. I think perhaps we should be leaving.' She looked across the table, catching her brother's
eyes. 'Are we ready to leave, Sarah—Will?'

'Yes, quite ready,' Sarah said. 'It has been an exciting day and I grow a little tired.'

It was agreed that they should leave and Lord Frant

called for his account and asked that the carriage should be brought round. Sarah and Will seemed content and did not say much as they were driven home but, after they had gone in, Jane asked if Paul would care for a nightcap before he left.

'Just for a moment in private,' he said and followed her into a small parlour, but, as she would have rung for brandy, he stayed her hand. 'Now that Melia will no longer be with you, I must visit her aunt and make arrangements for the contract for her marriage—and then perhaps I may visit you at home?'

'Yes, certainly you may, Lord Frant. I have already asked Will to invite you for the shooting in September, but if you wish you may call at any time.'

'I would hope to be with you before the month is out,' Paul told her. 'I can only pray that circumstances are more favourable by then…'

'Yet you will not tell me why you are troubled?'

'Jane, my love…' He reached out and drew her against him, looking down into her face for a long moment before he kissed her, softly at first and then with increasing passion. She felt a little shudder run through him as though he controlled his passions. 'I love you beyond reason, have done so since we first met—but I dare not ask you to be my wife until this business is finished…'

Jane felt herself melting into him as he held her close, her lips still warm and tingling from the passion of his kiss. 'I believe that I have come to love you, Paul,' she whispered. 'I did not think it could happen again but, though it is different this time, I know that I care deeply for you.'

'Oh, Jane, my love, I adore you,' Paul said and now she could not doubt it for she saw his love for her blazing in his eyes. 'I vowed to keep my distance to hold you safe, but how can I not speak now when my heart cries out for it? I want you for my wife, Jane—will you be mine, sweet love?'

'Yes, I will marry you—if it is what you truly wish.'

'I wish for it with all my heart, yet I must ask you that our love remains secret for a time—will you do that for me? Will you trust me, Jane? I think it better for your peace of mind that you do not know all my reasons, but hope that you will believe in my sincerity and wait until I can come to you freely.'

'Yes, if you wish it,' she said, for how could she refuse? She was swept away on a tide of happiness. 'I know there must be a good reason for what you do...'

'Believe me when I say I ask for your discretion only because I love you and seek to protect you from those who might seek to harm me through you. I have an enemy, Jane, and, though I am almost certain of his identity, I cannot name him yet.'

'Then I shall tell no one; even my brother and Sarah shall remain in ignorance.'

'Thank you, dearest Jane.' He kissed her softly. 'I shall treasure your promise and will return tomorrow after luncheon to bring you a token of my love...and now I must leave you.'

Jane smiled and kissed his lips and then allowed him to leave her. She was lost in a sweet dream as she walked up the stairs to her own bedchamber. Paul loved her and she knew that she loved in return. The future looked bright, for surely this time she would not be robbed of her happiness…

Leaving her, Paul felt a flickering of unease. He had meant not to speak openly yet of his feelings for Jane. Indeed, it would have been better for her sake if he had not taken her to the theatre—but he had needed to see her and then when she'd smiled his feelings had overcome him. He could only pray that his weakness in speaking would not endanger her safety. Yet surely what had passed between them was unlikely to reach the ears of his enemy…

Jane went shopping in the morning for some items she had remembered she would need when they got home. Paul was not coming until the afternoon and so she seized the last chance she might have to visit various establishments.

On her return she glanced through the visiting cards on the silver salver in the hall, a little surprised to find one from Lady Catherine. Flipping it over, she saw an urgent message.

> *I must see you privately. Please come to tea at my house this afternoon. I have something I must tell you.*
> Catherine Radcliffe

Jane stared at the message, frowning over it, for she could not understand why the lady should need to see her urgently. They knew one another but could never have been called friends and Jane had thought the other woman disliked her... But stay, perhaps she feared that Jane would speak of what she'd seen on leaving the theatre the previous evening. The young woman had clung to Captain Hershaw's arm, fluttering her lashes at him and flirting with him—at least until she became aware of Jane's gaze.

Paul meant to call that afternoon and Jane had no intention of perhaps missing him by answering Lady Catherine's summons. She did not wish for private conversation with someone she did not particularly care for. Instead, she would write and tell her that she was too busy to call that day but would be at home the next morning if Lady Catherine wished to see her.

She sent her letter off and spent the time during luncheon talking to Melia of her plans to leave London the next day with Miss Smythe and her brother, and discussing with Sarah any errands that needed doing before they too left London.

Will had promised to take Sarah driving and they left the house soon after the meal was finished. Melia went upstairs to write a letter to her aunt in her room and Jane retired to her parlour to wait for Paul's arrival.

He came at three, looking distinguished in a blue coat, long riding boots and pale breeches, his hat of beaver and bearing a silver buckle at the front. His gloves were of finest leather, his linen pristine and he looked every inch the wealthy gentleman about town.

Jane rose to receive him, holding out her hands. Paul took them and kissed them, and then handed her a flat red leather box. When she opened it she saw a beautiful diamond necklace.

'This is lovely, Paul,' she said. 'But we are not formally engaged; I ought not to accept it.'

'I have ordered a ring to be made, and perhaps tomorrow you could visit the jeweller and have your finger sized,' he said. 'The necklace was my mother's, given her by her father when she married and passed to me when she died. I know she would like you to have it, dearest Jane.'

'Thank you, I shall treasure it,' Jane said and closed the box. She looked up at him. 'I wish I understood why we cannot speak of our engagement to the world.'

'Forgive me—I want to shout it to the rooftops. I ought not to have spoken until these matters were settled, but I have waited too long already and feared to lose your regard. Please try to understand, Jane—it is difficult...'

'Hush, you do not need to tell me,' Jane said, making up her mind that she must trust him. 'You have your reasons and I accept that we must wait...'

'You fill my heart with joy every time I look at you,' he said and moved to take her in his arms and kiss her once more. 'I love you, Jane, and I want to marry you—as soon as it is...possible.'

She sensed that he had almost spoken a different word and wondered at it, but to question every word would show a lack of faith and she let the moment pass. Paul had told her that he loved her and she must accept and believe.

'Then I shall wait patiently for you to come to me,' she said and smiled up into his eyes.

'Tomorrow I have business I must see to,' Paul said, 'and the day after I leave for the country to visit Melia's aunt. I must see the date for the wedding set and talk contracts with her aunt and her husband-to-be—and by then you will be in the country. I may be able to call on you again tomorrow for a few minutes, but cannot be certain, so do not wait in for me.'

'Come if you can,' Jane said. 'You will stay to take tea with me now? Melia will be down shortly, though Sarah and Will have gone for a drive and will not be back until later.'

'Yes, I shall stay. I wish I had no engagements for this evening, but there are people I must see and I am engaged to dine with Major Harding…'

'Ah, yes, I believe he stayed in the country with you when you were last there?'

'Yes—and I was very glad to have him. If he had not…' Paul shook his head. 'I may have been wrong to ask you to tell no one of our understanding, Jane. You should feel free to tell your cousin and Will…perhaps your mama, if you wish? Yet it would be better if it went no further than your immediate family.'

'My brother and Sarah,' Jane said and smiled. 'I do not think Mama needs to know at this time because she would swear to keep it private and then tell everyone— and nor does Melia. She is a friend but no more and… she might not keep our secret.'

'No, she might not,' Paul agreed. 'I shall speak to your brother when I visit you at your home.'

'Yes, he will expect it,' Jane said. 'I am of an age to please myself in the matter of marriage, but my brother would think it a courtesy, I know.'

'I shall have your ring when I come down,' Paul said, 'but…' He broke off as Jane shook her head and realised that they were no longer alone. Turning, he saw Melia standing just inside the door.

'Forgive me,' Melia said. 'I did not wish to intrude, Jane, but I thought you might be waiting tea for me.'

'And so we were,' Jane said, smiling at her. 'Please come and sit down, my dear, and I shall ring for tea. Lord Frant wanted to speak to you, I believe. He intends to follow you down to the country in order to speak to your aunt about the wedding preparations…'

'Yes, I am sure my aunt will wish to discuss them with you, sir,' Melia said, but she did not look at him and Jane thought there was a sulky look about her mouth again, almost as if she had begun to regret her promise to wed Captain Smythe.

Chapter Thirteen

Jane was writing letters in her private parlour the next morning when the door was suddenly thrust open and Lady Catherine walked in, followed by a harassed maid, who apologised to Jane.

'Milady insisted, ma'am,' she said. 'I asked her to wait but…'

'It's all right, Tilly,' Jane said calmly. 'You may go. I was expecting Lady Catherine…' She stood up and greeted her guest with a smile and extended hand. 'I am pleased to see you, Lady Catherine.'

'Are you?' the other woman said rudely. 'I quite expected to be refused entry after your note.'

'Forgive me, I expected guests and could not come to meet you, as you asked.'

'You might be sorry that you did not. I've been told your guest was Lord Frant—and when you hear what I have to tell you, you may wish you had not been at home to receive him.'

Jane was puzzled. 'I'm sorry. I have no idea what you mean.'

'Have you not heard the latest gossip concerning Lord Frant?' Lady Catherine's eyes gleamed with spite. 'I know you two have been close so perhaps that is why you have not been told...'

'Told what?' Jane asked, her gaze narrowed. She had coldness at her nape and knew that she would not care for whatever it was that this woman had come to tell her.

'You may think Frant intends marriage,' the lady said and a cruel smile played over her mouth as she taunted, 'but you shall be sadly disappointed if you hope to be his wife. No decent woman could consent to marry him now...'

Jane's fists clenched at her sides, but she refused to be drawn. Lady Catherine had come here hotfoot to tell her this news but Jane would not press her.

'Don't you want to know?' The other woman laughed. 'Oh, you think yourself so secure—but I had this from Lady Moira, and she has been in his confidence...as well as from other lips...'

'Lady Moira was to have been Miss Bellingham's chaperon but Melia chose to stay with me. I do not see what you think so amusing in this...'

'Lady Moira told me herself. She was shocked when she heard it and confronted him, for she would never have agreed to chaperon the girl in the first place if she'd known...'

'Melia is a perfectly respectable young lady,' Jane said, feeling angry; although the girl had hurt Will she would not allow her character to be besmirched.

'It is not the girl but Lord Frant himself...' Lady Catherine's eyes gleamed with malice as she chose her words with deliberate spite. 'Lady Moira has been told by someone who knows the facts that he was married to a girl…a half caste Indian whore…'

'Ridiculous!' Jane said. 'Paul would never…' Her words stuck in her throat because Paul had spoken of circumstances that prevented his announcing their engagement or marrying her. 'He couldn't be married to a girl of that class…'

'Oh, she isn't of the lower class,' Lady Catherine said with great satisfaction. 'Her mother was the daughter of an earl but she became an Indian prince's concubine and her daughter is a whore—she gave birth to Lord Frant's child soon after he left India. It seems she claims he wed her in secret and she named him as her child's father…'

'No, I do not believe you,' Jane said. She refused to believe the other woman's spiteful words; they must be spoken out of malice, for there was no other reason to come here and speak so to her. 'Paul does not have a wife or…a child…'

She looked proudly at Lady Catherine. 'I do not know what you hoped to gain by coming here this morning, but you have failed if you believed I would listen to your lies. I do not know the truth of the matter, but I am certain Lord Frant would not have left his wife in India, nor would he have kept her existence a secret.'

'Men are all deceivers,' Lady Catherine said coldly. 'You may believe what you wish, Lady March—but I have been your friend in this by coming here. People are whispering about the way he is received here. You have no chaperon and you have been to his house with just his ward. Some say you are his mistress—a single gentleman and you still too young to be a true chaperon to any girl...'

'I hope I know Lord Frant well enough to be certain that it is perfectly proper for his ward and her chaperon to visit during the morning hours.' Jane raised her head proudly. 'We were hardly alone, for there were servants present. You will please leave my house, Lady Catherine. I have no wish to continue this conversation.'

'You will learn soon enough,' the other woman said. 'Be careful that you do not lose your reputation in the meantime. Believe me when I say that several ladies believe you to be his mistress. If you continue this way you may find you are not welcome everywhere, as you have been in the past.'

Jane took a step towards her. She was seething with anger and wanted to slap Lady Catherine's sneering face but held her temper in check, her hands clenched at her sides.

'Leave now or I shall ring for a footman to escort you from the house.'

'I'm leaving...' The other woman laughed scornfully. 'At least I know what I'm getting when I marry. I shall give the marquis an heir and take as many lovers as I choose—but I shall not be fool enough to lose either my heart or my reputation...'

Jane stood frozen to the spot as Lady Catherine swept from the room. Tears were burning her eyes but she refused to let them fall, despite her humiliation. She stood motionless for some minutes and then sank down to her chair. It couldn't be true—Paul could not have a wife in India and a child...

He would not have spoken to her of love if that were the case. She could not believe him so false and yet...he had begged her to keep their attachment secret for the moment. He had seemed so strange but she'd thought he was telling her his own life might be at risk when he'd spoken of an enemy.

Slowly, the tears began to trickle down her cheeks. For a while she left them unchecked, but then she dashed them away. She would not let Lady Catherine's spite hurt her because she believed it arose from jealousy. The night they'd all met on the balcony at the duchess's ball, Jane had seen something in the other woman's eyes. Lady Catherine had tried to make Paul notice her that night but he hadn't; his eyes had been only for Jane, and that would have aroused the other woman's ire. She was used to attention and to getting what she wanted—but was that enough to make her come to Jane with a vicious rumour?

That was all it could be—just a rumour. Paul loved her, Jane, and he would never do anything to hurt her... and yet he had told her that he was not yet free to wed her...

Might it be that he needed to free himself of a wife he no longer cared for? No, no, that was dishonourable and cruel and Jane could not love a man who would treat a woman who loved him thus.

Getting to her feet, Jane went slowly from the room. The housekeeper called to her as she began her ascent of the stairs but she did not answer. She needed a little time alone in the privacy of her bedroom.

'Thank God I caught you before you left,' Major Harding said. Paul was dressed for visiting and on the point of leaving to keep his promise to Jane. He'd had little time for anything these past few days, but intended to spend the afternoon with her, even if it meant he left some work undone.

'Something wrong?' Paul asked with a lift of his brows. 'I was just on my way to visit Lady March. You could walk with me if you chose.'

'I think you need to hear this,' his friend said, 'and in private—it's being whispered of all over town. A scurrilous lie, I am sure, but you should hear it, if only to be prepared…'

Paul sat down and invited the major to sit, but he continued to stand, looking uncomfortable.

'They say you have a wife…and she a royal bastard of mixed blood…in India. Apparently she had a child soon after you left and named you as the father. She claims to have married you in secret…'

'That is a lie,' Paul said but felt as if a jug of cold water had been thrown over him. 'Annamarie is not my wife—and I have never lain with her. The invitation was there but never taken up.'

'I have no doubt you speak the truth, but you know what the gossips will make of such a tale as this…' Jack Harding hesitated. 'Unfortunately, it is not the worst of what they are saying…'

'Go on,' Paul said grimly. 'Get it out, man.'

'They are linking Lady March's name with yours and whispering that she has been too free, visiting your house without a proper chaperon and allowing you access to hers... They begin to hint that she is your mistress...'

'Damn their wicked tongues to hell!' Paul said furiously and jumped to his feet. 'I care little for what they say of my having a wife in India. It is not true and I can prove it—though if Annamarie had a child it would be harder to prove I was not the father...' He struck one fist into the other. 'I should like to strangle whoever started the rumours...'

'Lady Moira told me what people were saying. She pretended not to believe it, but there was something about her manner...'

'I thought her a friend, but when I told her that I no longer needed her services for Melia she was angry—but I cannot think she made up the tale. How would she know of Annamarie? No, someone who knew me in India has done this...'

'We knew you had an enemy. He has tried to kill or injure you three times now. Once on the way home from Newmarket, in Ireland—and again in the country, when your saddle was tampered with...'

'Fortunately, you suspected something and discovered it before we went riding that day...' Paul was thoughtful. 'Yes, we knew I had an enemy who wanted me dead—but this is different. It is spiteful and meant to hurt another as much as I...'

'Yes, I detect a woman's hand in this,' his friend said. 'Which lady have you so mortally offended?'

'I have no idea,' Paul said. 'I knew Lady Moira was not pleased to be told she was not needed as Melia's chaperon—but there is no one else…' He paused, his gaze narrowed and thoughtful.

'You have thought of someone?'

'Lady Catherine…' Paul said. 'I thought it of no importance, but she did make the attempt to engage my interest on more than one occasion. I greeted her politely but could not give her the attentions she craved.'

'Lady Catherine is a flirt and proud, too spoiled for her own good. Yet how would she know of this girl in India?'

'I do not see how she could—unless…' Paul stared at him. 'I saw her the other evening at the theatre with Hershaw…. He followed me from India by the next ship, I think…'

'Then I think we have our answer.' Jack smiled grimly. 'Adam is in Ireland and could not have tampered with your saddle—and he certainly has not been seen in town with Lady Catherine.'

'Yes, I begin to think I wronged Adam even to consider that he meant me harm,' Paul said. 'It was something Melia said to me… I thought he had told her lies and that made me believe he might have had a hand in the bungled shooting…'

'Your ward? She has no cause to hate you or spread malicious rumours?'

'No sensible cause, though she thinks I did not give her a large enough dowry—or she did, but now she is to marry someone else and has forgot she ever wanted Hargreaves…'

'Then I think we should concentrate our efforts on Hershaw,' Jack said and Paul nodded.

'He is the most likely to be behind this latest attempt to bring me harm. Three attempts to kill me have failed, and now he thinks to ruin me by casting filth on my reputation. I shall find a way of letting it be known that I am not married and the child is not mine.'

'I doubt you will be believed, as far as the parentage of the child is concerned,' Jack warned him. 'The men will not blame you for that—but the women may not wish to welcome you as warmly as they did.'

'It is Lady March I think of,' Paul said. 'If it were not for the whispers concerning her, I should ignore them and let them do their worst.'

'Yes, it is her reputation that I care for too,' Jack said grimly. 'I shall do my best to scotch the rumours, believe me.'

'Thank you, my friend. I care not for the wagging tongues of spiteful women—but I would not have Jane hurt for all the world and, as for the other business, I think we must lay a trap for my enemy...'

Jane washed her face and changed into a walking gown of dark green, which she wore with a velvet bonnet tied with ribbons to match her gown. A silk shawl was draped over her shoulders. She had refused luncheon, telling her housekeeper that she had a headache and asking to be left alone, but now she needed to go out in the fresh air. Sarah would accompany her if she wished it, but Jane needed to be alone.

Sitting on her bed had not served. She was in too

much agitation to settle or sleep, and now her head really had started to ache. One thing she was certain of: she could not receive Paul that afternoon if he called—so she must make her escape and give herself time to think before she spoke with him again.

He would no doubt wonder why she had gone out rather than receiving him as she had expected to do, but Jane did not feel like asking the questions that raced through her mind. Paul had spoken of love and trust and she wanted to trust him, but it was difficult to forget the gleam in Lady Catherine's eyes. Clearly, she had enjoyed passing on the shameful gossip—for if Paul had deserted his Indian wife when she was carrying his child, he had behaved badly.

Yet would he have spoken to her of marriage if the stories were true? Jane could not believe it, but her treacherous mind would not let it go. She loved him and she ought to trust him, because with love came trust—and if it did not could it be true love?

Leaving the house, Jane told her footman that she would be back in time for tea. She did not want her family to worry if they discovered her room empty, but she wanted neither company nor sympathy and she was afraid that her emotions would show too easily. She felt as if her heart would break because she was tortured by her doubts.

What had Paul meant when he said he was not free to marry her yet? He wanted her, loved her, but he had asked her to keep their understanding secret—what honourable man would do that?

The thoughts kept going round and round in her head

and she could find no answers to her questions. She wanted to believe that his reasons were honest and that he was not the man Lady Catherine had implied. *Her* motive was easy to read, Jane thought. She'd wanted Paul for herself. Although promised to a man much older and with a respected title, she would have jilted him, had the opportunity arisen for her to marry a man as wealthy as Paul. He might not have the marquis's title but he had youth and strength and his fortune was vast, so it was said… Yes, Jane could think of reasons why both Lady Moira and Lady Catherine might want to spread poisonous lies…but why had Paul wanted to keep their engagement a secret?

If it were not for that, Jane would have dismissed the whole story as nonsense, for she could not believe Paul would seek to keep such a scandal from Society. It was almost certain to leak out if there was any truth in it. Only a fool would believe they could keep such a secret and Paul was not a fool. Indeed, she found him intelligent, amusing and honest…and she was the fool to let Lady Catherine distress her.

Jane found that she was heading for the park. It was a pleasant afternoon and she felt that a good brisk walk would help to clear her head, both of the headache and her doubts. All she knew of Paul was telling her that she should trust him and yet it was hard not to let the doubts creep in… If only she could be certain that he truly cared for her…

If she was sure that Paul loved her Jane would care little for the gossip. Some of the more spiteful ladies might watch her to see if she quickened with child but her friends would dismiss the tales of her being Paul's mistress as nonsense. Yes, perhaps she had been a little careless, calling at his house with just Melia—but the girl was his ward, and Jane had been married previously. She was not a vulnerable young girl. Surely only those with nasty minds would make anything of such meetings. There had been nothing clandestine in them, for Paul's servants had been in the house and Viscount Hargreaves and Melia…

Entering the park, Jane saw an acquaintance and nodded to her, but the woman looked through her. She sighed because the dowager Lady Benbow was a stickler and just the sort who would cut Jane if she believed the rumours. Oh, well, there was nothing to be done. She would simply have to ride out the storm and hope at the end she would still be accepted into the homes of her friends.

It was very hot. Jane felt beads of sweat on her brow and more trickled down her back. She headed for the trees because it would be cooler there and she was not yet ready to walk home. In her haste to leave the house she'd forgotten her reticule and had no money with her, so that meant she must walk all the way home again. Had she thought, she might have taken a cab when she was ready to return…though she could ask the cab to wait and ask her footman to pay for her. Yes, perhaps she would do that when she was ready, but for the moment she would simply walk in the shade.

She had been strolling, lost in thought, for almost half an hour when she heard a sound behind her. Turning, she gazed into the face of a man she knew and a shiver ran down her spine as she saw the look in his eyes. It was a look of malice and intent to harm.

'What do you want?' she asked, looking about her as she took a step back. 'Have you been following me?'

'Yes, of course, for weeks, but I never expected you to make it so easy for me. Lady Catherine must have done her work better than she knew...'

'That was you?' Jane gasped and moved back. 'Why did you send her—what did you hope to gain?'

'Exactly what I have,' he replied and grinned. 'You alone and vulnerable. There is nothing like sowing doubt in a woman's mind to make her do something foolish—but I thought you would be harder to deceive...'

'Get out of my way,' Jane cried defiantly. 'It was all lies. I know Paul doesn't have a wife...' But her words ended abruptly as a cloth was placed over her nose and mouth from behind and she felt herself losing her senses. She was falling...falling, though she did not know it, into the arms of the man who had followed her.

'Forgive me, my lord,' the viscount's footman said when he admitted Paul to the parlour. 'I believe Lady March went out earlier. If you would care to wait I shall make enquiries as to whether she has returned. Perhaps some refreshment while you wait?'

'Nothing, I thank you. I thought Lady March was expecting me. Did she say when she was to return?'

'I will enquire for you, sir.'

Paul stood looking out at the rear gardens, frowning because he had expected Jane to be here. Surely she knew he meant to call and spend some time with her before he left town? Why would she have gone out when she knew she would have company—unless Lady Catherine had been here before him? No, that would not make her leave the house. Jane must know it was a wicked lie—surely she did?

He turned as someone came into the room and he recognised a footman he'd seen before on his visits to the house.

'Lady March went out two hours ago, my lord. She said that she would be back in time for tea…'

'Ah, I see…' Paul looked at his watch. Perhaps Jane had an errand and did not expect him until then. 'I shall leave and return later…'

He was frowning as he walked from the house. He would call into his club and make the situation clear to one or two trusted friends who could be relied upon to refute the scurrilous lies that were circulating. Just as he reached it, however, he saw someone coming out and looked at him in surprise.

'Adam, you here?' he said. 'I thought you settled in Ireland?'

'Yes, I am, but there was a small matter of business that my lawyers wanted me to settle. I intend to return this evening. Our horses are being well cared for, Paul. There is nothing to concern yourself with…'

'I was just surprised to see you,' Paul said and placed a hand on his arm. 'You were in the club—did you hear a rumour concerning me?'

'If you mean that nonsense concerning Annamarie, I told the man who uttered it that I would knock it down his lying throat if he said such a thing again. I know you did not marry her—nor is the child yours...'

'Then she has a child?' Paul wrinkled his brow. 'I can scarce believe it.'

'If there is a child I have heard nothing of it—though there could be one,' Adam said. His expression changed to one of anguish. 'I cannot tell you here; it is too public. I never intended anyone to know, but now I must tell you. Where can we go to talk in private?'

'Come home with me, Adam, and I will listen to your story.'

'I should have told you sooner, but she begged me not to...'

'Come, my friend, walk with me and we shall speak in private...'

'I fear you will think the less of me once you know the truth.'

'We are friends,' Paul said. 'You saved my life on board ship when I lay ill of a fever—and I might have died that night as we returned from Newmarket. I believe you are not my enemy, though there were moments when I wondered.'

'And I gave you cause,' Adam said. 'I was bitter and resentful when I learned the true extent of my father's debts—but there were other reasons, as you will soon learn...'

'I wish you had told me this sooner,' Paul said when Adam had finished his story. 'I always sensed that you cared for Annamarie—but you told me she would not look at you...'

'For a long time that was true,' Adam said and grimaced. 'She wanted you, but one night after she learned that you had booked your ship for England, she came to me and...' He faltered, his voice caught with emotion. 'She declared that it was always I that she had loved and she gave herself to me. Yet afterwards she cried bitter tears and I knew that it was you she truly loved.'

'I could never love her, though I felt sympathy for her, caught between two worlds and never belonging to either.'

'When she learned that I had become the viscount she begged me to wed her and told me that she was with child—my child...though I wasn't sure whether she lied...' Adam hesitated. 'She believed that I would be rich and would send for her to come to me here... and I promised she would be received in society as my wife...'

'So when you learned you had nothing you resented what I had...' Paul looked at him hard. 'Knowing that Annamarie was your wife, why did you let my ward think you cared for her?'

Adam had the grace to look ashamed. 'I suppose I wanted to punish you a little for having everything that I wanted and I knew that you were concerned for her...'

'Not the action of a gentleman,' Paul said severely. 'You might have broken her heart.'

'I doubt she has one to break,' Adam said. 'She is a flighty little madam, Paul—yet I should not have let her think I cared. There is only one woman I have ever loved—but when she learns that I have only a small house in Ireland and a share in your racing stables...'

'If she loves you, it will be enough for her, Adam.'

'No. Annamarie loved you. I was second best and she took me only because she'd given herself to me in a fit of pique and feared the consequences. She will not want me when I tell her I have nothing to give her...'

Paul turned from him and took a few paces about the room, his thoughts working furiously. 'There is a way you might appease her,' he said. 'It is not what she hoped for or what you might wish...but it is a way for you to do what is right, Adam.'

'If you can tell me what I need to do then I shall do it,' Adam said. 'I have racked my brain, but I can find no solution—my wife would never consent to live in Ireland.'

'Yet she might be content to remain in India in her own palace—the palace I was given as a reward for saving the Prince's life...'

Adam stared at him in disbelief. 'You would do that for me? I could not ask it of you, Paul. I do not deserve such generosity...'

'No? You saved my life.' Paul smiled oddly. 'I have no need of pink palaces, my friend. My future is here in England—but if it can be of use to you...and it seems I owe a debt to Annamarie, though it was not of my making. Yet if my rejection of her made her come to you as she did then I share the responsibility...'

'She will never love me as she loved you but I have a title and if we live in a palace I think she will accept her fate.'

'All my lands there will be under your care and you will be my agent. I shall trust you, Adam, and in caring for my business affairs in India you will find both respect and wealth for yourself.'

'I can never thank you enough.' Adam squared his shoulders. 'As for the money you let me think was mine to invest in the land in Ireland—the stables are yours, Paul. As soon as you find another partner to take my place I shall return to India.'

'First there is something you may do for me,' Paul said and smiled. 'You may come with me and tell Lady March the truth of your marriage to Annamarie…'

'Yes, of course. When would you have me visit her?'

'Come with me now,' Paul invited. 'She should be at home now—and do not look so chastened, Adam. I've always suspected that you loved Annamarie. I am sure she will be happy when she has your child and you beside her. As for any coolness between us, it is forgotten now that you have told me the truth.' Paul smiled wryly. 'I do understand the power of love, my friend, and I think at times it makes a man lose all reason.'

'Indeed, you are right.' Adam looked rueful. 'Yes, I shall tell Lady March, and I must also see Miss Bellingham and beg her pardon if I led her on…'

'There is no *if* about it,' Paul said severely. 'Yet it hardly matters now, for she is to marry Captain Smythe and I truly hope she will be happy…though, as you said, she is flighty and it would not surprise me if she leads him a merry dance, but that will not be my concern…'

Chapter Fourteen

'Did Jane say nothing to you of her reasons for going out?' Will asked of Sarah as she came back to the parlour and told him that Jane was not in her room. 'It is unlike her to go off on her own like this without telling anyone.'

'She told John that she would be back for tea and it is now half past four,' Sarah replied. 'I have not seen her since she said she had a headache…'

'I know that my sister likes to walk when she has a headache, but it is so rare that she does—and she ought to have been home by now…'

'My lord—Viscount Hargreaves and Lord Frant are here.'

Will frowned at his butler, and then inclined his head. 'Pray show them in, if you please. Perhaps they may have some news of Jane…'

'Salisbury,' Paul said and held out his hand, 'I was hoping to see Lady March—she has returned from her walk?'

'No, she has not and I grow anxious,' Will replied. 'It is so unlike her to go off alone and not tell anyone where she is going...'

'I fear you have good cause to worry,' Paul said and handed him a piece of crumpled paper. 'I was about to leave my house when this was delivered—by an urchin who immediately ran off, I'm told.'

Will scanned the paper and then stared at him in bewilderment. 'Why was this sent to you, sir? If my sister has been kidnapped, the demand for her ransom should surely have been addressed to me?'

'We had not yet got round to announcing our intentions to the world,' Paul replied. 'I see I must be plain with you—I asked Jane to be my wife and she accepted me, but I begged her to keep it secret for a while.'

Will was puzzled. 'I do not see why you need to keep it a secret—unless you meant until you had told the family?'

'No, sir. It was more serious than that...though I had not told Jane. Would that I had warned her to be careful of him, but I did not imagine that he would do such a vile and desperate thing as to kidnap her.'

'Your enemy?'

'Yes. You may have heard some scurrilous rumours?' Will shook his head. 'No? There is talk of my deserting an Indian wife, who has since had my child. It is a lie, as Adam can confirm, for she is his wife and the child his—but before this there were three attempts on my life. I did not wish to worry Jane so I did not tell her everything, but it was my reason for keeping our understanding a secret—to protect her.'

'Someone knew of it,' Will said, his gaze narrowed. 'Someone must have passed the news on to whoever has used it against you.'

'I have told no one,' Paul asserted. 'If it was learned of, it must have come from Jane or someone here.'

'If my sister said she would keep a secret she would not speak of it, even to me,' Will said and frowned. He glanced at Sarah. 'You did not know?'

'Jane said nothing, but I suspected it,' Sarah said. 'I would never have spoken of it…' She hesitated, then, 'I think Melia might have heard something… She might not have been so circumspect. I believe she could be… spiteful and she was a little jealous of Jane.'

'Yes,' Will admitted. 'I had not realised it until recently, but she was spiteful about Jane and you, Sarah, on occasion. Yet would she have deliberately set out to harm Jane?'

'I doubt she meant to harm her,' Paul said. 'She is thoughtless and probably did not think telling someone could cause harm…'

'But who did she tell—and why should that cause harm to my sister?'

'If she told the man who hates me he would feel it cause to strike against her in order to harm me—this note is proof of that, if proof were needed.'

'You know who this man is?'

'I believe so,' Paul said. 'Years ago I spoke out against him because I believed he was a cheat at the card tables. He was sent away from the regiment on active service and I did not see him for many years—until he returned from India some weeks ago. Yet I would not have believed he could hate me so much—unless he has other cause...'

'Hershaw!' Adam spoke. 'He was not of our regiment, but he came to the region some months before you left...he asked me about you and I told him you had grown rich and powerful because of what you did the night you rescued the Prince from the flames.'

'While you and the others held the tribesmen at bay,' Paul said. 'I have not forgotten your part in the affair, Adam.'

'I but did my job,' Adam admitted. 'You broke down the door of that burning hut; you dashed in and brought out the Prince at some cost to yourself. You deserved the praise and the rewards.'

'But what does this have to do with Jane?' Will demanded. 'Why has she been kidnapped?'

'Because my enemy knows that it is my vulnerable spot. If anything happens to Jane... I do not think, I could bear it.'

'It would kill Mama,' Will said. 'In God's name, why didn't you tell us, Frant? I could have had her watched wherever she went...'

'That was my duty and I believed she was being watched over,' Paul said. 'I came straight here in the hope of finding it a hoax and Jane safe with her family, but I shall seek out those I had paid to watch for her and demand an explanation for this...'

'We must find her,' Will said. 'Jane is my sister. I care for her—as does Sarah and my family. We must get her back unharmed.' He frowned, then, 'You will pay the ransom?'

'I would pay three times over what he demands,' Paul said, 'but I fear he would take the money and laugh in my face—perhaps send her back more dead than alive. No, I must find her and bring her home…'

'How do you expect to do that?' Adam asked, looking grim. 'I shall help you, Paul. Whatever you ask, I am happy to do…but where do we start?'

'I must consult the men I employed to watch her back and mine. One of them should have followed her. It surprises me that he did not report this abduction himself before the rogues could do so themselves…'

'Tell me what I can do to help,' Will said. 'If you need more agents, more men to help you find her, you know I shall do all I can to aid you.'

'Yes, of course,' Paul said. 'For the moment there is nothing you can do but keep your cousin safe. You will hear from me again as soon as I have news. Come, Adam, we have work to do…'

Jane came to her senses slowly. Her head hurt and she was conscious of feeling sick, a dull aching sensation all over her body. As the light in the room strengthened, she could feel soreness at the back of her head and her wrists hurt. She touched one wrist and winced because she could feel where the ropes had chafed against the softness of her skin.

She had been drugged and dragged off to a waiting carriage. Her memory of what happened then was cloudy, but she seemed to recall that she had tried to fight off her captors and almost got away—until one of them had hit her on the back of the head. After that they must have tied her hands, though she had at some time since been released from her bonds.

How long was it since she'd been captured? Jane had no idea, but she thought it must be morning now. There was a faint light coming from the windows, which had thick drapes over them but were not quite drawn together. She rolled over and tried to put her feet to the floor but the feeling of sickness swept over her and she vomited, the foul-smelling bile spilling out of her to the floor. Her mouth tasted as bitter as gall and she thought they had forced her to drink a few sips of something, probably to drug her, as the cloth soaked in some foul mixture, which they'd put over her nose in the first place, had not put her right out. She'd recovered enough to kick the shins of her captor and run, but of course they'd caught her because she'd been disorientated and frightened. Jane had seen real hatred in the eyes of the man who had captured her and she did not think that he intended to let her go. She had not been taken for a ransom.

If she could get to the window and discover where she was… Had they brought her to a house in town or were they in the country somewhere? She listened hard, but could not hear anything that would help her to identify her whereabouts.

She stood up, immediately felt dizzy and fell back onto the bed. It was no use; she felt too ill to even think about making an attempt at escape, even if there was a chance of it.

Jane lay back against the pillows and closed her eyes.

Her head was throbbing. She could not remember feeling this ill before, even when she'd had the influenza.

Hearing a key in the lock of her door, she kept her eyes shut as heavy footsteps came towards her, sensing that there were two men in the room even though she could not see them.

'She's still out. I reckon 'e 'it 'er too 'ard. If she dies it'll be us that swings fer it. Mind me words, Herb, he'll be off scot-free and us'll be for the 'igh toby.'

'He's a rotten swine, the captain,' Herb said. 'I 'ates 'im, but I daresn't do other than wot 'e says. If'n I'd known it was a woman I'd never 'ave gone along of it. But I dare say the devil would 'ave shot me if'n I'd refused 'im.'

'I reckon you'm be right,' the other man said. 'Put the tray down there, Herb. If'n she wakes, she might want a drop of water and a bit of this 'ere cheese. As I says it meself, it's a rare bit o' cheese, that—tasty and fresh.'

'Seems a waste ter leave it if she's gonna croak…'

'He's payin fer it, and there's a pot of soup downstairs. Reckon we'll leave this in case she wakes and have our soup and bread in the kitchen with Sophie.'

'Sophie'll 'ave me guts fer garters if'n this one croaks. She created somethin' awful when she see it were a lady… She says we'll all be 'ung fer this night's work…'

Jane heard the men leaving and locking the door behind them. She opened her eyes cautiously, but she was alone again. Sitting up carefully, she managed to pick up the small jug and pour some liquid into the thick earthenware cup provided. It tasted good, cool and fresh, like spring water. Jane seldom drank water in town that had not been boiled first because it was often contaminated—this water was good and she thought they must be in the country. As if to confirm her thoughts, she heard a cock crowing the hour. Yes, that was a country sound—but they could surely not be too far from town, unless she had been unconscious for more than one night.

Suddenly becoming aware of a need to relieve herself, Jane struggled to first sit up and then to put her feet to the floor. She was still a little unsteady but she managed to walk to the window and pull back the curtains enough to let in some light. Glancing round, she saw the room was furnished with heavy ill-fashioned pieces made by a carpenter rather than a cabinet maker, but there was a rather crude commode chair, and she sighed with relief as she made use of it.

She saw a washstand in one corner, and on examination found water for cleansing herself, a lump of coarse soap and a rough cloth to dry on. It was all of the poorest quality, but the cloth was clean and she was glad of the chance to wash her face and hands. Returning to the bed, she looked at the tray and saw that the cheese and bread were fresh, though the bread was not white but thick dark bread that looked home baked with coarse-grained flour. However, the tiny piece she broke and ate with a morsel of cheese tasted good and she ate half the bread and all the small slice of cheese.

At least she wasn't to be starved, Jane thought. The men who had checked on her sounded reasonable enough, though clearly the kind of rogues who sold their services to a man they feared. She imagined that they would not baulk at murder if she were a man, but the thought of killing a gentlewoman had given them cause for concern—and Sophie sounded as if she might have some influence with at least one of them. It was Sophie she had to thank for the soap and towel, and the bread and cheese. If she had any chance of getting out of here alive, it must be through Sophie—and she would hope that next time food was brought it would be the woman herself.

Jane sat on the bed and hunched her knees to her chest. She knew the name of her captor and she'd seen hatred in his eyes. Right from the time of their first meeting, Jane had been wary of Captain Hershaw but she could not imagine why he wanted to harm her. What had she done that had so offended him?

Yes, she had perhaps made it clear that she did not wish him to make himself free of her brother's house, but was that cause enough for him to abduct her? It seemed so strange that he should look at her in that way—as if he wanted to inflict pain on her...or someone else.

Was it possible that the person he truly hated was Paul Frant? Jane came to the conclusion in a flash, because it fitted with the rest. Lady Catherine had been at the theatre with Hershaw and she knew they'd been noticed—was it because of that Jane had been told of Paul's wife in India? Had they hoped her distress would lead her to do something foolish? If so, they must be pleased with themselves for she'd walked neatly into their trap.

Her brother would be frantic with worry—and Paul, would he be anxious too? Yes, of course he would. He'd sworn he loved her and she ought to have trusted him and ignored Lady Catherine's lies, for she was now certain that they had been concocted especially for her sake, to make her act foolishly—and that was her own fault. Paul had told her that he wished to keep their attachment secret in case his enemy sought to use her against him—which was exactly what he had done, but it was Jane's own foolish behaviour that had put her into danger. Will often told her that she ought to take a maid when she walked out in town, but she'd laughed and told him she was perfectly safe. While that was probably so in the grounds of their country home, it was clearly not the case in London—but she had not realised she had enemies.

Hearing a sound outside the door, Jane sat on the edge of the bed. She'd eaten food and made use of the water for washing so there was no point in pretending to be asleep.

The door opened and a woman entered. She looked at Jane and nodded, smiling as if she were pleased to see her sitting up and relatively unharmed.

'My man said as he thought you was awake, milady,' she said. 'I came up to see for myself and see to things… he said as you'd been sick earlier.'

'He spoke of Sophie—are you she?'

'Yes, milady, and I must tell you that I was angry with Herb and my brother for bringing you here in that state. It was a wicked thing to do—but you mustn't think too hardly of them, for it was that wicked man as made them do it. He's a rare cruel devil that one and they be fools for havin' to do with such a one as he.'

'Tell me,' Jane said, 'were you once in service to a lady, Sophie?'

'Aye, my lady, I was—and a sweeter, gentler lady was never to be found. I loved her and stayed with her until she died of a fever and they turned me off; 'twas then I married Herb and came here—and there's times I curse myself for a fool. He's not a bad man, milady, but easily led—and my brother was never to be trusted, though as a boy none had a sweeter nature.'

'Do you know what Captain Hershaw intends to do with me?'

'Ah, you know him then,' Sophie said and looked concerned. 'It would be better had you not seen his face for he will not let you go now—for a crime such as he plans the penalty is death at the end of a rope.'

'Do you know why he hates me?'

'I doubt it's you he hates, milady—but the man you care for. My man heard him in his cups one night, vowing to be even with his enemy. He thinks he can deal him a blow through you from which he will never recover.'

'Did your man hear the reason for his hatred?'

'None that he told me, but it seems it was something that happened long ago...'

'Yes, I see,' Jane said and bit her lip. 'I think he means to hold me here to lure Lord Frant to his doom—and then he must kill me too...'

'Aye, 'tis what I suspected from the start, milady.

I've told Herb that if he stands by and does nothing I shall leave him…'

'If you help me to escape I would see you all rewarded for your trouble.'

'I dare say you would, milady, but money won't help my Herb if the captain suspects us.' Sophie gave her a measuring look. 'I would help you but you must play your part—are you brave enough to fight for your life?'

'Yes, I believe so,' Jane said. 'I have never had cause before—but what would you have me do?'

'He has gone somewhere for the moment,' Sophie told her. 'When he returns for his meal he will probably call for drink. I could make sure that he became drunk more quickly than he thinks and when he comes to gloat over his prisoner, as he surely will…you must be ready.' Sophie brought out a heavy iron bar with a hook on the end, used for hanging meat in the kitchen. 'Hide behind the door when he comes and then hit him as hard as you can, but do not drop the weapon for I would not have him know I gave it to you…'

'I shall do as you suggest,' Jane promised and took the weapon from Sophie.

She was aware that even in his drunken state Hershaw would not be easy to knock down and if she attacked him he would most certainly retaliate—and yet she knew it was her only chance, for he could not let her live.

'I wish I could simply let you go now while he's out,' Sophie told her. 'Yet he is an evil man and I fear that he would kill us all.'

'Have you considered that he may do so anyway

when this is over?' Jane said. 'Once you have served your purpose it would be an unnecessary risk to let you live.'

'Yes, I've considered it, but my man thinks he's too useful to the captain,' Sophie said and shook her head. 'I think this mad venture will be the end of us all, milady—but I've done what I can for you and there's an end to it.'

'You know where they've taken her?' Paul stared at Jack Harding with a mixture of disbelief and wonder. 'How—please explain?'

'I happened to see Lady March enter the park yesterday afternoon,' Jack said. 'She looked to be in distress and I wondered if I should go to her and ask what was wrong, but, knowing that you worried for her safety, instead I followed at a distance. For a moment I lost her as she sought the shade of some trees. Forgive me, Paul, it all happened so quickly and they had her before I could do anything. I was unarmed and there were four of them. I thought it best to follow and watch—and that is what I did.'

'Is she in town? A prisoner in some low house?'

'They had a carriage waiting and took her out of town. I had no horse, but I commandeered one from a friend who rode by in the park and followed. The house in which she is a prisoner is some two hours ride beyond the town, a deserted place tucked well away near some sheltering woods. I remained there all night and then I saw two young lads and asked if they would keep watch over the place. If anyone took a woman away they were to follow and discover the new hiding place and one must return to tell me when I came back…'

'Do you think they will do as you ask?'

'Yes, for I gave them half a guinea and promised the other half on my return—and one asked if I needed a groom and I said yes, I would take him if he did as I asked.'

Paul gripped his shoulder. 'We must return at once. I shall send word to Jane's brother and gather my men. I pray God that he has not harmed her.'

'You know who took her then?' Paul nodded grimly. 'It was no surprise to me that Hershaw should be a villain. I have thought it but there was never any proof. He will not be admitted to any house in England again when I have finished with him.'

'If I get my hands on him, he will not live,' Paul muttered. 'If he has harmed her I will see him dead before nightfall.'

'Better to leave him to the law,' Jack cautioned. 'We have enough evidence to hang him now—and I would see justice done.'

A nerve flicked in Paul's cheek and for a moment his hands clenched and then he smiled oddly. 'It is as well you are here, my friend, for I have been in agony all night. I knew not where to search. I feared her already dead and my anger has been building. Yes, the law shall have him—but if they do not take his life I will…'

'We must waste no more time in talking,' Jack said. 'Gather what you need and let us go. The longer she remains in that devil's power, the more likely that he may harm her.'

* * *

It had been a long day for Jane, cooped up in the stuffy bedchamber with nothing to read and only water to drink. Sophie had brought her some soup and bread at midday, but since then no one had been near her. She thought someone had arrived an hour or so earlier, for she heard shouting downstairs, but since then nothing.

How long must she sit here and feel the anxiety gnawing at her stomach? She'd told Sophie that she would use force to protect herself but she knew she would find it difficult to strike hard enough to fell Hershaw, for he was a big man—and she could never bring herself to kill him, even though he might deserve it. She would beat him about the shoulders and body if she could and then make her escape.

As she heard sounds outside her room, her body tensed and she gripped the iron bar tightly, her heart racing with fear. Standing so that she would be behind the door when it opened, Jane took a deep breath. She would only have one chance to escape, for if she attacked and did not succeed she was sure he would kill her.

The door swung slowly back. A man entered and moved towards the bed, looking at the shape Jane had formed beneath the covers.

'Still asleep, bitch?' Hershaw demanded, his voice slightly slurred. Sophie had done her work well, plying him with strong drink and perhaps more.

Jane rushed at him and struck a blow against his back. He gave a yell of pain and rage and turned on her, his eyes blazing. Jane struck out again and caught him on the shoulder, but it was her last blow for he caught the bar and held it, wrenching it from her by force of his superior strength.

'You damned bitch!' Hershaw cried. 'Murder me, would you? I'll see you in the ground afore the night is done, but first I'll have a taste of what you give to him…'

'No!' Jane struggled as he grabbed her by the arms. 'Don't you dare touch me, you filthy brute.' She pushed him back and then heard sounds in the house. Shouting and screaming and one shot and then Sophie's voice yelling in anger. Hershaw grinned and looked towards the door. 'He comes at last—the one I hate…and he shall see you die before his eyes.'

To Jane's horror, she saw him pull a pistol from inside his jerkin and point it at her. His hand was not quite steady but his finger was on the trigger. Did he mean to kill her or Paul first?

She heard voices outside the door. It was flung back and Paul charged in, armed with two pistols, Jack Harding close behind.

'Stay where you are,' Hershaw warned. 'I shall kill her before you can get to her, Frant. You may kill me but come one step closer and she dies first.'

'Don't be a fool,' Paul said and Jane thought that she had never seen him look so grim. 'I have this place surrounded. You cannot get away. If I don't kill you, one of my men will…'

'Do you think I care what happens to me once I have my revenge? You took all from me when you made those charges against me…and she swore to me that you had ruined her life. Her child is yours and you plan to marry another…and now I have been told she lies ill on her bed in India because of what you did, her child lost and her mind wandering…'

'If you speak of Annamarie, I am sorry to hear of her tragedy but she was never my wife and I have never laid a finger on her,' Paul said calmly. 'If she lied, it was because she hoped you might do something foolish—but I have only your word that she named me when she knew it was a lie…'

'Damn you, Frant, I loved her and I'll have your life for her pain if I die for it…' Hershaw took a firmer aim, holding his right arm with his left in an effort to keep it steady. His finger was on the trigger when Jane bent to retrieve the iron bar and struck. She brought it down on his arm with all the force she possessed. He screamed in pain and his finger squeezed before the pistol dropped to the floor and the ball embedded itself in the wall. 'You bitch…' He lunged at Jane but before he touched her Paul's pistol spoke and the ball struck his leg. He fell, writhing in pain and cursing them both. 'I should have killed her first…' he muttered and promptly passed out.

'Jane, are you hurt?' Paul asked as he covered the ground between them and drew her into his embrace. 'Forgive me, I should have instructed my men to keep a closer watch, but I did not expect him to abduct you. Oh, my love, I have been so afraid. I knew he hated me, but not the extent of his hatred or the true reason for it.'

'Annamarie—is she the Indian Princess that Lady Catherine said was your wife?'

'Yes. She is very beautiful in her way,' Paul said gravely. 'I think she expects homage and if she does not get it, it makes her angry. I angered her because she made it clear she wished to be my wife and live in my palace but I ignored her—indeed, I am guilty of treating her as though she was a spoiled child. I did not think her capable of such lies…and I pity Hershaw, for she would never have had him. Yet I pity Adam more, for she is his wife…and I must tell him what Hershaw revealed and I know it will cause him pain.'

'And the child is his?'

'Yes, so he claims, but I wonder…'

'Poor Adam,' Jane said softly, for she understood what he meant. This woman who would lie to set one man against another was not to be trusted and her child might already have been conceived before she married him, but it was not for either of them to speculate. 'No wonder he was adamant that he could not marry Melia—and yet it was not kind in him to lead her on…'

'No, and I have told him. I think he regrets it now… as he regrets other things, but he will return to India and live in the palace that I have given him. He will be my agent there, for I shall never return to India. My home is here now, Jane, with you…'

'Oh, Paul, forgive me for causing you so much trouble. I was distressed and did not think what I was doing…'

'Do not think of it,' he said and kissed her softly. 'Come, I shall take you to the carriage and you will return to town with your brother. I must remain here until the magistrates have been and have this rogue under lock and key.'

'Is Will here?'

'Downstairs, seeing to the woman and her husband, I imagine. He knew I should not be satisfied unless I dealt with the rogue myself, though he would have come had I not told him his part was keeping an eye on the others.'

'Be careful, Paul. He would still kill you if he could and he is only unconscious…'

'His men have dispersed,' Paul said. 'Only one of them put up a fight and once Jack fired over his head, he surrendered and begged pardon. He claims he was forced to help Hershaw and I believe him.'

'Yes, I am sure it was so,' Jane said and sighed. 'Must you truly stay?'

'Yes, for my word will be needed; otherwise Hershaw will lay false charges. I must see this thing through, my love—but when all is done I shall come to you and we shall begin to plan our wedding…'

'Was he the reason you wanted to keep our understanding secret?'

'He had already made three attempts on my life— and then he heard from someone that we were promised to each other and changed his plans to include you…'

'Three attempts to kill you…' Jane stared as the horror of it finally hit her and she realised how close they had both come to death. 'You did not tell me.'

'I did not want you to worry for my sake, but I did not suspect that he intended to harm me through you until I was told of the rumours. I made arrangements for someone to watch over you, but for some reason my man did not see you leave your house. But I hardly thought Hershaw would kidnap you and hold you hostage in order to torture me before he killed us both.'

'Paul…he must be evil or mad…'

'Perhaps a mixture of both,' Paul said. 'I believe he had a run of bad luck on the horses recently. He tried to make up for his ill luck at the tables and was caught placing a card he had secreted from his sleeve into his hand. He managed to hush it up, but once the story got round he would have been ostracised and I think he lived by what he managed to win cheating some young fool at the tables.'

'And so he decided to take his anger out on you— is that it?'

'Yes, it seems that way.'

'Who told you all this?'

'Adam told me when he learned of your abduction. One night when Hershaw was in his cups he'd spoken of his misfortunes and blamed you, though his reasons were incoherent…'

'Why did Adam not tell you before?'

'He had his reasons,' Paul said. 'Perhaps he too felt some jealousy, Jane—but it is over now and we are friends again. He will return to India to his wife and I shall stay here and run my stables…and marry you, if you will have me.'

'You know I shall,' she said and kissed his cheek. 'But if Adam is to return to India, how will you manage your stables?'

'Perhaps he will have me for his partner,' Jack said, coming to the doorway to look at them. 'We have them all under control, my friend. The magistrate is on his way—and perhaps Lady March should be if you wish to protect her good name...'

'Yes, of course,' Paul said and gripped Jack's arm. 'Take her down to the carriage, my friend, while I see that he is taken care of...' A moan from the man lying on the floor gave warning that he was coming to his senses. 'I'll bind his wrists and bring him down—and then we'll talk...'

Chapter Fifteen

'Oh, Jane, I am so glad to see you back,' Sarah said and rushed to embrace her. 'I wanted to come to find you, but Will said I must stay here in safety. He would not hear of my coming but I have been so anxious for you all...'

'There was no need,' Will said. 'Between us we had more than a dozen men, all armed and ready to do whatever was required of them, but no blood was spilled—except that of the rogue who began this. He was wounded in the leg and will be lame for what little time remains to him. If my evidence has anything to do with it, he will pay the ultimate price for his perfidy.'

'I am surprised he still lives,' Sarah said. 'I thought one of you would kill him, for you were all so angry— as you should be. He treated you shamefully, Jane.'

'It was through my own foolish fault,' Jane said and laughed as Sarah looked outraged. 'If I had stayed safe inside the house instead of rushing out like a fool he could not have taken me so easily.'

'Yet he would have found a way,' her brother told her gravely. 'If he meant to harm you both he would have waited—and you could not live your life under the shadow of fear, Jane. Had Paul begged you to be careful it would have irked you.'

'Yet he would have done so had he thought it necessary,' she said and smiled. 'No one could have guessed what would happen. I wonder that a man should bear a grudge so many years.'

'Yet perhaps it was because of his run of ill luck of late,' Will said. 'He had nursed various grudges against Paul for a long time yet did nothing. Only when his fortunes fell so low did he think of such wickedness. I am not sure what he hoped to gain from it, but perhaps he thought, as Paul's ward, Melia might inherit his fortune when he died. I believe she would have wed Hershaw had he asked…and with a fortune to call his own he could have done anything. In time he might have seen her dead and returned to India in the hope of securing Annamarie's affections…'

'She must be very beautiful,' Jane said, 'to play on the hearts and minds of so many men—Adam Hargreaves and Hershaw, and who knows what others lie victim to her charms?'

It was in her mind that the beautiful girl had wanted the only man who had resisted her. Yet was Paul completely blind to her charms? For a moment jealousy raised its ugly head, but she squashed it before it could take root. She could not doubt that Paul loved her and she would not let herself wonder any more. Instead, she would think about the future with the man she loved…

* * *

'I suppose you think you have won.' The injured man threw Paul a look of hatred as he was pulled roughly to his feet. The magistrate had taken his evidence and a secure coach was waiting to take the prisoner into custody, yet still he was defiant. 'She promised to reward me if I made you suffer—she wants your life, Frant, and I doubt I'll be the last to be swayed by her.'

'She is another's wife, not mine—and her child was his,' Paul replied. 'Do not blame her for your decisions, Hershaw. She knew of your bitterness and played on it. All that has happened to you has been your own fault, because you resented me and thought to gain great riches from the woman you wanted. I doubt she would have kept her word, for her story was built on lies.'

'Damn you!' Hershaw said and tried to lunge at Paul even though his wrists were bound, but was restrained by the magistrate's men. 'You were always my enemy.'

'No, you were your own enemy,' Paul said and turned away as Hershaw was taken off, cursing and spitting defiance, his injured leg dragging on the ground.

'He will trouble us no more,' Jack said with satisfaction. 'You and your lady may walk in safety now, my friend.'

'Yes. I thank God for it—and you, Jack. Had it not been for your quick wits, I might have been searching for weeks and still not found her.'

'Oh, he would have let you know eventually, for your death was his intention, but she might have suffered in the meantime. I do not like to think what he had in mind this evening.'

'She had found a weapon from somewhere and was defending herself, but I think he must have overcome her resistance in the end.'

'Then it was a mercy we arrived when we did,' Jack said and jerked his head at the woman and her husband, who had been silently watching the proceedings awaiting their fate. 'What do you want to do with this pair? The other rogue ran off when we arrived.'

'That was my brother, sir.' Sophie spoke up. 'It was I gave milady the weapon to defend herself. She came to no harm in this house. We but did what that devil commanded, my lord—he would have killed us all if he'd known.'

'Yes, I imagine so,' Paul said. 'Jane told me that you had helped her and I shall not move against you this time—but the magistrate warned you of your fate if you break the law again.'

'If my man attempts such a thing I'll take my hand to him,' Sophie said and gave her husband such a look that he jerked back as if he believed her.

Paul hid his smile. 'Very well, woman. Keep your man on a leash, because if he ever comes near my lady again I shall kill him.' He turned back to Jack. 'Gather the men. I would return to London and speak with Jane…'

Jane was sitting in her parlour at her writing desk when Paul was announced later that evening. She turned, gave a cry of pleasure and ran to him. His arms opened to receive her, holding her close to him for a moment before he spoke.

'You are safe now, my love. Hershaw is safely locked away and will harm neither of us again. He was a bitter, twisted man and a dangerous enemy, but I did not expect he would use you so ill, Jane.'

'That was my own fault. If I had not allowed Lady Catherine to distress me I should not have laid myself vulnerable to his schemes.'

'She has a vicious tongue and meant to hurt you, but I doubt she knew what lay in his heart, or what he was capable of.'

'No, I am sure she did not. Lady Catherine spoke out of spite and jealousy. I think you must have slighted her, Paul…or I have done something to arouse her hatred.'

'She was at the theatre with Hershaw. Perhaps she thought we might speak of it to her betrothed and spoil her marriage plans, for he was merely an amusement to her. She would not have married him, because she requires a prestigious title and a fortune.'

'I should never have dreamed of such a thing,' Jane said. 'Let us forget her and the other one…though I think her the more dangerous of the two. If Annamarie would move a man to murder because of some imagined slight…'

'It was the reason I could never like her,' Paul said. 'She is proud and beautiful in her way, but I thought her cold of heart. She offered herself to me and I refused her… I knew it angered her but did not imagine she would inspire a man to murder because of it.'

'Yet if he had not already hated you, she could not have done it. Adam loves her and has every reason to feel jealousy, but he does not hate you…'

'No, I must admit that for a while I thought he might be my enemy but, despite knowing that the woman he loves preferred me, he did not turn completely from me. I can only pray that his love for her will overcome her nature—for otherwise I think he will know only unhappiness...'

'What kind of a woman could be so vengeful?' Jane marvelled at it for she could never understand such wickedness. 'I could never urge a man to kill another, even if he had slighted me.'

Paul smiled softly at her. 'I know and it is that precious difference between you that makes me adore you, my sweet Jane. I loved you from the moment we met and if you had not found it in your heart to love me, I should never have married.'

'Oh, Paul,' Jane said, her throat catching. 'You know that I loved Harry. I never thought to love again, but I do—and as deeply. Harry was the mad, sweet love of first youth and you are the man I love now and will love all my life.'

'I thank God for it,' he murmured and bent his head to kiss her lips. 'How soon will you marry me, Jane?'

'We go down to the country soon and you must visit Melia and her aunt or she will think you have deserted her. As soon as you come to me, we shall set the banns and then we can begin our new life together...'

'Yes, you are right,' he said and sighed. 'The responsibilities of a guardian weigh heavily upon me, Jane. I would that I might stay by your side, but I must do my duty.'

'Do what you must and come to me,' she said and

lifted her head so that he could kiss her again. 'I shall look for you every day so do not tarry longer than you need, my dearest one.'

'You have my promise on that,' Paul said. 'We shall spend tomorrow together and then I really must leave for the country—when next we meet it shall be at your home...'

'I will accompany you to Miss Bellingham's home,' Adam said the following evening. 'I must make my peace with her—and then I shall sail for India. I cannot thank you enough for all you have done for me, Paul. You have stood as a good friend to me and there were times that I did not deserve it.'

'You loved a woman you knew had feelings for me and it caused you grief,' Paul said. 'Yet be comforted by the knowledge that I never once laid hands upon her. She is your wife and she must care for you or she would not have come to you that night, nor would she have wed you.'

'She wed me because she was carrying a child.' Adam frowned. 'I think she came to me out of temper and a wish to hit back at you through me—perhaps she thought I would be turned against you, but she never asked me to take your life.'

'You were not Hershaw and would not have done it,' Paul said. 'You had opportunity to see me dead by an-other's hand, but you did not take it.'

'No, for I am no murderer,' Adam said ruefully. 'I know Annamarie's faults, Paul. She can be both spite-ful and cruel, but she has been taught harshly by her father's people when they turned her from the palace after her father's death. Now that she will have a palace of her own and my title, I can provide her with the life she wishes, I believe she will be content. Besides, she is my wife and, if Hershaw speaks the truth, she is desperately ill. If she still lives when I return, I shall do my best to make her happy. I can only hope that illness will have driven the bitterness from her heart.'

Paul kept his silence. He was not sure that Adam would ever find happiness married to the beautiful but vicious woman he so obviously adored, but love was blind. Words would not change Adam's heart nor would he wish to try. Love was a strange but glorious thing, which brought both great happiness and terrible grief. Adam loved his wife despite all and he could only send him on his way in friendship.

'Very well, if you wish to say goodbye to Melia you shall come with me,' Paul said. 'We shall ride together, Adam—and then I shall take my leave of you, because I stay only one day before I join Jane at her home...'

The man looked down at the battered body of the fool he had so easily duped into bringing him the only weapon he needed—a bottle of wine. It had been a pity to waste good claret on the oaf but, broken over the head of the obliging turnkey, it had proved sufficient to gain his freedom.

He took the keys to the outer door. His prison had proved no stronghold and he'd known immediately that money would sway the fool they had given charge of him. All he had to do was steal a horse and he would be away. Then he needed clean clothes and money, which he had hidden safely in case he had need of them.

The horses were in the stables behind the magistrate's house. No guards patrolled the grounds and there was only one unsuspecting groom in charge of the stables that night. It was a matter of a swift blow to the neck with the broken bottle and the fool fell to the ground, blood seeping from the wound as he tried to call out but could not speak.

Once upon his chosen mount, the man sped away from house and stable to open countryside. His first plan had failed and that bitch Frant planned to marry would be on her guard, but there was one other who would not be so wary. He might yet find a way to ruin her and bring Frant to his knees.

Annamarie's promise was in his mind as he sped through the darkness.

'Kill him for me and I will share everything I have with you…' she'd whispered as they lay together in the darkness. 'I will take you for my husband and you will live in a palace…'

He had been mad for her from the first time he saw her, when he was sent with a diplomatic mission to her mother. At first the girl had not seemed to notice him, but then one night she had waylaid him as he returned home from dinner at the Governor's house. Her smile had sent his wits spinning and when she offered herself to him in return for a favour, he had not stopped to think. He would have killed anyone for her at that moment—but when she spoke the name of the man she hated, he'd laughed with pure delight. Frant deserved all that was coming to him.

He had taken his time planning the downfall of his enemy, but somehow luck had been on Frant's side—but this time he would no doubt be planning his wedding to that bitch and would know nothing of his ward's elopement until it was too late.

Melia was a flighty little thing and he did not doubt that he would have her eating out of his hand within a few minutes of speaking to her. She would run off with him...and then he would make Frant pay, both in money and with his life. A ransom first and then a ball in his heart...

Melia was annoyed. She had expected that Lord Frant would be here sooner. The plans for the wedding could not go ahead until he came and the marriage contract was signed. Her aunt was strict about keeping the proprieties and she said it would be discourteous to speak to the vicar or plan anything until Lord Frant arrived—and her betrothed agreed.

'Your aunt is correct, dearest,' he'd told her. 'Besides, what does it matter? We have a lifetime ahead of us—and it is but a few days' delay.'

Melia did not know why she felt so frustrated. Until they came down to the country she hadn't truly known either her betrothed or his sister very well. Spending each day in their company, she was beginning to be bored. Anne was forever with her nose in a book, and her brother spent most of his time riding or speaking to the grooms. He did walk with Melia in the afternoons and was attentive in the evenings, but that was almost worse than when he left her alone to go riding or played cards with her aunt's guests.

The truth was that she had provoked Captain Smythe into speaking by saying that she was to return to her aunt's house and did not know if she would ever return to town. Managing to shed a tear, she'd had him gallantly trying to comfort her and when he'd suddenly proposed she had accepted him—and now she wished she hadn't.

Oh, what a bother it was! She had been so sure that Viscount Hargreaves was in love with her, but when she'd tried to push him towards a declaration he'd told her he couldn't afford to marry her. Melia had blamed her guardian, because Adam had told her of the rewards her guardian had received while he had only a few guineas. She'd resented that, because she was sure that Adam would have wed her if she'd had more fortune.

Then, after it was made clear to her that she would never persuade the viscount to wed her, she had met Captain Hershaw. He'd set out to captivate her from the start and, though she did not think him as handsome as Adam Hargreaves, he'd seemed to like her—but he had not spoken and so she'd seized her chance when Captain Smythe proposed. Now she wished that she had waited, for it seemed that only a lifetime of boredom lay ahead.

So it was with a mixture of anticipation and surprise that she heard Viscount Hargreaves announced as she sat alone in the parlour that morning. He entered and her heart raced at the sight of him. How handsome he was and she loved him. Yes, now that she saw him again, she knew that it was Adam Hargreaves she had always wanted.

'Miss Bellingham, forgive me this intrusion,' Adam said and looked awkward. 'Your guardian has allowed me a short time to speak with you alone…'

'You wanted to speak to me alone?' Melia asked and her heart raced. There could be only one reason for him to come all this way to speak to her! Her engagement had made him realise that he cared for her and he had come to beg her to break it off and marry him. The excitement was so intense that at first his words did not penetrate her mind.

'It was very wrong of me to let you think I was free,' Adam said and at last the words reached her. 'I found you attractive and I was disturbed by other things. I should not have been so free in my manner towards you, because I have a wife and child in India…'

'You have a wife…?' Melia stared at him in dismay. 'You let me think and you knew…you always knew that you were married…'

'Forgive me. I have regretted what I did and perhaps, had I been free…'

'How dare you come here?' Melia demanded. 'Why should I care what you have to say?'

She threw him a look of malice and ran from the room before she could shame herself and weep before him. Adam called her name but she did not look back. Her disappointment was such that she could scarcely bear it and she ran from the house, through the back gardens to the orchards beyond.

Leaning with her back against a tree, Melia let her tears fall. How could he come here just to tell her that he had a wife? Oh, how she hated him, and her guardian. Lord Frant must have known of the wife—why had he not told her at once? Why had he allowed her to humiliate herself by running after that hateful man—and why had he brought him here to hurt her in this way?

She hated them both. She wanted to strike out and hurt someone—to punish those who had wronged her.

'Miss Bellingham, I do not like to see you in distress…'

The voice broke into her fevered thoughts, bringing Melia's head up. She gasped as she saw him and dashed her hand over her cheeks.

'Captain Hershaw,' she said. 'I did not expect to see you here.'

'I could not stop thinking of you,' he said softly and smoothed his fingers over her cheek to wipe away the tears. 'I should have spoken sooner, my dearest Melia, but I dare not because your guardian hates me.'

'And I hate him,' Melia said, firing up immediately. 'He does not care for me—no one truly cares for me…'

'Then come away with me now,' he urged. 'Let me take you to France, where we can live and be happy. I shall find a way to…'

Before he could say more, a voice called out to him. 'Stand away from her, you dog! Melia, move away from him. He is a coward and a murderer…'

Melia saw her guardian striding towards her and, a little distance behind him, Adam. She lifted her head defiantly.

'You have never wanted me to be happy,' she said. 'I am going with Captain Hershaw now and you cannot stop me.'

'Think about what you're doing,' Paul warned. 'He is wanted for a hanging offence and means only to lure you away to get at me...'

'And I nearly had her,' Hershaw snarled, reaching out to grab Melia around the throat with one arm. He levelled a pistol at her head. 'I am taking her with me and I shall dishonour her and you, Frant. When I've done with her I shall kill her—and if you come near me I'll kill you too.'

Melia gasped. Her throat hurt where his arm pressed against it, but the pain of humiliation was far worse. She had come here to weep in private and he had offered her comfort, but it was just a trick. Filled with rage and hatred against the whole world, Melia bit his hand as hard as she could and heard him scream and jerk his hand away. In that moment of freedom, she wrestled with him and tried to take the pistol he'd held to her head. In her thoughts was only one desire—to see him dead at her feet.

He knocked her back so that she was felled to the ground and then fired at her guardian. Hearing the muffled oath, Melia thought he must have hit him and she rolled over, flinging herself at his leg and pulling at it so that he stumbled. He kicked out at her, his boot landing hard against her mouth so that she tasted blood and then he fired again.

Getting to her feet, Melia glanced round and saw that Adam lay bleeding on the ground. She ran to him, screaming, as she flung herself down on her knees and looked into his face. He was dead, Hershaw's ball having found its target too well. A pistol lay beside Adam. Melia's hand reached for it. She took it, turned slowly and aimed. Her shot caught Hershaw in the groin and he screamed in agony but levelled his pistol at her, and in that moment another shot rang out and Hershaw pitched to the ground.

Melia fell back, faint and sick of heart. She wished that it had been her ball that had killed him, but knew it was her guardian who had fired. She was aware of being lifted gently and carried indoors. People were around her. She heard their voices but did not know what they said, nor did she wish to know. Adam was dead. He had loved another, but still she loved him and she grieved that his life was lost. She turned her face to the wall and let the blackness take her.

'It is so shocking,' Mrs Bellingham said as she came from her niece's bedchamber after the doctor had been. 'To think that he might have made off with her, had you and the viscount not been there and seen what he was about.' She mopped at her cheeks with a lace kerchief. 'My poor niece—and it was all to be arranged for her wedding this very day.'

'Yes, well, that may have to be postponed,' Paul said, looking grave. 'Adam was badly wounded. I am sure she thought him dead, which is why she fired. I had been wounded and it took me a moment to steady my aim and he might have killed any of us if Melia had not acted as she did—she is a brave girl, madam.'

'Yes, indeed, but I think it has shocked her fiancé and his sister. They do not know quite what to make of her actions—and I must say it was not what I would have expected of my niece, or of any gentle girl.'

'I had not expected so much of her,' Paul said. 'I hope that she will soon feel better and I shall delay my departure until I am sure she improves. I must speak with her and see what can be done to sort out this mess.'

'He…that awful man is dead now?'

'Yes. I should have made sure of it before this, but I thought to bring him to justice. If Melia or Adam had died I should not lightly have forgiven myself.'

'Well, I cannot like what has happened, Lord Frant. I do not think my brother would have approved of the company she has kept since you became her guardian.'

'I would willingly have given her care to you, madam,' Paul said. 'But now I owe her something and I shall make sure she is happy with her chosen course before I abandon her to you or her fiancé.'

Paul walked down the stairs to write a letter to Jane to explain why he could not join her as planned. His arm was painful, but he was fortunate to have escaped further injury. Adam's wound was far worse and had barely missed his heart; another inch to the left and he would indeed be dead. As it was, he would be ill for some time and the doctor had stressed that he must not be moved for the moment.

It would be awkward for all concerned. Melia had not taken his apology well and Paul believed that she had been on the verge of running off with Hershaw, perhaps to spite them all. She, like Jane, was safe from

Hershaw now, but she would be bitter and it would be painful for her to know Adam was lying in his sickbed in her aunt's house. Paul was not sure what he could do to help her, but he blamed himself for what had happened. Adam was his friend and, in paying court to her, he had not been fair to Melia. Perhaps worse still, Hershaw's actions had been meant against Paul and Melia had unfortunately been caught up in the sorry mess. It was a miracle that she was not badly wounded or dead. Her bruises were superficial and Paul suspected that it was her broken heart that had caused her to turn her face to the wall.

Had he been careless in his duty towards her? Paul knew that he had been caught up in his own affairs, labelling the girl as a flighty miss. Yet now he felt that he might have been remiss and if there was a way to help her, he must find it. For the moment his own affairs must wait, even though he was impatient to be with Jane once more.

Chapter Sixteen

Paul's letter did not reach Jane for four days and she had begun to wonder why he did not come as he'd promised. Wild thoughts went through her mind and she pictured him lying dead or injured, so the truth was not so very shocking. He had a flesh wound, but Adam's was so much worse he feared for his friend's life—and Melia had taken to her bed and refused to leave it.

I wish I might be with you, planning our wedding. Yet I know you will understand why I cannot leave this house for the moment. I must make arrangements for Adam to be properly cared for when he is well enough to be moved—and I feel in part responsible for Melia's despair.

It seems I wronged her in believing that she would soon recover from her infatuation. I now believe she truly loved Adam, and his confession that he was married to Annamarie deeply wounded her.

Had I not followed she might have gone with Hershaw and, in his hatred for me, he would have used her ill.

I would not ask it of you, Jane, but I believe she needs a friend she can speak to of what is in her heart. Her aunt is a good woman in her way but she fusses foolishly. Come if you can, and perhaps together we can heal her wounded heart.

Jane took her letter to Will and showed him. She found him with Sarah in the parlour. They had been talking earnestly, but Will saw at once that Jane was in distress and read the letter she handed him. He agreed that she must go to Melia and Sarah offered to go with her.

'The viscount will need nursing and I have some skill in that,' Sarah said, and looked at Will shyly. 'We have something to tell you, Jane...' She faltered and he smiled and nodded.

'Yes, my dearest sister. I am sure you have long guessed it was my intention—but I must tell you that I have asked Sarah to be my wife. We shall announce our engagement but the wedding will wait until after your own has taken place.'

'I had hoped that might be quite soon,' Jane said, 'but, should it be long delayed, you must not delay your plans to suit me—I can quite easily stay with Mama until my affairs are settled.'

'I knew you would say that,' her brother said and gave her a quick hug. 'Sarah insisted we must wait, but we shall call the banns for one month hence and hope that Lord Frant's friend will have recovered before that…'

'He is severely wounded, but wounds of the heart may heal sooner than a broken heart,' Jane said. 'I think Paul is more concerned for Melia than he has written. I shall go to him this very day, Sarah. Are you sure you wish to accompany me?'

'Yes.' She looked at Will and he nodded. 'We must all help each other and I shall come with you, Jane.'

Jane accepted her offer and went at once to set plans in motion for their journey. She could not know how long they would have to stay with Mrs Bellingham and would take clothes for a few weeks, as well as all the medicines and clean linen bindings she thought necessary.

Will had decided to accompany them. 'I shall not stay to be a burden to Mrs Bellingham,' he said, 'but I have friends nearby who will welcome me and shall ride over each day to see how you go on.'

'I am glad of it,' Jane said, because she did not wish to be the cause of their parting at a time when they should be planning their wedding.

The journey took several hours and it was past six when they arrived at Mrs Bellingham's house. She had been expecting them and her relief was obvious for she welcomed Jane with open arms, sniffing into her lace kerchief.

'I am at my wits' end,' she declared to Jane as she ordered tea and cakes to sustain them until supper. 'Melia will not even speak to me…'

'Is Paul here?' Jane asked, looking about her, for she had expected he would meet her.

'He is with the doctor attending the viscount,' Mrs Bellingham said and gave a little sob. 'That such a thing should happen here! I have never been so shocked. We have had the magistrate here and doctors... Lord Frant was not satisfied with our local man and sent for a man from town. I am sure I do not know what things are coming to...a man shot dead, another dying and my niece refusing to eat or drink...'

'I shall go up to her,' Jane said. 'You may send a tray of tea with two cups and a little bread and butter and some chicken to the bedchamber, if you please, and I shall do what I can to encourage her to drink.'

'I will show you to her room,' Mrs Bellingham said. 'If your brother and cousin will take some tea...' She seemed torn between being polite to her guests and Jane's request.

'Your footman may show me up,' Jane said and pressed her hand. 'Pray do not worry so, ma'am. I am sure that Melia will be better soon.'

'Oh...well, if you think so...'

Jane left her with Sarah and Will and enquired direction from the footman who had admitted them. He took her up the stairs and she thanked him as he directed her to Melia's room. She knocked and entered, though Melia did not invite her to do so. The room was in darkness and Melia was lying hunched up on the bed, still dressed in what she had been wearing for days judging by its state. She had her face turned to the wall and did not look round as Jane spoke to her.

'Why are you in such distress?' she asked. 'Your aunt is distraught because you will not speak to her—and with Adam so ill...'

She saw Melia stiffen and then she rolled over on to her back and pushed herself up against the pillows, staring at Jane in disbelief.

'I saw him die...he was so pale and still...that devil killed him and it was my fault...'

'How could it be your fault?' Jane asked. 'I must tell you that Adam is badly wounded, but he is yet alive. I had it from your aunt but a moment ago. A new doctor has been summoned and Lord Frant is with him now.'

'He is truly alive?' Melia looked at her and for a moment there was light in her dull eyes. 'He was not killed?'

'No, he lives. I cannot promise he will not die, but he lives at this moment.'

'I am glad...' Melia gave a little sob. 'I hated him for a time that morning. He told me that he has a wife—and I loved him. Why did no one tell me that he was married? Had I known...'

'The viscount told no one of his marriage. It remained a secret until Hershaw spread a whisper that Lord Frant was secretly married to the Indian Princess and had deserted her. I was told in such a way that I became distressed and left the house alone—which led to my capture and imprisonment.'

She saw the shock in Melia's face. 'Yes, I was imprisoned by Hershaw's men, and he meant to kill me when he had finished his evil work against Paul—as he would have killed you, my love.'

'Oh, Jane, I did not know what was in his mind,' Melia said and tears rolled down her cheek. 'It is all my fault…I brought him to your house and encouraged him. I told him all the things he wanted to know about you and my guardian…I told him you had an understanding…'

'Yes, I thought it must have been you,' Jane said and saw the girl flinch. 'No, do not blame yourself for what happened, Melia. He would have found a way even if you had not told him anything…'

'I am to blame,' Melia insisted. 'I was selfish and thoughtless—and if Adam dies it will be my fault.'

'If you regret what you have done, give up this selfish remorse that is so distressing for your aunt…' There was a knock at the door and then a maid came in with a tray and Jane asked her to set it down.

After she had gone, Jane poured two cups of tea, giving one to Melia and taking one herself. 'There is a little bread and butter and some cold chicken, my love. Please try and eat a little and drink your tea. I have been travelling and truly need mine.'

'You are so kind to me and I do not deserve it,' Melia said and sipped her tea. She discovered that she was thirsty and drank it all. Jane poured them both another and Melia ate a few mouthfuls of the bread and butter and Jane tried one of the delicious cakes.

'Your aunt has a good cook, Melia.'

'Yes, she does,' Melia said and put down her empty cup. 'What am I to do, Jane? I am not in love with Captain Smythe—but I have promised to wed him…'

'You know that even if the viscount lives he will return to India—to his wife and child?'

'Yes...' Melia's complexion was pale but her expression was set. 'He never loved me. I was foolish to fall for a pretty face and charming manners. I see now that when he made excuses he was only being kind...'

'I fear there was a little more to it,' Jane said. 'He felt some resentment towards Paul and perhaps he flirted with you in a mood of mischief. It was not kind in him, Melia—but I think he relented when he realised the damage he had done. Paul has forgiven him and perhaps in time you will be able to do the same.'

'I do not know if I can forgive,' Melia said, 'but I pray that he will live and...be happy with his family.'

Tears were running down her face. Jane wiped them away with her kerchief. 'In time the pain of a love lost will lessen,' she said. 'I think you must decide whether you wish to marry Captain Smythe or not and tell him. He left to take his sister home, but said he would return in a few days. You should tell him at once that you cannot marry him if that is your wish.'

'I shall be an outcast from Society,' Melia said. 'When word gets out there will be a terrible scandal.'

'No, I do not think it need be so. Some people may be cool towards you and think you a jilt, but others will be kinder—as for the other business, it will be hushed up and your name kept from it, I am sure. Lord Frant will do all he can to protect you.'

'I shall never marry...' Melia said and looked so miserable that Jane leaned forward to kiss her.

'Do not despair, Melia. For a time you will grieve

but in time your heart will mend. One day in the future, Paul and I will take you travelling—perhaps to France and Italy. You may find happiness again. Besides, in a year or two your brief engagement will be forgotten.'

'Yes…' Melia sighed. 'I suppose it will…'

A knock came at the door then and Paul asked if he might enter. Melia said that he might and he came in looking apprehensive, but smiled as he saw her sitting up and the teacups.

'You are feeling a little better,' he said. 'I am glad, Melia—and I beg you to forgive me for all that has happened to you.'

Melia smiled, perhaps the first natural smile she'd given him. 'You were never anything but generous to me, sir. I was foolish and greedy, and I beg your pardon for the hurt I have caused.'

'I came to tell you that Adam is conscious. He asked after you, Melia, and said that he would like to see you when you felt able…'

'I will go and see him,' she said and then looked down at her crumpled gown, as if she had not realised the state she was in. 'Perhaps I should change first… this has his blood on it.'

'I shall help you,' Jane said and looked at Paul. 'We will talk later, my dearest.'

'Yes—and thank you for coming to our aid…'

He left the room and Melia stood while Jane unfastened her gown and helped her to change into a clean one. Melia chose a plain blue dress that had none of the fashionable style she had adopted in London, her hair caught up in a simple knot at the back. Jane thought she looked prettier than she ever had before.

'I shall leave you,' she said. 'Perhaps you will come down to supper later?'

Walking down the stairs, Jane went to the parlour where the others had been taking tea earlier. Paul was alone, drinking a glass of brandy. He turned as she entered and held out his hands to her. She went to him and he took her hands, drawing her into his arms and holding her.

'You spoke of a wound?'

'It was a mere scratch to my arm,' he said. 'I should not have mentioned it, but I had to explain… I needed you here, my darling. I could not reach Melia, no one could…she would not listen to us.'

'She thought Adam dead,' Jane told him. 'She blamed herself for his death. I think she both hates and loves him. He hurt her badly—and yet she could not bear to think her foolishness had led to his death.'

'Even if he had been dead it could not have been her fault,' Paul said. 'The blame is mine. I should have been more careful. I thought it right to leave Hershaw to the law, but I should have known that he would never rest until one of us was dead.'

'Why should he hate you so?' Jane touched his cheek.

'It was many things…mostly envy and greed, I think,' Paul sighed. 'Truly, I hardly understand such hatred myself. I once warned our superior officer that he cheated at the card tables and he was sent away in some disgrace, but that was many years ago. I can only think that he fell prey to the charms of a jealous woman…or perhaps it was his losses at the card tables…'

'We shall never know for certain,' Jane said. 'I am relieved that he is dead, Paul, though a man's death is never cause for celebration, I know.'

'No, it cannot be,' he agreed. 'Yet, unless the law dealt with him harshly, I think a shadow would have hung over us. He tried to kill Adam and he would have killed Melia had I not fired first.'

'Then it ended the only way it could,' she agreed. 'I hope that we shall never have to speak of him again, Paul.'

'I see no reason why we should,' he said. 'All has been settled with the magistrates and, though an inquiry may be held, there is naught to fear. We must wait until Adam is on his feet again—and then perhaps we can be married…' He smiled at her. 'You must decide where we go on our wedding trip, my love.'

'I think we should live a week or so alone somewhere—and then perhaps we could take Melia on a trip to France or Italy…'

He gazed into her eyes. 'I know of no other woman who would be willing to share such a precious time with her but I am grateful to you for the offer. I feel the need to make some recompense for her hurt.'

'Yes, I know, and I have promised that she shall go travelling at some point,' Jane said. 'Her heart weeps now for her grief but she is young and I believe she will recover well, given the opportunity.'

'Has she decided against marriage to Captain Smythe?'

'Yes—how did you guess it?'

'I knew from the way she wept over Adam that she still loved him. I wasn't sure whether she would marry for position and wealth.'

'I think she believed she could go through with it—but perhaps she was too young to know herself, Paul. I think she knows now that it will not do for her. I think this has made her wiser and perhaps better—and we must hope that she finds love in the future.'

'Yes, I shall pray for that,' he said and then bent his head to kiss her. 'Perhaps we need not wait too long to be wed, now that Adam is out of danger?'

'My brother and Sarah wish to wed soon. Mama will come down for the wedding—and we may have ours soon after. In six weeks, perhaps? It should give your friend time to recover and...'

Jane could say no more for Paul's lips were touching hers, caressing them with a tender sweetness that filled her with love and pleasure. She melted into his arms, murmuring his name as his kiss deepened.

'Jane, my love,' he whispered huskily. 'If I had lost you I do not know what I should have done...'

They were married in the church at Jane's home some seven weeks later. Although Adam had turned the corner and was now conscious, it had taken him some time to recover. Melia had helped Sarah with the nursing after the first few days and, as Adam no longer needed constant watching, Will and Sarah had married two weeks before Jane. They had gone away for a few days, but returned in order that Jane's brother could give her away, and Sarah stand with Melia as her maids of honour.

Will's wedding to Sarah had been lavish, but Jane had chosen to celebrate hers with just a few good friends. Major Harding was Paul's best man, and Adam was able to attend the wedding, even though he did not stay long at the reception, but retired to the room provided for him after the toasts were drunk. He had booked his passage to India in one month and everyone wished him a fair journey and happiness at the other end.

Melia had broken off her engagement from Captain Smythe and it was with a little smile on her lips that she told Jane he had seemed mightily relieved.

'It was all I could do not to laugh when he assured me he would always be my friend and did not hold my decision against me.'

'You will choose more carefully in future, I think,' Jane said and Melia nodded.

'I am not sure I can love again, but I shall certainly be more careful in future.'

On the morning of her wedding, Melia and Sarah helped Jane to prepare. She looked lovely in a gown of pale ivory silk shot through with rose and silver threads. Her bonnet was fashioned of pink velvet and tied with silver ribbons, her boots of soft cream leather and her gloves a pink lace to match the bonnet.

'You are beautiful,' Sarah said, her face glowing with happiness as she handed a posy of pink roses tied up with lace to Jane. 'Lord Frant is very lucky to have you as his bride, Jane.'

'I think I am lucky to have found him,' she said and

smiled at her dear cousin. 'I know you are happy with my dearest Will—and he looks as if he has the world in his pocket. If we are as happy I shall be more than content.'

'I am sure you will be,' Melia said. 'Lord Frant is both generous and caring—and I was a spoiled silly girl to ever say anything else.'

Jane knew that Melia had been thoroughly chastened, but she had recovered well enough to face the world with a proper dignity and was looking forward to the trip to Italy that had been promised her when Jane and Paul returned from the first part of their wedding trip.

In private she'd told Jane that she had forgiven Adam for hurting her and they had made their peace. She was able now to wish him happiness with his wife and Jane prayed that he would indeed find it—though, from what she'd heard from Paul, she doubted it. Annamarie was beautiful but cold, and it was more than likely that hers had been the voice that urged Hershaw to murder Paul.

India was a world away and Jane believed that all the bitterness and pain that Paul's enemy had caused was over and she had nothing now to think of but her life with the man she loved. She hoped that Adam too might find happiness; perhaps illness and loss would have softened the Indian girl's heart and she would learn to be happy with the man who loved her.

For her the future held only happiness and the pleasure that would come from being Paul's wife. Walking down the aisle towards him, she saw a shaft of sunlight pierce the stained glass windows and light up the altar with gold. It seemed a blessing on their marriage and, as she looked up into her husband's face, she felt her heart overflow with happiness.

They were wed and all Jane wanted now was to live in peace and happiness with Paul.

He came to put his arms about her as she stood near the window, looking out at the view across the park to a lake in the distance. In the dying embers of a summer sun, its waters looked almost pink as the huge ball of fire seemed to sink below the horizon.

'Your home is lovely, Paul,' she said and her cheek was close to his as his lips touched the arch of her white neck.

'This belonged to a friend,' he told her. 'He knew my mother well and loved her all his life and so when he died he left it to me. I had thought I might sell but when I saw the view from this window I knew it was the perfect place for us.'

'Yes, it is perfect,' Jane said. 'The gardens are lovely but in places unfinished and the work will be a pleasure to oversee.'

'You must order everything as you wish,' he murmured against her throat. 'You made my house in London a home and I pray you will do the same here.'

'I think there are improvements to be made, but it is already a home,' Jane said. 'I felt it when you brought me to it this afternoon. I believe it is a happy place, Paul.'

'It was and will be again,' he said and turned her in

his arms to kiss her. 'I love you…want you so much, my darling…'

'And I you,' Jane said and gave herself up to his kiss.

Paul swept her up in his arms and carried her to their bed. The fresh linen sheets smelled of lavender and felt cool to the touch as they lay together, wrapped in each other's arms, touching and kissing, becoming one in a sweet embrace that lifted them to the heights of pleasure. Their bodies fitted as one in a sweet bliss that neither had known before. Jane had been married and was able to give herself freely to the man she loved, his touch different from that of her first husband but just as sweet, and perhaps because the years had taught her the meaning of loss and sorrow she was able to experience an even sweeter joy in finding love once more.

They loved and slept and loved again, entwined as one, for ever in perfect harmony, the need of one perfectly matched to the other. And in the morning when Jane woke, she discovered that he was still deep in slumber beside her. All the worries and cares of the past months had melted away and he looked almost boyish as he slept, and then she bent and kissed him and his strong arms surrounded her, pulling her down to him so that her silky flesh surrounded him and his desire leapt once more to white-hot passion.

'You have made me the happiest man alive,' Paul whispered as they lay quiet once more. 'I shall always love you, my darling—and I thank God that I have found you.'

'Oh, Paul,' she whispered. 'I thought I should never

know true happiness again. Life is good and I know that, whatever the future brings, we shall be together.'

'Until the years pass and we are old and grey,' he teased, touching her nose with his fingertip. 'I dare say you will grow fat and I shall grow bent and grouchy...'

'Me? Fat? You wretch! Never!' she said, and threw herself on him, pummelling him with her fists until he began to kiss her and she could only smile into his eyes and give herself once more to his loving embrace...

* * * * *

LET'S TALK
Romance

For exclusive extracts, competitions
and special offers, find us online:

- facebook.com/millsandboon
- @millsandboonuk
- @millsandboon

Or get in touch on 0844 844 1351*

For all the latest titles coming soon, visit
millsandboon.co.uk/nextmonth